Long Time
No See

Also by Susan Isaacs

Novels

Screenplays

Nonfiction

Long Time
No See

SUSAN
ISAACS

HarperCollins*Publishers*

ISBN 0-06-019570-3

To Larry Ashmead
   my editor and my friend
   with love

Acknowledgments

I sought advice and information from the people listed below. All of them gave it freely and cheerfully. I am grateful for their generosity and hope they will understand that on the occasions when their facts did not fit the needs of my fiction, I gave the facts the heave-ho: Michael Adler, Jennifer Stern Bernbaum, Paul Blackman, Kevin Caslin, Mona Castro, Gerard Catanese, Cesar Collier, Jr., Teena Deocales, Jonathan Dolger, Frank Guidice, Lawrence Iason, Robert M. Kaye, Robert W. Kenny, Erica Johanson, Edward M. Lane, Susan Lawton, Chris McCandless, Alice T. McGillion, Robert McGuire, Robert G. Morvillo, Marcia Riklis, John Royster, Cynthia Scott, Lisa Bochner Sims, Greg Suridis, William Wald, Roger Widmann, Jay Zises, and Susan Zises.

As always, I am grateful to the staff of the Port Washington (N.Y.) Public Library.

Owen Laster has represented me for more than fifteen years. He is a splendid agent and a great man.

My editor, Larry Ashmead, is a legend. He is revered for his instinct, admired for his ability, and adored for his humanity by everyone in publishing. What a guy! What a mensch!

The following people made generous contributions to charities. Their prize (I hope they will find it so) was to have a character in this novel named for them: Susan Viniar, Cecile Rabiea, Andrea Leeds, and Dana Friedman for her mother, Zelda Friedman. Beth Cope became a character because she was exuberant, goodhearted, and got me to the train on time.

Elizabeth J. Carroll's research for this novel is a book in itself, and a well-written one at that. Liz is not only marvelously smart, she is creative, tenacious, and patient.

My assistant, Michelle E. Goldberg, is a blessing in my life. A list of laudatory adjectives to describe her would run pages, so let me briefly say that she is kind, intelligent, intuitive, cheerful, thorough, indefatigable, and diplomatic. She is also great fun.

My children and their spouses give me love, warmth, support, humor, and editorial advice. An infinity-infinity's worth of gratitude to Leslie Stern and Andrew Abramowitz and Elizabeth and Robert Stoll. Thanks also to my grandson, Nathan Henry Abramowitz, for pure joy.

Lastly, my love and appreciation to my first reader and my one and only, Elkan Abramowitz. He is still the best person in the world.

Long Time
No See

Chapter One

On an unseasonably warm Halloween night, while I was reading a snappy treatise on Wendell Willkie's support of FDR's war policies and handing out the occasional bag of M&M's to a trick-or-treater, the fair-haired and dimpled Courtney Logan, age thirty-four, *magna cum laude* graduate of Princeton, erstwhile investment banker at Patton Giddings, wife of darkly handsome Greg, mother of five-year-old Morgan and eighteen-month-old Travis, canner of peach salsa, collector of vintage petit point, and ex-president of Citizens for a More Beautiful Shorehaven vanished from Long Island into thin air.

Odd. Upper-middle-class suburban women with Rolexes and bi-weekly lip-waxing appointments tend not to disappear. Though I had never met her, Courtney sounded especially solid. Less than a year before, there had been a page one feature in the local paper about her new business. StarBaby produced videos of baby's first year. "I thought it would succeed because I knew in my heart of hearts there were thousands just like me!" Courtney was quoted as saying. "It all started when Greg and I were watching a video we'd made of Morgan, our oldest. Fifteen minutes of Morgan staring at the mobile in her crib! A beautiful, intelligent stare, but still . . . After that, another fifteen of her sucking her thumb! Not much else. Suddenly it hit me that we'd never taken out the videocam for Travis, our second, until he was six months old!" (I've never been able to understand this generation's infatuation for using last names as first names. Admittedly it's a certain kind of name: you don't see little Greenberg Johnsons gadding about in sailor suits.) Anyhow, Courtney went on: "I was so sad. And guilty! Look what we'd missed! That's when I thought, it would be so great if a professional filmmaker could have shown up once a month and made a movie starring my son!"

Though not unmindful of the *Shorehaven Beacon*'s aggressively perky style, I sensed Courtney Bryce Logan was responsible for at least half those exclamation points. Clearly, she was one of those incorrigibly up- beat women I have never been able to comprehend, much less be. She'd left a thrilling, high-powered job in Manhattan. She'd traded in her brainy and hip investment-banking colleagues for two tiny people bent on ex- ploring the wonders inside their nostrils. And? Did even a single tear of regret slide down her cheek as she watched her children watching *Sesame Street*? Was there the slightest lump in her throat as the 8:11, packed with her Dana Buchman–suited contemporaries, chugged off to the city? Nope. Apparently, for can-do dames like Courtney, being a full-time mom was full-time bliss. Ambivalence? Please! Retirement was merely a segue into a new career, motherhood, another chance to strut their stuff.

However, what I liked about her was that she spoke about Shore- haven not just with affection but with appreciation, with familiarity with its history. Well, all right, with its myths. She mentioned to the reporter that one of the scenic backgrounds StarBaby used was our town dock. She said: "Walt Whitman actually wrote his two-line poem 'To You' right there!" In truth, Courtney was just perpetuating a particularly dopey local folktale, but I felt grateful to her for having considered our town (and our Island-born poet) important.

I think I even said to myself, Gee, I should get to know her. Well, I'm a historian. I have inordinate warmth for anyone who invokes the past in public. My working hours are spent at St. Elizabeth's College, mostly squandered in history department shriek-fests. I am an adjunct professor at this alleged institution of higher learning, a formerly all- female, formerly nun-run, formerly first-rate school across the county border in the New York City borough of Queens. Anyhow, for two and a half seconds I considered giving Courtney a call and saying hi. Or even Hi! My name is Judith Singer and let's have lunch. But like most of those assertive notions, it was gone by the end of the next heartbeat.

Speaking of heartbeats . . . Before I get into Courtney Logan's stun- ning disappearance and the criminal doings surrounding it, I suppose a few words about my situation wouldn't hurt. I am what the French call *une femme d'un certain âge.* In my case, the *âge* is fifty-four, a fact that usually fills me with disbelief, to say nothing of outrage. Nonetheless, although I still have the smooth olive skin, dark hair, and almond-shaped eyes of a mature extra in a Fellini movie, my dewy days are over. My children are in their twenties. Kate is a lawyer, an associate in the corporate department of Johnson, Bonadies and Eagle, a Wall Street firm whose founding partners drafted the boilerplate of the restrictive covenants designed to keep my grandparents out of their neighborhoods. Joey works in the kitchen of an upscale Italian deli in Greenwich Village making overpriced mozzarella cheese; he is also film critic for a surprisingly intelligent, near-insolvent Web 'zine called *night.*

As for me, I have been a widow for two years. My husband, Bob, the king of crudités, flat of belly and firm of thigh, a man given to barely suppressed sighs of disappointment whenever he saw me accepting a dessert menu from a waiter (which, okay, I admit I never declined), died at age fifty-five, one-half day after triumphantly finishing the New York Marathon in four hours and twelve minutes. One minute he was squeezing my hand in the emergency room, a reassuring pressure, but I could see the fear in his eyes. As I squeezed back, he slipped away. Just like that. Gone, before I could say, Don't worry, Bob, you'll be fine. Or, I love you, Bob.

Except when the love of your life actually isn't the love of your life, the loss still winds up being devastating. Golden memories? No, only vague recollections of passionate graduate-school discussions and newlywed lovemaking fierce enough to pull the fitted sheet off the bed. Except those times had blurred in direct proportion to the length of the marriage, and after more than a quarter century together, Bob and I had wound up with sporadic pleasant chats and twice-a-month sex that fit neatly between the weather forecast and the opening credits of *Nightline.*

But back to Courtney Logan. "Something's very, very wrong with this disappearance business," I announced to my friend Nancy Miller a few days later. We were strolling around Gatsby Plaza, an upscale shopping center named, without a trace of irony, for Fitzgerald's *nouveau riche* character. It was one of those places that offers the woman who longs to spend two thousand dollars for a handbag a myriad of venues; it also provides the setting in which passersby, with one discerning blink, can acknowledge not just handbag owner's status, but her worth.

Anyway, the evening was lovely, clear, although too balmy for early November. The early stars were outshone only by the twinkly lights wrapped around the trunks and branches of the slim, pampered trees that sparkled Christmasly all year round. The air, heavy with the pungent autumnal scent of designer chrysanthemums, felt thick and humid, as though it had been shipped from the greenhouse along with the mums. Supposedly, we were on our way to a restaurant. For me, six-thirty is dinnertime. For Nancy, it's late lunch. Naturally, we were nowhere near a grilled salmon.

She'd halted in front of a store window, transfixed by a dress, a clingy, tubular thing in white cashmere with a hood. It was displayed on one of those chichi mannequins. This one had a barbed-wire head and Ping-Pong-ball-sized breasts that, for some reason, had nipples so prominent they looked like a pair of teeny Uzis.

"You like that dress?" I demanded.

"I more than like it," she replied. Her response came out something like "Ah mo thun lak it." Although Nancy had rarely been back to her native Georgia in thirty years, she'd clung to its syrupy accent, convinced, correctly, that it added to her charm. "I *love* it."

"It's a white cylinder."

"That is the point," she replied, too patiently.

"It probably costs a fortune," I warned.

"Of course it costs a fortune!"

"With that hood, you'll look like one of your white trash Klan relatives."

She gave one of her sighs of Christian forbearance. "You have several areas of competence, Judith. Haute couture is not among them."

"What *do* you think about Courtney Logan just vanishing?" I persisted as she was pulling open the heavy door to the shop. It was the Thursday after the disappearance, a night the stores stayed open until nine.

"She probably had some kind of secret life," Nancy said offhandedly. "That white dress in the window," she murmured to a saleswoman who, naturally, had walked straight to her after passing right by me, as though my wearing a not-genuine camel's-hair coat had rendered me invisible. The woman took Nancy's measure in a single flutter of her eyelashes, each one of which appeared to be individually mascaraed, after which she rested her chin on the pad of her index finger. Her long, squared-off nails were the color of prunes. (I, for one, find fingernails with right angles strangely disturbing.) A true size eight, the saleswoman intoned. Nancy, who had never been able to exorcise completely her inner Southern Belle, said nothing, merely lowering her eyes with sweeter-than-molasses-pie modesty: I concur. The woman left on her mission.

"What the hell is a 'true' size eight?" I inquired. "As opposed to what? A false size eight? Do sixes and tens try to pass?"

"I thought you wanted to discuss that Courtney woman."

"I do," I quickly answered.

"There's nothing to discuss."

"Your arteries are hardening."

"You do loathe reality, don't you?" Nancy observed. "Not that I blame you. Reality is hardly ever amusing. But my guess as to what happened is, Courtney Logan, woman of mystery, ran off with her kitchen contractor." She shook her head. "So fucking tedious. All these broads searching for meaning with anything that has eight inches."

"First of all, there's no indication that Courtney had anyone—"

"How do you know she didn't?" Nancy challenged.

"I don't. But women like her don't just disappear into the night. If she wanted to leave, she'd confide in a friend, talk to a matrimonial lawyer . . . tell her husband directly, for God's sake. She was hardly some passive-aggressive wimpette. She'd been an investment banker. Even if she were going to run off, would she just bring her little girl home from trick or treating, drop her off, and leave without a word?"

"What should she do, take the kid along?" Nancy crossed her slender arms over her true size eight chest, clearly miffed I was not anticipating the arrival of The Dress with sufficient enthusiasm.

"Nancy, focus: I've read everything about this and seen whatever they have on TV."

"For me," she declared, "this case is mildly interesting. For you, it's unhealthy. I don't like seeing you—"

"Relax. I'm fine! Listen, this is what seems to have happened: Courtney brings the little girl home. She says to the au pair: 'I forgot something. I just have to run to Grand Union for a minute.' Then she *doesn't come back*." I chewed my lip for a moment. "Have you heard any gossip or about anything the paper *hasn't* printed?"

Several years earlier Nancy had given up freelance writing to become first an assistant, then an associate editor of "Viewpoints," *Newsday*'s op-ed pages. Before she could even tell me she was too overwhelmed with work to listen to reporters' gossip, a blatant lie, the saleswoman returned. She carried the hanger aloft. The white dress wafted in the breeze she created. Together, she and Nancy fingered the hem reverently, in the manner Catholics might touch the Shroud of Turin. Then off they strode toward the dressing room.

Halfheartedly, I leafed through a rack of gray clothes which appeared designed to fit a Giacometti sculpture and thought about Courtney. According to both *Newsday* and Channel 12, the Long Island all-news cable station, no one had seen her at the supermarket or in its parking lot. That was not in the least remarkable, as the market was about a mile and a half from her house, and her car, a 1998 Land Rover, was later found right where it usually was, in the garage. Not one neighbor had seen or heard anything unusual. That was no big deal either. In that part of town, Shorehaven Farms, the houses stood at least an acre apart.

The following day, an announcement was made in the middle school and high school's homeroom classes requesting anyone who had been trick or treating in Shorehaven Farms between five and six P.M.—the time the au pair believed Courtney left for the supermarket—to please come to the main office ASAP. A few minutes before three, after a proffer of full immunity was broadcast over the PA, six juniors who had spent a productive night toppling mailboxes finally came forward. All swore they had seen nothing of Courtney.

Nancy returned from the dressing room, gray-green eyes shining, cheeks aglow. It was clear the dress had done for her precisely what she'd hoped, an event that has not yet occurred in my life. But then, Nancy is one of those natural . . . Well, not quite beauties. One of those women in their fifties who remain natural lovelies, all peaches-and-cream skin and long legs and auburn hair and huge eyes and wasp-waistedness, although the last had been facilitated by Jason J. Mittelman, M.D., F.A.C.S., Long Island's premier plastic surgeon, and his gluttonous liposuction machine. "The husband," Nancy postulated.

"Feh."

"What do you mean, 'feh'?"

"Too obvious," I told her.

"You're clearly not as bright as you think you are. It happens to be a thesis that's so obvious it's actually subtle."

"Wrong," I informed her. "If there's a shred of proof they would have arrested him." Then I mused: "I wonder what they actually have, if anything."

"Judith, you're not going to—"

"Please! Of course not. I'm just wondering. It's a sign of intellectual curiosity, not that you would know. Now what about the husband?"

"Somebody Logan."

"Greg Logan," I said encouragingly.

"Well, you asked if I'd heard any gossip," Nancy went on, tossing her head back so her hair flopped prettily, the southern belle gesture that accompanies any reaction from mildly pissed off to utterly hysterical. "I did hear one thing. He did not come into this world as Gregory Logan. He changed his name from— Are you ready?" I nodded. "Greg *Lowenstein*." She began to spell it for me.

"Don't waste your breath," I interrupted. "So big deal. People anglicize their names. Three generations ago half the Eastern Europeans and a quarter of the Italians who came through Ellis Island—"

"Greg's father is Fancy Phil Lowenstein. The gangster. The one who wears all that jewelry. He's the guy who brokered the truce between the Italian mob and Russian Mafia and he's this close"—she held up her index and middle fingers so they looked glued together—"to the Gambellos."

I switched from chewing my lip to gnawing my knuckle for a while. "So what are you getting at?" I was finally inquiring just as the sales-woman came into view. A garment bag with Nancy's KKK robe was hooked over her index finger; her other hand held the sales receipt and charge card. As she seemed to be advancing at the pace of a bride coming down the aisle, I kept going. "Are you saying some two-bit hood with an asinine nickname was dispatched to throttle Courtney Logan, the mother of Fancy Phil Lowenstein's grandchildren, and dump her body in Long Island Sound?"

"In Fancy Phil's circle," she replied, "that's a quickie divorce."

What Nancy did not reply, but which I learned when I picked up the papers from the driveway the next morning, was that *Newsday* was going with Greg Logan's pedigree as their front page, along with a photograph of Greg carrying his small son and holding his daughter's hand, heading toward a BMW in the driveway. The picture might have been taken with a telephoto lens because Greg did not look intruded upon and outraged. Merely sad. Possibly exhausted. Good-looking, though not convention-ally; his face was more valentine-shaped than standard rectilinear Wheaties box. Still, with his high cheekbones and thick, dark, upslanting eyebrows, he seemed intriguing in a slightly Genghis Khan way, even though the perpetually off newspaper color gave his skin that odd tone which makes people look as if they belong to a race with mauve skin.

Fancy Phil's picture—a black-and-white mug shot—was inset. He did not look like a Calvin Klein model. The headline made a semiclever reference to "family," which anyone more worldly than Travis the Tod-dler would know was intended to mean not only a group of people re-lated by ancestry, marriage, or adoption but also the old *la famiglia* so beloved by Mafia genre movies—dialogue inevitably accompanied by glasses of Chianti held high by men with inordinately hairy arms.

The *New York Times,* naturally, buried the story in the depths of the Metro section, allotting it three short, untitillating paragraphs. The *Shore-haven Beacon,* which was tossed onto driveways on its customary Friday, said nothing new about the Lowenstein connection, only that a "spokesperson for the Logan family" asked for the community to pray that Courtney would turn up "alive and well." What the *Beacon* did print was the photo of Courtney they'd run earlier with their original feature on StarBaby. It was captioned: "WHERE IS SHE?"

In the picture, Courtney, wearing slacks and a sweater set and an open, friendly smile, leans against a tree in front of what seemed to be a pretty nifty Georgian-style colonial. It was hard to tell precisely what she looked like because the *Beacon* is printed on such tissuey stock—the sort used for toilet paper in Second World countries—that the ink was always smudgy. Her nose and eyes, scrunched up in the act of smiling, offered too much nostril and too little eye; it was hard to read her expression. But her dimples were so deep that, even under the sad circumstances, I found myself smiling back. Her blond, shoulder-length hair was surprisingly full and wavy, more Grand Ole Opry than Princeton, although perhaps it had just been the humidity.

"Where is she?" took over the town. In the bakery, a neighbor gazed covetously at a cheesecake while proclaiming Courtney the victim of a serial killer. Leaning against the Shorehaven Triplex's popcorn machine—not cleaned since the Carter Administration—the kid behind the counter held a monster cup of Sprite and opined that Courtney Logan was an FBI agent, undercover to get evidence on the Logan-Lowensteins, and, at that precise moment, was probably being debriefed in Washington. Or maybe dead. In my book group the favorite theory held that Courtney's body was in the trunk of some hood's Lincoln Continental, courtesy of Fancy Phil, who wanted his son to marry some other Jewish gangster's daughter from Scarsdale, thus creating an unstoppable Long Island–Westchester organized crime axis. (This was no more idiotic than their interpretation of *Mrs. Dalloway.*) At work, the perpetually overwrought history department secretary suggested in her usual choked voice that maybe the au pair had buried Courtney alive in a graveyard, *where nobody would think to look for her.*

For the next few weeks, with increasing desperation, I read the papers and listened to the news hoping for a driblet of information about the Courtney Logan case. But Courtney had disappeared from the media as completely as she had from Shorehaven. People who'd only wanted to gossip nonstop about the Logans went back to warring over the "No Right Turn on Red" sign on Main Street and Harborview Road: Neighbors shook fists at neighbors at Town Hall meetings over whether the sign was a prudent traffic control measure or an edict that violated the due process clause of the U.S. constitution. Who else could I carry on with about the mystery? My children were busy being adults. Nancy suddenly had even less free time than usual, having tumbled for her new Jaguar mechanic. My other friends were involved with their own less interesting, less adulterous affairs.

I was so hard up for someone with whom to analyze the Courtney case that I actually wound up trying to discuss it with Smarmy Sam, aka Samuel P. B. Braddock III, the department chair. As always, because he thought of himself as a patrician and me as his inferior, the Smarm had simply pushed open my office door without knocking and stuck in his head. With his limp-lidded eyes and awesome overbite, this was no treat. He looked as if a couple of crocodile genes had glommed onto his double helix. "I'd liiiike an answer," he was saying. Well, he'd come to my office to again try to persuade me that teaching an additional two classes of America from Reconstruction to the Cold War in the spring was not just good for the commonweal, but for me as well.

"Before we get to that," I said with unseemly animation, "did you happen to hear that a woman from my town vanished into thin air?" Before Sam could get a word in edgewise, I offered a synopsis of what had been reported.

Sam understood that before he had a chance at my jumping at his offer, he'd have to let me jabber. "Is this Greg Loooogan a suspect?" He spoke more in a honk than a voice, that lockjaw Long Island accent still extant among polo players, random debutantes, and fakers. "By the by, is this Logan related to the Logans of Oyster Bay?" Sam inquired.

"No. He's related to Fancy Phil Lowenstein, a mob guy. Actually, Fancy Phil's his father."

"Oh." The Smarm, predictably, was doing his best to hide that he was appalled by the likes of me. His best, as usual, was not good enough. He was a man who not only taught American history, but believed he owned it. An ambulatory anachronism in our age of diversity, Sam was an East Coast WASP who not only thought he and his ilk were better than, say, me and my ilk—or anybody's ilk—but also believed we needed constant reminders of what our place was, for our own good. Was his accent the real thing? Was he genuinely wellborn? None of us had a clue. Well, he did keep his pens in a mug with a St. Paul's insignia and he managed to work the phrase "preparing at Sint Pol's" into a sentence at least once a week. Naturally, the entire department was on continuous Sint Pol's alert, all sworn to report an occurrence the second it passed the two-dimensional lines that were his lips.

"Caaaan we return to the business at hand?" Sam asked. "Your class load, or, if I may be so bold, your lack of it?"

So my need to talk about Courtney and what had happened to her was, yet again, frustrated. After the Smarm left, I told myself it was better he wasn't interested. Many mysteries in life remain unsolved. No matter how much I yearned, it would not be productive for me to try to insert myself into a situation that was none of my concern, even though every fiber of my being, and I had a fair number of fibers, cried out to do precisely that.

A few words of explanation might be appropriate here. Here they are: I am passionate about whodunits. The fictional kind. Hand me a Robert Parker novel, a John Dickson Carr locked-room mystery, even one I've read three times before, and you'll be giving me the gift of pleasure. But I love real-life whodunits more. About twenty years ago, as I was passing over to the bleak side of thirty-five, at a time when my now-lawyer daughter and film-critic son were little more than tykes, a local periodontist, M. Bruce Fleckstein, was murdered. I recall hearing about it on the radio and thinking: Who could have done such a thing? Before I knew it, I was investigating, and feeling thrillingly alive.

I am not sure why. Maybe it had to do with my sense of fair play—trying to bring the scales of justice back into balance. Murder is an attack on the body politic as well as on a particular body, and perhaps I felt the need to set things aright in my home town. Maybe I liked solving the puzzle, or maybe I was simply drawn to the dark side of the street. Believe it or not, I actually was instrumental in determining just who the killer was. But in the course of my detective work, I came into contact with a real homicide detective, Lieutenant Nelson Sharpe of the Nassau County Police Department.

To make a long story short, I had an affair with him. That was it. Six months of faithlessness in a twenty-eight-year marriage. Even for a historian like me, aware of the persistence of the past, it should have been ancient history—except I fell in love with Nelson. And he with me. For a time we even talked about leaving our spouses, getting married. We simply couldn't bear being without each other. Not just for the erotic joy, and there was plenty of that, but for the great fun we had together. But even more than my secret belief that a marriage that rises from the ashes of two other marriages is doomed from the start was our mutual, acknowledged awareness of what our leaving would do to our children. At the time Kate was six and Joey four. Nelson had three kids of his own. So he stayed with his wife June and I remained with Bob Singer. Nelson and I never saw or spoke to each other. For almost twenty years.

And then, less than a year before, we'd caught a glimpse of each other. For barely an instant. Unplanned. Nelson looked even more shocked than I felt. All he could manage was a brief nod as he kept walking. The next morning at eight-thirty—the time he used to call me knowing Bob would be on his way to the city—my phone rang.

However, the three seconds of seeing him and that very short phone conversation proved, for me, three seconds too long and one talk too many. After Bob's death, I wasn't exactly going to win any mental health awards. It took me months to get over that fleeting encounter with Nelson. I lifted the phone to call him a couple of thousand times. The only reason I hung up before the connection was actually made was that he was a cop and could no doubt trace any call. Naturally I couldn't sleep. Some internal motor kept racing. Some inner voice wouldn't stop screaming Fight or Flight; all that held me back from fighting or fleeing was a cloud of despondency so thick I couldn't see my way through it. Since I was already the Zoloft Queen, I tried to cure my ills with more therapy. Relaxation cassettes. Self-help books. A yoga video. Ben & Jerry's Chunky Monkey. Finally, what helped was time. So no more detecting for me. I'd vowed as much to Nancy. The previous week, when I discovered my Jeep straying onto Bluebay Lane, the street on which the Logans lived, I made a U-turn and drove straight home.

With Smarmy Sam gone, I turned back to my computer screen. There were the same three paragraphs of what was supposed to be a seven-hundred-fifty-word review of a book about the Glass-Steagall Act I'd promised to email two weeks earlier. Yet instead of a fourth paragraph, I typed an outline of what I knew from the papers, radio, and TV:

GREG . . . SHOULD HE BE SUSPECT IN COURTNEY DISAPPEARANCE?

1. Spouse usually 1st suspect.

2. Greg owns small chain of take-out places called Soup Salad Sandwiches. One in Huntington. Rest on the South Shore.

    A. Smart. Graduated from Brown, MBA from Columbia.

    B. Got into food business when father, Fancy Phil, gave him 2 fast food franchise stores in N.J. called Mr. Yummy's. Sold them for the $$$ to start own business from scratch.

3. SSS: Stores sell 3 varieties of soups, salads, and sandwiches daily. Big on quality ingredients. Stores in upper-middle-income towns.

4. An au pair living with Logans. University student. Depending on which account, from Austria or Germany. She was one Courtney told, "I forgot something. I just have to run to Grand Union for a minute." Any funny business with au pair and Greg??????

I also noted all the information I could recall about Courtney and her company, StarBaby. The following morning, on my way to work, I became one of those pitiful sensation sniffers and drove (shamefully slowly) down Bluebay Lane. It was the day before Thanksgiving. I should have spent those extra minutes at home with an orange so I could toss a few dozen strands of zest along with a tablespoon of Grand Marnier into the canned cranberry sauce—an old family recipe. Instead I found myself scrutinizing Greg and Courtney's red-brick colonial.

The house was set well back from the street on a velvet carpet of lawn. On each side of the dark green front door, three white columns stood tall and proud. The shutters were painted that same old-money green. Nevertheless, despite its classic Georgian features, the scale of the house was slightly off. It was set back on an acre, and though the builder had wisely not hacked down the property's impressive old trees, the Logans' place seemed overly large for a single family. It looked more like the Romance-languages department at a New England college.

In mysteries, it always annoys me when houses in which strange doings have occurred are described as "strangely still." What are they supposed to do? Cha-cha? Nevertheless, there was absolutely no sign of life in what the *Post,* obviously hoping to prevail in some tabloid alliteration competition, was calling the "lush Lowenstein-Logan Long Island estate." It really was strangely still. No BMW in the driveway today, no tricycle left out overnight. The curtains were drawn. A stubby flagpole over the door, the kind that displays those flags mail-order catalogs have managed to palm off on the public, was not flying the national colors of Pumpkinland or United States of Pilgrim Hats or whatever hideous banner suburbanites run up for Thanksgiving. However, if the *Post* could be trusted, Greg Logan was still in residence, having been "advised by Nassau County police authorities to remain in the community." Well, with Courtney having been missing for almost a month now, that advisement was no surprise.

The only surprise was that I had sunk so low that instead of going straight home after work to prepare what my kids referred to as Mom's Secret Sweet Potato Recipe (which, even with its optional canned crushed pineapple, was no different from the thirty million casseroles of marshmallow-covered golden glop that grace the tables of American households every fourth Thursday of November), I drove straight to the house of Mary Alice Mahoney Schlesinger Goldfarb. Nancy and I had known Malice since our college days at the University of Wisconsin, so I guess she was something between a longtime, unwelcome acquaintance to Nancy and a semifriend to me.

Mary Alice talked more than anybody in Greater New York and said the least. Was she annoying? Usually. Vacuous? Indubitably. Stupid? Probably. However, somehow her pea-brain was optimally structured for the absorption and retention of every item of Shorehaven gossip that flitted through the air, no matter how vague.

"Who's catering you?" Mary Alice inquired as we stood in her dining room. Her gold-and-white outfit, with its skintight pants and embroidered bolero jacket, would have looked better on a matador. I sensed it was the work of one of those avant-garde designers she had, sadly, grown to favor. Naturally, she was not cooking, but, as her third husband, Lance Goldfarb, urologist to the North Shore's best and brightest, was suburbane enough to understand, only first wives cooked.

Mary Alice, however, was preparing for the next day's feast. She leaned over her table (gleaming black wood with red and yellow glints, made from what was doubtless an endangered species in the Amazon rain forest), her long, thin fingers rearranging squashes, purple grapes that I guess were supposed to look slightly moldy, sprays of bittersweet, and some ruby-petaled flowers that looked like a cross section of female genitalia. The arrangement overflowed a sterling silver tureen the size of a footbath. Mary Alice's engaged-to-Goldfarb ring, a diamond dazzler, sparkled in the genteel light of a Venetian chandelier.

"No one's catering for me," I responded. "I'm cooking."

A saddened "Oh" popped out from between her high-gloss lips, but she quickly put her index finger against them, as if she were a kindergartner who'd just been signaled to shush. For a woman halfway into her fifties, Malice had an astonishing repertoire of little-girl mannerisms. I knew what she was thinking: Bob had left me practically in the poorhouse, i.e., unable to afford a caterer who could bring in baby squabs stuffed with wild mushroom polenta which would be touted, by the caterer's Manhattan-actor-waiters, as much more authentically Native American than any turkey. However, poverty was not an issue for me. Bob had grown into the sort of man who could never resist a frolicsome lunch with an insurance actuary. He'd planned for everything except his own early death and had left me, though not rich, well fixed enough to spring for a squab or two.

But I repressed a powerful urge to babble a defensive: I *like* cooking my own food. Instead I asked: "What's new?" Then, before she could utter her first word in what would be an exquisitely detailed description of how she was having her chinchilla jacket relined, I immediately tossed in a "Oh, Mary Alice, I keep forgetting to ask . . . Has anyone seen Greg Logan around town?"

"Not that I've heard about," she replied, pulling out one of her Empire dining-room chairs (from Husband Mahoney) and sitting. I did likewise, although the large Napoleonic bee design on the center of the burgundy damask of each seat had always seemed slightly menacing. "But you know who *has* been seen around town?" She waited, patient. I was, too, so finally she pronounced: "The au pair! In the patisserie. Buying rye bread." I noticed Mary Alice was still rolling her *R*s intermittently, so "rye bread" came out vaguely Gallic; she'd recently returned from a weeklong urethra conference in Lyons with Husband Goldfarb. "She was wearing what everyone was positive was an Hermès scarf." She gave a humorless, monosyllabic laugh. "You know what *that* means." She rested her left arm on the table and, with her right fingertips, caressed the gold threads of what was either a leaf or a duckling embroidered on the jacket's sleeve.

"She knows how to accessorize?" I suggested.

"No. Most people were saying, Well, *we* know who's dipping into Courtney Logan's scarf drawer."

She waited for me to respond, so I said "Wow." Actually, I was impressed with the notion of an entire drawer dedicated to scarves. Mine were kept in two Hefty One-Zips that resided with my nightgowns and a lifetime's collection of half-slips I couldn't bring myself to throw out.

"But then I heard, no, she isn't stealing. It was one of many, many, many *gifts*." To make sure I understood, she added: "From Greg Logan."

"So people are saying he's taken up with the au pair?"

"Not now. *Before*." Malice took a deep breath to compose herself after imparting this electrifying news. As for me, I'd already said Wow, and a gasp would have been extravagant, so I just sat quietly. "Before Courtney disappeared," Mary Alice explained. "They say what happened is that Courtney came home with their little girl Morgan from trick or treating. One guess what she walked in on?"

"Greg Logan and the au pair?" She gave a knowing nod. I was still trying to get used to the notion that "Morgan" had become more than a financial institution or a surname. It was what former investment bankers named their daughters. Then I asked, "Where was their little boy during this liaison?" Mary Alice shrugged. "And wasn't Greg at a business dinner in the city that night?" I went on, "That's what I've been reading, that when Courtney didn't come back, the au pair made no attempt to call him. She just put the kids to bed and waited until he got home. Then she told him she didn't know where Courtney had gone."

"Not according to my sources."

"Who are your sources, Mary Alice?"

"Everybody." She adjusted one of Husband Schlesinger's three-carat diamond-stud earrings. "Everybody knows about them, Judith."

"Well, let's say Courtney did walk in on that kind of a thing," I conceded. "What is she supposed to have done? Or what was done to her?"

"Ha!"

"They're saying Greg and the au pair murdered Courtney?"

"That's the number one theory. They did it, maybe to keep her from screaming or something and—"

"Where did they stash the little girl with a bagful of candy while they were murdering Courtney Logan?"

"I don't know." Trying to appear blasé, she pretended to be absorbed in a cuticle, although knowing Malice, she could have been genuinely engrossed.

"And then?" I demanded.

"Well, it could be they buried the body someplace. Everyone said the police had a dog and they looked in the wooded area in back between the Logans' and—I think it's the Lanes' house, Judy and Ed. He's the ear, nose, and—"

"But they didn't find anything."

"The other theory," she said, recovering quickly, "is that Greg's father, Mr. Big, did something with the body. I mean, that's his meat and potatoes." Mary Alice had the gift of unfortunate metaphor. "Or . . . But not too many people believe this one."

"What?"

"It's a psychoanalytic theory. You'll probably laugh."

"Tell me, Mary Alice."

"That Courtney was, you know, traumatized. She just ran off when she saw them together. And it was *so* traumatic she got amnesia. She could be anyplace, not knowing who she is. You've got to admit, that's better than being beaten to death or knifed or strangled or something by your own husband and a foreign au pair, for God's sakes, who then gets free range to your scarf drawer. And everything else, if you get what I mean."

"How about this: Maybe Courtney went outside and met up with someone weird. Halloween's the one night of the year you have lots of people—a lot of them in masks—roaming around, even in the quietest neighborhoods."

"But *everyone* says in this kind of thing, it's usually the husband. Isn't it?" Mary Alice reached over to her Thanksgiving centerpiece and tapped a sprig of bittersweet forward an eighth of an inch. *"Isn't it?"*

Isn't it? Sleeping with a homicide cop for six months does not qualify one as an expert on criminal detection. Neither does reading Maj Sjöwall/Per Wahlöö and Ed McBain police procedurals. Not even once having helped solve a murder. Still, if I hadn't distracted the ever-distractable Mary Alice Mahoney Schlesinger Goldfarb by inquiring what, as Thanksgiving hostess, she was going to wear (and then listening to her pleat by pleat description of an Issey Miyake skirt), I would have had to say yes, absolutely, it usually is the husband they suspect when the wife suddenly and inexplicably disappears.

Throughout that winter, I heard whispers and mutterings that Greg

Logan's arrest was imminent. None of the rumors panned out. It wasn't that I forgot about Courtney. One bitter night, when the snow on the spruce outside my bedroom window grew so heavy that my light sleep was broken with the ominous crack of a limb about to crash, I lay in bed knowing in my heart that she hadn't been grabbed by some monstrous Halloween deviate and was being held against her will, but that she was lying in some shallow, icy, suburban grave. I'd think about her children: One day they'd had a mother who adored them. The next day she was no more. Were these poor kids told Mommy will be back, or Gosh, honey, we don't know where Mommy is but we hope she'll call? Were they told anything?

But because it seemed there would be no conclusion to the Courtney case, it was easier to push it from my mind. I threw myself into work and lived for the times I'd see Kate and Joey or my friends. When I was by myself, mostly I thought about Bob. True, he and I hadn't had a fairy-tale marriage. Still, even when all that's left is polite conversation and low-wattage marital sex, you have to remember (I'd told myself during those years we were together) that once upon a time it *must* have been a love story. I guess I always half expected the plot would get moving again: Some incident will touch off a great conflict in our relationship. Then, lo and behold, not only will the air between us finally clear, but there'd be romance in it! The two of us will walk hand in hand into a sunset, happily ever after—or until one of us went gently into the night in our eighth or ninth decade. Imagine my surprise when he died before my eyes in the ER of North Shore Hospital.

So not only no husband. No prospect of another one. Not one more blind date, that was for sure, not after the two geriatric wonder boys Nancy had dubbed Old and Older. After Christmas break, I began to go out occasionally with Geoff, a postmodernist from the English department at St. Elizabeth's. I rarely understood what he was talking about, his clothes smelled as if he patronized a discount dry cleaner, and unfortunately he had a healthy sex drive. No one else was knocking at my door.

I had long before disciplined myself not to think about Nelson Sharpe. And to dwell on the Courtney Logan case would be to invoke him: What would he make of all this? Would he be putting pressure on the husband? Would he be investigating other leads?

I didn't want to jeopardize again the life I'd fashioned for myself because, whatever it was, it worked. I had kids, friends, library and Block-buster cards. I had a job that evoked remarks like, Gee, or Ooh, how intellectually stimulating. The truth was, my work occasionally had my mind. Never my heart.

So winter warmed into spring and early one evening in the middle of

May I came home from St. Elizabeth's and raced straight to the garden to cut lilacs. When I came back inside, in the way of so many people who live alone, I reflexively turned on the radio for company. My face was buried in my armful of lavender, purple, and white blooms and I was getting dopey on those first ecstatic sniffs. So it took a few seconds before I actually tuned into the sandpaper voice of Mack Dooley, the Logans' pool man. He was telling WCBS radio: "Like, this morning, about eleven, I'm taking off the Logans' pool cover with this kid who works for me—you know, pump it out, acid-wash it, get it ready and—" The reporter did attempt a question but Dooley kept going. "So listen. The cover's fine, tied down real tight like I left it in the middle of September when I closed them up. The kid and I are kind of rolling it back and I see something. I say, Holy—You know how big raccoons can get? Except for the life of me I can't figure out how even a raccoon could work its way under that cover. Well, that second I see, you know, it's . . . It's a body! Jeez. Believe it or not I'm still shaking."

Chapter Two

The news about the body in Greg Logan's swimming pool consumed local TV and radio, a tristate info-blob engulfing any news about Al Gore's plummeting poll numbers or the raging wildfires in Los Alamos. Everyone was broadcasting: I heard about it at teeth-grinding length from my next-door neighbor, Chic Cheryl, in her skintight silver racewalking getup that highlighted each buttock as if it were a separate trophy. Mary Alice Mahoney Schlesinger Goldfarb left three breathless messages on my answering machine, during which I sent up three prayers of thanks for the invention of Caller ID.

I also heard from two of my colleagues at St. Elizabeth's, from my doctoral adviser at NYU, and from Bob's college roommate, Claymore Katz, a criminal lawyer. Needless to say, postmodernist Geoff called; he wanted to know (a) Was it not beyond irony that the paradigmatic suburbanite was found dead in a backyard swimming pool, and (b) Did I want to see a revival of *Krapp's Last Tape*. I called his voice mail and retorted (a) I wasn't sure what lay beyond irony, and (b) No thanks. Nancy phoned from *Newsday*, but that was to verify I was actually home, not skulking about in Holmesian drag in a pathetic attempt to attract the attention of a certain member of the Nassau County PD. Not one of them could add a single factlet to what I'd initially learned on the radio, although that didn't stop them (or me) from discussing it.

Late the following morning I was at my kitchen table grading my classes' final exams, determined to dismiss all thoughts of murder, mostly because I felt obliged to give my students a fair shake. The majority were either good kids or hardworking get-a-college-education retirees. None were born scholars. (The most elementary of my four essay questions, "Describe the programs Franklin D. Roosevelt's first administration put forth to help 'the forgotten man at the bottom of the economic pyramid,'" evoked answers as exhaustive as Darci Lundgren's "FDR's Brain Trust" and Seymour Myron Bleiberman's "emerg. banking bill + hire men for govt relief projects + helping farmers.") In the interest of full disclosure, I have to admit that once I achieved my goal, teaching history on the college level, I discovered a disturbing truth about myself: I didn't like to teach. What I wanted was to read history, or talk history, preferably with someone who knew more than I did.

After an hour I gave myself a coffee break, hopped onto the Web, and discovered that the Nassau County medical examiner had already completed the autopsy. He had determined (no doubt employing a procedure so revolting I wouldn't even begin to contemplate it) that the woman in the Logans' pool had died from a bullet in the head. The condition of the body indicated that death could have occurred around the time Courtney disappeared on Halloween night. Furthermore, his examination of dental records confirmed what all of us would have been glad to tell him: The body was indeed that of Courtney Logan. Then, thank God, the phone rang.

"Hey!" My son had such an astounding basso voice that, on hearing it, you half expected him to burst into "Some Enchanted Evening." Clearly this wasn't to be. Joey was not a Rodgers and Hammerstein kind of guy. "Mom, did you hear? They found that woman. She was in her own pool, over in Shorehaven Farms!" For a cinéaste and ironist who never wore a color inappropriate for a state funeral, he sounded remarkably cheery. "Did you know her?"

"No," I said regretfully. "I don't think I ever even saw her." I set down my red pen atop a blue book on which I'd written a large *C*. Then—what the hell—I picked up the pen and added a conspicuous plus sign after the C. "Isn't there some movie that begins with a body in a pool?" I mused.

"*Sunset Boulevard,*" he suggested in an overly gentle manner.

"It's just mild senility." I chuckled but received not even a polite heh-

heh in response. "With . . . You know who I mean. William what's-his-name."

"Holden." An offspring's sigh of tedium is inaudible to all human ears except a parent's. Boring your child who, at one point in his or her life, found you unspeakably delightful is humbling. "So what do you think?" Joey asked, slickly changing the subject before I could blurt out that the director was William Wyler instead of Billy Wilder and further humiliate myself. "I mean, about the woman they found."

"Her name was Courtney Logan," I said.

"Who did it? The husband?"

"Only if he's a total moron." Chewing the top of the pen for a moment, I debated whether to self-censor all talk of murder. I would probably become excessively enthused and knew from experience that giddiness in the postmenopausal was generally less than appealing to the recently postpubescent. Nevertheless, I found myself bubbling, "Listen, kiddo, the *minute* a wife is missing, there's speculation about the husband's guilt. But let's assume for the sake of argument that Greg Logan, Brown graduate, is not self-destructive. And that he's smarter than Fred Mac-Murray in *Double Indemnity.* Okay? And let's also assume he plans a murder."

"Okay," Joey said in bright anticipation, the way he had when he was ten and I'd allowed him to see *Return of the Jedi* yet again.

"Now, I don't mean Greg actually sat down and plotted anything. Let's say it was a spur-of-the-moment crime of passion. But tell me, why would he stash his wife's body in the one spot where—*guaranteed*—she would be found the following May, if not earlier? And on his own property? Why not simply let her stay missing? Even if everyone assumed she was dead, no one would have the foggiest notion where she was."

"So if there wasn't any body . . ." Joey thought aloud.

"Where's the physical evidence a murder was committed? Nowhere, that's where. All there'd be is a *belief* Courtney was dead. Everything I've ever read says it's very hard to get a conviction without a corpus delecti. But now her death—her *murder*—is a fact."

"Except maybe this Greg guy *is* a total jerk," Joey mused. "Or some kind of psycho. Or okay, maybe it was temporary insanity but then he panicked and just wanted to get rid of her. Except once he calmed down, he couldn't figure out a way to fish her out of the pool."

"Maybe," I submitted, "he didn't do it."

"Maybe," he countered, "he did do it because it was part of some scheme."

"Are you giving me an Oliver Stone conspiracy theory?"

"No. Listen, Mom. Maybe he was willing to take a huge risk, because he needed the body to get insurance money—except he needed a few months to make sure he'd covered up all his tracks. Or maybe it wasn't the husband. Maybe it was his old man, Gangster Guy, who ordered the hit."

"Why? Because Courtney forgot to send him a birthday card? Joey, even if Fancy Phil Lowenstein wanted his daughter-in-law dead, is he going to deep-six her in the one place sure to incriminate his son?"

"Maybe Fancy Phil has issues with Greg."

"Still, would he stash her where, God forbid, his grandchildren could conceivably see their mother's body?"

"You're talking as if Fancy is a normal human being. What if he's an animal? Do you think he'd care about his grandkids' mental health?"

A few minutes later, after tossing a few more theories back and forth and discussing whether the plot of *The Big Sleep* made any sense and agreeing that it probably didn't, we said our good-byes. I must have flaked out for a minute because when I glanced down, I noticed that pen was still in hand. Mine. And it had jotted:

1. Greg Logan?
2. au pair?
3. did Courtney have boyfriend???
4. enemy from Courtney's investment banking days?? or earlier??
5. Greg girlfriend??? + was she jealous???
6. stalker/psycho???
7. mob hit by Fancy Phil/Fancy Phil's enemies???

It was only then that I realized I'd been scribbling on an exam booklet of one Amanda Gerrity, a whispery, milk-white young woman with a distressing number of body parts pierced by studs and hoops. I ripped off the cover with my notes, transferred the C+, jotted an apology about spilled coffee. Trying not to think about the process of getting a silver ball embedded in one's tongue, I studied my list of possible perps. Back to work, I finally commanded myself. Crumpling Amanda's bluebook cover, I strode purposefully across the kitchen and lobbed it into the garbage.

Three hours later, by the time my daughter Kate called, I had lunched on suspicious three-day-old deli tuna salad and survived, and graded seven more exams.

"Mom," Kate began efficiently. The law firm for which she worked billed two hundred and sixty dollars an hour for their second-year associates; as she'd always been an honorable child, she dispensed with gratuitous words like "hi" when calling on office time.

"Hi, sweetheart!"

"I cannot believe you haven't called me," she said.

"About what?"

"About who done it." Kate sounded playful, a quality I was some-times afraid she would lose practicing corporate law; Johnson, Bonadies and Eagle's clients did not sound like a pack of merry madcaps. Stretching the telephone cord until its curlicues became an almost straight line, I re-trieved the red-penned list from the garbage. It smelled, not surprisingly, like suspicious three-day-old deli tuna salad. Holding it as far from my nose as I could, I read off the possibilities. "What do your detective in-stincts tell you?" my daughter inquired.

"Hard to say. I have no sense of what the husband's like. Do you have time to talk now?"

"No problem," she said, indulgent, generous.

"Well, there's an au pair, German or Austrian. Maybe she's gorgeous. Maybe she's Voof-voof the Dog-faced Girl. Who knows? But people are definitely gossiping about her and the husband. So far, though, no one's described her in any way except to say she's twenty-two."

"Not a capital offense in New York," Kate suggested leisurely, as though the debt restructuring of Southeast Pulp and Paper she'd been slaving over fourteen hours a day including weekends was a trivial detail she could attend to at her leisure.

I was about to continue down my list of possible perps when I had one of those belated "aha!" moments. It was no coincidence, my children calling on the same day, wanting only to chat about Courtney Logan's murder. They'd had a conference, Kate and Joey, and had obviously con-cluded that with semester's end at St. Elizabeth's imminent, there was nothing to keep me amused. Amused? More likely, the last time they'd seen me, a few days before on Mother's Day, they'd intuited the limita-tions of psychopharmacology. So here they were, my two good kids, demonstrating a way for me to get some life back in my life: get revved up about a murder. A few minutes later I gave my firstborn what I hoped was a reassuringly upbeat good-bye. Then I went searching for the Yel-low Pages.

Two days later, Mack Dooley of Pools, Etc. was standing in my back-yard, a very short man with a very long tape measure. "I hope you're talking gunite, Mrs. Singer." As he spoke, he kept flapping back his hand again and again, ordering his assistant, a blond, buzz-cut, blank-eyed kid to move farther back with the tape measure to give me an idea of the length of the pool.

"Well, Mr. Dooley—"

"Call me Mack," he said cheerfully. For such a short man, he had re-markably long arms. Except for the lack of hair, he resembled those jolly chimpanzees in baseball caps who are perpetually being trotted onto TV by anthropologists to prove that human beings aren't the only primate with language and tool-making skills.

"As I told you on the phone," I told him, "I'm only *considering* a pool right now. I'm not ready to commit to—"

"Sure, sure, but with a place like yours—" Mack Dooley glanced back at the house. It's a Tudor-style of brick and stone with a fine mullioned bay window. It's not imposing, but solid, the sort of house Henry VII's favorite furrier might own. "—how could you go with vinyl?" He was not entirely successful in suppressing a shudder at that thought. "Now, you're probably talking a lap pool, about four feet deep, right?" I nodded. "And fifty feet long, although you could do sixty here easy and in the end you'd say, 'Mack, thanks for pushing me to sixty.' "

"Maybe you can give me estimates for both," I suggested. I pulled back my head and eyed him. "Were . . . Were you the one I saw on TV?" He nodded modestly, although his light eyes, bright against his tanned-to-leather skin, sparkled at the recognition. "God, it must have been terrible for you, finding her like that."

"Yeah, well, it was no treat. I mean, every couple of years, you open a pool and there's somebody's ex-cat. But trust me, nothing like this."

"Were you able to see who it was?"

Mack Dooley shook his head. "She was like floating—you okay, hearing this kind of thing?" I nodded encouragingly. "Except what I saw was her back. At first I thought, This is some kind of big animal, a raccoon, or one of those eight-hundred-dollar big dogs—I forget what you call them—that drop dead when they're seven years old. But then I see, Sweet Jesus, it's a *person*. I could make out the back of her neck and a little of her ear. So I say to John—" he pointed with his chin at his assistant at the other end of the tape measure. " 'Get out of here.' Then I threw him my cell phone and I told him, 'Get 911.' You don't want a kid like him having to see something like that."

"Was the body badly decomposed?"

"What can I tell you? She was facedown. But what I seen of her, you wouldn't call her composed." Mack didn't appear to resent the questions. After three days of interrogation, not just from cops but from reporters and neighbors, he seemed to be resigned to the attention that comes with celebrity.

"Was she clothed?" I asked.

"Yeah, but what she was wearing didn't look so good either."

"What was she wearing?"

He looped his thumbs over the waistband of his lightweight gray sweatpants, pursed his lips, and moved them left, right, left as he thought;

this was a question no one seemed to have posed. "Looked like some kind of jacket. My best guess? One of those blazers."

"What color?"

"Hard to say. Probably used to be dark, but it was kind of faded. I guess from the chlorine. All I could see was the shape at first. The back. That's how come I thought: Raccoon? I didn't see the rest of her. You know how they say 'dead man's float' when you're learning to swim?"

"Right."

"Well, for some reason it wasn't like that with Mrs. Logan. I couldn't see her arms and legs. They must have been hanging down in the water, and after—what is it?—all those months, the water isn't what they call crystal clear. Now don't think that's a problem for you, poolwise, Mrs. Singer. All pools get algae and stuff over the winter no matter how much chemicals we dump in the fall. One acid-wash in May—takes hardly no time—and you'll have perfect water all summer."

I had to admit, the notion of a pool was sounding not so ridiculous. Laps in the morning before work, laps in the evening. I could have unimaginably firm upper arms and be one of those women who wear sleeveless turtlenecks. I could have friends over for a swim and a barbecue, or drift alone on a float with a plastic cup of Chardonnay and watch the sun set. My head began making up-and-down motions as if I were already saying yes to Mack Dooley. "Did you know her?" I asked quickly, to divert attention from my bobbling head. "Courtney Logan, I mean."

"Yeah," he said, "because she was the one I had to deal with, putting in the pool. She signed us up for the maintenance, too."

"What was she like?" I paused. "I guess you've been asked that too many times."

"I don't mind," Mack replied graciously. "She was really nice. But businesslike. Know what I mean? A lady. Hello, how are you, did you have a good weekend—that kind of stuff. Not snotty or snooty or whatever you call it, like some of them—I hope you'll pardon me, but you're not one of them . . . The younger ones. The yuppie ladies. They leave the business world to raise their kids, but you know what? They still gotta show you what big shots they are. They're so . . . tough. Not Mrs. Logan. She was just nice to deal with."

"Was she a hard bargainer? Did she accept your first price?" He seemed to hesitate. "Don't worry," I reassured him. "If I decide on a pool, you'll make a profit. I'm not such a good negotiator." He pressed a button and the tape measure whizzed back into its receptacle. The blond kid moseyed back to the truck.

Mack Dooley smiled again, a pleasant, crooked-toothed smile in an orthodonticized universe. "She had one shrewd business brain, I'll tell you that. Every time the husband was ready to sign on the dotted line, she'd say to him, 'Greg, let's sleep on this.' But in the nicest way. She handled herself so nice you couldn't resent her."

I thought back to the photograph the *Beacon* had published: Courtney *had* looked genuinely nice. "Did the husband seem browbeaten by her?"

He shook his head. "I don't think so. I kind of assumed he was more the easygoing type."

"Did the police want to know all about him?"

"Did they ever!"

"Like what?"

"Did he have a temper. Did I ever see them fight. How they got along."

"How did they get along?"

"As far as I could see, good." He rubbed his chin thoughtfully. His beard made a sandpaper sound. "What else? Oh, did I notice anything between him and the foreign girl who watched their kids." I raised my eyebrows in what I hoped was a subtle query. "I saw her a few times, with the little girl, by the pool. Quiet type. Not what they call a looker. With the hair that kind of separates into strings. Like a mop just before it dries. Except—I don't know—maybe it's how girls' hair is supposed to be these days and it's really pretty."

"What did you tell the police when they asked you about this au pair and Greg Logan?"

"The truth. I didn't see nothing. If I was Logan, I guarantee you, I wouldn't be tempted with such a nice wife, blond hair, dimples. Except the girl didn't have a bad shape. And listen, how the heck can you tell what's doing in some other guy's heart? Right?"

Right. And three days later on a gloomy Sunday afternoon, with the sky a ceiling of gray steel, I said zero to Nancy about hearts or about Mack Dooley. I didn't want to listen to another lecture on what she'd decided was my fixation not on solving a puzzle—figuring out whodunit—but on Nelson Sharpe. Instead I politely inquired: "Besides looking at it, does anyone actually *use* a gazebo?" We were making our way through the acre and a half of woods on the side of her house, taking minuscule elflike leaps to avoid the poison ivy and nettles that were already choking to death the spring wildflowers. "Besides, if it's stuck all the way out here, you wouldn't see it from the house." We turned to look behind us. Only a dark shingled edge of the roof of the Millers' sprawling Victorian was visible through the newly leafed trees. "I guess you could bring a book out here. But would you want to read on a wooden bench or one of those wrought iron garden chairs that make your ass numb? Plus—" I glanced up at the lofty oaks, maples, and other assorted trees—"in this light, what could you read? The first two lines of an eye chart?"

"I need *someplace*." Nancy sounded less huffy than desperate. "Larry's going to trash the house again." Every five or six years her husband, an architect, would be gripped by a new artistic vision: *This* is what the world should look like. Then the grand old house's guts would be ripped out and replaced—with all white walls, floors, and furniture. Or with a single, immense terra-cotta-tiled space that was kitchen-dining-room-living-room-den-library. Or with such rococo moldings and fixtures that even the downstairs guest bathroom looked as if a Bourbon king could be in there signing an entente.

"Well," I said, stopping to admire a miniature forest of knee-high ferns, "better Larry finds a new aesthetic when he gets bored than a new wife."

Nancy shrugged. "I am no longer certain that is true. What do I need him for?"

"You love him."

"You are an incorrigible romantic, Judith." She shook her head, saddened by my foolishness. "Of course, being a romantic is a cinch once you don't have a husband. Tell me, how can I love someone who wants his creative legacy to be a Gothic media room? Do you know what he confided to me last night, *post* the usual *coitus nauseus*?: 'Nancy, the Gothic style is the only morally correct form of building.' Any moment he'll get a tonsure and a hair shirt." She shrugged. "The man is fifty-eight years old. This is probably the beginning of dementia. I'll be changing his diapers soon."

"Would it blight this day even more if I reminded you that the age difference between you and Larry is three years, not thirty-three? But so what? For a woman in her mid-fifties, you look fabulous. You even look fabulous for a woman in her forties. Why get hung up on age—"

Setting her hands on the slim hips of her tight, low-slung jeans, Nancy snapped, "Hush!"

"You know what my new motto is?" I asked her.

"Regurgitate every syllable of psychobabble I hear on *Oprah*?"

"No," I said. " 'Never be afraid of the truth.' "

"The truth is, it's Viagra three nights a week. The only thing *not* limp about Larry is his dick. His very essence is limp. And speaking of limp, it's high time you reconsidered your adolescent fantasy about that cop. If you don't think he has to put a splint on it these days you are seriously deluded. You're deluded anyhow. A few months' fling twenty years ago and he's the love of your life?"

I slammed my hands onto my hips. "I did not bring him up."

"He's in the air. I can sense his continual presence in your head."

"You're way off base," I lied.

"You wonder why you're not meeting any decent men—"

"No. I don't wonder. You do."

"He's married, Judith."

"Not to the same one."

Nancy stopped short before a copse of bamboo. "No. You're right. To a new one."

"It's not working."

"How do you know? You ran into him a year ago for a couple of seconds."

"But then he called," I protested feebly.

"And you had a four-second conversation."

"It lasted a few minutes. I could hear it in his voice: He wasn't happy. Anyhow, he's not in Homicide anymore. He's head of some other unit, Special Investigations. Something like that. But if you're thinking I'm obsessed, it so happens *I* was the one who said 'Nice talking to you again' and got off the phone."

"Sure. So you could faint."

"I don't faint." I hated fighting with her. It was one thing to be assertive professionally, to tell a history department chair you will not teach four sections of America from Jamestown to Appomattox the following fall, especially if he's going to stick forty students in each section. It's another thing to go head-to-head with your dearest friend. But Nancy possessed what I guessed was a journalist's ability to withstand unpleasantness and keep going. In fact, confrontation seemed to refresh her. So I turned away and got busy studying her house. All that was visible was the roof and what I was pretty sure (but not a hundred percent) was the top of a linden tree. I didn't really want to ask if it was, because it would clue her in that I wanted desperately to change the subject. Naturally, Nancy would know if it was a linden. It has always been my belief that Protestants, born with innate knowledge of the names of all things botanical, cannot help but think less of you if you have to ask.

"In three-quarters of an hour," she observed, "I haven't heard one word about Courtney Logan from you. Why? To prove to me you're really not interested in a murder, i.e., not interested in *him*."

Precisely. So I snapped, "No. I've been listening to you nattering on about gazebos." I decided not to add: and couldn't get a word in edgewise.

"I was expecting you to ask me to hit up our reporters for unpublished tidbits about the head wounds."

"Wounds?" I demanded. "I heard about *a* bullet." Nancy made a big

show of casualness, taking off her sweater and tying it around her waist. It was a peach-color wisp of a thing, made from some suddenly chic fluff I think was shaved off the gonads of Indonesian goats, the must-have knit now that cashmere had become a bore and pashmina a cliché. "Wounds?" I repeated. "Did I hear a plural?"

"I heard something about there being two bullets in her head. The first shot killed her. The second one was . . . I don't know. Maybe insurance."

"Do they have any idea what the weapon was?" I demanded.

"The medical examiner may. I don't."

"Are you sure both shots were from the same gun?"

"No."

"Can you find out?"

"No, Judith. I don't do crime. I assign and edit op-ed pieces—other people's diatribes about health care. Or bilingual education. Friday I cut a thousand-word paean to desalinization to seven hundred." She shook her head. Her expertly cut auburn hair swung gracefully a quarter inch above her shoulders. "It still sucked the big one."

"You could ask the reporter who's covering the Courtney—"

"Listen to me. You know how you think my drinking is bad for me? That's what I think this detective business is for you. Okay, fine, twenty years ago you had some fun figuring who did it to that dirty dentist. It showed you there was a world that extended beyond your car pool. And you got laid. Maybe even made love to. Fine. I do it all the time." In Nancy's mind, Mount Sinai was the place God had given Moses the Nine Commandments. In her thirty-one years of marriage, at least fourscore lovers had come—and gone. "Gives you a glow that beats a paraffin wrap. But you're not me. You take fucking seriously." Somewhere in the deepest south there is a finishing school that teaches young ladies a thousand and one wiles—from the moist-lips-slightly-parted-as-if-anticipating-fellatio-while-hanging-on-every-word trick to cunningly contrived cleavage displays. Only when belles have mastered all thousand and one stratagems are they given carte blanche to say anything that comes into their heads, any place, any time, no matter how obscene or shocking, along with a guarantee they will be deemed far more enchanting than conventional eyelash-batting magnolia blossoms who mind their tongues. "There's nothing *wrong* with taking fucking seriously, even though it's a tiresome way of looking at the world."

"It's not," I told her, although I was just keeping up my end of the argument. For all I knew, Nancy was right, and I'd pissed away my juicy decades. Now all I could ever hope to attract was someone like postmodernist Geoff with his ear hair. "But if you think there's no advantage to

doing it because it would be tedious or because Nelson would need a der-
rick to get it up, then what would be so terrible if he and I were to get
together—which I swear I'm not planning."

"Because you're emotionally vulnerable now."

"I'm much better."

"Do I have to hum 'The Merry Widow Waltz' to remind you?" She
picked up a dead branch and, with a final glance toward her house, staked
it in the dirt: Ground Zero for her gazebo. "You lost a husband. You lost
him to death, not to a twenty-something with perky tits and a law degree
from Harvard. So you can't hate him for leaving without feeling guilty,
which being Jewish you have a genius for anyway. And you lost him—"
She snapped her fingers—"like that. Whatever you felt for him, you're
still getting over the loss. It would be one thing if you took up with a cute
guy with a wad in his jeans to offer you a little temporary comfort. But
not this cop. All he can offer you is *Sturm und Drang* and *maybe* middle-
aged fucking and champagne for one on New Year's Eve—none of which
you need." She pulled the branch out of the ground and started walking
again. "So no cop."

"No cop," I said quietly.

"And no murder."

"Fine." Thirty hours later I knocked on Greg Logan's front door.

Chapter Three

"I'm Judith Singer." I'd rehearsed what I would say to Greg as I was putting on eyeliner. Not bad, I thought: both the makeup and the introduction. As far as the makeup went, for once both eyes came out as if they belonged to the same person. As for the second, I thought the simple intro sounded pleasant, self-assured. Not pert. Pert was the last thing a guy needed one week after his late wife was found in his backyard pool.

Except as I introduced myself, I went hoarse either from nerves or the cheapo estrogen my HMO was foisting on me. My "Judith Singer" sounded like Marlon Brando's Don Corleone—not a plus at the front door of the Son of Fancy Phil. I cleared my throat and offered Greg Logan a small, sad smile. He stood in the doorway, gazing at something beyond me, so I glanced back.

Nothing. Although technically night, after eight, a band of sky just above the horizon was still pearly with light from the just-set sun. In the deep twilight, the front walk, a path of blue-black stones, appeared to be pools of water. No floodlights were on, but probably none were needed. People weren't dropping by this house. It was only me and Greg.

I waited for him to ask What can I do for you? or return my mini-smile. But he said nothing. His face was blank. So I said hello. It was so quiet I could hear the jets of a distant plane heading for La Guardia, then the *pop!* of an automatic sprinkler head emerging from the grass. After that, silence again. Not a bird, not a car, not a rustle of a leaf: silence so intense it felt as if life had stopped. My gut started poking me in the ribs: Get going! My mind was soothing: Relax. What's he going to do? Put a gun to your head?

The widower Greg, in olive shirt with a crossed golf club insignia over his heart stood before me in khaki slacks and bare feet. He was cen-tered in the green door frame against a background of the celadon-on-celadon wallpaper in his front hall. I'd been wanting him to look at me? Oh God, now he was staring into my eyes. Unblinking, unless he and I were having simultaneous blinkage again and again and again.

Trying to find the humanity behind those eyes, I looked deeper. All I saw was more nothing. No intelligence, no dullness, no compassion, no belligerence, no bereavement. Merely two eyes of that ho-hum hue be-tween blue and gray. True, they were those thick-lashed, perpetually moist eyes that, with some men, evoke bedroom thoughts. Except any intimation that Greg was hot stuff in the whoop-de-doo department would have been instantly nullified not just by his silence but—I cleared my throat—by his hair. Potentially, it was gorgeous hair, the blackest brown, that lustrous, heavy hair a gigolo would wear long and gelled back. Greg Logan, however, wore it clipped so close on the sides and in the back he looked less like a lover boy and more like the congressman from Raleigh-Durham on his way to a prayer breakfast. Few sights are less erotic than pallid scalp with brown birthmark viewed through sheared sideburn.

Besides, Greg was too intriguing looking to be conventionally hand-some. His eyes and cheekbones slanted upward, and his nose had a slight northerly tilt that gave him the delicate quality I'd spotted on the front page of *Newsday*. In the illumination of a brass chandelier, all that kept his heart-shaped face from being downright girly was his end-of-day stubble and his eyebrows—the crazed, curly kind that look like a pair of inverte-brates creeping across a forehead.

I tried to look at him without appearing to stare. Despite Greg Lo-gan's valentine of a face, the word "effeminate" did not come to mind: The delicacy of his features was more than countered by a tough-guy physique. He had a thug's thick neck, barrel chest, legs like two giant se-quoias. He looked like a man who had to work out double-time to trans-form the family flab to muscle, and who only seemed to be managing time-and-a-half. His heft made him a presence you had to look up to.

Not that I actually had to look up all that far; he wasn't more than five-nine or ten.

The encounter was moving from uncomfortable to disturbing. I swallowed hard. Whatever gland pumps adrenaline was working overtime; a wave of nausea was accompanied by tingling skin and a spike of heat that sent perspiration washing down my cleavage.

The silence was broken at last by the deafening tinging of a wind chime. Immediately after, I heard Greg Logan's breathing, noisy, rapid. I vaguely remember praying, Oh please let this be his adenoids and not some prelude to frenzy, a mere awkward silence with both of us mute from the paralyzing dread that we'll start blithering at the same instant. But his nonresponse was lasting too long. If I hadn't been frozen by his stare I would have squeaked Whoops, wrong house and made a break for my Jeep. How the hell could I not have rehearsed anything beyond "I'm Judith Singer"?

At last, thankfully, Greg took a deeper, quieter breath. A flicker of hope: Maybe the deadness in his face was because he was so taken aback by having a visitor that he was in shock. Social shock. He was, after all, the prime suspect. After Courtney's disappearance on Halloween, through winter and early spring until this very instant in the month of May, I doubted that few, if any, Shorehavenites had stood on his doorstep offering kind words or homemade gingersnaps. Those who had rung his chimes most likely had been more bad news—cops, journalists, crackpots.

But that instant, Greg Logan showed me that no matter if he was murderer or victim, he was still clearheaded enough to recall the suburban motto: Congeniality now, congeniality forever. Even at this moment, just one week after the discovery of his wife's body, he was able to flash me a mechanical and inordinately white smile. Once more, time could march on.

Exhaling so loudly with relief I almost whinnied, I decided this was not the moment to get distracted figuring out whether Greg's teeth were capped or bleached. I forced up the corners of my mouth and declared brightly: "I'm on the board of the Shorehaven Public Library." This was true.

"Oh," he replied. He opened the door wider and stepped back into the house, letting me come in.

The house smelled of macaroni and cheese which someone had sought to mask with room spray—not the sort that spritzes fake strawberries but the expensive kind that has the scent of genuine apricots. Greg Logan and I stood two squares apart on the dark-green-and-white marble checkerboard floor of the entrance hall beneath the chandelier. I glanced up, beyond his face. Each flame-shaped bulb at the ends of the chandelier's brass arms had its own miniature celadon lampshade, which in turn was edged with a deeper green trim—sort of like rickrack, except instead of zigzags it was scalloped, so it seemed an unending chain of teeny-weeny smiles.

"Is there anything I can help you with?" Greg inquired, too politely. He was plainly expecting me to ask for a donation. Or to make some grotesque pronouncement: Your wife borrowed *The Lively Art of Pumpkin Carving* in October and it's seven months overdue.

"I'm sorry to be dropping in like this, Mr. Logan. I know you've had a family tragedy—and still must be going through a terrible time." I waited for him to say Thank you for your concern, or something. But all I got from him was a bigger dose of nothing. I managed to say: "I'd like to talk to you for a few minutes."

I stared boldly at him once more. This didn't seem to bother him, but once again, the lifelessness in those eyes unnerved me. I averted my glance and peered down, until I got nervous he would think I was staring either at his personals (which I wasn't, not that you could see anything with those baggy khakis) or at the swirls of hair on top of his feet that looked unnaturally plopped down, like two tiny toupees. Then, ever hopeful, I looked up again. I shouldn't have. His stare was still as dead as Courtney.

I quickly glanced over at four gilt-framed botanical prints hanging from satin ribbons just to have something other than eyes and foot hair to concentrate on. Was Greg thinking I was some kind of nut? That silent voice inside me started screeching again: Get out, you jerk! *He's* the nut! A smiley, Ivy League psycho whose dead eyes are going to be sparkling with merriment as he squishes your hacked-up body parts into his compost bin. At which point my intellect's sweet voice of reason inquired: Judith, is there any need to make yourself crazier than you already are?

Greg gave me a quick once-over. I'd gotten dressed to look more stereotypical library board member than casual neighbor: a navy skirt, a powder blue cotton sweater, a complementary blue silk scarf with butterflies, and only enough makeup so as not to look gruesome. My blue trustworthy look was evidently working because at last Greg said, "Please come inside."

He led me down the long center hall into a living room so expansive it had four seating areas, like the lobby of a Ritz-Carlton. The house, with its grand rooms and soaring ceilings, seemed precisely the sort of place that would be built by the upwardly mobile too young to remember the 1973 Arab oil embargo. He switched on a lamp or two and offered me a seat on a long, fat-armed couch covered in green, cream, and yellow striped silk—that heavy, nubby stuff. Unfortunately, the couch was heaped with so many throw pillows that despite its vast length, there was only room for a couple of anorexics to sit. I wound up with a giant, over-stuffed yellow square on my lap. Each of its four corners had a big tassel, the kind strippers twirl from their nipples (a talent, like playing the xylophone, I've always vaguely wished I possessed). Another pillow, a thickly fringed rectangle with a petit-pointed yellow dog, competed for space with my right hip.

"Professionally, I teach history at St. Elizabeth's College. I was thinking that an oral history from you—" In that instant, Greg Logan froze, his backside inches from the dark green wing chair cater-cornered to the couch. "I understand my being here may seem an intrusion, but I was hoping you might have something important to tell the community about how the criminal justice system operates—or fails to operate."

He did sit, but his bushy, dark eyebrows were now raised so skeptically high they came close to being curly bangs. "I don't understand," he replied, still courteous. Or at least not discourteous.

From the depths of my shoulder bag I pulled out a copy of my curriculum vitae in a clear plastic sleeve—along with a bonus, a petrified wad of Trident wrapped in an ancient shopping list. As I slipped the gum gob back into my bag and handed over my CV, I answered his unasked question. "It seems to me you've been the victim of leaks to the press, of knee-jerk assumptions that have more to do with prejudice than reality."

Greg's eyes didn't mist in gratitude, as I suppose—subconsciously, arrogantly—I'd hoped they would. Instead, he responded to my proposal pretty much as he'd been responding from the instant he opened the door. You could say it was the way you'd expect a guy with an MBA to respond—with polite neutrality that really was no response at all. Or else you could say it was the behavior of a well-mannered psychopath. He glanced down at the CV. He was less tentative now, more the businessman. His eyes darted back and forth at an astounding rate. I hoped he wasn't one of those entrepreneurs who take up speed-reading because they have time for nothing. Obviously he was: In seven seconds he knew what I had to offer and didn't want it. "This is all very nice, Ms., Dr. Singer."

"I don't use the 'Doctor,' " I told him. "And please, call me Judith."

He didn't call me either: "A Ph.D. in history from NYU. I'm sincerely impressed." He was neither sincere nor impressed. I felt so let-down. He was talking like a well-programmed android: "And I appreciate your sympathy. Although I don't really understand what an oral history would do." He gave what was supposedly an apologetic shrug, which was nothing more than a brief, robotic shoulder lift.

"It might elicit some understanding of what you're going through.

Maybe even some empathy that could translate into community support." I kept waiting for him to start nodding in comprehension. But he sat unmoving, neck frozen, arms bonded to the arms of the wing chair, so I went on. "It seems to me you've gotten a raw deal. You've been convicted without even being tried." He did nod then, but barely, merely to indicate he was listening as he tried to figure out the real reason why I was there, and who'd sent me. "I'm also here because I don't believe you had anything to do with your wife's murder." As I said the word "murder," his right hand slid across his lap to his left and he began to twist his wedding band around slowly. My mouth went dry. My tongue stuck to my palate, which made my next words sound gluey. I managed to say: "You're too smart to have done it so stupidly."

"I'm sorry," he snapped. At last he had an expression. Disdainful. His nostrils flared in impatience, as if I had come to his door peddling a frivolous product. "I don't have time for this." With each word of the sentence, his voice grew louder and more contemptuous. His fingers curved until his hands turned into fists.

"Don't you see?" I pleaded. "The police have only been focusing on you. And while they are, they're not looking for the person who *did* commit the crime. Also—please hear me out—I'm a first-rate researcher. If you'd like I can look into it, see if I can find anything that might lead to someone else."

Now he was shaking his head. No. A definitive no. Worse, he was standing. "My lawyer has hired a private investigator." I could hear the contempt behind his words.

"Please, give me one more minute," I pleaded, looking up at him. "When I say look into it, I'm not talking about canvassing the neighborhood and asking who saw what on Halloween. Or what, if anything, your neighbors told the police. That's a legitimate job for your private detective. What I can do is go deeper, follow a paper trail, search into people's pasts. Also, I have some small experience investigating homicide and—"

It's so mortifying, to watch someone who's been trying to dope you out finally conclude *Shit! A wacko!* So I stood as well. I was on the verge of grabbing him by his golf shirt, shaking him and shouting, Please believe me. *I am not a wacko!* Which probably would have been as convincing as Nixon announcing he was not a crook.

We were saved from whatever—maybe only another agonizing silence—by the *clomp-squeak, clomp-squeak* of heavy rubber soles, through the dining room, across the center hall, *clomp-squeak, clomp-squeak* until their noise was hushed by the lush wool of the Persian rug. For an instant he and I glanced at each other, embarrassed, as if we'd been caught doing something illicit.

A tall, rawboned woman crossed the living room and stood before Greg. She looked like Janet Reno in a henna-rinsed pixie cut. Her tan shoes, laced up, had inch-thick, orange rubber crepe soles. Her slacks and matching T-shirt were the hue of canned salmon. The phrase "older woman" sprang to mind, along with the word "polyester," until I realized she was not that much older than I, albeit dressed in some unnatural fabric that did not reflect kindly on her.

"Mr. Logan, sir?" A bizarre speech impediment? A heavy Scottish burr?

"Yes, Miss MacGowan?" Burr. He made no attempt to introduce us.

"The little ones are asleep." She offered a professional nanny's benevolent smile, which didn't last long. So, I mused, the au pair did not seem to be part of the Logan household anymore. What had made her leave? Had she been fired? Could the au pair and Greg actually have been lovers and were now playing it cool? Or had her departure been due to something else—like fear of Greg Logan? Was I nuts to keep dismissing my own fear of him? I'd watched enough TV news to know: The most dangerous people weren't maniacs with eyes that swirled like pinwheels. They were the guys who looked virtuous enough that you would invite them over for dinner. "I thought I might drive to Dairy Barn," the nanny was saying, "and buy those berry pops Morgan's been asking for."

"Great!" Greg declared. His eyes were no longer dead; they were sparkling at her. His manner was vigorous. It was as if Greg Logan had vanished and instantly been replaced by an extroverted identical twin. "Excellent! Thank you very much." Miss MacGowan pursed her lips, a gesture that might have been Scottish for "you're welcome." Then, with barely a glance at me, she hurried off. The only sound was the *clomp-squeak* of her shoes.

In those few seconds of silence, my eye drifted to the table beside the chair in which Greg had been sitting. On it was an artful juxtaposition of a pile of antique leather-bound books beside a bottom-heavy onyx vase. Their dark browns and greens glowed in the gold light spilling from a lamp fashioned from a porcelain urn festooned with dragons. On the other side of the lamp, in an old tortoiseshell picture frame (the shell probably yanked off the back of some luckless Edwardian-era tortoise) was a photo of Greg and Courtney Logan. They wore tennis whites. Their arms were around each other, pulling each other close so there was no space between. Her blond head, bound in a terrycloth headband, rested against the chest of his cable-knit sweater. His darkness was a pleasing contrast to her pastel prettiness. They weren't merely smiling for the camera, they were laughing: two people made for each other, like pieces of jigsaw puzzle that formed a picture of marital happiness. God, what a sickening loss he'd sustained.

Suddenly Greg switched off the lamp and said, "I have a great deal to do, Ms.—"

"I wish you'd call me Judith," I urged. But Greg Logan didn't say anything. The light from the front hallway was more than enough for me to see that he was shaking his head. No.

And good-bye.

I passed that night squirming in my dark bedroom, feeling my face flame again and again as I cringed over my visit to Greg's. Over and over I asked myself What in hell possessed you to try such an idiot move? Forget humiliating yourself. He's Fancy Phil's boy. Daddy could arrange to have someone dispatched to take care of Singer, J., 63 Oaktree Street. Your address right there for all to see in the *Shorehaven Nynex Community Directory*. And even if he were to turn out to be a sweetie, the world's most benevolent man, he obviously thinks you're a major creep, to say nothing of a loser. You've blown the whole damn investigation.

I tried not to tune into house sounds: the clunk as the refrigerator switched off downstairs, the creak of absolutely nothing on a floorboard. I hated being alone at night. In bed. In life, come to think of it. I didn't feel so bad when I was working, or out with my kids or a friend. But dating, at least with the major and minor drips I'd met, only made my loneliness feel not just painful, but pathetic. Postmodernist Geoff wasn't even a nice guy; he was merely the least dreadful. He had asked me to go to the English Lake District with him in June ("Naturally we'll share expenses," had been his second sentence). But I'd said no. Having made out with him on Long Island, I knew there was no point in taking the show—this time with three complete acts—on the road to Windermere.

The truth was, yes, sure, I was a person in my own right. Historian. Mother. Friend. Reader. C-SPAN junkie. Movie lover. Library board member. Nassau County Coalition Against Domestic Violence volunteer. But what I yearned to be was a wife again, to hear Bob's sleepy voice murmuring "G'night" as he turned over, to sense the warmth of a man's body across a few inches of bed, to inhale the homey bouquet of the fabric softener on his pajamas, to know we'd have boring sex every other week. Of course, if I'd left Bob and married Nelson, I thought, he and I would still be in a state of postcoital ecstasy, sitting up in bed discussing the Courtney Logan case and—Stop!

Over the years I'd become my own tough cop, policing myself from crossing the line from the occasional loving or lustful memory of Nelson to hurtful fantasy: What is he doing this minute? Is he happy? Would it be *so* terrible to call him and offhandedly say, You just popped into my head the other day and I was wondering how you . . . Stop! An hour later I finally managed to lull myself to sleep by thinking about who could have killed Courtney Logan.

The next morning, I had some business to attend to: detective business. I hunkered down at the end of my driveway pretending to be preoccupied by the fate of a dwarf juniper or malnourished baby yew to which I actually had very little emotional attachment. Look, I was desperate for some kind of lead and knew this was the time for Chic Cheryl, my next-door neighbor, to come careening home after driving Spike (husband) to the 8:11. Sure enough, her Mercedes wagon, capacious enough to transport a *Schutzstaffel* battalion, was roaring down the street. Chic Cheryl had to race home in order to have quality time with TJ and Skip (children) and Danny, Colleen, and Bridget (Irish water spaniels) before she had to floor it to get to her nine A.M. golf lesson on time.

Her brakes didn't squeal as much as give a squawk of panic as she slammed them on when she was a foot away from me. "Ju!" she blared. Then, modulating her usual roar, she shouted at me: "How *are* you?"

"Fine," I told her. She nodded sadly, secure in the fact I was no such thing. I couldn't say exactly why Chic Cheryl always condescended to me. It may have been that I was a woman without a man, although more likely it was that I drove an American sports utility vehicle. I knew better than to ask her about the Logans, since she'd conveyed the only unique piece of information she had months before (while simultaneously pointing out to me the features of the soles of her new Nike Streak Vengeances), which was the riveting news that she'd heard Courtney Logan had cooked on a La Cornue range with a built-in simmer plate. "Cheryl," I said, "do you happen to know anyone who used StarBaby, Courtney Logan's—"

"Not me!" she thundered, shaking her head so vigorously that the morning sunbeams caught each of the Merlot highlights she went to Manhattan for every six weeks; Cheryl had patiently explained, without my ever asking, that truly first-rate highlighting was unobtainable anywhere east of Madison Avenue until France. "I mean, don't you think it looks"—her voice grew even louder—"T-A-C-K-Y to show a video of your kids that looks *professional*?" I was never sure about Chic Cheryl, if she talked so loudly to me because she thought hearty voices were the cat's meow or if for some reason she'd decided that, at fifty-four, I was so old I ought to be deaf. "Can you imagine? 'A StarBaby Production' *right up there*? I mean, God, does that spell Long Island *or what*?"

"Right. Did you know anybody who ever used . . . ?"

And so the next day I paid a visit on Jill Badinowski.

Chez Badinowski was what those shelter magazines—the ones that

feature homes of couples so rich you know they don't sleep together—
would call "a small jewel." It had been the gatehouse on some late-nineteenth-century robber baron's estate, but now the mansion (Greenbough)
and the baron (Jeremiah Eccles Stumpf) were history, and the Badinowskis' mini Norman villa stood in the shadow of eighteenth-century
trees a respectable fifty yards inside the border that separated patrician
(i.e., cost more than anyplace else) Shorehaven Estates from the rest of
our town.

I'd prepared an explanation about why I was interested in StarBaby
and Courtney Logan that would have satisfied anyone not prone to ana-
lytical thought, but the minute Jill Badinowski saw me on her doorstep
and heard "Shorehaven Public Library Board," I was welcomed inside
without having to say another word.

Jill was in her early thirties, although her prominent freckles, wide-
spaced eyes, and fair number of extra pounds gave her the sweet, goofy
look of those excessively adorable cartoon kids on greeting cards. By the
time I got finished telling her I was trying to get some information on
StarBaby and Courtney, I was seated at a big, round, rough, made-to-
look-worn wood farm table in her granite-countered, oak-floored dream
of a kitchen watching her grind beans for a fresh pot of coffee. This last
was no mean feat, as a chunky toddler who was either a short-haired girl
or a long-haired boy clung to her leg and shrieked "Chips! Chips!" no
matter how many times Jill gently responded with "No more chips!" (I,
of course, would have given in and handed over a king-size bag of whatever high sodium, additive-suffused carbohydrate would stop that nerve-
grinding duet of gasping sobs and hiccups. Jill, however, was obviously
one of those mothers so placid they can remain sympathetic but unmoved
by screaming, breath holding, and even turning blue.)

"Were you friendly with Courtney?" I called out over the din. "Was
that how come you had the video made?"

Jill's response was a loud single-syllable laugh of the you've-got-to-
be-kidding variety. "No," she boomed back. "I mean, could you see
someone like Courtney Logan and someone like me being friends? Not
that she wasn't nice."

The toddler's screeching subsided, so I was able to ask: "Why
wouldn't the two of you be friendly?"

"Let me tell you," Jill said slowly. "In every town there are two kinds
of women home with their kids. Typical women like me who can't imagine *not* being home. Then, you know, the high-powered ones. The ones
who were executives or journalists or high-finance types like Courtney."
Cautiously, as if concerned the machine might spit back the coffee, she
sifted in the ground beans. "Their motto is"—she made the sort of half-

amused, half-sneery sound that, charitably, might be called a chuckle—
" 'achieve, achieve, achieve.' Which, if their husbands are raking it in, becomes 'buy, buy, buy' once they're full-time moms. Not that they do
much mothering. Maids. Sitters. Nannies. Au pairs. Believe me, with
these two types, never the twain shall meet, if *they* have anything to say
about it."

"But aren't all of you mothers now?"

"Yes," she said, slowing down even more. Maybe this was her pensive
mode. You could practically take a nap between each word. "But giving
birth and staying home doesn't . . . you know, kill the 'achieve, achieve,
achieve' bug, does it?"

I gave what I hoped was a knowing laugh and quickly changed the
subject. "How long have you lived on Long Island?"

"We're pretty new." Jill seemed to think she still owed me something
more, so while she straightened the curled-up elastic waistband of her
bright yellow shorts, she added kindly: "We really like it here."

"Where are you from?"

"You mean a thousand years ago? From Indianapolis. But Pete—my
husband—is with Delta." Then she added: "The adhesives—not the airline, not the faucet. We've moved seven different times." She tossed off
the Delta business in the overly affable manner of someone who had
grown weary of explaining a thousand explanations ago. "We started in
Houston, then Pittsburgh, Chicago . . ." One of the subsequent cities was
either so abominable or so dull all that came out was a sigh. "That's why I
needed StarBaby, because Luke—this little guy here"—the kid's shrieks
for chips had modulated to whimpers and now became mere whines—
"was five months old and we couldn't even find our videocam. It's probably in one of the cartons we never got around to unpacking in Denver.
That's where we were before Long Island."

"How did you hear about StarBaby?"

Jill turned to pour water into a well in the great coffee machine. Even
from the back she would have looked like a pudgy cartoon kid except for
her varicose veins. "Half a second," she murmured. She appeared befuddled until she found which button to press to start the thing; it was one of
those oversize shiny contraptions with so many valves, buttons, and spouts
it looked capable of playing the Italian national anthem. "It's new," she
explained, although that seemed to be the case of everything but the
house itself, and even that was suffused with the smell of freshly hung
wallpaper. "Oh, StarBaby, right. I saw the ad for it in one of those give-
away papers. My husband—Pete—and I talked it over. Then I called."

Unfortunately, the Saga of Jill Badinowski, from Delta Adhesives to
her StarBaby connection, was still emerging with unbearable slowness. A

yeast dough could rise in the time it took her to move from sentence to sentence. I couldn't tell if this was just her midwestern style (unlike New York talk, in which natives tend to shove out each phrase in their hysteria to get to the next, even more brilliant one) or if she was so lonely she wanted to keep me around longer. My longing to snap, Spit it out! grew in direct proportion to the length of her narrative.

"She came here the next day. Courtney Logan, I mean," Jill went on. Then she shuddered, probably recalling the murder, although it might have been the house's overenthusiastic central air-conditioning, unwarranted on such an exquisite May morning. She was wearing a yellow-and-white striped tank top that matched her shorts and the skin on her rounded upper arms was dotted with pink goose bumps. "Are you writing up something about her for the library?"

"No. I happen to be a historian. I'd like to try some sort of oral history." She nodded, impressed. "But before I start taking down the history," I went on, "I just want to get a sense of all different aspects of Courtney's life. I was looking for someone who had used StarBaby. My neighbor Cheryl mentioned you."

"Cheryl's little girl TJ is in my daughter Emily's class. First grade." A brief, soft smile made her face glow. Since it would be impossible to achieve that look of tenderness thinking of Chic Cheryl, I read it as the expression of someone who not only liked the idea of having children, but who actually enjoyed their company. Absentmindedly, Jill stroked Luke's head.

"You have two children?" I asked because I sensed she expected me to.

"No. We also have twin boys, Michael and Matthew. They're nine. Oh, they're all in the video! The StarBaby video. Do you want to see it?" She seemed so desperate for me to say yes I found myself nodding with maniacal eagerness, if only to prove to her that we Long Islanders are decent folk.

I sat on a new-smelling brass-studded leather couch in a wood-paneled TV room that had once been a small library. Shelves that had been built for hundreds of volumes were now filled with family photos, athletic trophies, and arrangements of silk flowers; everlasting ivy and wisteria drooped from shelf to shelf, obscuring the spines of the Clancys, Jude Deverauxes, and diet and parenting books that constituted their library. Together, Jill and I watched sixty minutes of Luke and family.

I was a movie buff, not an expert on film. But from what I could see on the TV room's giant screen, StarBaby's efforts were the work of a pro, giving genuine value for the year's worth of videotaping. Of course, whether that one cassette was worth the three thousand dollars Jill told me it had cost was another story. There were slick opening credits: A logo of a five-pointed star rocked cradlelike on a crescent of film. Seconds later the word "StarBaby" in chubby pink-and-blue letters appeared beneath it. Then the star dissolved into a shot of baby Luke Badinowski's toothless grinning and the video began.

Throughout winter, spring, summer, fall, there were relatively few of the predictable home movie scenes most parents show to tolerant relatives and friends: no baby waving bye-bye, no toddler cautiously touching baby goat at a petting zoo, no tyke gnawing on a new Christmas or Hanukkah toy. Instead, Luke and family walked along the Shorehaven waterfront and checked out the progress of a horseshoe crab, ate swirls of frozen yogurt and watched sailboats from the town dock, visited the pediatrician's for a checkup, and explored every room of their house. The Badinowskis' seven moves had paid off, I guessed; Pete's last promotion must have been a big one, because the furniture, rugs, and window treatments in each of the rooms were not just newly acquired, but expensive.

"Did Courtney do the filming herself?" I asked. For an instant Jill looked startled, as if I started blabbing in a movie theater, unnerving her, taking her out of the mesmerizing story up on the screen. She shook her head no. It was clear she wanted to keep watching the video, and almost as clear that she was hoping an outsider would revel in her family with her. Seven cities, I thought. If you have to say good-bye to friend after friend, there must come a point when you finally cannot allow yourself friendship. I could hardly imagine a life in which I had to ask a stranger to watch my home movies.

So I turned back to view Luke peering up at *Blue's Clues,* pulling up a carrot from the family vegetable patch, playing a baby version of football with his two brothers, being taught how to climb up a playground slide by his sister. Watching wasn't that great a sacrifice. The Badinowskis seemed a good-hearted clan, although crew-cut Pete of Delta Adhesives carried himself as if he'd gotten an M-16 up his ass in some marine boot camp.

StarBaby had done not merely a professional job, but an intelligent one. Throughout the video, someone offscreen must have been asking specific questions, because everyone—from the pediatrician to siblings to the mailman to shoulders-back, chin-up Pete—spoke of Luke affectionately and occasionally articulately, with none of the predictable, awkward *Hi! It's me and I just want to say, uh, hello to, uh, the big boy on his birthday.*

When it was over, I offered my praise of Luke, who was sitting on the floor taking apart a red-and-yellow plastic truck which I assumed was meant to be taken apart. Then I asked Jill: "Did you spend much time with Courtney?"

"Oh sure," she replied. With her midwesterner's passion for Rs, her sarcastic response emerged as Eww shrrrr. "Actually, she came with a sample video and talked to me about what I wanted. She was probably here for less than an hour."

"What was she like?"

"I can't honestly say. I guess . . . We must be, must have been, around the same age. But I felt like she was a lot older." Jill pulled at a loose thread on the hem of her shorts, causing a giant pucker. "She was so so-phisticated. She wore slacks and a plain white blouse. It had to be silk. And a gold watch but no other jewelry. Except her wedding and engage-ment rings. She just looked . . . perfect. Not like in *Vogue*. But you know that quiet good taste people in the East have? And she was so self-confi-dent I couldn't imagine *not* signing up for the video."

"Well, it looked great to me."

Jill offered me a sunny smile. "To me, too."

"You called her sophisticated. Is that Indianapolis for cold?"

She flushed and cocked her head to one side to consider my question, and I had enough time to notice that if you played connect the dots with the darker freckles on her left cheek you got a snowman with one arm. "Not cold," she finally replied. "She was nice. I didn't feel like she was looking down on me or anything. But then again, she wasn't judging me as a potential friend. I guess you could call her charming. But it was strictly business charm. I knew not to take it personally. She wouldn't be interested in me." She glanced down at Luke. "Well, why should she be? Even though Pete's chief operating officer of Delta now, my job hasn't changed. *My* motto isn't 'Achieve, achieve, achieve.' Why should I inter-est someone like her?" Jill may have been waiting for me to protest, but I took too long. She continued: "Not that I'm finding fault with Courtney. She was a type. And a businesswoman. She didn't come here to be my friend."

"But her business was kids," I suggested. "That's kind of a warm and friendly way to make a living."

"Warm and friendly is what sells these days," Jill snapped, so sharply that I was still sitting frozen on the leather couch recovering from her tone while she was bending over to disengage Luke from the pieces of red-and-yellow truck he'd started to heave at the blank TV screen. "That's what Courtney Logan was here for. Selling something. Making money on a product. Babies. But her business could have been making cookie cutters." Then she added in her amiable, middle-America way: "Or poison gas."

Jill's poison gas floated over my head all day as I read an article—a revisionist analysis of Harry Hopkins's administration of the lend-lease program by a Tulane University historian besotted by his own audacity—and planted my lettuce and arugula. It stayed with me, too, as I pushed my cart up and down the supermarket aisles, looking over a recipe for "French cutlets" on the tofu container, knowing in my heart—wishing it could be otherwise—they would not turn out *délicieux*. Everywhere I'd turned in Shorehaven, all I had heard about Courtney was "smart" and "nice." Very nice. Really, really nice. Genuinely nice. Jill's was the first not-nice. I didn't have to open the can of Vanilla Almond tea leaves in my cart to read the animosity behind "poison gas."

It was nearly seven when I set my bag of groceries in the back of my Jeep. Too much time studying frozen cheesecakes, scrutinizing sponge mops. Living alone, I'd noticed a tendency to check and recheck the unit price on Ultra Charmin and to squeeze far too many nectarines in order to put off going back to an empty house. So, I mused as I drove back up Main Street and down Beacon Road, was Jill simply reacting to a real or imagined condescension to a housewife on Courtney's part? Or had she, even subliminally, picked up on a ruthlessness that everyone else, gasping or tsk-tsking over Courtney's murder, had been eager to overlook?

What an evening it was, sugary with the mingled scents of flowering crabapple, dogwood, cherry, and apple trees. Except I kept thinking about poison gas. For me, better than nice. Because, I told myself as I pressed the garage-door opener, nice women do indeed get murdered, but nice cuts way down on motives:

Q: What did Courtney Logan ever do to you?
A: Nothing. She was incredibly nice.

But a cold woman, a ruthless woman, a poison gas woman might give me something to work with.

I drove the car into the garage, got out, and opened the rear gate of the Jeep thinking, Hmm, Boston lettuce with sliced mushrooms and how could I get leads to the investment bankers who'd worked with Courtney, and oh, to her close friends, too, and—

"You Judith?" a rough voice demanded. And, from a cobwebbed and shadowed corner in the back of my garage, out stepped Fancy Phil Lowenstein.

Chapter Four

In a voice that had the delicacy of sulfuric acid, Fancy Phil Lowenstein demanded, "You Judith Singer?" Simultaneously, he put an arm around my shoulders that weighed enough to compress the disks between each vertebra. I thought of all those movies in which the heroine plunges her hand into her pocketbook and retrieves one of those femme items, like a metal nail file, that can be instantly converted into a weapon. But the notion, Aha! I'll poke my Jeep key into his eyeball to distract him, did not occur to me. My brain, fear-frozen into suspended animation, did not instruct my hand to unzip my shoulder bag, plunge in, and retrieve my house keys—with the nifty little panic button for the alarm system I kept on my key ring. In fact, all I could think to do was nod, like one of those dopey dolls whose heads bop up and down on a spring: That's me, uh-huh, yes, right, I'm Judith Singer.

Fancy Phil muttered: "I'm asking . . ." His voice trailed off as his eyes peered upward, at the motor of the garage-door opener. Then they scanned the rear wall, at the rake, snow shovel, and mysterious-object-left-by-children-that-might-have-pumped-up-basketballs-or-served-as-hookah-or-bong-or-whatever-they-call-it that dangled from the Peg-

Board. Apparently, he suspected my garage was bugged because he murmured: "... because of that research stuff you mentioned to . . ." His eyebrows lifted in a gesture I suspected was Felonese for "my son."

With that, I found myself being transported toward the door that led from the garage into the house. I wasn't being shoved or dragged so much as simply having my location altered by an elemental force. "You know who I am?" Fancy Phil inquired as his fingers grasped my upper arm. It was like being held by five bionic bratwursts, the smallest of which sported a ring with a diamond the size of one of Jupiter's lesser moons.

I stood before the entrance to the kitchen, my heart banging against my chest like some desperate creature pounding on a door, begging to be let out. In, actually, was the place I wanted to go. Nevertheless, I knew there was no real sanctuary: Garage, kitchen, this guy could kill me anywhere. I stood paralyzed, my face inches from the door, my handbag gripped under my free arm. My car keys were clenched so tight their metal teeth bit into the flesh of my palm. I didn't realize I was hugging my grocery bag with such passion until I heard a dull *bloop!* of splitting plastic and immediately inhaled a whiff of vanilla yogurt. Finally some words emerged. "You're Mr. Lowenstein," I replied.

"Yeah. Phil Lowenstein. And you know whose father I am." I nodded. I'm pretty sure I didn't actually turn to look at him, although I vaguely recall allowing my eyes to drift sideways. Fancy Phil's head had been plopped midway between his shoulders without benefit of neck, so his second chin rested against the heavy gold neck chain exposed by the open collar of his shirt. He'd put on quite a few pounds since his last mug shot. "Call me Phil." He released my arm and wiped his forehead. His skin, glazed with perspiration, was flushed an ominous red that, as I watched, was darkening to purple. "Hot in here," he observed. A flash of gold caught my eye. A snake bracelet entwined around his meaty wrist, the mouth and tail separated by an inch of over tanned skin and graying arm hair.

"I know it's hot," I acknowledged. "And you having to stand in a garage, waiting for me, with the door shut and no air circulating—"

"Lemme help you with that bag."

"No. No thanks," I chirped much too quickly. "Really, I can manage!" I sounded revoltingly hearty.

"So you can get to your key." Obviously Fancy Phil was perceiving a smidgen of unease on my part because he took a step back—although he remained within easy stabbing/strangling/stomping distance. "We could sit down inside, where it's cooler. You don't have to be scared of me. I want to talk business."

"Business?"

"Yeah. I'm here on business. You *are* the history lady? Right?" His "his-tor-y" was three deliberate syllables. No uncouth "histry" for Fancy Phil. My guess was he picked up the pronunciation from watching Public Television against his will during his last stopover at the Elmira Correctional Facility. Two and a half years, according to the news. For aggravated assault on the person of one Ivan "Chicky" Itzkowitz during a contretemps over certain funds obtained by withholding gasoline sales tax from the state of New York. "You're a history professor."

"That's right."

He smelled clean but insanely citrusy. This was one badass lime cologne, a scent for capos and rappers. "A doctor of history. Now listen, Doc. Don't worry about Gregory, about him saying he wasn't interested."

Who knows what happened in that instant? It could have been I recognized that Fancy Phil had indeed bothered to put on aftershave, or made the effort to grant "history" its three syllables. But suddenly I sensed that if I wasn't safe, at least he had no intention of murdering me right away, although I was not unaware that he might delegate the job to some discount contract killer who hung out on the fringes of the Mafia or the Russian mob. My throat made a swallowing movement even though all my saliva was still sloshing in that secret reservoir to which bodily juices flow in times of terror.

"Maybe I overstepped my bounds," I began to apologize. "Going to his house—"

He cut me off: "It don't matter Gregory wasn't interested. I'm interested."

And then we were inside. Fancy Phil offered to help me unpack the groceries, but seemed relieved when I said no thank you. I sat him at the kitchen table, an overly long, narrow, rickety quasi-antique of dark wood that was more appropriate for a Castilian monastery than a Long Island Tudor. But I'd bought it (along with a Swedish wood-burning stove and a frightening Art Nouveau umbrella stand) in the year I'd taken leave of my senses, after Bob died.

Anyhow, I opened the back door, muttering something inane about loving the evening smells this time of year, although both of us knew I needed to see a way out. The air outside the screen door was cooling down fast: Summer was still a month away. I glanced around the kitchen. Being too nervous to think of a novel hors d'oeuvre to please the discriminating criminal palate, I microwaved a bag of popcorn and poured it in a salad bowl shaped like a deformed daisy—one of those hideous, indestructible wedding presents that lasts longer than the marriage. For a millisecond Fancy Phil's boulder of a head wobbled on his shoulders, which I took to mean "Thank you." He also accepted the only kind of beer I had in the refrigerator, some microbrew of Joey's, one of those concoctions that have the hue and aroma of rancid pumpkin pie.

"Essentially," I said, at last feeling capable of uttering a simple declarative sentence, "your son didn't want my services. He said he'd hired a detective."

After a couple of glugs of beer, Fancy Phil's chubby cheeks and domed forehead were no longer that alarming aubergine, as if he were on the verge of a cardiovascular incident. His color subsided to a rosy flush— almost an exact match for the bright pink in the gingham of his short-sleeved shirt, an odd choice of fabric, but perhaps one of his chums had hijacked the wrong truck. His slacks were a white linen that picked up on the white checks in the gingham and matched the white loafers. As did his white patent-leather belt. I decided it was not politic to mention one does not wear such attire until after Memorial Day or, ideally, ever.

"Gregory's lawyer's got some detective she works with," Fancy Phil continued. "His lawyer's a she. Anyhow, she says her guy—this ex-cop— knows his ass from his elbow. Pardon my French. But listen, an ex-cop . . . What can I tell you? You know how the world works."

"I have a general idea," I conceded.

"What I mean is, you're no kid." Wearily, I nodded. "I meant that as a serious compliment." With what I guessed was his suave gesture, Fancy Phil smoothed back his hair with the heels of his hands. The top had thinned, but the sides and back were thick and profoundly dark, a black that does not occur in nature. It was held in position by a mousse that apparently hardened into Plexiglas upon application. "Like, for instance," he went on, "you didn't scream when you saw me in the garage, which, to tell you the truth, I was a little worried you'd do. Not that I'd blame you. I mean, here I am, some guy you never met before. Except I figured, Hey, if she knows enough to think she should get hired, she probably saw my picture on TV or in the paper, with all the publicity about the thing with—" He looked away from me, past his snake bracelet, down into the jumble of popcorn, and in a mournful tone added: "Courtney."

For a moment after he uttered her name he seemed mesmerized by the yellow-white puffs, no two alike. Then he began playing knock hockey with one of the few unpopped amber kernels. At long last he shrugged and went on as if no time at all had passed: "So I figured about you, she's not gonna think I'm some dangerous lunatic in her garage. Sorry if I scared you. But it wouldn't be a good idea for me to sit outside in my car. You know how people are." He shook his head, disheartened by man's distrust of his fellowman. "One of your neighbors could dial 911."

"Where did you put your car?"

"I had a friend of mine drop me off. I don't want trouble with cops. Know what I mean?"

"I do." The popcorn, I was relieved to see, was a success, though some diet guru or woman in Fancy Phil's life had clearly coached him to eat only one puff at a time, not a handful. But his arm kept moving so swiftly between bowl and mouth it was almost a blur.

I fetched a Diet Coke and joined him at the kitchen table. "Anyway," he went on, "you not being a kid, you being someone who's a doctor of history, you probably could dig up stuff from a library or computer or whatever that this ex-cop won't even think of."

"I was trying to explain my research capabilities to your son," I said. "Also, I know the mores of this community. Your son's neighbors might offer me information they wouldn't confide in an ex-cop."

" 'The Moreys,' " he repeated. I saw he was trying to recall if the Moreys were a Shorehaven couple Greg had mentioned. Not that Fancy Phil was stupid. On the contrary. Even in the garage I sensed he was not just observing me, but was using my every word, my every action to add to his sum of knowledge. Moment by moment, he recalculated more precisely who and what I was.

"Mores," I said offhandedly. "Local customs. Also, I've had a little experience investigating—"

"Yeah, I know. The dead dentist. Dr. Dirty. I remember seeing your picture in the paper." I must have looked surprised, because Fancy Phil gave me a smile, a surprisingly likable flash of teeth and popcorn. "I got an incredible memory," he explained, in the modest manner of a man stating the simplest fact about himself. "I said to myself, way back then, 'Hey, that's one smart cookie.' So, Doctor, I want you on the case. You want to work for me?"

"You mean, for your son."

"No. When I say me I mean me. He don't want no part of you." Then, realizing he may have been a tad less than gallant, Fancy Phil offered an apologetic lift of his eyebrows. "Kids. Do I have to tell you?"

"Did he think I was one of the local crazies, coming out of nowhere, knocking on his door?"

"They grow up and what can you do with them?" A Kissinger-like response, I thought. "So, Dr. Singer, you charge by the hour or by the job?"

"Please, call me Judith. For you"—I looked straight into his dark eyes. They absorbed the light in the room, yet gave off none—"there's no charge."

"What are you not charging for? You still scared of me?"

"Less than I was in the garage." He nodded slowly—head down, head up—to show me he understood and that he was still listening. "I think it's best for me not to be your employee. But I really would love to do the work."

"Why would you work for nothing?"

"Intellectual curiosity."

The side of Fancy Phil's mouth began to twist, but the expression vanished before it could become a smirk. "Okay. I can understand curiosity. But you should know something. I'm retired. Not dealing with my former associates." He crossed his arms over his stomach, which was so rotund that his arms made their X right above his wrists. "I got grandchildren. You got any?"

"Not yet," I said.

"Well, when you do, your whole life changes. You don't want them thinking, Hey, because of Poppy Phil, I didn't get invited to some little kid's birthday party. So I had to stop being what I was. Know what I mean?"

"Sure." I was not sure this was a genuine change of heart. In fact, I wasn't sure if it was a change at all or simply the sort of line gangsters give girls with doctorates. I didn't have time to reflect, because he was waiting for me to say more. "Wise decision," I added. Not enough. "I bet it was a tough thing to do, not just to give up a way of life, but some of the friendships that go with it."

Fancy Phil thrust out his lower lip and gave me a slow nod of acknowledgment, a silent You get it. "So go ahead. Ask me anything."

"Well, as I told your son, the cops think they have their man. They're not looking to clear Greg." I stood to get him another beer. "So beside the fact that he's the husband, which automatically puts him under suspicion . . ." I handed him the bottle and the opener, sat, and leaned forward so I could look him straight in the eye. "Tell me, Phil. How come the cops are so damn sure it's your son?"

"Some money business." He offered this complete explanation proudly, then pressed the cold bottle against his forehead with a soft "Whew," just to let me know that such candor was enervating.

"That's it?"

"That's it. Money business." He got busy studying the label, perhaps to find out what in God's name the brewmeisters in the Bronx could be putting in their beer.

"The more information you give me," I told him, "the deeper I can dig. The less you give me, the longer it will take and the less effective I'll be. You know that."

"It's like this." Fancy Phil was one of those men with the dexterity to uncap a bottle of beer with one hand. "Halloween was on a Sunday, right? So the Monday before the Monday before Halloween . . . The cops found out Gregory transferred some money that day." He sat back, took a swig of beer, and appeared happier, relaxed, as if he'd finally told the whole truth and nothing but.

"Transferred whose money from where to where?"

"Most of what was in their joint money market account."

"To?"

"He transferred it to an account in just his name."

"How much?" I inquired.

Fancy Phil emitted a minor snort, which I assumed was to show me he was amused, not irritated, by my persistence. "Forty and change," he finally said.

"Forty thousand? Greg took forty thousand out of his and Courtney's joint account?"

He nodded. The sun had set. The patio and lawn beyond the open kitchen door lay black in darkness, but the window over the sink was still a rectangle of indigo. "The cops think that's suspicious," he sniffed.

"How did he account for moving the money?"

"He told them the truth." I waited. "Look, honey, Doc, what can I tell you? He's got a business."

"Soup Salad Sandwiches," I said.

"Right. But he's got a problem."

"What?"

"Me." Fancy Phil fiddled with the medallion on the buckle of his belt, a circle about the size of the average grapefruit. "I'm not what a CPA would call an asset. That's why I made Gregory change his name to Logan before he went to college. He went to Brown, in the Ivy League. Just like Harvard, only in Rhode Island. Anyway, Gregory's a straight kid. I swear to God. And smart. All he wants is to keep his business on the up-and-up. But if I'm the problem, here's the catch: Courtney."

"How was she the catch?"

Wearily, he shook his head. "StarBaby. You know about that?"

"Her company," I said. "Videos of baby's first year."

"Right. So here's my kid, who's dealing with bankers who are totally legit. If he wants to grow legit, expand his business, the bankers gotta lend him money. Understand?"

"I'm with you."

"So when they lend money, they gotta see all his business records. Plus his personal stuff. It's called net worth."

"I know what net worth means. Go on."

"He has to prove he's a solid citizen. Like, he has to be substantial enough so he's not gonna loot Soup Salad Sandwiches to, whatever, pay his liquor bill—not like he drinks, maybe a couple of glasses of wine. None of that single-malt yuppie crap."

"What did StarBaby have to do with Soup Salad Sandwiches?"

"Courtney thought 'joint account' meant 'Take me. I'm yours.' Two or three times she dipped into their money market account. She helped herself from their brokerage account, too: She sold stock from their Smith Barney thing that was also joint. One time she put it back. The other times . . . And the thing of it was, she didn't say, Hey, Gregory, I'm borrowing from the brokerage thing because I need to buy thousands of dollars' worth of"—for an instant Fancy Phil's generous-lipped mouth contracted into a bitter slit—"camera junk to take pictures of babies and to advertise. She just took it. Like it was all hers. She kept pouring big bucks into that *fershtunkiner* StarBaby. Gregory told me about that afterwards, after she was missing. He's never been, you know, a crybaby. Whatever was going on, he kept it between man and wife."

"What did he think was going on?"

"He said all he thought at the time was that Courtney was a little out of control businesswise."

"How come she didn't go to one of those legitimate bankers for a loan?"

"Trust me, honey, she did. And they said, Hey, not one thin dime more until you start doing serious business."

"Was StarBaby failing?"

"No. But she wasn't breaking her back carrying sacks of money to the bank vault either. She was doing so-so." Speaking about his daughter-in-law, Fancy Phil's face didn't harden into anything resembling hatred, but it didn't get warm and fuzzy either.

"Maybe she would have built the business up in time."

"Maybe. And in time maybe the bank would have given her a big loan. But meanwhile, she couldn't believe the real reason the business was slow: because it was a *stupnagel* moneymaking idea. No, Courtney was positive all she needed was capital. Capital, capital. She wouldn't shut up about having to capitalize."

"And Greg?"

"Gregory was scared she'd go through everything they had together without telling him. Then the banker would check his net worth figures and say, Hey, Logan, you're full of it. You don't got no fifty-five thousand in the money market account and eighty in stocks."

I must have blinked: a young couple in their thirties with so much. Even though Bob had done well, there were years we had to choose, especially early on, and the choice hadn't been between a BMW or a Mercedes; it was a new roof or a new septic tank. But the Logans had it all, along with money in the bank. "How much did Greg say Courtney took without telling him?"

"Fifteen from the money market. Twenty total from Smith Barney. So she took thirty-five. But she put back . . . I forget. I think ten. So they were down a total of twenty-five big ones for the cameras and for ads."

"When did this happen?"

"Around this time last year," Fancy Phil replied.

"Let me be clear about this." I stood, got my shopping-list pad and pen from near the telephone, and came back to the table to do the arithmetic and make a few notes. "Courtney's fiddling with their money happened about a year ago. But about two weeks before she disappeared—and was murdered—Greg transferred forty thousand dollars from a jointly held money market account into an account that was in his name only."

"Yeah. A coincidence. I mean, him moving the money and then Courtney getting killed. He needed another loan from his bank in October."

"Let's go over the math. If she'd helped herself to fifteen out of the money market account, that meant originally they had fifty-five thousand."

"Yeah."

"And how much was in their Smith Barney brokerage account?"

"Eighty minus twenty. Plus the ten she put back." He watched patiently until I wrote *70,000, Smith B.* "You don't got a doctor in arithmetic, do you?"

"No. So tell me, Phil, do you sense Greg was very angry about Courtney's money manipulations?"

Fancy Phil shook his head vehemently, as if the words "Greg" and "angry" could not occur in the same sentence. "Nah. Upset. Like he knew Courtney was going through a tough time, being home with the kids, trying to get used to going from being on the fast track to being a mother. And a businesswoman, but not in the city. What she couldn't get through her head was that now Gregory was the breadwinner. He couldn't let her keep sticking her hand in the till for a business that was—I hate to say it of the dead—stupid. Every young married couple has one of those video cameras. All they *do* is take pictures, like they invented babies and they've gotta show the world. Little Buster in the high chair. Little Buster out of the high chair. Little Buster in the grocery store. They take their babies out at night, for God's sake, to restaurants, so everybody can share their joy. So there's Little Buster screaming and puking that milky lumpy stuff all over the polenta and making everybody else crazy, and they're *still* taking pictures. 'That's Little Buster *breching* in Mario's.' "

"But you think Greg and Courtney's marriage was basically sound? They were just going through a rough time?"

"Yeah."

"You're sure? No serious trouble?" Fancy Phil raised his right hand as if taking an oath. His palm was oily from the popcorn. "What about the au pair?"

"What about her?" he snapped. "A hundred different languages in the world and they pick a girl who speaks German. Teaching the kids: *'Auf Wiedersehen, Grossvater.'* And she had a face that could stop a clock and probably did."

"Maybe. And maybe she had a great figure or a sweet vulnerability that attracted your son. I don't know. The police and half of Shorehaven obviously believe there was something between her and Greg."

"Well, there wasn't. Cross it off your list. Gregory loved Courtney. He didn't step out."

Fancy Phil's nostrils dilated. I sensed this was not a sign of pleasure. So I decided to skip any more questions about the au pair. Still, considering I was alone in a house with a gangster convicted of aggravated assault, I felt remarkably comfortable. There he was, my first client, sitting at the head of my narrow kitchen table. Fancy Phil was clearly a man who expected respect, or at least not condescension, much less a hard time. Still, even if I gave him an argument, I sensed I probably wouldn't wind up bloated, bobbing in the East River, a New York moment for the folks from Toronto on a Circle Line tour. But I felt I had to say: "Phil, from time to time I may ask you questions you don't like."

"That's okay."

"Good. I don't want to have to be concerned you'll hold a grudge."

"What are you worrying about?"

"I wouldn't say worrying. It's just those two and a half years you spent upstate because of an aggravated assault on a fellow—"

"Chicky Itzkowitz?" He snorted a dismissive laugh. "That's what *I* call history. Plus I told you, I retired. A new man. Anyway, with Chicky it was a business matter."

"Well, you and I are doing business even if I'm not taking money."

"Hey, Dr. Judith."

"What?"

"You got nothing to worry about."

He did look relatively benevolent, a hoodlum Buddha. So I asked: "What did you think of Courtney?"

"Me, personally?" I nodded. He thought for a minute, then shook his head sadly. "*Lukshen.* You know what that is?"

"Noodles?"

"Yeah, but the thing is, *lukshen* without butter, without salt and pepper . . . What's the word? Blah. A *b* word."

"Bland?"

"Yeah! Bland." He put his elbows on the table and rested his chins on the heels of his hands. "You send your kid to an Ivy League college because you want him to be better than you. But he winds up bringing home a bowl of *lukshen* from the West Coast with blond hair and blue eyes who went to another Ivy League college and is an investment banker and plays tennis and is even cute looking if you like cute looking. Looks like a great package. But then you look for a personality and it's not there."

"There is a kind of West Coast low-key style." Well, I wasn't about to interject that his son wasn't exactly a live wire either, although in fairness, I had met Greg under strained circumstances during a terrible period in his life.

"Excuse me, Doc," Fancy Phil said, "but bullshit. Low-key, laid-back, loafers without socks—that's how they are. But people from the West Coast still have a personality."

"Was she a good mother to the kids?"

"Yeah. Fine. I mean, she could talk your ear off about Travis's teething. She was always saying to Morgan, 'I need a huggy-buggy,' and Morgan would go running to her." With his thumb and index finger he massaged the bridge of his nose. An altered nose, the broad-bridged, slightly upturned schnozz many got in the fifties and early sixties, in the era of frantic assimilation, a nose which made thousands of second- and third-generation American Jews look as if they'd descended from Porky Pig. "And she was good to Gregory, too, except for putting her hand in the till. Always calling him 'sweetie' or 'honey' or 'Greggy,' but listen, she was a good wife. You saw their house?"

"It was lovely."

"She fixed it up herself. No interior decorator or nothing."

"On the other hand . . ." I prompted.

"On the other hand," Fancy Phil went on, "if she's quitting her job to stay home with the kids, how come she's not staying home with the kids? She's out all the time. Call the house and you got that kraut. 'Mizzus Logan is at her exercise class,' " he mimicked in what I assumed he believed to be a German accent. "A class? What kind of crap is that? Someone's gotta teach you to touch your toes? Or she's at a meeting, or having lunch with her girlfriends, or taking a run, or in her office—"

"Did she have an office outside the house?"

"Nah. She took over a bedroom. Anyway, she's in her office doing business and cannot be disturbed."

"Did you meet Courtney's family?"

"Yeah. They're what you'd expect. *Lukshen* comes from *lukshen*."

"Where do they come from?"

"Washington. The state. Olympia. It's somewhere, but I don't know where."

"Are both parents alive?"

Fancy Phil gave an exaggerated sigh of boredom. "You want to call that alive, then they're alive. The old man's a comptroller of some two-bit lumber company. The old lady designs flowers. Puts them in bowls or something."

"Did they come east to the funeral?" He nodded. Not one of his fleshy features moved, yet I sensed a change in his expression. "How did they act?" He shrugged. "Phil, I'd like to get a sense of the people Courtney came from. Was the finding of the body a shock to them? Or do you think they had a sense she was dead in the months before, when she was missing?"

"They think it had something to do with me," Fancy Phil said, his tone so flat it might have been one of those computer-generated voices. "At the funeral. Episcopal. But I go over to the mother and try to hug her." He lowered his arms so they were rigid against his sides. "She goes like this. It was like hugging a little block of cement. She's short, like Courtney. And neither of them—her or the husband—would look in my direction. And not one word."

"What made them think you had something to do with it?"

"Just—you know, what I was supposed to be."

"You never had any arguments with Courtney? Or with Greg about Courtney?"

"No!"

"Did they think Greg had anything to do with it?"

"I don't know. At least they talked to him."

A night breeze blew through the open kitchen door and gave me a chill. One of my neighbors' dogs began that hysterical staccato bark you hear from nutsy dogs or from dogs with nutsy owners. Fancy Phil glanced at his beer bottle and seemed surprised to find it empty. "Did they put up any kind of a fuss about Greg having custody of the children?"

"What are you talking about?" he asked, annoyed. Then he answered his own question: "You mean, if they thought Gregory did it, they would want to get the kids away from him. No. They didn't say a peep about custody."

"Right. Okay, the first few days after Courtney disappeared: Did the cops ask Greg to see if anything of hers was missing?"

"Yeah, and as far as he could tell, nothing was. The only money that was touched was the money Gregory took out of their joint account two weeks before. The sapphire earrings he got her for her thirtieth birthday were where she kept them, in a little safe they have in a closet. Some other jewelry. Her mink was in the closet."

"Did she have an engagement ring?"

"Yeah, sure. She was wearing it, you know, when they found her. And her Rolex, too."

"So all that was missing was the twenty-five thousand she'd taken from the money market and stock brokerage accounts months before she disappeared?"

"Right," he agreed.

"So now what I've got to do is find out if she paid out twenty-five thousand dollars for video equipment and advertisements."

"And if she didn't?"

"Then I'll need to figure out what was going on in Courtney's life right before her death."

Chapter Five

StarBaby's videographer, Zee Friedman, bent over the railing on the landing outside her fifth-floor walk-up. "Just one more flight!" she called out encouragingly. She lived in a run-down neighborhood just north of the grand, high-ceilinged apartments around Columbia University and south of the renovated brownstones of Harlem's latest renaissance. The stairwell of her building exuded that Old New York smell which has nothing to do with Henry James and lavender; for nearly a hundred years, the yellow-brown walls had soaked up garlic and onion vapors from the various ethnic groups that had used the place as their first step up from New York's bleakest tenements. Now optimistic twenty-somethings and disillusioned thirty-somethings paid nearly a thousand bucks a month rent for each room.

Zee graciously ignored the mewling sounds that came from my throat with each breath as I made my way up the fourth flight of ridiculously steep stairs that seemed designed for a longer-legged species than *Homo sapiens*. In her leaning over, cascades of her black hair fell forward, forming a curtain around her face. It wasn't until I finally clomped up to her landing that I got a good look at her. Zee definitely outclassed her surroundings. She had the pudgy apple cheeks of one of those Victorian bisque dolls, except instead of the expected vacant blues, her eyes were alert, sparkling black. "Hi!" Her handshake was like a stevedore's, although she wasn't much more than five feet tall.

"Hi," I gasped.

"Half Chinese, half Jewish," she replied to my unasked question as she led me into her studio apartment. I nodded, not yet trusting myself to speak two consecutive words without snorting. "Twenty-four. Years old, I mean. The Zee's for Zelda. After Zelda Fitzgerald. Why, you may ask, did my parents think it was a good idea to name me after some poor demented woman who burned to death in a mental hospital? The answer is: I don't know."

Her not-very-large studio was divided into three areas: a kitchen that was simply some shelves above a sink and a two-burner stove; what I assumed was the bedroom, although it was hidden behind a curtain that looked fashioned from hula skirts; a five-by-five square that was the living room. Zee escorted me in and gestured toward a Baby Bear–size club chair. It was covered in one of those sage green, one-size-fits-all slipcovers that are better in catalogs than in life, although on her chair it had the schleppy charm of a child playing dress-up in her mother's clothes. She sat across from me on a love seat draped with three or four flowered fringed shawls, the ones you see on pianos and fortune-tellers. None of the floral prints matched.

Obviously Zee Friedman possessed that gift I'd always longed for, flair, the intuitive sense of when less is less and when less is more. Her outfit, plain black cotton pants cut off mid-shin and an ordinary white T-shirt, was stylishly minimalist. I, on the other hand, was in navy slacks, my perpetual blue sweater with butterfly scarf, and gold button earrings. Hopefully she'd think my retro look was intentional.

I'd spent the two previous days doing research and making calls. At last, through a friend of a friend of a neighbor of Jill Badinowski, I came up with another StarBaby client who had taken down Zee's phone number. "Sorry to bother you on Memorial Day weekend," I told her.

"No problem," Zee assured me. She had the voice of a more imposing woman, the contralto the Statue of Liberty would have if she could speak. She pulled her feet up on the cushion of the love seat so her heels touched her backside. She hugged her knees. Her toenails were the pale blue of bleached denim. "Are you a detective?" she asked hopefully.

"Let's just say I've been hired to see what I could find out about Courtney." Zee gave me an enthusiastic nod. Her dark hair bounced cheerfully, as if eager to know more. "Do you have any idea how many other people she employed?"

"At least one other guy, but I can't say for sure if there were any

more. I worked for her freelance, on weekends." Between us was her coffee table, an old wood toy chest with peeling decals of the Little Misses
Muffet and Bo-Peep.

"Only on weekends?" I asked.

"Well, that's when both parents are home. You want the two of them
interacting with the baby, since the video's at least partly to prove to the
kid how great his parents were, no matter what he remembers. Anyway, I
work full-time, so Saturday and Sunday were it for me."

"What do you do?"

"I'm a production assistant for Crabapple Films."

I nodded respectfully, as if to say, Oh, but of course, Crabapple,
though I'd never heard of it and prayed they didn't make movies about
adolescent girls being chainsawed. "What do you do there?"

"The stuff nobody else wants to do," Zee replied, smiling happily.
She seemed inordinately content, one of those people miraculously missing the resentful gene. Not only was her voice big, her smile was also:
overwide, the grin you'd see in a nursery school drawing. "Like I get per-
mits from the mayor's office, copy and file stuff, run back and forth to the
set. That's how I got onto Courtney. One of the guys on the set was filming for her and he moved to L.A. He passed the job on to me."

"Do you want to be a cinematographer?" I was tempted to drop the
fact that my son was a movie critic, but decided it sounded undetective-
ish. Also, just in case her cheeriness was a sham and she'd pumped two
bullets into Courtney, the less she knew about me the better.

Zee shook her head definitively. "Actually, I enjoy the managerial
stuff a lot more—knowing where the money's going, making sure a sev-
enty-foot crane is at Grand Army Plaza in Brooklyn Tuesday at six A.M."
She had managed to get her legs into a knot so complex all but one pale
blue toenail was hidden. Her arms, meanwhile, were stretched out along
the back of the love seat, as if about to embrace two invisible friends. "As
far as Courtney goes—eeesh, sorry . . . As far as Courtney went, I was
surprised she stuck with me. I'm just another Columbia film major whose
parents got her a digital camera for graduation."

"Did Courtney ever talk about her background with you?"

"No. After you called I started thinking. I realized how much I don't
know about her. Except like obvious things. Married, two kids. She'd
been an investment banker. I mean, we talked a little. Like how much
we'd loved college and hated high school. But who loved high school?
Maybe one dumb jock and an Epsilon semimoron Most Popular. Anyone
who still has a clear memory knows how awful it was."

"Why did Courtney hate it?"

"I think . . . The usual. You're either skinny or fat or puny or a giant and you don't have a boyfriend. And you like to read. Courtney was sawed off and scrawny, although she said she filled out by college. But most of the time she was all business with me."

"Was she good at her business?"

"She definitely didn't have a cinematic eye—which was why she decided I was a good videographer. She seemed nice, I guess."

"What do you mean, 'I guess'?"

Zee pursed her glossed lips and gave it several seconds of thoughts. "It's terrible to sound New Age-y," she said slowly, "especially when you have tendencies. But some people emit niceness rays. You know?"

"Did Courtney emit not-niceness rays?"

Zee shook her head. "No. Not at all. But at the beginning I thought, Wow, what a woman! I mean, this bundle of energy. She'd talk about StarBaby and make it sound like I was joining her on some kind of crusade: *Courtney and Zee's Excellent Adventure.* That StarBaby would really *do* something. People would be able to see themselves as they were, as their parents and siblings were. Maybe an idealized version, because they were being filmed, but at least not filtered through fantasy or an imperfect memory. Courtney was going to franchise it all over the country. And probably the world—though she didn't say that."

"Did she have a plan?" I asked.

"I remember she showed me a list of all the zip codes and what the per capita income was for each one plus lots of other demographic boring stuff. She was so optimistic, so *positive.* I could almost see her on the cover of *Time.*" Zee put her feet up on the seat again, wrapped her arms around her legs, then rested her chin on her knees, a feat of elasticity I found impressive. "At first anyway."

"She changed at some point?"

"Yeah, I guess last summer, probably in July. She'd said something a few months before then that summer might be a little slow for business because parents were around more, kids could do more outdoors and all that. I'd have thought that was a good time for filming, except I had this feeling that if I liked my job, I shouldn't contradict her. But business didn't pick up after school began again." Before I could ask she added: "It didn't slow down either. Courtney just seemed kind of bummed to me, although that was strictly me and my ESP. For all I know I could have been reading her totally wrong. Because she wasn't all that readable. She never made small talk. And she had zero curiosity."

"What do you mean?"

"Like when people meet me and hear 'Friedman,' they tend to squinch up their eyes because they're thinking: Asian and adopted? Half-and-half? Or because of the film-major business, they're curious about what my favorite movie is. But with Courtney, zilch. She read my ré-sumé, checked out the first two minutes of my student film, and told me what the pay was. I was less a human being and more the mechanism that operated the camera. She was Total Business Person."

"She was cold?"

"Not what most people would call cold. With a truly cold person, you're always wondering, Shit, what did I do wrong? But she never made me feel inadequate. In fact, I could tell she liked the way I worked. She'd even say Good work! and sound as though she meant it. So I felt she had her code of privacy or sense of boundaries and it wasn't anything personal."

"Did she stay so dispirited about the way the business was going?" I asked.

"Not really. By the time mid-September came she . . . I honestly don't know. She did what she had to do—go over what each family was looking for, how much to shoot. But she acted disengaged, like her mind was someplace else. Before that, even when she was going through her bummed phase, she'd always brainstorm ideas on where to film, or think of ways to get the parents to ask for more time, which equaled money, but essentially she said to me, Whatever."

"I'm trying to get a handle on her," I explained to Zee. "She doesn't sound as if she was the world's warmest person," I mused.

"Except that's really not right because with her kids she *was* Mrs. Warmth. Mrs. Mom. I mean, Travis, the little boy, came into the room once. She put her arms out for him and her face got this blissed-out ex-pression. Madonna and child—the Virgin Mary, not the singer. And from the way her house was fixed up, she was really into that Mrs. Homebody role. She had no eye in terms of film, but she did have . . . I guess you'd call it Rich Suburban Lady good taste." An uh-oh expression came over Zee's big-cheeked face.

"Don't worry," I reassured her. "I'm not rich. And if left to my own devices—although fortunately my friends restrain me—I'd probably put up purple plaid wallpaper. But I know what you mean. Nothing offensive."

"Right. But nothing imaginative. Nothing personal. Everything *done*. I mean, you couldn't pee there without good taste. Sorry. My mom hates it when I say 'pee.' Anyhow, you'd go to the bathroom—the guest bath-room, downstairs. She had a pile of guest towels—the kind you're afraid to use because they have to be ironed, but then you've got to because you're scared she'll think you didn't wash your hands. And then on the sink counter—pink marble—she had this basket with eensy-weensy Tylenol and Motrin tins and a teeny sewing kit. Tampaxes with a pink bow around each one. I swear to God!" She shook her head and added: "Courtney lined the bottom of the wastebasket with a paper doily."

Zee Friedman's breezy manner was actually not that distant from my own children's more sardonic Long Island style: Both were true to the Generation X credo that when one is profoundly cool, life can hold no surprises, and thus, there is never any reason to act excited. "You couldn't go into that house without feeling awe," Zee went on, sounding noticeably unawed. "It was the apotheosis of its kind. Did you get that? 'Apotheosis'? That's four years at Columbia. Anyhow, her house is to upper-middle-class suburban houses what the Parthenon is to Doric architecture."

I nodded, recollecting the miniature decorated lampshades over each candelabra bulb in the chandelier in the front hall, the impeccable arrangement of photograph, lamp, and leather-bound books on a small antique table in the living room. How Courtney must have loved what she created. Then I said: "I saw the StarBaby video you made of Luke Badinowski." Zee simultaneously grinned and pressed her fingertips against her temples, as if Luke or his parents had been a headache. "Your work looked professional to me."

She shook her head. "Thanks, but it's just competent. I've got an editor friend with super-rich parents. She's got a monsterly expensive piece of computer editing equipment, an Avid. Trust me: If you used one, your videos would totally look Kar-Wai Wong."

"What kind of equipment did Courtney Logan have?"

Zee ran her fingers through her hair, pulling it back from her face and shoulders, then twisting it into a bun. "Not that much. Lights for indoor shots. No big, expensive deal. I forget what they're called—the things those guys who make wedding videos use. Maybe eight, nine hundred bucks' worth of lights."

I thought about the fifteen thousand bucks Fancy Phil had claimed came out of the Logans' joint money market account plus the ten thousand Courtney had ultimately kept from the Smith Barney brokerage account. Fancy Phil had said that sum, twenty-five thousand dollars, was spent for "camera crap" and promoting the company. "What about cameras?"

"I used my own," Zee replied. She let her hair fall back to her shoulders.

"Any other equipment?"

"No. The other guy she had filming kept the StarBaby equipment in his house. He went to Wesleyan."

"Did you ever meet him?"

"No. Typical Courtney. She said practically zero about him. I got the impression she didn't want us to get to talking, which probably meant she was paying one of us more than the other. Anyway, she expected I'd use my own equipment. I did rent a mike because the one on my camera makes everybody sound like King Kong."

"Did she spend a bundle on ads or publicity?" I asked.

"That I don't know. If she did, I couldn't see any serious results. The whole time I worked for her, the level of business seemed about the same."

"Did she ever talk shop with you?"

Zee leaned her head against the back of the love seat and gazed up at the carved molding at the top of her wall. The decoration could have been a series of grapes or rosettes, but obscured by a century's worth of paint, it was just evenly spaced bumps. "One time. She said businesses fail for two reasons. Lack of capital and one other thing. Patience or a plan or something." She looked apologetic. "I'm interested in production, but what she was going on about was more like a business school rant. I tuned out."

"What made her chatty about business all of a sudden?"

"It must have been when I asked her if she had any more work, around July, when she started to act bummed. I'd been hoping she'd give me more to do. But she sort of intimated that she wanted to spread whatever work there was around, not to have to rely on one person."

"Did that make sense to you?"

"If you believe the clichés about film people—that we're undependable and narcissistic—it did, even though the truth is making movies is a highly organized operation. If people aren't reliable they don't work again. But to me her talk about patience and stuff sounded defensive. I couldn't see that she was on any road to franchising."

"How often did you work for her?"

"Two or three weekends a month."

"What did you think of StarBaby?" I asked. "As someone interested in the producing end of making movies."

"I guess it's not a bad idea for wealthy communities, where people have a lot of disposable income and not that much time. Probably there are, like, rich dot-com couples with babies who buy videocams but then are too busy to read the instruction book. Except unless Courtney could get the price down, StarBaby wasn't going to become the McDonald's of kiddie video. I mean, she'd been talking about wanting to trademark everything with the word 'star' in it: StarChild, StarKid, StarGirl, Star-Boy. And before the summer, she'd been looking into all sorts of other stuff. She'd gotten two pediatricians to let their exams be photographed, which had to have been a brilliant con job on her part because of doctors' malpracticephobia. And she was thinking about renting or buying some cuddly dog—a beagle or a collie—the kids could snuggle up to if the family didn't have its own dog. But she said there was a liability problem, like if lovable dog decided StarBaby was lunch."

"What about her husband?"

"I only met him once—the last time I saw her. He came in after golf. The way she looked at him you'd think he was this combo of—I don't know—Gary Cooper and Jude Law. You mentioned warmth: She acted pretty warm with him, as if he was really, really hot. To me, he was a majorly boring golf guy with good facial planes."

"Do you think the hot stuff was an act on her part?"

Zee cocked her head to one side for a moment of introspection. Finally she said: "I never had enough of a sense of the real Courtney to know if there was a false Courtney. For all I could tell, she was deep and unknowable. Or shallow and what you saw was all there was."

"But with you she was just businesslike?"

"Right, but . . . In the last couple of months, she did seem kind of detached. I mean, not upset or sad it wasn't doing better. Indifferent. Distant. Her mind was someplace else."

"Where?"

Zee offered an I-don't-know shrug. "I couldn't begin to guess. But Courtney went from trying to inhale for me—which was a real pain, I'm very organized—to basically letting me wing it."

"Could she have been depressed?"

"Well, she always acted so peppy. It was hard to see beyond that. She'd say hi and it would come out 'Hi-ee!' with this cute little squeak at the end. I'd say she was pretty low in July, but she was still squeaking. And by September she was squeaking Hi-ee, except her head was someplace else that wasn't StarBaby country."

"Did she seem afraid of anything? Nervous in any way?"

"Not that I could see, but then again, how much was she going to let me see?"

"Could she have been in love? Having an affair?" Zee offered me an I-don't-know shrug. "Did you ever see her emotional about anything?"

Zee shook her head slowly, though I could see she was still mulling over my question. While she mulled, I concluded she wasn't a homicidal psychopath and would be terrific for Joey. "It was weird," she said finally. "One time she got a phone call. We were in her office, which was an upstairs bedroom she'd converted. Cool. She used a beaten-up table that *had* to be an antique for her desk. There were tons of real flowers in vases. The room was done to a tee, like everything in the house. Anyhow, she put whoever was calling on hold and then went someplace else. But she must have stayed on the second floor, maybe her bedroom, because I could hear her, although a lot of it was muffled. She seemed pretty upset: 'Why can't you . . .' And what else? Oh. 'You *promised* . . .' That was all I heard, but boy, did she sound hassled. Almost desperate. I don't know, I could be reading too much into it."

"Could you tell if she was talking to a man or woman?" Zee shook her head. "Do you happen to remember when it was?"

"Late afternoon, when she was making out my check. That's why I was in her office. It must have been my last check—which would have made it a Sunday. The Sunday before Halloween. The Sunday before she disappeared."

"Was that before or after you met her husband that afternoon?"

"After. Definitely after."

From Zee's I drove from Manhattan over the Williamsburg Bridge—a structure that does not inspire confidence in the profession of civil engineering—into Brooklyn to keep a lunch date I'd made with Joey two weeks earlier. Ever since Bob died, I had to force myself out of the house to live something that vaguely resembled a life.

Except whenever I was out, all I wanted to do was get home. It wasn't so bad the days I was teaching at St. Elizabeth's, because my classes were all in the morning. I could be safely home by twelve-thirty. But for the first few months after his death, when I had days off, and I'd be doing volunteer work or running errands, I found myself scurrying to my car and rushing back to the house at lunchtime. And once I got there, my face damp from the tension, my breathing harsh . . . What? What was I expecting? Bob calling really long distance?

So for the last eighteen months or so I'd pushed myself back into the world, making lunch and dinner dates weeks in advance. Some nights I went to meetings, lectures, concerts. I was in an adult-ed class for beginning conversational Spanish. Or I let Nancy drag me into the city, to the galleries or the theater. When I was alone I buried myself in piles of term papers or exams. Or I'd reread a favorite book—nothing new, nothing unexpected for me. I played endless, numbing games of computer solitaire. Or I'd watch my favorite old movies until I'd become so enervated by Rosalind Russell's pluck that I'd fall asleep.

Maybe Socrates was right and the unexamined life was not worth living, but I was giving it my best shot. Weekends were harder. Everybody else knocked themselves out with leisure. But unless Nancy or one of the kids was free, or I had a date, I'd have no answer for the universal Monday-morning-at-work question: What did you do this weekend? For a while I made elaborate to-do lists in eighteen-point boldface and taped them up on the refrigerator. However, by Sunday night the only crossed-out item would be something like "Find Jane Fonda low-impact video," which, instead of inserting into the VCR as I'd pledged to myself, I'd inserted into the garbage can. All I seemed able to do was clean house. Along with the cassette I'd toss out stuff I'd previously been unable to part with: a bag of potting soil from around the time of the Reagan–Carter–Anderson race, five thousand pounds of *Gourmet* magazines, Bob's collar stays.

Anyhow, Joey took me to a new, hot restaurant near his apartment. The waiters, in white, short-sleeved shirts, black slacks, and skinny black ties, looked like funeral directors from Tuscaloosa. The food, however, was not southern but a trendy fusion, Californian and Cuban, which seemed to mean vertical stacks of rare fish, greens, and assorted legumes over *al dente* rice. Joey had not only heard about Crabapple Films but had actually given their latest release, a film set on Staten Island but based on *As You Like It,* four and a half out of his five stars. But he said no, I could not call and ask Zee if she was interested in being fixed up with him. And no, movie critics do not casually saunter into production offices and ask half-Chinese, half-Jewish PA's for information on their latest projects.

When I got home, I weeded my flower beds and vegetable patch until it was too dark to find weeds. It wasn't only the loss of Bob, the change of my status from wife to widow, that made weekends so tough. It was the other loss in my life—Nelson Sharpe. For twenty years I'd spent too many Saturdays and Sundays in a reflective fog, summoning up every episode of our relationship—and there were plenty of episodes. Worse, the previous year when I'd accidentally bumped into him for a total of three seconds: I compulsively replayed that scene again and again, choosing it hands down over anything the present had to offer.

Okay, the scene: It had been almost twenty years since Nelson and I had last laid eyes on each other. Suddenly there he was, walking right past me. The truth? He looked semilousy. His salt-and-pepper hair had hardly any pepper left. His face was the chalky, indoor color of a lifelong civil servant, though later I tried to tell myself he'd simply gone pale with shock at seeing me. While I had neither the time nor the presence of mind to give him the once-over, his body still looked fine. His eyes, still beautiful, large, and velvety brown, were wide open—with amazement or horror. For those three seconds they did not leave my face.

It's amazing how long three seconds can last. Naturally, I immediately thought there was some ghastly flaw he'd spotted, one of those hideous imperfections of middle age I'd missed because my eyesight had gone to hell— a giant hair growing out of my chin, an entire cheek covered by a rampaging liver spot. I held my arms tight to my sides so as not to reach up and feel for what was wrong. But then I reassured myself that for someone who, in her youth, had assumed that by her mid-fifties she'd resemble Albert Einstein, I was still fairly attractive. However, before I could think of something unmortifying to say, or offer him a serene nod, he had passed me by.

When I reported the encounter (in encyclopedic, adolescent detail) to Nancy, she made me swear not to do anything crazy like call him. I swore. Nevertheless, she insinuated I'd try some cute trick to get around my oath—like faxing him Bob's obituary—so I slammed down the phone.

Actually, it was Nelson who called me the next morning. He explained he hadn't meant to be rude, but was so shocked to see me he couldn't think of anything to say. We talked for just a few minutes. He told me there was a new political regime in the department. He was out of Homicide and head of a unit called Special Investigations. He also said he and June had gotten divorced fifteen years before. He'd been married for three years to a woman named Nicole, a high-school guidance counselor. Naturally, being the Compleat Schnook, I asked how old she was. Thirty-nine, which technically made him old enough to be her father and untechnically made me speechless with something pretty close to despair. He filled the silence by asking what I was doing, so I told him I'd gotten my doctorate and was teaching college. I didn't say a word about Bob. Nelson said, Maybe one of these days we could get together, have a cup of coffee. I said no, I didn't think that was a good idea.

And that was it. End of conversation. Later I was positive that when he spoke of his new wife his voice hadn't had a lilt, but Nancy declared I was *non compos mentis* or, alternatively, engaged in the most pathetic sort of wishful thinking. So I demanded, Then how come he wants to have coffee with me? She replied he's probably an old lech who reflexively whips out his wonker for an airing every time a woman passes by. He's not *that* old, I chimed in, and he was never a lech. Drop this, Nancy warned. Whatever it was you had together, it never meant to him what it meant to you.

But back to the Courtney Logan case. Since it was Memorial Day, I had the leisure on that Monday morning to attempt to come up with a reasonable suspect for the murder who could take the place of Greg. However, I soon realized I didn't know anywhere near enough about Courtney's friends and associates to begin. Since I couldn't interrogate Greg, I did the next best thing and called my client, Fancy Phil Lowenstein. He said he'd meet me that night in a new restaurant. In Port Washington. La Luna Toscana. Eight o'clock. You get there before me, you tell Antonio, Listen, I'm the doctor of history who's here for Phil. He'll take care of you till I get there.

But Fancy Phil had arrived before I did, and was seated at a corner table. He faced the room, his back toward a mural of a moonlit olive grove that for some reason was overrun by a herd of cross-eyed sheep. At first all I could see of Phil's outfit was a giant red napkin over his chest. Then I saw it was tucked into the neck of a black sports shirt that had a minuscule pattern of what appeared to be chartreuse boomerangs. He wore a gold link bracelet and a gold watch with twelve diamonds instead of numerals. Maybe to go with the watch, he had on his doozy of a diamond pinkie ring.

Before Fancy Phil was so much antipasto that what must have been the large oval platter beneath it all was completely camouflaged. Cheese vied with peppers for air. Artichoke hearts tried their best to squeeze in between the bresaola and pepperoni. His pudgy fingers were busy rolling up slices of prosciutto and provolone into a cigar shape. He stuffed the entire cylinder into his mouth, chewed once, swallowed with a big bounce of his Adam's apple, and commanded: "Sit down, sweetheart. I ordered some stuff. If you don't like it, Antonio'll have the chef make whatever you want. So, you come up with any, uh, theories?"

"I'm working on it," I answered as he poured me a glass of red wine. He held my glass up to the light. "Rosso di Montalcino." His accent would make an Italian shriek with laughter. Not to his face, of course. Someone might have the nerve to laugh with Fancy Phil, but never at him. "It comes from Tuscany. That's what 'Toscana' means. Tuscany. It don't mean parrot."

I decided not to inquire why anyone might think such a thing. "I need to speak to more people who knew Courtney," I told him. "I've got feelers out trying to get the names of her close friends, but I could get going quicker if you could help me."

"No problem." He picked up a dark olive so huge it looked like a major organ from a small mammal. He popped it into his mouth and it disappeared. He did not seem to know or care if it had a pit.

"When do you think you could come up with some kind of a list?"

"Now," he said.

"You have it all written down?"

"Not written. I know stuff from Gregory. I spoke to him and then I went there after you called me."

Iron sconces on the wall held flickering bulbs that were supposed to approximate the gleam of candles, but instead of a soothing glow, the continual sputter of light made you wonder if your retina was detaching. La Luna Toscana. For some reason I never could explain, whenever a new culinary trend got under way in Manhattan, like Tuscan cuisine, it spread to the other four boroughs, then went west, straight out to Kansas City—with a side trip to Emporia—before it could manage to cover the twenty-six miles east to the north shore of Long Island.

"Greg gave you specific names?" I asked, pondering a chunk of white cheese that felt hard enough to break a tooth. I set it on the side of my plate and picked up a bread stick. "For you to give to me?"

Wearily, Fancy Phil shook his head. Naturally, not a single jet black hair changed position. "Nah. I asked him what he told the lawyer. One of the things he told her were the names of Courtney's friends, her business people. Then when I was upstairs with Morgan playing Candyland, I walked out for a few minutes and went into her office." He paused. "This is strictly between you and me."

"Sure."

"So I'm in her office. I don't know about computers, but I look at the fat leather book she had, with a calendar and addresses and other crap. A map of the Underground in London."

"It's called a Filofax. It's made in England."

"Bully for England."

"So you took notes of what was in her Filofax?"

"No, no, no. I didn't need to take no notes. I never forget nothing." He snapped a celery stick in two and shook one of the pieces at me the way a teacher would shake a pointer at a deliberately dense student. "You should remember that, Doc."

"Is that a veiled threat that's supposed to make me feel chilled to the bone?"

Fancy Phil laughed a deep, big-bellied laugh, said "Nah," and recommended the Tuscan pot roast.

The next morning was one of those exquisite end-of-May days, the air sweet with the fragrance of new-mown grass and so clear that from the highest hill in Shorehaven you could see the Manhattan skyline shining gold in the sunlight. But I was in a carrel at the library. The unending creak of the elevator transporting books was my background music while I studied Fancy Phil's list of names. Unlike him, I'd had to write things down. I was awed by his ability not only to remember the spelling of each name, but to spew out the phone numbers and addresses that he'd cribbed from Courtney's Filofax.

I didn't know where to begin, so before I took on Courtney's friends, women who might also tie their tampons with ribbons, I flipped a quarter. Heads meant that Steffi Deissenburger, the Logans' former au pair, was German. Tails she was Austrian. She'd been reported in news accounts as being from both places. Austria won. I got out my cell phone and called the consulate in Manhattan and—*Mein Gott!*—finally got connected to a man who clearly knew who she was.

Nevertheless, Herr Toasty—which was the best I could make of his name, since his speech was exceedingly clipped—told me, in a huffy manner that all but said *Dummkopf,* that it was the United States embassy in Vienna that issued visas to Austrian citizens, not the Austrian consulate in New York. So I addressed him, in an even huffier tone: Excuse me, Herr Toasty, but it's one thing for an Austrian national to be an innocent victim of our overeager media, and it's quite another (I raised my voice) FOR FOREIGNERS TO USE OUR LIBRARIES AND THEN RUN OFF WITH BOOKS THAT ARE PROPERTY OF A PUBLIC INSTITUTION! After some mutual, guttural harrumphing, Herr Toasty agreed that if he could *possibly* find someone who *might* know Fräulein Deissenburger's whereabouts, which was *highly* unlikely, he would mention my name, the Shorehaven Public Library, and overdue books in the same sentence.

Naturally, I considered all the reasons why I should not have used the name of the Shorehaven Public Library in vain not before I'd hung up with Herr Toasty, but after. Like if Steffi Deissenburger actually had taken out *Madeline and the Bad Hat* to read to little Morgan but had borrowed it on Courtney's card and ergo knew that the library having her name in its records was fishier than last week's flounder. Like if Steffi (or worse, her lawyer) did call but, instead of calling me at school, decided to call the library and demanded to speak with the head of the library, thereby getting me kicked off the board and well on my way to becoming a town scandal. And then of course there was the little question I'd been avoiding answering: Was I nuts? Nuts to think I could set myself up in the detecting business, nuts to risk chasing down a murderer, and even more nuts to take on a client like Fancy Phil Lowenstein.

For most people, this sort of anxiety leads them to say: I'm so upset I can't eat a thing. Usually for me, it's: I'm so upset I need a grilled-cheese-and-tomato sandwich and a glass of milk and multiple Fig Newtons. So by the time I went out to dinner with a historian who taught at Queens College, I could only gaze into the brown depths of the Spicy Chicken Soong feeling something between existential nausea and plain pukey. However, that awful feeling evaporated as we wound up comparing and contrasting Watergate and the Whitewater/Lewinsky debacle, alternately howling with laughter and nodding sagely with the usual wild abandon of two historians sharing a half bottle of Chardonnay.

So if I wasn't singing "Life Is Just a Bowl of Cherries" by the time I got back, I was in a pretty decent mood. No messages at home. I listened expectantly to the one that was on my voice mail at the college, hoping to hear Steffi Deissenburger's girlish Teutonic tones advising me she had no library books and leaving a phone number, but it was only Commodore Patrick Daley, USN, Ret., one of my oldest students, telling me he had recovered still more memories of Admiral Hyman Rickover and the development of the *Nautilus* and would I consider writing his memoirs with him?

I was thinking semideep thoughts about how so many older students at St. Elizabeth's would find excuses to come to my office and then not talk about the course, but their own personal histories. It wasn't simply because they were lonely. They needed the solace of knowing that their lives had meant something. So when the doorbell rang I didn't think, Gee, it's nine forty-five and people don't just drop in at this hour. I sauntered over to the front door and peered through the peephole I'd had put in after Bob died, along with an alarm system and an overzealous motion detector that warned me of any squirrels humping within a five-mile radius. At first all I saw was an eye squinting back at me. And then I realized it was Nelson Sharpe.

Chapter Six

Nelson Sharpe.

Faced with the precise scenario I'd been dreaming of for twenty years, I was, of course, completely unprepared. My entire body, from my scalp to the soles of my feet, was jolted by an electric *Yikes!* With each beat, my heart slammed harder until my entire chest filled with what felt like life-threatening hammering. Except it wasn't my heart, but the geyser of blood erupting in my head that made me sure my imminent death certificate would read "cerebral accident" instead of "myocardial infarction."

After a couple of seconds, relieved to find myself alive, I managed to put the chain on the door and open it its three inches. Nelson looked significantly better than he had the year before, when I'd bumped into him for that instant. Casual now, his sports jacket (a houndstooth check patterned after a hound who needed orthodontia) was open, displaying an admirable section of broad, white-shirted chest, bisected by a yellow knit tie, and what appeared to be a still-flat belly. His coloring was no longer the civil-service parchment I'd been shocked by a year earlier. Actually it was now a fairly furious red. "Come on, Judith, open the damn door!"

Never a girl who could play hard to get, I eased off the chain, grateful I was still wearing slacks and a silk blouse and hadn't changed into one of my tantalizing bits of lingerie, like an oversize T-shirt and stringy terrycloth robe, neither of which disguised the fact that my breasts were no longer looking up. Anyhow, the instant the chain came off, Nelson used his suburban variation on the old TV cop routine, though instead of slamming his body against the door, he used a discreet combo of knee and shoulder that pushed the door open far enough that I could not change my mind about letting him inside.

Like I would change my mind. Except his first words in the front hall as he stood beside the umbrella stand were not: "Ah, Judith, eternally my beloved," but "What the hell were you doing last night?" Well, I thought, at least he wasn't shouting. In fact, his volume control was turned down suspiciously low.

"What are you talking about?" I whispered back. Not a particularly scintillating response, but I was so flustered being with him, alone in the house, that it was a small miracle that five consecutive words emerged. I couldn't really listen for his answer, being too busy focusing all my energy on breathing slowly so he wouldn't think I was panting with desire—or wheezing with the über-hysteria of postmenopausal women in Freud's lesser case studies. Also, with the exhilaration of Nelson's presence, I couldn't think straight enough to recall what I had done the previous evening. Plus, my cognitive processes weren't helped by his sports jacket. A thought flitted through my head: If you're dressing to drop by at your former lover's house, even if you don't have an iota of feeling left, you spiff up. What could have possessed him to wear a sports jacket that belonged in a smutty vaudeville act?

So for an interminable time that probably lasted four seconds, we stared into each other's eyes and I think were mutually embarrassed to discover that, despite twenty years' worth of crow's-feet and hideous houndstooth, the old flame was still blazing.

I got busy clearing my throat while Nelson recovered from the moment's awkwardness by acting like a detective, i.e., glancing over at my mail that was strewn over a small, skinny-legged half-an-oval table across from the umbrella stand. Since all that was in sight was a Long Island Power Authority electric bill, a thank-you note from Human Rights Watch for the contribution, the June issue of the *Journal of American History,* and a Williams-Sonoma catalog, he turned back to me and snapped: "Last night." His snap, however, was still pretty damn sotto voce. What was with him? In the old days he'd never been a sotto voce kind of guy when in snappish mode. Not that he was a screamer, but boy, could he be loud.

Then it dawned on me that the reason for his self-control was his conviction that I was not alone, that Bob must be upstairs. In our briefest of brief phone conversation the previous year, he'd told me about his new wife. I hadn't mentioned my late husband. However, since my hands were now on my hips (my acutely pissed-off position) with my unringed ring finger clearly visible, I concluded his deductive skills might have dimmed a tad.

"Okay," I said, "I give up. What about last night?"

"You were seen in the company of a certain Philip Joseph Lowenstein."

"A certain Philip Joseph Lowenstein? You mean out of all the Philip Joseph Lowensteins in Nassau County—"

"Fancy Phil Lowenstein, damn it!" He made a fist, but before he could smash it against the wall for emphasis, which, as I recalled, was one of his Top 10 Intimidating Cop Tricks, he thrust his hand into his pocket. "Look," he said more calmly, "I know what you like to do." Then quickly, abashed, he added: "Are you involved in looking into his daughter-in-law's murder? Or are you . . . Is Phil Lowenstein some kind of an acquaintance, or a business associate?"

"How about my paramour?"

"Come on, Judith."

"How come you're asking me about Courtney's murder? Didn't you tell me you weren't in Homicide anymore?"

"I'm heading up the unit called Special Investigations."

"Which does what? Investigate with whom your ex, uh, lady friends are dining?"

"It deals with organized crime. And so does Fancy Phil."

"Let's see . . . What happened?" I asked. "You have a tail on him and . . . Give me a minute to think this through. You or someone in your unit saw him coming out of La Luna Toscana with me. Being a gentleman, Fancy Phil walked me to my car—"

Peeved that I wasn't awestruck by his unit's investigatory prowess, he cut me off: "Yeah, right. And my guy ran your license plate. And there was your name and address on my desk this morning." He permitted himself a small smile: "The report had you down as 'an alleged history professor.'"

"That's what they say where I teach, too. Listen, do you want to come inside and sit down so you can grill me more comfortably?"

"I don't want to grill you," he was saying as he followed me into the kitchen. We sat across from each other at the table, which sounds proper, but being a narrow refectory kind of thing, it brought us close enough together that I could sense the heat radiating from his knees. Every few seconds his eyes would dart around the room, maybe searching for some familiar landmark still there after twenty years. But the white-flecked beige Formica counters had turned to blue-black granite and the GE refrigerator with the kids' artwork had been replaced by a Sub Zero the size of a small kitchen. Or maybe he was checking to see if Bob was shuffling about in slippers and robe. I offered, but he declined anything to eat or drink. I flipped open the tab of a can of Dr. Brown's Diet Cream and took a sip. "Do you know who Phil Lowenstein is?" he continued. "I mean, beyond whatever it is you read in the paper?"

"I have no doubt you'll fill me in." The next second I panicked that he'd think what I'd said was a double entendre, so with enormous nonchalance I took another sip of soda, which naturally was too ambitious. I leaped up for a napkin sensing it less than suave to wipe my dripping chin on the shoulder of my turquoise silk blouse.

"He's got high-level ties to both the Italian Cosa Nostra *and* the Russian Organizatsiya," Nelson said as I sat back down. "He's done everything dirty—dealt in stolen checks, diamonds, stock manipulation, bootleg gasoline, all sorts of stuff. Phil Lowenstein stinks to high heaven."

"Some might call him the personification of the American entrepreneurial spirit."

"Don't blow this off, Judith. Look, he took a vacation for aggravated assault, but we think he's been behind at least half-a-dozen hits."

"Are you saying Fancy Phil himself pulled the trigger?"

"Fancy Phil makes bad things happen."

"When?" I demanded. "Recently?"

"Over the years," he responded coolly. He rubbed his lower lip. I warned myself: Don't start picturing what it would be like to kiss him there. So naturally I got a graphic mental image of kissing his finger, then brushing it aside and kissing the very place he'd been touching.

"How come you haven't arrested him?" I asked.

"Grow up."

"I have. And I know if you'd had any real evidence, he'd have been convicted of murder. But the truth is, all Fancy Phil was convicted of was aggravated assault. One conviction. Fine, I'm the first to concede it's not nice to hit people."

"Especially not in the face with a brick," Nelson remarked.

"But Phil paid his debt to society. Now he's a grandfather, and he wants to play it straight for the children's sake."

"I can't believe you fell for that."

"And also for the sake of his son, especially since suspicion's fallen on Greg for Courtney's murder. I think Phil feels if it weren't for the way he's lived his life, the authorities would be doing what they should be doing—investigating who killed Courtney Logan—and not harassing Greg."

Nelson leaned back so the chair rested on its two rear legs and crossed his arms over his chest. "Tell me you aren't that naive," he said quietly.

"I'm not naive at all," I said to the cream soda. I was thinking it was actually a plus that the light over the table was strong enough to show him I hadn't become a shriveled-up crone when, all of a sudden, looking down at his big hands resting at the edge of the table, I got a flash of the past, how Nelson used to undress me as we made love, how so many times I'd looked down at those hands unbuttoning my shirt.

"Phil Lowenstein is an animal," he said harshly. "Don't pretend you don't know that."

"Phil Lowenstein is a human being."

"Don't start shoveling the liberal bullshit, Judith. I don't like seeing you getting involved with—"

"I can take care of myself." He shook his head: No, you can't. "Is Phil a suspect in the Courtney business or is it just Greg?"

"What's your involvement in this?" he demanded.

"I'm curious. You didn't answer my question."

"I'm not in Homicide anymore."

"That's not an answer."

"Your 'I'm curious' isn't an answer either." He shifted forward so the chair again rested on all four legs and stood. "Listen, I know better than almost anyone that you've got brains and guts. So if you want to pursue your detective thing, fine. Personally and legally I would warn you to stay out of it, but if that's what you gotta do, you gotta do it." Reluctantly, I got up, too. "Except find yourself another case," he went on. "Dealing with this guy: Listen to me. There are top-level mob guys too scared of Fancy Phil to go near him. You should be, too." He turned and walked to the door that led back to the hallway. When we reached the front door, he took a deep breath and said: "Someone like you, a person of your station in life, shouldn't have her name in the folder that comes to my desk every morning. And I want you to hear me on this . . ."

"Go ahead," I told him.

"If you step over the line in his company, don't count on any favors for old times' sake." Having said that, he at least had the decency to look embarrassed. On the other hand, he didn't take it back.

Since I couldn't think of any response, clever or insipid, I simply reached around him and pulled open the front door. "Does your husband know you're involved in this?" he asked as he stepped out into the balmy May night.

"I very much doubt it," I replied. Quickly, before there could be that instant of awkwardness followed by something he might regret and I might not, I closed the door behind him.

Naturally I didn't sleep much, being busy playing over the scene with Nelson a few hundred times, coming up with all sorts of reasons for his dropping by, from strictly business to he-wants-to-be-completely-certain-before-he-leaves-his-wife-for-me. Much of the time I substituted sparkling repartee for what I'd actually said. Nevertheless, when my alarm rang at seven, I didn't go back to sleep, perchance to dream of Nelson. Instead, I called my voice mail at St. Elizabeth's.

To my amazement, Herr Toasty of the Austrian consulate had actually come through! Steffi Deissenburger, in a minimal German accent—the sort that makes the speaker sound like an American who just needs a little time with a speech therapist—said she was certain she had returned all her books to the Shorehaven Library, but to call her. She left a number with a Connecticut area code. Two hours later, when I called, I explained that Herr Toasty might have misunderstood: I was a historian who happened to be on the library board. I'd been asked to write a historical overview of crimes against the wealthy on Long Island for an academic journal. Could I have just a few minutes of her time to get some background on Courtney Logan?

Well, Steffi thought aloud, her employer, Ms. Leeds, would be taking the twins to a breeder to look at puppies. That would be at one o'clock. Therefore, Steffi would be free from one until two. Although she wasn't supposed to have visitors at the house. But then again, the brakes on her car were being relined, so she couldn't get out. If I was prompt . . .

I drove about an hour and a half northwest, up to one of the farthest of Manhattan's bedroom communities. Whitsbury was a town of flawless lawns sheared to velvet, patrician trees, and houses so stately they could con their owners into believing they were to the manor born. From the roots of the English ivy to the tops of the stone chimneys, homes and grounds were unrelievedly refined, as if exuberance had been banned by local ordinance. This was stiff-upper-lip country. No new waves of immigrants reinterpreting the American dream the way we do on Long Island. No Tudor with a skylight to outrage the neighbors; no Dutch colonial resurfaced in ersatz fieldstone. Not even a château with a hot tub: Whitsbury was orthodox Anglo-Saxon.

I tooled up a cobblestone driveway to a red-brick house so splendidly solid it made the Logans' impressive Georgian look like something made from Lego pieces. Steffi Deissenburger stood at the front door, watching with apprehension as I narrowly missed scrunching half a flower bed under my right front tire. As I exited the Jeep, I gave her an all's-well wave that must have been a little too hearty because she inched backward into the house, perhaps fearing I'd do something embarrassingly Long Island, like bear-hug her or screech Hey, fancy-schmancy!

"Hello," she said cautiously.

"Hello," I said genteelly, though with extra warmth, in my be-nice-to-German-speaking-people-so-they-don't-think-you-think-they're-all-Nazis manner. From everything I'd heard, I'd assumed Steffi would be plain, and in khaki slacks, a white shirt, and sneakers, she definitely wasn't fashion's fool. Still, she would never be mistaken for an understated lady of the manor. Instead of the au naturel Connecticut horsey set's no-makeup look, in which a woman strives for a family resemblance to her mare, Steffi was cosmeticized to the nth degree. What looked to be ivory skin was agleam with a heavy coat of that shiny, slimy foundation and cheek color that I guess is supposed to make the young look dewy but winds up making most of them look like hookers who need astringent. Too bad: She had a classic oval face with placid gray eyes touching in their gentleness. Her nose, unfortunately, was ice-cream-cone-shaped and stuck a bit too close to her mouth. But if she wasn't actually pretty, at least she was better than advertised, projecting an aura of calm and kindness.

She was working as an au pair for an advertising-agency owner and his wife who had twin three-year-old girls. "Gwendolyn and Gwyneth," she informed me as she led me through the house, stopping to hand me a silver-framed photograph as we tippy-toed through a living room that was so vast it needed three different Oriental rugs to cover its dark wood floor. She waited eagerly for a reaction, as if wanting to make sure she had communicated her fondness for her charges.

"Very sweet," I replied. Gwen and Gwyn were fat-faced and red-cheeked, with identical puckers above their noses; to me, they looked more like anxiety-prone Munchkins than preschoolers. I handed back the picture. Reflexively, Steffi buffed the frame with her shirttail before leading me into the glassed-in porch she referred to as a conservatory.

A white wicker couch and chairs were covered in a chintz of tulips, hyacinths, and daffodils that practically sang "Spring Is Here." Expensive picture books on flowers and glossy gardening magazines were fanned across a marble table resting on a short Neoclassical pedestal. Leaves and flowers cascaded down a high, graceful steplike structure like chorus girls in a Busby Berkeley movie. I wouldn't have minded taking the room back with me to Long Island. "Do you miss Travis and Morgan?"

"Of course," she said quickly. "Now, you're here because you wish to get a sense of what Courtney was like?"

"That's right. As background for my project." Steffi, like Gwen and Gwyn, seemed older than her years. Her brown hair had frosty platinum and copper streaks, the sort of color job a woman my age, desperate for top down, hair-wild-in-the-wind youth, might inflict on herself. Sunlight shone on her hair and gave the dyed streaks a green, phosphorescent gleam. "As I told you on the phone," I continued, "this chat can be off-the-record. It's for my benefit, so I can be better prepared when I begin to write."

"Yes. Okay."

"Good. Then we'll get on to Courtney."

"Yes, well, you see I am calling her Courtney as well because she asked me not to call her Ms. or Mrs. Logan. She was so kind." Steffi pursed her thin, scarlet lips, meticulously outlined in darker red pencil, while she pondered what Courtney was like. Meanwhile, her index finger was busy tracing the outline of a large, pink hyacinth on the creamy chintz on the arm of her chair. "She was not at all formal. But neither was she . . . friendly. No, that is not the word I want." Though she was taking her sweet time thinking about adjectives, she didn't strike me as pedantic as much as concerned about being precise. " 'Accessible' is what I mean," she finally said. "Most people in the U.S. are very free with information about themselves. Courtney was not. She was, I would say, a lady."

"Can you give me an example?"

Steffi massaged her forehead with her thumb and index finger. In an American, I would have called the gesture full of baloney, but for all I knew it could have been a common posture for thinking Austrians. "I am sorry but . . . It was not that she did not talk. Sometimes she could talk a great deal. She would ask me about my country and would speak of how it was here." Her massaging left two dull lines in the sheen of her makeup. "But I learned little of her from all her talk, if you understand me. She spoke of government or economics or about the children, of course. So for instance, I did not know she came from the state of Washington until, you know, I read it in the newspaper when she was missing. I think I knew about her only that she went to Princeton College and worked as an investment banker."

"Was she specific about what she wanted or didn't want with the kids, or your duties around the house?"

"Oh yes. Very specific. Only fruit snacks. One hour of television a day. She must approve all videos and play dates. For the children, I mean. She asked me please not to let them see me eating sweets. Or watching television. I had a television in my room, so I could watch programs after they were asleep. But she was so kind. She said, 'I hope this won't put you out, Steffi,' and I said, 'No, of course not, Courtney.' "

"What about Gregory Logan?" I asked.

"I saw less of him." Under the layer or two of makeup, I thought I saw Steffi flush. I couldn't tell if it was because of some sexual memory, or a crush on her employer, or simply from chagrin at having been whispered about in connection with him. "He worked late many times. When he was home, naturally he was with the children or Courtney."

"Did you call him Greg or Mr. Logan?"

"Neither." Her violet-lidded eyes gave a single blink. "He never asked me to call him by his Christian name, but as Courtney had invited me to do so with her, I never knew what to say." She shrugged. Just for an instant she looked flustered, like the postadolescent she actually was. "I didn't call him anything."

"What happened on the night Courtney disappeared?" I asked softly, praying she would find this an appropriate question for a historian to ask.

"She came home from tricking and treating with Morgan and went to the kitchen. She said we had no more organic apples. She did not wish the children to eat too many sweets, you see, from Halloween. So she said to give them an apple for dessert, then one sweet. After the apple they would not be so hungry and ask for extra sweets. I told her: I will go to the Grand Union and buy the apples. No, she said, because it was the one night of the year children run around the streets, tricking and treating. They wear masks, so they could not see properly. She would prefer to drive. You see? Always thoughtful."

"What time was that?"

"Between five-thirty and six."

"Did you hear her car? Or actually see her drive away?"

"Yes." Steffi came across as one of those naturally tranquil people, with her gentle eyes and low-pitched, calm voice. Until you looked at her hands. They would not stay still; they traveled down to her khakis and rubbed her knees. "We always saw her go, because in the beginning, Travis used to cry when she would leave the house. Courtney said we should, you know, make a game of Mommy going bye-bye. Morgan would climb onto the window seat in the family room and look out the window where, you know, you could see the car leaving the garage. I would pick up Travis. We would all wave and say: 'Bye-bye, Mommy. See you soon.'"

"And on Halloween night, as she left to go for the apples . . . Did Courtney seem preoccupied or fearful or in any way not herself?"

Steffi's hands slid back from her knees and began to knead her thighs. "No. I am certain. I have thought about this many, many times. She played Mommy going bye-bye with us in the same way. She waved good-bye. She smiled."

"What happened next?"

"Nothing. I waited. It was seven o'clock. Then seven-thirty. I couldn't understand, but I gave the children each a small Snickers bar— from the bag I bought to have for trickers and treaters, not the sweets from Morgan's bag because I knew Courtney would not want them eating candy from other people. I put them to bed."

"Where was Greg Logan then?"

Steffi's hands came together as if in prayer. She rested her chin on top of her middle fingers. "In Manhattan. A dinner for business."

"Did you try to call him there?"

She shook her head, wearily. Clearly, she had repeated this account over and over to the police. "No. I did not call him."

"How come?" I tried for that look of benevolent curiosity women friends have in laxative commercials.

Her scarlet lips formed a tight fish mouth. "I was afraid that Courtney would become—what is the word?—upset with me."

"For bothering her husband?"

"No, no. For letting him know she was not at home. One time early that month he called. I told him I did not know where Courtney had gone. It was about four in the afternoon. He called back several times. When she did come home, at seven o'clock, she was angry with me. Angry in a quiet way. That was her way of being angry." Steffi hugged herself in consolation, as though still shaken. "It was my fault. I had forgotten what she had instructed me."

"What was that?"

"That when I did not know where she was, I should say she was shopping so her husband would not worry." I probably lifted an eyebrow or two skeptically. "Courtney worried that *he* worried," she explained. "She said to me, 'My husband has enough on his plate.' "

"What did she mean by that?"

"That he had much to think about. As they say, 'pressured.' "

"Did he seem that way to you? A pressured businessman?"

"No."

"What was he like?"

"Quiet."

"Nice to you?"

Steffi nodded, but I thought I caught her swallowing hard. Was Greg not nice? Had there been something between her and her employer, either before or after Courtney's disappearance? Did she simply have a lonely young woman's crush on her boss? Or was it about those rumors floating around Shorehaven? Could there be some darker reason for that swallow? "Yes. Nice. Very polite."

"He's an interesting-looking man."

"Yes, interesting. Somewhat Asian in the upper part of his face, I think, but his manner is very American."

"How were he and Courtney together? I'm asking because in preliminary interviews, I heard several different accounts. You have the advantage of being in the house."

"They were fine. They were in love." Steffi's eyes left mine and gazed out the glass wall of the conservatory at the high stands of pink rhododendron on the far side of what was either a huge puddle or a small fishpond. "Her face—when he walked through the door she would become . . . like a bride on her wedding day. So happy. He would always kiss the top of her head and ask her, 'How is my Courtney?' "

"Any sign of violence or threat of violence? Did he ever hit her or threaten—"

She jerked back her head, startled at the suggestion. "Oh no!"

"Was she out of the house often—I mean, where you didn't know where she was?"

"No." Reluctantly, she brought her eyes back to mine. "Well, more so in the week or two before Halloween. Three or four times, I think. Mr. Logan did not come home until eight, so she could be out until then."

"How did she dress those times she went off?"

"I don't understand."

"Was she dressed in casual clothes, as if she were staying in Shorehaven? Or dressier."

She took a deep breath and exhaled slowly. "I think . . . She was in—yes—a suit and high-heeled shoes."

I recalled Jill Badinowski reporting how simply and elegantly Courtney had dressed, in slacks and a silk blouse. "The sort of outfit she would wear when she visited couples to tell them about StarBaby? Or dressier?"

"As though she was going to something important. I would say in Manhattan, but I do not know, of course."

"A sexy suit?"

"No, no. Business, I think. A beautiful suit. Although she put on makeup and once put her hair up on her head. But she wore a blouse. Not sexy. You could not see her, you know, her breasts."

"Let's get back to Greg Logan. He came home around eight during the week?" Steffi nodded. "Every night?"

"Yes. His business was food, take-out food. People bought their dinners in his stores, so he had to be in his office, above the commissary where the food was prepared if something was not correct. And these times she was away so long, she would be gone from after breakfast to seven or once even seven-thirty. If he called, I had her beeper number and was to call her right away. But he had her cell phone number, of course, so I am sure he could always speak to her."

"But most of the time?"

"She was home. In her office. Courtney spent many, many hours there. She worked so hard."

"What time did Greg Logan come home the night she disappeared? He wasn't working, was he? Halloween was a Sunday."

"He was meeting a Chicago man in the city. I believe for an early dinner. He came home about fifteen minutes past eight o'clock." Steffi's voice was flat, as if she'd recited this story so many times that the words were without meaning.

"Did he look the way he always did?"

"His face, yes." I waited. "He usually wore what is called a sports shirt to his office. But that night he wore a suit and tie."

"How was he behaving? Same as always?"

"Yes."

"Not excited or upset? His clothes not messed up?" I was looking to find the truth and, hopefully, clear Greg. But I also wanted to find out what Steffi had told the cops.

"No. He acted"—she clasped her hands in her lap like a schoolgirl—"as always. Appeared as always."

"Which was . . . ?"

"Neat. Very neat. Pleasant. And, you know, a little tired."

"Was he worried when you told him Courtney had gone out for apples— How long before was it?"

"She left between five-thirty and six o'clock."

"So was he worried that she'd been gone so long?"

"Not at first. But as it got closer to nine I would say he was maybe concerned. He said she might have met some friends."

"And then?"

"He went upstairs. The children were asleep. I think he stayed upstairs in his bedroom."

"His bedroom? Did he share a bedroom with Courtney?"

"Oh yes. I meant *their* bedroom."

"Do the windows up there overlook the swimming pool?"

Steffi closed her eyes and put back her head to think. There was a U of beige glossy makeup around the white skin on the underside of her chin. "No. Their bedroom windows are in front and on the side of the house. The pool is in back."

"Did Greg come downstairs again?"

"Yes. About nine-thirty or nine forty-five. He looked worried. He said he'd called the police, but there were no auto accidents, so I need not worry. She might have gone to a friend's and forgotten to tell him is what he said."

"He'd tried her beeper and cell phone?"

"Yes, he said he did that. She did not call back. He left a message on the voice mail of her cell phone, but she did not call." She lowered her head until she appeared to be gazing at the hands in her lap. "He stayed downstairs after that. Walking from room to room. I did not know what to do. He kept looking at his watch. I thought I should get out of his way. I went upstairs—"

"About what time?" I inquired gently.

"About ten o'clock. From my room I can hear the garage door open, but I heard nothing."

"Did your windows overlook the pool?"

"No."

"Okay. Please go on."

"I came downstairs at about ten-thirty. I asked him if he thought he might call the police to say she was missing. He said no, not yet, that Courtney might be out to dinner or a movie with some friend and be angry if he called the police. He seemed, you know, calm. But then he started going from room to room looking for a note she might have left. More than one time he asked me: 'Are you *sure* you didn't throw away a piece of paper?' I tell him I am sure, but a few minutes later I go into the kitchen because I thought I hear sound from there and he is going through the garbage pail."

"Did he call his father?"

"I don't know. He used the telephone, but I do not know who he was talking with. I just see the telephone line light up again and again. And then I went upstairs because I thought, if Courtney comes in, it is not my place to be there when he greets her. Just before midnight there is a knock on my door. It is Mr. Logan and he tells me, 'None of Courtney's friends know where she is. I called the police. They are coming.' "

Chapter Seven

"Sounds like a bullshit case to me," remarked Claymore Katz, criminal lawyer and bon vivant, as he stroked his luxuriant mustache.

Clay resembled Theodore Roosevelt or a walrus, depending on whether or not he was wearing his glasses. He had been Bob's roommate at Columbia College. As long as Bob lived, they'd had lunch every six months or so to talk business, politics, and relive the 1955 World Series. There had also been an annual dinner in Manhattan with me and the girlfriend or missus of the moment, during which—usually seconds before the entrée was served—Clay would lean over for his sincere moment with me: Tell me, Judith, how are the kids doing?

Clay stirred his martini with his index finger. Two tiny white cocktail onions chased each other madly around an ice cube as if trying to conjoin, breed, and form a string of odoriferous pearls. "Then again," he was saying. I pulled my eyes away from the glass. "I've seen one or two guys like this Greg Logan go up the river on nothing more than dumb-ass circumstantial evidence." He tore off the end of a sourdough-fennel roll and popped it into his mouth.

"*Totally* true," Heather Peters-Katz, the latest wife, said as she reached across the table and solicitously brushed several crumbs off the husbandly mustache. Heather should know. She'd been an assistant United States attorney, a federal prosecutor. Now, evidently, she was Clay's junior partner, not only in his firm, but also in his life. Giving no sign he'd heard his wife speak, the barrister cleared his throat to go on.

The Katzes of East Sixty-eighth Street and East Hampton had such an active social schedule that I hadn't anticipated getting an actual dinner with them. I'd called Clay to invite him to lunch and pretty much expected a damn-I'm-all-booked-up-how-about-Wednesday-at-3:07-in-my-office. My guess about his dinner invitation? He felt guilty for having called only a couple of times to find out how I was doing sans Bob in the more than two years since the shiva. Or else he had visions of me sliding my hand over his generous thigh in a midday paroxysm of widowy lust while he was halfway through his broiled-without-butter arctic char. His hearty courtroom voice had boomed over the telephone: Judith, Heather would never forgive me if I kept you all to myself. She's dying (having let "dying" slip out, Clay was too cosmopolitan to falter, though I did sense a millisecond's pause) to see you. The restaurant he'd chosen was one of those new chic wonders with a one-word name—Esplanade or Thyme or Gala—with bare ecru walls and so many candles that you feel you're not getting enough oxygen, the way you do on a long flight.

"The police seem to think the husband did it," I said in a sprightly voice. I'd brought up the Logan case as if it were a lively bit of suburban lore to amuse these city slickers, not as though it were a crime I was investigating. "Everyone says they've stopped looking for the killer and are bent on making a case against this Greg Logan."

"Another Boulder." Clay sighed, taking his final forkful of a salad composed largely of beets and kidney beans. Clearly, we were living in what would become known as the Year of Maroon Food.

"Boulder as in the JonBenet Ramsey case?" I inquired.

"In the sense of the cops not wanting to do the work, going for the obvious solution." Though to me it seemed likely that Boulder had been an inside job, I kept my own counsel.

"What's the *evidence*?" Heather demanded. Clay, his lower lip thrust out in vague annoyance, peered around the restaurant as if someone at another table had been talking too loudly. I began to ache for Heather. Her husband's generic female companion was thirty-two and bosomy, and Heather looked on the verge of receiving those birthday cards of dubious hilarity, the sort with "Look out! Here comes the big 4-0!" on the front.

"The evidence?" I responded. "Well, Greg took over forty thousand dollars out of their joint account and put it under his own name. His ex-

planation is that Courtney was withdrawing money for her business and
he needed to keep a certain amount of cash on hand to keep his bankers
happy. Evidently the cops aren't buying his story. Oh, and her body was
found in the family pool."

"Was *he* having an *affaire de coeur*?" Heather inquired.

"Well, there were the usual rumors around town, about his taking up
with the au pair either before or after the murder. But I doubt that happened."

"Why not? It's been *known* to happen." Heather Peters–Katz was one
of those people who italicize at least one word per sentence, making
everything she said sound sarcastic, which I didn't sense was her intention. Actually, she was polite enough, if not truly benevolent.

In looks, she was the picture of good-natured simplicity, reminding
me of the Strawberry Shortcake doll my daughter Kate used to have, with
that toy's pinchable, fat cheeks and ridiculously red hair. Unlike Ms.
Shortcake, however, Ms. Peters–Katz was built like a brick shithouse. She
generously exhibited her endowments by means of an out-of-court pea-
green silk dress so clingy it gave evidence she had cleavage both front and
rear.

Seated beside her, alas, I'd noted that with lackluster eyes and nostrils
the diameter of the average garden hose, she wasn't particularly pretty.
Clay, I suspected, like many presbyopic middle-aged men, probably didn't
know precisely what his new wives actually looked like except for the
more obvious features: breast projection, ankle thickness, hair color.

"Well, I can only give you my impression of the case," I replied,
throwing in an "uh" and an "um" to show I'd only just begun to think
about the Logan murder. "I don't know what the cops really have on
Greg. But the au pair is working up in Connecticut now. People tell me
she still speaks of him respectfully, as a former employer—not as a lover or
an old lech or anything. I'm sure she told the cops the same thing." Husband and wife propped their chins on their fists and waited for my next
question, which I addressed to a neutral sliver of space halfway between
them: "You're both defense lawyers. If you were representing Gregory
Logan, how would you handle the case?"

"I would—" Heather began.

But Clay was already mid-sentence: "I'd make the DA and the cops
sweat. Why the hell should it be easy for them? I'd dig into this Courtney's background." Instead of looking peeved at being beaten to the
punch, Heather's head bobbed up and down, agreeing with her husband's
every sentence as if to say: That's *precisely* what I would have said. It was
as though Betty Friedan had never lived. "Any men in her life?" Clay demanded. "Unsavory characters? Criminal associations?" I told him about

Fancy Phil. "Ah," he sighed. With evident fondness, he smoothed his hair with the tips of his fingers. Both his hair and mustache were dark brown, but with that mysterious orange Ronald Reagan tinge that occurs when men hit the dye bottle. "Okay, so he set aside that forty thou. Now how much did she take from their account?"

"Between their money market and brokerage accounts I hear the total she actually wound up with was twenty-five thousand. She told Greg it was for StarBaby, her business, for camera equipment and I guess what you'd call promotion—ads and stuff."

"Well?" Heather asked, twirling the stem of her wineglass impatiently between her thumb and index finger. "Has anyone *seen* a twenty-five-thousand-dollar camera or a full-page ad in the *Times*?"

"Not that I know of," I responded.

"That's my point!" Clay trumpeted, banging his empty martini glass on the table for emphasis. "Too many unanswered questions." You're telling me, I said to myself. "There's been a rush to judgment," he continued. "I'd have private detectives and forensic accountants all over the place looking for stuff on this woman, following the money, finding out who her friends were. Of course, with Logan's old man, Lowenstein, there could be some organized crime angle and Courtney could be pure as the driven snow. But I'd buy time demanding a lot of forensic tests. And I'd look for anyone who might have a reason to want her dead." The waiter, probably an actor whose career was already kaput because he looked like Leonardo DiCaprio's older, less handsome brother, slid our entrées in front of us and faded out.

"Who had reason to want her out of the picture?" Clay demanded. His hands gripped the edge of the table. Leaning forward, he jutted his head toward me as if he were Queen's Counsel in some British courtroom drama and I an accessory to murder standing in the witness box. "Who?" he repeated.

"As far as I can tell," I answered, "no one. I mean, who'd want to kill a woman out to buy organic apples for her kids? On the other hand, there is the inescapable fact that she was shot in the head twice."

"Does the husband *at least* have a decent alibi?" Heather interjected. Clay had fallen momentarily silent during the Sniff, Swish, Swallow, Cerebrate, and Nod Ceremony over the Burgundy he and the sommelier had earlier conferred about exhaustively. When I took a sip, it tasted like Manischewitz without the blessing of sugar.

"Greg had an early dinner meeting that night," I told her. "Unfortunately, he was still driving to it around the time Courtney drove to Grand Union—or wherever she went—between five-thirty and six." I'd heard that from Steffi, who had seemed observant enough. "He got home about eight-fifteen—" I would have gone on, but all of a sudden a man about my age was standing behind the fourth chair at our table, the empty one. He sighed and shook his head: "Just got in from D.C. All the flights were delayed."

I waited for Clay to suggest to the man that he was at the wrong table. Instead, he leaped up, vigorously pumped the man's hand, and announced to me: "This is Dan . . ." I didn't get the last name because Heather was cooing "Dan!" and springing from her seat, leaning forward to offer her cheek to his cheek. They briefly smooched the air then switched cheeks only to peck once more to conclude their Euro-kiss. Immediately after that Clay and Heather began a battle of words: "Judith, this is our *dear* friend—"

"Dan Steiner," Clay cut in. "He retired last year from running his own—and may I add—very, very successful hedge fund—" Dan Steiner was approaching six feet, although he hadn't gotten there. Still, he was inches taller than Clay, who, unsettled being so near a man of greater height and vaster wealth, began to stroke his already smooth tie uneasily.

"But the *real* point is Dan is going for a Ph.D. in Russian history *at Yale*—" Heather, I thought, was being excessively delightful. I surmised her sparkle was not evoked by his academic credentials. Dan the Man himself did not appear the sort to inspire such enthusiasm. Although he fairly could be described as slim, or at least trim, he had developed one of those mush faces that are visited upon many in their fifties; it had lost not just color, but definition, so precisely from the point the jaw rose out of the chin he resembled an overkneaded oblong of dough topped with thin gray hair. The chin itself, however, a hard-edged rectangle, protruded out of his face as though it were an appendage donated by another species; it was so long I kept marveling he hadn't grown a beard to camouflage it, especially now that he was one with Academe.

"He drives up to New Haven every week to take—"

"Dan—I hope Clay told you—Judith *has* a Ph.D. in American history and teaches at a *very prestigious* small Catholic college—"

Since the three of them were standing, I decided it might appear surly to remain seated. But just as I was about to rise, Dan reached across the table and gave my hand the limp shake of a man who's never gotten over the notion that women are the weaker sex. His eyes looked past me, or nearly so; an observer would have thought he was saying Nice to meet you to my earlobe. Then he took his chair. Now that Heather and Clay had only each other to look at, they, too, quickly sat. Within two seconds Dan was asking about one of Clay's SEC cases and Clay immediately began simultaneously declaiming and violating the Canon of Ethics: "The guy's in a sweat. He's leveraged beyond belief." Dan intoned: "You know, when you get that kind of leverage, certain moves in the market are magnified and—"

Not that I cared that they were (a) boring and (b) rude. Okay, I did care. But also, I was so agitated by being half of what I gathered was a blind date that all I could do was stare at my Tender Young Chicken in a Rosemary-Mustard Marinade Grilled over Apple Wood and try to calm down. What was as galling as the presumption of fixing me up without asking me if I'd be interested was the fact that Dan appeared utterly uninterested. He was spouting to Clay about unlearned lessons of the Longterm Capital Management scandal while disregarding me with such intense concentration that I could tell he'd been strong-armed into the dinner and wanted to be either at home with a tome about the terribleness of Ivan IV or on the town with whatever his definition of a hot number was.

Heather leaned so far over to me her left breast brushed across the fruit salsa atop her halibut, leaving a small dark stain and a fleck of what I guessed was peach but could have been some new fruit I'd never heard of. "Judith," she whispered, unaware of the to-do on her left nipple. "We didn't tell you about Dan because we didn't want you to get your hopes up." As I was literally dumbstruck she filled in the blank: "In case he didn't show." Then she sat back, waiting for me to attempt to entice Dan.

Except as I sat there, watching two middle-aged male hotshots vying to say something so insightful it would stun the other into silence, watching the exquisitely cleavaged Heather, this litigator who confronted for a living, say "Um" three times in an attempt to join the conversation only to have her husband and Dan reflexively raise their voices so her "Um" could be ignored without blatant discourtesy, I realized there was nothing I could say or do that would entice Dan Steiner.

Someone might ask: Why the hell would I even be tempted to entice a guy I wouldn't want even if he exhibited the politesse of a Lord Chesterfield and a schlong that went from here to Cleveland? Well, because he was a prime catch, what someone like me ought to go gaga for. Smart enough to get into Yale, or so astoundingly rich he could buy his way in. Definitely rich enough—from the sheen of perspiration on Clay's forehead to the gleam in Heather's insignificant hazel eyes—to be the sort of magnate revered for his cool instead of being blown off as the cold fish he was.

What saddened me most was that in his snazzy pale gray pinstripe of exquisite summer-weight wool so painstakingly cut it (almost) concealed the mini-love handles no exercise or diet could expunge, Dan was precisely the man my late husband had always yearned to be.

The worst of the worst was, a sweetie pie smile kept trying to take over my face in a pitiful attempt to win the favor of the man who was ignoring me. Two more seconds and I'd be batting my lashes, complying with Article Two of the Girl Constitution: If he rejects you, try harder. I actually had to command myself: Wipe off that sycophantic smile. "Excuse me," I said to Dan in an Elizabeth Cady Stanton voice. "There was a murder in my town on Long Island. I was asking Clay and Heather about how they would defend the chief suspect."

"A murder?" he echoed. There followed an instant of silence during which we could hear the clink of fork against plate as a waiter deboned a fish at a nearby table. Dan seemed to recognize another sentence was required of him, which he evidently found vexing. For him, this was a dismal evening after a rough day in Washington. His cheeks inflated, prelude to a petulant exhalation. Clearly he knew intuitively (as well as from studying the Houses of Rurik and Romanov) that, as a rich and powerful person, he had an absolute right to behave badly. Finally, however, he exhaled his pissed-off sigh through his nose and in a resigned voice inquired: "Who was killed?"

So while the waiter dashed off to get him a Salad of Baby Greens with Four Variations on Duck, nothing else, thanks, which was no doubt how Dan the Man kept himself slim to trim, I offered a précis of the Courtney Logan case. "Clay told me the lawyer for Greg, the husband, should be hiring a forensic accountant. The goal seems to be to follow the money."

"No one knows where the twenty-five thousand she took went to?" Dan asked. His suit was one of those trendy, three-button numbers that expose shirt and tie only to mid-sternum. It had the effect of making him look straitjacketed, and the impression was underscored by his stiff bearing and the way he held his upper arms close to his sides, even when he reached for his water glass and took a sip. It was not the posture of a guy who could, in any way that counted, be fun.

"From what I've heard, all Courtney said was that she needed the money for her business," I replied.

"If she didn't hide it really well, that should be easy enough to find out," Clay interjected. "I mean, for the husband's lawyer."

What I was thinking was: No one had actually seen any expensive cameras, had they? Zee Friedman had told me she'd used her own stuff: Could the equipment Courtney told Zee was at the Wesleyan graduate's house be a fiction? If so, then what could she have used the money for? Why would she lie about it? "Just out of curiosity," I inquired, "what would a woman in her position need thousands and thousands for if not the business?" I halted for what I hoped was a meaningful pause, although it was probably a little overdramatic. "Blackmail?" I proposed. No one said no. On the other hand, I didn't hear any resounding yeses.

"Face-lift," Heather offered to break the silence. "Seriously, the works can *easily* be around thirty-five thou. Or could she have had a jewelry habit?"

"She didn't seem the type." Could the Wesleyan student himself be a fiction?

"Drugs?" Clay was asking.

"Courtney seemed to function very well—at everything," I told them.

All I wanted to do was ransom my Jeep from the overpriced Manhattan garage, tool back to Long Island, and again read over my notes on the case. Maybe this time they would tell me something. Yet I kept talking to Dan, trying to get something out of him, at least some snippet of financial expertise that might shed some light on the Courtney Logan case. "You were a businessman before you became a scholar?" He nodded, a single nod, clearly not being profligate in the nod department. Still, he seemed gratified enough by the word "scholar" that I half regretted using it. (The other half, sad to report, was preening that I'd finally done something to please him.) I went on: "Let's forget what the murder victim needed the money for. Let's just say she needed it, ostensibly for the business. If she'd been turned down for a loan by the banks but still needed more money, where would she get it?"

"Family money?" Dan suggested. I shook my head, which seemed to disconcert him. He rubbed his shovel of a chin and, after a few seconds, "Money in the market?" emerged from his pale lips.

"There was some. I think eighty thousand in one particular account." Dan blinked, probably in shock at such a chicken-feed number. "She took out twenty, but put ten back. Her husband wouldn't let her get at the rest."

"Well, maybe she only needed a small amount," he replied in a rather hushed tone. "She did have a small business." He appeared slightly dazed to find himself in a discussion whose subject he hadn't set.

"But she had big ambitions for it," I explained. "Franchising, stuff like that."

"Maybe a loan shark?" Clay ventured. "Someone whose name she heard bandied about by her father-in-law?"

"She'd been an investment banker at Patton Giddings," I explained to Dan.

"Could she have used the money for on-line trading?" Heather chimed in. "Or for day-trading?"

"Possible," Dan replied, "but only barely. Most of these people, even the so-called sophisticates . . . Cocksure of themselves. They wind up losing it far easier than they run it up. She'd have had to be very, very good just to break even over the long term. Day-traders are addicts, no better than the blue-collar guy who squanders his salary on offtrack betting week after week."

"But with her background in finance?" I reminded him.

"Please," he said, in the overly patient manner of someone who is trying to appear open-minded rather than supercilious. He pointed his fork straight at me. I pulled my eyes away from the drippy leaf of baby spinach woven between the tines and looked right at him. His lips were compressed into a hyphen. Despite his mush face, the flesh above and below his lips was protuberant, well muscled, evidence that his disdain for me was almost nothing personal, that Dan's native expression was one of scorn. "Ask yourself," he said. "If she were really first-rate, would she have quit Patton Giddings? To live in the *suburbs*? To be a *mommy*?"

Dan was so odious I actually skipped dessert. The worst thing about the evening was that it would be too late to call Nancy and recount it, thus giving her the chance, in her role as official best friend, to rage against Claymore Katz's ill breeding and sexism in fixing me up without asking my consent, to orate on Heather's self-victimization, and to offer a diatribe about Dan Steiner's boorishness, egotism, pomposity plus, naturally, several scathing, southernly accented sentences about how teeny his penis must be—that being the universal and official female put-down. Alas, I've always felt it a form of vengeance (while not without its immediate satisfactions) that is sadly impotent.

Driving home on the Long Island Expressway, I put Dan out of my mind, tried not to devote even one neuron to Nelson, and didn't waste a microsecond on post-modernist Geoff. Musing over murder most foul, I decided, was far more comforting than contemplating the unholy trinity of me, men, and my future. Except I found little comfort. I was beginning to feel uneasy about the case. The more I learned, it seemed, the less I knew, not the sort of progress I wanted to report to a client like Fancy Phil.

What could I tell him? That I'd spent the day at the library searching databases for all variations on Courtney Bryce Logan, Courtney Bryce, StarBaby, Courtney AND Princeton, and Courtney AND "Patton Giddings." All that popped up was a wedding announcement, the fact that Courtney had been treasurer of Princeton's Class of '86 Fund, and an article from *The Olympian* in Washington state, Courtney's hometown paper, reporting her murder with quotations from a few of her Summit High classmates, one of whom had used the adjective "shrewd" where "smart" might have been more seemly.

And when I'd gotten home from the library in the late afternoon, there had been a message on my voice mail: "The clock's ticking. You got anything yet?" No name of course, but there was no doubt it was Fancy Phil. With more than a hint of strained patience in a gravelly baritone unaccustomed to expressing forbearance. *"You got anything yet?"*

Did my client simply and sincerely want to discover the truth? Or had he wound me up and sent me searching to find out all that was findoutable, that is, to see if there was any evidence the average detective might miss that could lead back to Fancy Phil himself, or to Greg, evidence he could then destroy—along with the historian who'd dug it up?

Nelson Sharpe hadn't warned me about Phil Lowenstein just so I could swoon and throw myself into his arms. Basically, Nelson was saying: This guy doesn't just have a nasty temper. This guy can order a murder, although if he likes you, he'd probably ask one of his associates just to maim. What kind of lunacy or presumptuousness had led me first to knock on Greg Logan's door, then after that let me think I could handle his old man?

So the next morning, feeling a little shaky, I phoned Mary Alice Mahoney Schlesinger Goldfarb and my next-door neighbor, Chic Cheryl, to try to track down some of Courtney's friends. Mary Alice said she knew "tons" of them, but, under not very rigorous cross-examination, was unable to come up with any names. On the other hand, Chic Cheryl blared out not only names, but net worth and country-club memberships. Also, according to CC, the explication I'd gotten from Jill Badinowski of the social stratification among younger, stay-at-home mothers was in error: They formed cliques not based on the status of their occupations in their former lives—cosmeticians vs. bankruptcy lawyers—but on the wealth of their husbands, a notion that would have desolated me for weeks had I not been so eager to gather enough information that I could get to Fancy Phil before he decided to get to me.

After writing down Chic Cheryl's candidate for best friend, Kellye Ryan, I must have had some "When Irish Eyes are Smiling" stereotype in the back of my head, because the tall, tan, slender, long-limbed nearbeauty who rang my doorbell that Friday afternoon was a surprise.

"Hey," she greeted me.

"I appreciate your coming over," I told her.

"No prob." Kellye didn't seem to notice the missing "lem." "Nice house. Hey, I'm glad you're doing something to—what's that word?— whatever, to honor Court." Although she did appear to be vocabularily challenged, she was alert and self-confident. I led her through the house, out the back door, and offered her a seat on an old cedar bench. Unobtrusively, she flicked off what might have been an atom or two of pollen before executing that deft bent-knee, ass-to-seat maneuver that indiscernibly transforms the naturally graceful from a standing to a sitting position. "So much publicity. Yuck. It's nice someone wants to hear nice things about her."

"I do want to hear nice things," I assured her. "But if I'm going to write about it, or turn it into an oral history, it's my obligation to ask all sorts of questions. My job isn't to commemorate Courtney Logan, even though I'm sure she deserves it."

"Gotcha," she replied. Kellye Ryan did not look like the average Shorehaven mommy, in a T-shirt and khakis with just enough forgiving Lycra to get her through dinner at Burger King without having to open her zipper. Instead, she wore one of those dresses of palest peach silk and lace that is barely distinguishable from a full-length slip. As she was at least five feet ten, it ended mid-thigh, which in her case was not a problem.

With the dark hair pulled back into a bun at the nape of her neck and her almost black eyes, Kellye looked like a beautiful flamenco dancer. That is, until she smiled. Then she looked like a flamenco dancer from Transylvania. Dracula teeth: Her upper canines were so elongated they appeared to pierce her lower gums. I had to stop myself from lowering my chin to protect my neck.

"Tell me a little about yourself," I prompted. "What's your background?"

"You know." Sensing this might not be quite enough, she went on. "College, Bard. After, Bill Blass."

"Were you a model?"

"Uh-uh," she said, while giving me a modest little shrug to acknowledge the compliment. Then she got busy aligning the two spaghetti straps on her slip-dress.

"What did you do there?"

"Marketing."

I sensed a little more small talk was needed before I started asking her about her murdered friend. "Did you like working in the fashion industry?"

"I mean, to work for Bill Blass? Total, total dream job."

"Uh-huh," I found myself saying.

"The whole line. Quality. Down to the seams. Beautifully finished. You *never* have to be ashamed to take off your jacket."

"Right. And now?"

"Married, two kids." Her smile slowly faded and a sorrowful expression elongated her face. "Same as Court."

"How did you meet her?"

"Tennis tournament. Rolling Hills."

"That's a country club?"

She nodded. "Yeah. They paired us. Doubles team. I mean, Mutt and Jeff. Short and tall. But we were great. Together. We started playing singles. A powerhouse, that girl! Fridays. Strategy, strategy. And a killer serve."

"And you became close friends?"

"Right."

"What was she like?" I asked.

As Kellye considered she scraped some invisible lipstick or crumbs from the corners of her mouth with the tips of her pearl-colored pinkie nails. "Court? Smart. Adorable. I used to kid her. Call her Miss Perfect," she said, smiling sadly. "But she was. Always there for you. Great friend. Totally, totally in love with her kids."

"And what about her husband?"

"In love with him, too," she said quickly, although I noticed the "totally, totally" was dropped. "She was cute looking, too. But smart enough not to wear ruffles, you know? Princeton, and it's not easy to shake that boring, Ivy style, so she was a little too safe fashionwise. But who's going to argue with Armani?"

"Not me," I said.

"And always . . . *doing*. StarBaby. Before that Citizens for a More Beautiful Shorehaven, president one time. Volunteer, Island Hospital. Something else with cancer. Tennis, running, learning golf. And doing for Trav and Morgie? Like the day she . . ." Kellye, suddenly breathless, pressed her hand against her chest and paused to compose herself. "The day Court was missing. Got killed probably, but who knew that then? She made a Halloween pumpkin cake. You wouldn't believe it! Two cakes in bundt pans. Put them together, one on top of the other—you know, bottom to bottom, with frosting for glue. It honestly did look like a pumpkin. Orange frosting, black frosting eyes, and she smushed together green gumdrop thingies for the stem. I said, 'Court, you don't have enough to do?' and she said, 'Yes, but wait till the kids see this. They'll be' . . . Some word like 'so happy.'" Kellye's eyes grew moist. A tear rolled out onto her black lower lashes. She carefully dabbed it off with the side of her index finger to avoid smudging her mascara.

"I'm sorry," I told her.

"'Sokay." Her tears kept flowing. Kellye Ryan might have been deficient in language, but perhaps not in intelligence and definitely not in feeling. I found a tired Kleenex in my back pocket and handed it to her. "When she was missing," she finally went on, "I couldn't stop thinking. Sicko people out there, you know? Like the guy who killed Versace. Except not gay. And creepier. So I was petrified. Like what could be happening to her? I didn't want to think about all the things that could be—oh, Jesus!—done to her. But I couldn't help it. And then when they found her body . . . I just pray whoever shot her in the head just did it, not later after doing like sex things or torture things." She folded the tissue and inserted it under her lashes, holding it at one eye, then the other until the tears finally stopped. "Sorry."

"Don't be sorry," I replied. Kellye closed her eyes for a moment to regain her composure. Then she nodded—I'm okay now—patted around her nostrils with the tissue, and swallowed hard. She crossed her legs at the ankle, and swung them over to the left, in that uncomfortable posture women's magazines urge upon you to look ladylike and/or to prevent on-lookers from having an I-Thou relationship with your pudendum. "Did Courtney ever talk about her past?" Kellye shook her head. "Old boyfriends?"

"Uh . . . Some guy at Princeton. Chip? Chuck? One of those names."

"Any last name?" I asked.

"Uh-uh."

"Did she ever talk about her family?"

"Uh-huh. Only child. Crazy about gymnastics, but even though she was skinny then . . . You know how they say: 'You can't be too thin.' "

"Anything else?"

"Her mother was born-again for a little while. She talked about Jesus *really* loud at Taco Bell or one of those places. Courtney said she was so mortified she wanted to die."

I waited. Kellye got busy twirling a silvery bangle around her wrist. I said: "I'd like to ask you a painfully direct question."

"Okay."

"You're describing a terrific person. So who in the world would want to hurt Courtney, or get her out of the way? I'm trying to get a handle on her for this history and I can't seem to get past that question."

"I can't either. I guess . . . maybe . . . one of those serial killers."

"Is that what you told the police when they questioned you?"

Kellye shook her head and her white-gold or platinum earrings made a tiny tinkling sound. "They didn't question me."

"Did they call you or—?"

"No. Nothing. I was surprised. Best friends. They called a couple of the others. But not me. I asked Denny, my husband, should I call them? I was at Court's the day she was missing. Or killed. But early, when she put the cake together. My Dexter is seven and her Morgan is five, so . . . What you'd expect. Boy, girl, age difference. Would they trick-or-treat together? Of course not. So Denny, my husband, said: 'Do you have something to tell the cops? Something that would help them?' So I said: 'No.' So he said: 'Then don't get involved, babe.' Denny's a lawyer. Tax, but . . . hey, they know. Right?"

"Right. Did Courtney herself seem to change in any way over those last few months, before she disappeared?"

Kellye bit her lip while she thought, a youthful gesture that might have been endearing except for her fangs: "Yes and no," she finally responded. I waited. "Like I said about her being perfect." Kellye bit again. "But you know when a friend is just going through the motions. Court was doing that for weeks. Toward the end. Maybe months. At tennis she'd call out 'Good shot,' but I could tell. She wasn't *in* it. And she kept canceling. Her mind was someplace else. And Halloween, with the cake. She couldn't *not* bake—I mean, Veterans Day cake, Chinese New Year cupcakes, and like, is she Chinese? Every holiday. But she was, you know, at least fifty percent flaked. For like a month, maybe two or three, before."

"Did you ask her if anything was wrong?"

"Sure."

"And what did she say?"

"That she was—what do you call it?—preoccupied with StarBaby. But it was starting to take off. Everything was fine."

"The marriage?"

Kellye shrugged her exquisitely tanned shoulders. "She said it was. I mean, she would have liked it if Greg had, whatever. Bigger ideas. She wanted him to open up on the West Coast. New York was okay, but it's, like, ethnic and they want dinner to be a dinner. Not soup, salad, or a sandwich. Even *and* a sandwich. But California is spelled L-I-T-E. Except Greg said no."

"Why?"

"Capital."

"Is that what Courtney told you?"

"Uh-huh."

"But other than that?"

"They were fine." She nodded, satisfied with her account. But a second later she was shaking her head.

"What made you think it wasn't fine?" I asked.

"ESP." I offered what I hoped was a nod more encouraging than her own had been. "And ask yourself: Why do people get flaked?"

"Did you think she was frightened?" I asked. "Or under pressure of some sort?"

"Not *that* kind of flaked."

"You mean Courtney might have been interested in someone else?"

"I hate to say this, but I did kind of think: Some guy? I mean, what could make Court go, like, through the motions. Not have her heart in her pumpkin cake. And she *bought* Morgan's costume. Queen Amidala." I was trying to think of a way to ask Kellye who that might be when she added: "If you said to me, Hey, here's a billion dollars. Who could Court possibly get hot for, even though she was always hinting Greg was the hottest guy ever." At this thought, Kellye covered the front of her neck with both hands, then stuck out her tongue as if she were choking. Then, in case I didn't get it, she added: "Gag, double-gag."

"What's wrong with Greg?"

"Q-U-I-E-T."

"What?"

"He's too quiet. It's creepy. Denny, my husband, says it's because his father is a Jewish Mafia guy. Greg's father. Not Denny's. Denny's father has an air-conditioning company in Glen Cove. And not Jewish. Half Irish, half Polish, or something else foreign. I think. Whatever. But Greg wants everyone to think he's got class, not that he's like a gangster. That means low-key. So when he's with you he acts so low-key it's like he's not there. So you won't think he's—what's that word? For always pushing people around and stuff?"

"Pushy? Aggressive?"

Kellye gave me a grateful Bride of Dracula smile. "Right! But maybe Courtney didn't know better."

"About?"

"About what was hot. But maybe he really was. Is. Do I know? Except I don't think so, and I swear to God, I have radar. All my friends say so. They say, Kellye, is so-and-so hot, and I say—"

"So if your theory's right and Courtney was involved with someone else—"

"But who? Except even for a billion," Kellye said, shaking her head sadly, "I couldn't tell you who it could be."

Chapter Eight

Here I was again, shuffling down the road that I was less and less sure would lead me to the killer. Everyone around Courtney was so pleasantly nonhomicidal. Who in God's name could murder a woman who cut bunny stencils for Year of the Rabbit cupcakes? Even the Lowenstein-Logan boys, my top two candidates (if Fancy Phil hadn't been my client) seemed incapable of such an atrocity.

Yet two bullets in the head didn't appear on any list of Common Household Accidents. Someone had pulled the trigger—twice—and I had to find out who. So here I was, sitting in another kitchen with yet another of what the politicians and media now, universally and nauseatingly, call a "mom." At some point, I suppose, it was decided "mother" sounded too old-fashioned. Or too prim. Or maybe in the minds of the boomers it was forever linguistically tainted by its linkage to "fucker."

Anyhow, the mom in question, Susan Viniar, sat at the head of her table. I, by default the guest of honor, sat at her right hand. My own hands were nearly frozen onto an iced beer stein into which she'd poured the thick, freezing drink she'd blended for me.

"It's a Lime Refresher," she explained, her firm chin high with self-assurance.

I had to give her credit. I, for one, wouldn't have been that confident. The bright green stuff in the mug, with flecks of frost dispersed throughout, looked like mad-scientist poison in 1950s horror movies. Still, feeling I was getting noplace fast on the Courtney front, I couldn't be too fussy. So I waited till Susan sipped, then I did, too. It tasted like a blend of green Chuckles, Gatorade, and crushed ice. That sounds fairly revolting, except to my relief, not only didn't I die, I found the Refresher, well, refreshing.

"How close were you and Courtney?" I asked.

Unlike Kellye Ryan, Susan had no tears for her friend. Then again, she explained, she and Courtney hadn't actually been friends. "My son Justin and Travis Logan are in the same play group." She shrugged, apologetic she couldn't be of more help. As she did, the deltoids under the straps of her chartreuse-piped-with-apple-green tank top gleamed darkly. I decided I wouldn't want to be on the opposite side of a school bond fight with this dame. Her muscular, unspeakably firm upper arms were bisected by the sleeves of a coordinating apple-green sweater with chartreuse trim that was fashionably tied around her shoulders. Though slender, Susan Viniar looked weight-trained beyond buff: She could probably bench-press Fancy Phil.

Outside her kitchen window, a bolt of lightning ignited the low-hanging sky. Instead of startling at the flash, as I did, my hostess seemed to be silently counting the seconds until the rumble of thunder began. Then her head bobbed a single bounce, as if to let God know she was satisfied with His performance.

The Viniars' pine kitchen table was tucked into an alcove with a bay window and framed by the pale and dark leaves of hanging plants. Outside, beyond a brick patio, we could see the drenched velvet carpet of backyard lawn going on forever. Its perfection was interrupted only by a picket-fenced lap pool and a dark green swing set elaborate enough for Justin to train for the 2016 Olympics. Gorgeous greenness. Even the thick gray storm clouds at second glance seemed to have taken on an olive-drab tinge. In my red pinstripe shirt, I felt like an interloper in Emerald City.

"One time we did have a conversation about signing the boys up for Pre-Swimbees," Susan was saying, obviously believing she owed me another sentence or two. "But it was part of a larger conversation with a bunch of mothers of one- and two-year-olds."

"Oh," I said, feeling I'd taken her Lime Refresher under false pretenses. "Someone told me you were a good friend of hers."

Susan shrugged again, her deltoids rising, to say nothing of her triceps and biceps brachii. She was such a perfect specimen that, except for the covering of her dark brown skin, she might be the model for one of those charts of striated muscle the teacher pulls down in high-school biology. "I guess it's understandable, someone thinking we were friends. I mean, we run with the same crowd."

"What crowd is that?"

With her thumb, she wiped a spatter of Lime Refresher off the rim of her stein. "Maybe 'crowd' isn't the right word. That makes it sound as if we're the fast country-club set in a John O'Hara novel. What I'm talking about is seven or eight women. We're mostly in our thirties, with preschoolers Travis and Justin's age."

"Better a crowd than going through it alone," I remarked.

"I guess so. A United We Stand, Divided We Fall mentality." For about two seconds the teacher in me overcame the detective; I gave her a *Very good!* smile of commendation for her historical reference. Except the last thing I wanted was for Susan Viniar to decide she'd invited a grinning madwoman into her house, the way Greg Logan had. So I tried converting my smile into a genial I'm-all-ears expression.

"But you're not really close with these women?"

"In the group? I have one good friend. But it's like this." She spoke to the sky as it darkened even more. "If you go the mommy route"—her eyes came back to me—"even if you love your kids more than anything, there's still only so much gratification you can get from hearing them saying 'coo-kie.' " Not only did I recall that time, I found myself nodding so empathetically I nearly lost an earring. Susan didn't need more incentive to go on. Clearly she'd been thinking about this for a long time. She gestured to the panorama beyond the glass, to the acre of lawn, its color deepened to June lushness from the ethereal green of spring, although that more intense hue might just have been shadows of storm clouds. "Living here, you feel so disconnected. You keep asking yourself: Where's all the suburban kaffeeklatsch stuff, the sisterhood that's supposed to be coming my way?"

I swallowed my mouthful of Lime Refresher. "I remember. Until I met the woman who's still my dearest friend, I was so damn . . . I guess the word is isolated. No. Lonely."

"I think a lot of us are," Susan agreed. "Especially if you worked in a big office the way I did. You go from all that collegiality to pureeing peas in a food mill by yourself. And there's no one except your husband to discuss all the other things you care about besides children. He becomes your only connection to the world beyond Pampers." I was about to ask her: What did you used to be? But then I worried that Susan would conclude the question assumed her present identity was less than satisfactory. Meantime she was saying: "You start to ask yourself: Oh my God, what have I done to myself, quitting work, sentencing myself to life in the suburbs? So we travel in packs, taking the kids to all their activities."

"And Courtney Logan was part of your pack?" Susan nodded and her ponytail bounced. She had the silky black hair of African-American women with six-figure incomes. "But she wasn't a friend?"

"No."

"As far as you know, did the police question any members of your circle about Courtney's habits, connections?"

"They spoke to a couple of the women."

"And?"

"And what could anyone say? That Courtney loved her family. That she was smart. That StarBaby was not just a great idea, but that she actually brought it to fruition, so maybe she was more focused than the rest of us. And she was a nice person."

"So how come you and Courtney weren't really friends?"

"No particular reason." I waited. "We weren't on the same wavelength."

"What was her wavelength?"

"This is some project for the library? You mentioned you were on the board." Susan posed the question with the cool of someone who already knew the answer, so I didn't play it cute.

"No, more for me. I can't seem to get a handle on Courtney Logan. I suppose I shouldn't be . . ."

Susan Viniar didn't immediately leap up to proclaim, No problem, your asking me questions about personal matters that are none of your business. For a moment that felt uncomfortably long to me but obviously not to her, she gazed at the vapor from the air-conditioning register as it misted up the bay window and considered what I'd asked. "Moms," like Susan and her crowd, I decided, had remained out in the world a lot longer than we mothers had. They'd worked longer, married later, had children later. They seemed cooler cookies than my contemporaries. These younger women mulled, they pondered, they deliberated. They seemed less desperate, or at least slower, to please.

Finally, as my Lime Refresher began to separate into its somewhat grotesque-looking components, Susan seemed to conclude that: a) I could be trusted; b) it couldn't hurt for her to be accommodating and for me to owe her a favor; and c) it might be pleasantly kaffeeklatschlike to talk about Courtney. I sensed she had the self-possession of a diplomat. Not a Talleyrand. Her flawlessly plucked arched eyebrows and bitter-sweet-chocolate-brown eyes were far too expressive for her to hammer out a strategic-arms-limitation treaty with, say, the foreign minister of Ukraine. However, I sensed that for someone like Susan, negotiating a trade agreement with a petulant neutral power would be a snap.

"There was nothing *wrong* with Courtney," she began diplomatically. "In fact, who could be righter? Good school, glamorous Wall Street job. Then came the nice husband, two adorable children, mommyhood. What else? Her house—Lord, when we went there for play group! It was so complete, so decorated, but in that undecorated old-money way. It looked as though there'd been Logans in it for centuries. And I guess you know that with all her volunteer work, she was highly thought of in the community. Plus she had a new business that could go through the roof. She was a decent athlete, too, and pretty—if your idea of pretty is the blond rah-rah type. As far as I could see, the only fly in her ointment was the father-in-law."

"In what way? Did he interfere in their lives?"

"No. Not that I know of. I'm talking about the simple fact of him. He's a . . . whatever, a gangster. That's not a social asset in most circles. But I liked the way Courtney dealt with it. Directly. She actually referred to him as Fancy Phil Lowenstein and—I'll bet not in front of Greg—mimicked him." Susan cleared her throat, then pitched her voice to a low bad-guy growl: " 'Hey, sweetheart, how're t'ings?' "

"She sounds like fun," I remarked.

Susan tilted her head to one side to consider. "Actually, no. I mean, you never had to hold your sides to keep them from splitting. But Courtney was definitely an upbeat person."

"So if there was nothing wrong with her, what wasn't right?"

She turned from me and looked outside, and for a moment seemed lost contemplating the masses of green curled around the grape arbor that formed the portal to her backyard. For all I knew, it might actually have been a genuine grapevine. Finally she turned back. "Did you ever see the movie *The Invasion of the Body Snatchers*?" she asked sheepishly.

"Sure!" I decided that since she seemed convinced of my sanity I'd better not mention that I'd seen all three versions, the Donald Sutherland one twice. "So what are you saying? That there was a pod person inside Courtney?"

Susan's index finger slowly traced the whorls of a knothole in her pine table. "I guess what I'm saying is that the Courtney I came into contact with didn't feel totally real." She shook her head, dissatisfied with her answer. "It wasn't that she was phony. But there was something . . . unusual about her. I sensed she had some other, inner life that the pod person was running—a pod person who had researched the culture of the north shore of Long Island but who'd only gotten an A-minus on the term paper. Almost perfect, but not quite. Or if there wasn't a pod person, maybe part of Courtney Logan was missing and that's why she didn't feel real."

"Like what?" I inquired.

"The part that makes us *not* unique, but like everybody else." Another brutal slash of lightning. The lights flickered, then stayed on, although across the kitchen the digital clocks on the wall oven and microwave began flashing in a crazed bid for attention. Susan didn't notice. "That part that gives us the sense that a stranger is okay, that he or she shares our humanity and isn't off in some way, or empty inside, or a threat." She set her glass down on her napkin, then crossed her powerful arms and turned so she was facing me directly. "Saying this straight out, it sounds asinine."

"No, it doesn't sound asinine." It was easy to sound reassuring because, aside from her evident devotion to her own musculature, so much about Susan—her impressions of suburban motherhood, her historical and movie allusions, her recognition of her own isolation, her introspection—reminded me of me at her age. "It sounds as if there's good communication between your intellect and your gut. You know, the longer I'm around, the more I believe that if your gut says something's going on here, something usually is." Then I added: "Just one question. Couldn't it be a less cosmic explanation? Like Courtney's mind might have been someplace else? Business reverses? Maybe she was having a fling?"

Susan tried to come up with an answer, but in the end all she could come up with was another shrug of her impressive shoulders. "It's hard to say, because I really didn't know her. I never had a sustained one-on-one discussion with her. She could have had some secret problem weighing on her. But as far as an affair? That gut of mine you think I should trust? It says: No way."

"Why not?"

"That thing that makes us feel real to each other?" She paused for a moment to organize her thoughts, then spoke carefully. "Sexuality is an aspect of it, the sexuality we sense in other people as part of their he's-normal, she's-normal package. You know, the fact that a person *has* sexuality. Forget whether somebody's hot or cold or into bizarre practices. Real people give off subliminal signals that some aspect of sex—wanting it, not wanting it, being able to do it only when wearing spike heels—has some value in their lives. Pod people don't."

"And with Courtney?"

"God rest her soul and all, but she was the chirpiest, least sexual human being I'd ever met."

It wasn't just muscles that gave Susan Viniar her air of authority. Unlike the pontificators and the boasters who aim to wow you, she spoke with quiet simplicity, as though her words came from both her heart and head, such a decent heart and a good head that they had to be right. Then again, I reflected, she could be one of those people so bedazzled by their own fantasies that they truly believe their fabrications are truer than truth.

"Okay," I said, "so if we assume no lover, but a husband who adored her, neighbors who thought highly of her, friends who liked her, or at least saw her as a decent person, then it comes down to: What kind of person would want to kill her?"

Susan's arms crossed even tighter, as if she were beginning a set of isometrics or warding off a chill. "Based on what I saw? What I knew Courtney to be?" I nodded encouragingly. "Absolutely no one," she declared.

So no one had anything against Courtney Logan. I thought: Then how come she won't be making a strawberry, blueberry, banana Flag Day cake this year?

That night, the storm finally exhausted itself around ten-thirty, leaving behind it the intoxicating smell of ozone and wet grass. A soft breeze blew through my open bedroom window and touched me gently, as if aware I needed special handling. I pressed the eject button and a tape I'd made years earlier of *Old Acquaintance* slid out of the VCR. I probably sighed, an audible *hommage* to Bette Davis, Miriam Hopkins, and female friendship, and with another flick of the finger turned off the TV.

It was one of those rare, lovely nights that I wasn't feeling at least a little depressed-lonely or frightened-lonely. Depressed, that I'd wind up alone in an assisted-living facility rife with denture-clacking, Trotskyite bridge players and Lucky Strike–smoking, anti-Semitic Republicans. Or frightened, that I'd have an anaphylactic reaction to the sting of a bee which had slipped through the quarter-inch rip in my bedroom window screen: I'd be discovered a week later, the phone receiver clutched in one decomposing hand, the other having had only enough life left to dial 9-1 . . .

But this night was good. I lay at ease in bed, my pillow perfectly fluffed, my blanket just the right weight, enjoying the sweetness of almost-summer in a dreamy way that carried me back and gently set me down in the backyard of my Brooklyn childhood. As far as I can recall, I wasn't even thinking about who killed Courtney Logan, though I might have subconsciously weighed Acquaintance Susan Viniar's No Possible Extramarital Funny Stuff theory against Good Friend Kellye Ryan's Courtney Was Having a Fling hypothesis. I turned onto my side, flipped over the pillow so it was cool against my cheek and closed my eyes. Ahhh. So naturally when the phone rang, the sound shot through me the way current zaps a convict in the electric chair. My legs kicked and I made one of those Nyah! noises and answered the phone with a croaky "hello."

"Hi," he said.

"Hi." Even had I been more composed, I don't think I would have pretended I didn't know it was Nelson Sharpe.

"How's it going?" he asked.

"Not bad."

"Good. Is it too late?" He wasn't actually slurring his words, but he was inordinately slow. He'd had a touch too much of something. "Can you talk now?"

"Sure."

"How've you been?"

"All right," I told him. I pictured him leaning against the dark-paneled wall of a smoky Irish bar, talking into a pay phone. Except he wasn't Irish. He was a WASP, a Methodist, but I couldn't conjure up a Methodist bar. Or else he was sitting at his desk in the Special Investigations bureau, his bottom drawer with its half-drunk bottle of whiskey still open. Then I realized I was thinking in black-and-white, which no doubt came from watching more noir movies than were healthy for me. So I opened my eyes to the reality of my dark room and asked: "How have you been, Nelson?"

"Good. Hey, listen. I was out, talking with a couple of guys."

"Uh-huh," I said encouragingly.

"Couple of buddies from Homicide. That Courtney, the one who's Fancy Phil's daughter-in-law. She had this car, a Land Rover."

He seemed to be waiting for something from me, so I said: "Right."

"You didn't hear this from me, but the mother's helper who was working for them reported she saw Courtney drive away in it. But then later that night, when the husband called and the precinct cops went over, there it was, in the garage—the garage in their house."

"Right," I said again. My heart was beating faster than it should, though it was less the fact of Nelson calling me than that he was calling me about the Logan case. I think. Anyhow, I reached up and switched on the lamp to kill any fanciful thoughts. "So do they have any idea who brought the car back? The murderer with Courtney dead? Courtney alive and the murder was done at the house?"

"The only physical evidence in the car was evidence of Courtney— and the husband and the au pair. Lots of kids' fingerprints in the back."

"Husbands drive their wives' cars," I told him. "It's not a felony in New York."

"Right. Sure. But there wasn't a sign that any other adult had been in it besides the two of them and the au pair."

"But anyone else who would have planned for even two seconds to kill her would have worn gloves," I protested. "And the fact that Greg Logan's prints were on it might have meant he took her car out to get his lawn mower blade sharpened or something."

"The guys from Homicide said it was warm that day." He'd pretty much dropped the *d* sound from "Homicide" and "said," as though lifting his tongue to the front of his palate was too great an effort. "Warm for Halloween. Anyone wearing gloves would get looked at funny."

"Maybe it was someone wearing a Halloween costume," I suggested.

I waited for the Nelson I knew to give me an argument. But all I heard was breathing so slowly I thought he might have fallen asleep. Then he surprised me. "For all I know, you may be right," he said. "Not about the costume. You probably read all those idiot serial-killer books."

"I do not."

"But there is enough talk on TV these days about DNA that, okay, if it wasn't a spur-of-the-moment thing, even a dope would have taken precautions, like wearing a hat so hair doesn't get on anything. Maybe gloves, too, and he'd stick his hands in his pockets or something so no one would ask questions."

"Or her hands." All I got was silence. I had a sense Nelson was waiting for me to continue, since he was just pie-eyed enough to have forgotten that it was he who'd made the phone call. "So the car was in the garage," I prompted. I wasn't about to shout hosannas of gratitude since the detail that the Land Rover was back in the garage was in practically every news account I'd come across. "Anything else?"

"About what?" he demanded, annoyed, as though I was trying to pump him for police secrets. "Oh, she'd had the car serviced on October fourteenth."

"Right. And she disappeared on the thirty-first."

"And between those two times, do you know how many miles she put on the car?"

"How many?" I asked, probably too eagerly.

"Seven hundred sixty-two," he replied coolly.

"Wow. That would be a lot of car pools."

"Yeah, Judith. A lot of car pools." And before I could ask him anything else, or even say thank you, he hung up.

And that should have been that. The next morning, a Saturday, I put hot rollers in my hair so I'd look sleek at the New-York Historical Society's exhibit on female allegories of America. With luck, and enough hair spray to increase the hole in the ozone layer, I could get to my daughter's apartment in an unfrizzled state so that she and her boyfriend could serve me a dinner of shockingly expensive, oddly mated foreign dishes—bouillabaisse, tandoori chicken, and gnocchi the size of softballs had been their last offering—from their local gourmet take-out joint.

Kate's boyfriend, Adam, was a slender young man who worked in MTV's legal department. He dressed in slacks so baggy that it looked as though he were carrying a load in his diaper. He wore only black shirts, like Il Duce's thugs. Never a tie. What kind of thirty-year-old guy (who spoke as if he'd spent his youth in a Watts rap group instead of being what he was, Mr. White Boy at Palos Verdes Peninsula High School) would be that susceptible to fashion that he would actually don a zoot suit? Could someone like him be man enough for my beautiful and brilliant Kate? Every time I visited them (for he and his wardrobe of fascist shirts had moved in with her), I worked myself into a fair case of melancholia, to say nothing of indigestion.

Except at ten o'clock, Kate called and said she had to cancel, that she'd been called into the office to work on a hostile tender offer. I refrained from demanding what I wanted to demand, which was What the hell is so important about a tender offer that it can't wait till Monday? And I emitted not a single guilt-inducing sigh of resignation: Women without husbands are dependent on the kindness of children. So I told her I was looking forward to seeing her as soon as the pressure let up. Then I trudged into the bathroom, removed the hot rollers, ran my fingers through my hair until, regarding myself in the mirror, I was pleased to discover I didn't look like Mike Myers playing Linda Richman. Rather, I looked sensuous, albeit slightly world-weary, a combination of Anna Magnani and Simone Signoret—though admittedly I had the advantage of having forgotten to turn on the light.

Then I clomped downstairs, determined not to wimp out of going to the Historical Society simply because it held no prospect of human contact. However, I gave myself permission to take a later train. So when the doorbell rang a little after ten-thirty, I'd had just enough time to get sweaty and crabby from unsuccessfully trying to get my new Palm Pilot to form a relationship with my computer.

Of course as I called out "Who is it?" in nauseatingly mellifluous tones, I was picturing Nelson at the door: Having found my voice on the phone so Siren-like the night before, he'd been compelled to come over. So when I looked through the peephole and saw him, then heard "Nelson Sharpe," I stood rather stupidly for a moment, astounded that it actually was he. Quickly, I patted my damp forehead with the hem of my skirt, stretched out the neck of my T-shirt to blow two blasts of cool air under my arms, and opened the door.

"I, uh . . ." he said. This time there was no houndstooth sports jacket to make me think twice. Evidently, this was dress-down Saturday for the

Special Investigations unit, and he looked so good in a plaid shirt and jeans I temporarily forgot about the gold ring on his left hand.

"Would you like to come in?"

"I don't want to disturb anybody." I knew him well enough to know he was simply double-checking. Nelson was nothing if not thorough. He'd probably already driven past the house a few times, staked it out for a while, then looked in the garage, where he'd seen only one car—mine, the car registered in my name whose license plate the cops in his unit had called in the night of my dinner with Fancy Phil. No doubt he'd concluded Bob was, in all likelihood, in the city, clearing off his desk on a Saturday morning.

Okay, it did surprise me that Nelson hadn't considered that my husband's MO might have changed sometime during the last twenty years. On the other hand, had Bob been alive, without a doubt he would have been at his office.

Nelson's wedding band flashed its cold light at me a minute later, when we were sitting four feet apart on the living-room couch. "Listen," he said, "last night . . ."

"You're not sure what you said to me. You're afraid you might have whispered sweet nothings in my ear. Don't worry. You didn't embarrass yourself."

"No, no," he countered, with an isn't-that-ridiculous chuckle. Then he applied his detective skills to checking out the weave of the upholstery on the arm of the couch. "I'm concerned I might have repeated some, uh, casual conversation about the Courtney Logan case I heard from a couple of guys."

"Guys in Homicide."

"Guys in Homicide," he repeated quietly.

"Well, you didn't blab any state secrets— Stop pulling at that thread. You'll unravel the whole couch."

"I wasn't pulling on it."

"What were you doing? Investigating it?"

He shifted so his body was facing mine. His legs parted and I found myself staring into his eyes to hypnotize myself so I wouldn't even take a quick peek at the bulge in his jeans. It's bad enough when you're simply attracted to a guy; it's much worse when you already know what the prize inside is. What had I expected, that it would retract when he hit his fifties?

The problem was gazing into his eyes, which were big and a beautiful satiny brown. Soft, like cow eyes, except that implies a bovine quality, and his were, as they had been, intelligent, aware. And sexual. Women know: Some guys have the heat that makes their eyes almost feverish when they're looking at someone they want. Nelson had probably had those eyes at age ten. He'd definitely had them when he and I had been lovers, in his late thirties. I knew he'd have them for the rest of his life. "Look, Judith, can we have an honest talk?"

I quit looking into his eyes. "No."

"No?" He acted shocked, as if I'd said something that would scandalize any decent human being.

"Unless you want to have an honest talk about the Courtney Logan case," I added.

"Listen, don't you think . . . when we happened to run into each other last year, don't you think that was meant to be?" Nelson's voice was low enough to be bedroomy.

" 'Meant to be'? What's happened to you? Are you buying CDs of pounding surf and wind chimes? The answer is no, it was not meant to be. You and I had an accidental meeting because of a shared interest." His eyes had narrowed, which meant he was probably burning over my associating him and wind chime recordings, so I quickly added: " 'Shared interest' being homicide."

"I'm out of Homicide. I told you that."

"Why did you leave?" He didn't answer. "Did you jump, Nelson? Or were you pushed?"

"Pushed," he said quietly to his knees.

"What happened?"

"Nothing important." He seemed to be waiting for me to say something. When I didn't he added: "Department politics. They said it wasn't fair, me being there so long and so many guys wanting in and wouldn't it be a great opportunity to establish my own unit which would be elite and all that shit."

"What's the real translation?"

"Take this or take nothing."

"Did you think about leaving, collecting a pension, and doing something else?"

"Homicide is the top of the game. What could I do if I took my pension? Be chief of security at some mall and bag a teenage girl shoplifting lipstick?"

"Do you like what you're doing now?"

He was already shaking his head as I began formulating a sentence about how Special Investigations could be interesting, important work. "It's more baby-sitting than investigation," he said. "Wiretaps, tails, following a paper trail of fraudulent financial schemes that bore the hell out of me. These days a guy like your boyfriend Fancy Phil is mostly doing stuff like on-line trading with the Russian mob, so the FBI gets it, not us.

Of course, if he wants a skull cracked, Phil doesn't do it himself. He hires a guy who hires a guy who hires some dumb kid to do it."

"Is that why you were having him tailed? You think he ordered a hit?"

"You know I can't tell you that."

"Don't you think that the work you're doing is still important? You're going after the bad guys."

His mouth expanded into what I guess he thought was a cynical smile. "At least I'm not in uniform saying, 'Hi boys and girls, and welcome to Safety Town.' "

Even after a break of twenty years, it's amazing how fast two former lovers can fuse and become a couple again. Rules have long ago been agreed upon, parameters are still in place. Aside from the good news and bad news of getting older—the self-confidence Band-Aids we've managed with time to put over the wounds of childhood versus the decline of our bodies and our dreams—those same old cues still set us off.

As Nelson's hand was reaching across the cushion of couch that separated us, mine was ready to offer a concerned squeeze, eager to be enveloped in his hand's familiar size and warmth. Unfortunately, the hand he was extending was his left, the one with the ring from his new wife. I clasped my hands in my lap and said: "I sense there's more than one thing going on in your life that you're not thrilled with."

"I was so *right* in Homicide. When they created the new unit for me, it was like getting tossed out of the Garden of Eden. I kept telling myself, 'Well, at least I still have one thing to make me happy. I'm Adam and I still have Eve.' Actually, her name's Nicole. But then one night we were watching TV and I looked at her—and she wasn't. Eve, I mean. When we talked, I kept thinking, Who the hell is this woman and—"

"I can't help you."

"And the worst of it is, I think she feels the same way but—"

"I don't want to hear about your marriage—either one of them."

"Judith, trust me. You're not cool enough for the I-don't-want-to-get-involved stuff."

"As I'm sure you know, I was involved with you. Maybe I still am, or could be. And if that's the case, most likely it'll always be that way. When we agreed never to see each other again, it wasn't because we'd gotten bored or had grown to detest each other. We were still in love. So even though there's been a hell of a lot of water under both our bridges, it's tempting to think we can start up where we left off, or at least begin something new. Maybe I shouldn't be saying this. Maybe all you're looking for is a friendly pat on the head and my thinking you want something more is hideously uncomfortable for you because your tastes now run to nubile nineteen-year-olds."

"Cut the crap."

"So let me explain why this isn't going to happen."

He gave a sigh of boredom, as if he already knew what I was going to say. "You found you really love Bob and even though there's still whatever, a mental and physical attraction, it doesn't justify blah, blah, blah."

"The blah, blah, blah is that Bob died two years ago, suddenly." For an instant incomprehension turned his intelligent face slack and stupid. Then he lowered his head. I couldn't see his expression, but the flush on his cheek was spreading to his ear, so I knew he was embarrassed about the blah, blah, blah business. "I'm less of a mess than I was," I went on, "but I can't afford to get involved with a married man who has a sad story." I expected him to give me the sad story of his marriage anyway—since a fair number of men believe that women cannot fight their natures, which is to nurture everything from baby goldfish to depressed, middle-aged cops.

Instead he said, "I'm sorry for your loss. Really sorry." He stood and so did I.

"Thank you."

"I won't bother you again."

This last bit of business nearly had its intended effect: having me sniffle, then sob, then rush into his arms for comfort. But I couldn't let myself. Since junior high, I'd always been one of those girls/women who would lose all reason in the face of love. I'd allow a guy to so inhabit my head that every act, from dicing celery to offering the defense of my doctoral dissertation, could not be executed without three-quarters of my brain occupied by thoughts of him. This was one time I wasn't going to let that happen. "I appreciate that, Nelson."

Wearily, like two explorers retreating after having failed to reach the Pole, we trudged back to the front door. "Oh," he said. "I forgot to tell you what I came over to tell you." I gave him a go-ahead nod. "It's not much. I should be keeping my mouth shut, but it's not so terrible if I don't. It's this: The guys have pretty much given up looking for the gun that killed Courtney."

"What kind of gun was it?"

"Probably a Walther PPK/S. Do you know what that is?"

"I can look it up. Why have they given up? Where have they looked for it?"

"I don't know. I guess in and all around her house and grounds, the parking lot at the grocery store where she was supposed to have gone."

"Were there any groceries in her car?"

"Not that I heard of."

Which I sensed was a no. "I get the feeling," I told him, "that either you're obsessed with the goings-on in Homicide or you know more about this case than the head of the organized crime unit normally would."

"Well, you're involved in it. And with Greg Logan's father being Fancy Phil Lowenstein, I have a reason to be interested." The cuffs of his plaid shirt had been rolled up, and now he began smoothing them out and rolling them up again.

"Do you think they should still be looking for the murder weapon?"

"I can't comment."

"Nelson, I'm not a reporter shoving a microphone in your face. I'm—" He shook his head: No comment. "Well, let me talk, then. It seems to me that whoever is running this investigation, Lieutenant Some-body, I have the name inside, is not very thorough. Maybe he should look a little harder."

"Why do you say that?" he asked, finally satisfied with his cuffs.

"If you were handling the case, wouldn't it have occurred to you that if some pillar of the community, a wife and mother, is suddenly missing and you can't find her, you might consider taking a peep under the cover of the pool in her backyard, even if it looks tied down tight. Or am I mis-guided?" No answer, though his nostrils flared in a manner that I knew something was bothering him. "If you'd been in charge, wouldn't you have thought, What the hell, I'll just take a quick look to see if maybe there's a body? Or a weapon?"

"It's been a sloppy investigation," Nelson said, so softly I could barely hear him.

"Did they ask the neighbors if they saw anyone suspicious in the neighborhood that evening?"

"You don't ask it like that. Very often, the perpetrator belongs in the neighborhood. You ask: What did you see?" And before I could ask any-thing more, he turned the knob, stepped out into the sunny day, and closed the front door quietly behind him.

The next day, Sunday, was less boring than usual since Nancy's hus-band Larry was out of town. His newest client, a dot-com near billionaire who had probably played too many games of Dungeons and Dragons in his youth, was consulting with Larry on the design of a forty-thousand-square-foot-Gothic castle in Virginia hunt country. After I rejected tennis and Nancy vetoed my sport, porch-sitting, we wound up walking along the beach of Shorehaven Bay, an inlet of Long Island Sound that, at low tide, offered a flat path of wet, compacted sand, glossy seaweed, and paving of the blue-black shells of the mussels that had been lunch for the gulls.

"It doesn't matter that the cops are sloppy," Nancy was saying. "What bothers me is that you're avoiding the truth like it was some mangy old coon dog with hydrophobia."

"Shush! You sound like Strom Thurmond."

"You're missing my point."

"Which is?" I asked.

"That even if Homicide is as lame as Lieutenant Cutie Pie says they are—"

"He's a captain now."

"Even if Captain Cutie Pie is right about their sloppy methods, the Homicide guys are probably also right about Greg Logan killing Courtney. Why do they have to take off pool covers and ask a bunch of vexatious questions to half of Shorehaven? They knew damn well who done it." For a few seconds I enjoyed silence as we cautiously clambered over some boulders slick with seaweed. The afternoon June sun had turned from warm yellow to white-hot and beat down on us with the savagery of an August dog day. It evaporated the tiny pools of water in the empty mussel shells, perfuming the beach with the heady scent of dead fish. I turned away from the lethargic waves lapping against the shore to look up to a house of cantilevered white rectangles perched on a bluff above the beach. "Stop checking out real estate and avoiding what you have to do," Nancy commanded.

"Which is?"

"Call Fancy Phil and tell him straight out: 'Honey, looks to me like it's sonny boy that done the deed.' "

"You know," I told her, "even if you're wrong, you're right. Because except for Greg, I've probably spoken to most of the same people the cops spoke to. And so far I haven't been able to figure out why they're so in love with the idea of Greg having done it that they haven't looked elsewhere. They may be sloppy, Nancy, but they're not stupid."

"You say that with the confidence of someone not intimately acquainted with Nassau County's criminal justice system. Or at least, not intimately connected anymore."

"I can pretty well guess why they're onto Greg, besides his being the husband of the victim. Someone told the cops something they didn't tell me, something that made Homicide think, Hey, it's definitely gotta be the husband."

Nancy exhaled impatiently. "They're cops, for crissake! Genuine authority figures. Nothing personal, toots, but why would you expect peo-

ple to be as open with some history lady as with the Nassau County police?"

"First of all, I'm not *just* some history lady. I'm a good interviewer, an
empathetic human being. Why would any of them lie to me?"

"Maybe it wasn't a sin of commission. Maybe it was a sin of omis-
sion."

"Nancy, it was hold-nothing-back time. Well, at least they all talked
to me. And do you know what I learned Courtney was like? Nice, perky.
And cold, emotionally deficient. The sensual woman, the compleat asexual. Madly in love with her husband or maybe having an affair."

"You can do both, easy," Nancy assured me cheerfully.

"Now listen, after all those interviews—including a couple of people
the cops never got to, like her best friend—and all that snooping, what I
can't get is who Courtney Bryce Logan really was. But even so, whether
she was a cipher, an angel, or a bitch on wheels, who could possibly have
gained with her death? No one."

"Except if Greg had a reason to want her dead. He did take the
'theirs' money and made it 'his.' "

"But that was in response to her sneaking money out of their accounts. And it was forty thousand dollars he took. Major bucks to some
people, but not to him." Nancy was eyeing the ruins of an old seawall in
the distance and looked as though she might consider climbing it, with
me. So I sat on the sand and kept talking. "Unless, you're going to say, the
murder wasn't about money. Maybe he was having an affair and wanted
his freedom. But then you could say, if that were the case, he'd get a good
divorce lawyer. Unless . . . well, it might be better to have her dead than
squealing Fancy Phil's secrets, things she overheard in the house."

"As long as you're having this scintillating dialogue with me without
my participation," Nancy remarked, "I'm going over and check out that
old wall."

I shook my head and patted the beach beside me. Reluctantly, correctly thinking it one of my ploys to avoid walking the extra mile, she sat
beside me, took out the tortoiseshell banana clip that held up her hair, and
rearranged it into a distant relative of a French twist. "I don't think
Courtney Logan from Olympia, Washington, knew gangster secrets. Listen, Nancy, Fancy Phil's main thrust, you should pardon the expression,
was to keep his son out of the world of mafiosi and Russian hoods and all
the other scum. He's proud Greg went to Brown. He's proud that Greg
was borrowing for his business from a legitimate bank. He's proud of his
grandchildren."

"Maybe Fancy Phil was having a thing with Courtney and whispered
secrets in her shell-pink ear," Nancy suggested. "So she had to die."

"No. He would never betray his son."

"Why not? It was in that movie we saw. The father-in-law and the daughter-in-law. With Jeremy Irons and a one-word title. And the actress with the lips." Nancy, who could never sit completely still, began to stretch her fingertips down toward her toes. "Well, maybe Courtney was putting too much pressure on Greg. Get rich, buy me a pied-à-terre in the city or a Louis Quinze desk."

I recalled what Kellye Ryan had said about Courtney wanting Greg to open some Soup Salad Sandwiches stores on the West Coast, but that hardly sounded like enough pressure to drive a man to murder his wife. "You know, the cops didn't even talk to all of Courtney's friends. They felt—they feel they have the killer and the motive."

"Face it. Greg *is* the killer," Nancy said. "Although with that result, it's not likely Fancy Phil will write you a letter of recommendation."

For all I knew, she could be right. But I asked myself out loud: "Who *did* the cops talk to? Neighbors. Greg. Fancy Phil. And who else? Who could cast a shadow over Greg?" Nancy didn't reply, although she did grunt in triumph when the tip of her middle finger finally made it down her stretched-out leg and touched a toe. "I'll tell you who. Steffi, the au pair."

"But you talked to her, too, and said she only had nice things to say—"

"I guess that was only our first talk," I replied.

Chapter Nine

I can't say I raced to Connecticut, because that would imply eighty miles per hour up I-95 in a Porsche. Forget the Porsche: Besides the forty thousand dollars over the price of my Jeep, my delusion of myself as suburban sex goddess was more easily sustained climbing down from an SUV than heaving myself out of something low-slung, penis-shaped, and racing green. But after my hike on the beach with Nancy, I jumped into the shower, dressed, and was driving past an excessively quaint sign that said ENTERING WHITSBURY (in the colonial-style lettering that rendered Whitsbury as Whitfbury), when I realized two things. I hadn't called Steffi Deissenburger to ask if I could speak with her again and that four-thirty on a Sunday afternoon was not a swell time to pop in anywhere. So I gave myself an assertiveness lecture recycled from one of those Women Who Loathe Themselves/Women Who Love Themselves books I wind up ordering on the Web because I'm embarrassed to ask for it at the Dolphin Bookshop in town.

The next thing I knew, I was telling Steffi's employer, Andrea Leeds, that my name was Judith Singer—right, just like sewing machine—and she was telling me that Sunday was Steffi's day off and that she'd gone (parallel paths of foreboding formed between her brows) to Manhattan.

"I'm sorry to stop by without calling, Ms. Leeds, but I was visiting friends in New Canaan and forgot my little phone book." Three lies in one sentence. I wasn't sorry to stop by without calling, I knew absolutely no one in New Canaan, and having spent a wild Saturday night getting the Palm Pilot and the Dell to make peace with each other, I had transmogrified into an e-babe with no little phone book. "I'm on the board of the Shorehaven Library. That's how I know Steffi. She was always there with the Logan children."

"Please, come in." She was dressed in a yellow polo shirt and a short yellow skirt with green frogs all over it, so I assumed she'd just come home from the golf course. Andrea Leeds would probably be called rangy, being a head taller than I. She was definitely angular, almost bony, with knobs for elbows and knees. Though her face was technically an oval, with a broad forehead and Balkan cheekbones, it was more like an oval balanced on its side: Thus, with an impeccable pageboy curving under precisely at her wide jawline, she gave the impression of a woman who displaced far more space than she actually did. "Call me Andy, by the way." She led me along a hallway, taking such long strides I had to double-time it to keep up. The walls were covered with nursery school scribble drawings, matted and framed. "I'm spending quality time"—she smiled to signal I-know-it's-a-cliché, so I gave her an I-get-it smile in return—"with my girls."

She led me into a room I hadn't seen on my last visit. The library. Perfect. Tall windows and French doors welcomed the late afternoon sun. The light burnished the pale wood paneling so it shone gold. The cordovan leather couch had been so well used it looked as if the Invisible Man were lounging on its tastefully crackled cushions. On the shelves were books—genuine books—with those little bulges midspine to indicate they'd been read, or at least opened. With a single sniff you'd know these weren't the mildewed tomes homeowners buy by the yard to give the illusion of literacy. I had the sense that had Courtney seen the Leedses' library, she'd have understood in an instant that for all her botanical pictures on ribbons, and doilies in the bottom of wastebaskets, Andy Leeds, with her roomful of books (at a glance, a good but unsurprising white-guys-writing-in-English collection), was the one who'd gotten it right.

"Gwendolyn, Gwyneth, this is Mrs. Singer."

Together, the identical twins cheeped a happy hello as well as something that sounded as if it could be "Mrs. Singer," the sort of gracious greeting my children couldn't manage until they were in their early twenties. Then, side by side in a club chair, the children went back to studying

Horton Hatches the Egg. Gwen and Gwyn not only had their mother's wide Slavic features, pale brown hair, and long limbs, they were wearing the same yellow getup avec frogs. Since I doubted that three-year-olds golfed, even in Whitfbury, I decided the mother-daughter froggy business was a fashion statement that, by the grace of God, would not survive a voyage across Long Island Sound to Shorehaven.

After I complimented Andy Leeds on the girls' deportment—deportment being one of those words I figured would go over big—and she did her "Say thank you to Mrs. Singer, Gwendolyn and Gwyneth" bit, all of which seemed to take a half hour, she offered me a seat at a small table, probably an antique she and Mr. Leeds used whilst they played whist of an evening.

"I'm so relieved Steffi's found such a fine family to work for," I told her.

"We think the world of her." Beneath Andy's upper-class civility, I sensed authentic civility. However, I also detected an unuttered question mark. Any parent who leaves her children in the hands of a relative stranger, even one with a solid résumé and enthusiastic references, looks for additional reassurance, and all the more so when the young woman in question comes from a house in which a murder had been committed. "She seems like a lovely young woman," was all I would say, since I wasn't handing out endorsements for anyone connected to Courtney Logan.

"What a dreadful time she went through!" My hostess shuddered. The frogs on her skirt quivered sympathetically.

"To see someone just drive away like that"—I tsked-tsked—"and never . . ."

"Would you like some lemonade?" Andy Leeds asked meaningfully, glancing at her daughters. We left behind the gold glow of the library and the twins—who apparently could be trusted not to bean each other with Trollope and Updike novels they'd yanked off the shelves—and repaired to the kitchen.

Another mom, another kitchen. Yet another elaborate stove with six burners and several strange little ovens, as though all these suburban women were vying for three Michelin stars. Andy Leeds took a pitcher out of the refrigerator and poured the lemonade over crystalline ice cubes in a slender glass. "They still suspect the husband?" she inquired.

"From everything I hear."

"He sounds . . ." She hesitated. I nodded, as if I already knew what she would say. Yet my heart speeded up as if to outrace the dread starting to come over me: I was about to get news that Fancy Phil wouldn't want to hear. I was right. "To put it bluntly," Andy said definitively, "this Mr. Logan sounds horrid." Well, I decided, Fancy Phil would have to cope, although I wasn't looking forward to witnessing his anger-management strategies. Nevertheless, if I had/have any personal philosophical view, any slogan I'd want to put on a T-shirt, it's this: Never be afraid of the truth. "Perfectly horrid," she was kind enough to reiterate.

So the prime witness in the case, the Logans' au pair, Steffi Deissenburger, was saying Greg was horrid? Okay, not a plus. Had Steffi confided Greg's horridness only to Andy Leeds? Or to Nassau County Homicide as well? That would be a major minus. However, better to know the truth and deal with it. So I pretended to take "horrid" well. I even nodded—How horrid that Greg Logan was horrid!—then sighed with what I hoped sounded like commiseration. I felt Andy Leeds was bothered and on the verge of forgetting that gentlefolk are reticent. My biggest contribution would be keeping my lip zipped.

I received a thank-you-for-understanding sigh. Finally, before I had to come up with a you're-welcome exhalation, she went on. "What I can't understand is, how can it be a coincidence that his wife is missing just three or four days and he . . . you know, with Steffi?" I swallowed hard. And waited. "I mean, unless he had his eye on the girl all along and was just marking time until his wife quote disappeared unquote. I get ice-cold every time I think of it."

"It's amazing Steffi still managed to stay on there," I murmured. No wonder the cops weren't looking elsewhere for Courtney's killer.

"She was so devoted to those children. I suppose she felt a moral obligation."

"I suppose so," I said.

"Doesn't it break your heart when you think of them, their mother just vanishing and then . . . ?"

I nodded. It did. "But then Steffi did leave," I prodded.

"How could she not?" Andy Leeds responded. I sipped the lemonade wishing she'd come up with a cookie to go along with it. "The anonymous phone calls. The police knocking on the door there three, four nights a week to question him."

"I know," I said. "And once Steffi admitted to the police that Gregory Logan had been, you know . . ."

"Forward," my hostess politely suggested.

"Forward. Right." So Steffi had told the cops about Greg. Was he so obtuse or so utterly devoid of ethics that days after his wife was reported missing he decided to make whoopie with the au pair? "After his being forward," I continued, "it probably seemed suspicious to the authorities that Steffi *hadn't* picked up and left immediately."

"She told you about how he behaved?" Andy asked. I didn't lie and say yes. On the other hand, I concede that my head might have wobbled in an up-and-down direction. "The . . . the awfulness!" I heard a tremor in her voice and she didn't seem like the tremulous type, but Steffi's story about Greg clearly had shaken her. I gazed at the lemon circle resting on some ice cubes in the bottom of my empty glass. "Steffi's a strong girl," she went on, "but she broke down when she told me. Being in a strange country, going through this lovely woman being missing—and Steffi the last person to see her. And then having a detective try to make her say she had been . . . involved with the husband *before* the wife disappeared. Devotion or no devotion to those children, Steffi *had* to get out fast—before the police began to wonder what was keeping her there."

"Before they began suspecting her," I added.

"Absolutely!" said Andy Leeds.

About three minutes later, as I turned left out of the driveway, I asked myself whether I ought to stake out the intersection of Old Farm Road and West Pequot Drive to await Steffi's return from Manhattan. That way, I could confront her about what she'd told her new employer and the cops about Greg (lecherous slimeball) versus what she'd told me (quiet, nice, very polite).

A stakeout would definitely make me feel very sleuth-ish. On the other hand, it would probably be boring. And, without the requisite stakeout accoutrements that I'd gleaned from noir movies and novels— powdered doughnuts, cardboard container of coffee, a jar for relieving myself, which, not being a man, would no doubt result in a revolting mess involving me, the driver's seat, and a bag of Dunkin' Donuts—I'd probably be longing to get out of there within fifteen minutes. Besides, if Steffi had been duplicitous the first time I'd interviewed her, would she suddenly open up to me if I leaped from my car into the middle of West Pequot and forced her to slam on her brakes?

So I headed home. While waiting to pull out a week's worth of laundry before it could get scorched by my pyromaniacal dryer, I took a can of Diet Coke onto the patio and reread my notes on all the interviews I'd done. I was mulling over what my next step would be when Nancy called.

"How was Little Liebchen?" Uh-oh. Nancy's slooooow talk. "Did she fess up about Greg?" Generally, when Nancy drew out her syllables so long it seemed she'd never part with them, it was not Flower of Southern Womanhood Hour. It meant she'd had a vodka or two. Or three.

"Are you coherent?" I asked, nibbling on a no-fat cracker that tasted, predictably, like salted Styrofoam.

"Of course I'm coherent. Would you lay off about my drinking." The last sentence was more command than request.

"Why not stick a straw into a bottle of Absolut and just glug away?" I advised. "Save all that tedious pouring."

"Why don't you put a cork in it?"

With a sigh I hoped was sufficiently passive-aggressive to induce guilt, I went back to the subject at hand. "Steffi wasn't there. I spoke to the lady of the house, who had green froggies on her skirt. She told me Steffi had broken down and wept while telling her how Greg made a pass at her a few days after Courtney was missing."

"He must be très stupide. To say nothing of très tacky."

"I don't get it. Greg's not stupid. Not tacky either. And he didn't strike me as the type who would be swept away." Then jokingly, I added, "But what do I know about passion?"

"Not much," Nancy snapped. When she drank she tended to get a bit testy. "To tell you the truth," she conceded, "I don't know everything either. Do you want a for-instance?"

"I'm going to get one, so yes, I want a for-instance."

"For instance, I don't understand all these women you're speaking to—Courtney's friends, the Connecticut froggy woman. What do they *do*? They're all thirty-five, forty tops. Whatever happened to jobs? Remember jobs, Judith? Remember all those asshole husbands in 1972, yours and mine included, who said 'My wife isn't going to work,' and how we stood up to them and that idiot mentality. *So what are all these women doing home?*"

"What are you talking about?" I asked. "They're raising their children."

"I see. And may I inquire precisely why we went through a revolution in women's rights, why we bothered to have our consciences raised? So our daughters could sit on a bench in a playground and talk about whether Pampers or Huggies hold poopy better. That's how they talk: Cross my heart, hope to die. Poopy and peepee. Four years of higher education, graduate school—a whole world of possibility open to them—and they elect to sit on a park bench and talk shit."

"We fought so our daughters could choose—"

"We fought so our daughters would be allowed to do the work for which they were suited. Now what happens? They go to law school, medical school, business school and become lawyers or doctors or number crunchers for how long? Three or four years. But the minute they see they're just another cruncher or whatever, that they're not having *fun,* whatever that means, that they're flying to Milwaukee with their knees squished and will never get near the corporate jet, what do they do? They up and quit."

"Who's supposed to raise their children?" I inquired. "An illegal immigrant who doesn't speak English, who they underpay and overwork? Take a woman like Courtney Logan—"

"Courtney Logan!" Nancy huffed. "Give me a break."

"She had a business," I argued.

"She had a business that was going noplace fast," Nancy replied. "StarBaby was no star and Courtney was no business genius. On her best day she was third rate. I bet you she wasn't humping anywhere near the top of the totem pole at her old investment bank."

"Not everyone's a winner, Nancy. I'm not exactly a tenured professor at Harvard."

"But you *work*. Nobody's begging me to be executive editor of *The New York Times* either, but BFD, big fucking deal: I work."

"But I raised my kids, before I even finished my dissertation. And if you can remember that far back, you were freelancing, not working full-time."

"But we didn't have a path to follow. They do. Because we cleared it."

"Maybe they don't like the path."

"Maybe in a few years men will be saying: 'Hey, how come they're letting all these women like Courtney Logan into law school and medical school and into the hot jobs on Wall Street when all they do is work three years and quit? That's not fair. Why can't those places go to men who will stay the course?' And they'll be right."

"Women like Courtney are better, more involved mothers than we are," I told her.

"Women like Courtney quit good jobs and wind up banging tambourines on their heads in Mommy and Me class and fucking their golf pros and doing anything to avoid real work. Women like Courtney are up a goddamn creek without a paddle. What was she planning on doing when she turned forty-five? Fifty? Better someone shot her and put her out of her misery."

After delivering herself of that magnanimous insight, Nancy announced she had to wash her hair, although from the clunk of ice cubes against glass, not muffled by any liquid, I surmised she wanted to get downstairs to pour herself another drink. She was less than appreciative when I asked her what was the first letter of the alphabet, then suggested she double it and find the nearest meeting.

After wasting a half hour folding underwear and towels so meticulously they could be displayed at an *American Washday* exhibit at the Smithsonian, I broke down and called Fancy Phil and gave him the gist of what Steffi had told the cops. I expected a gangster-ish outburst: thunderous Fucks! and fists breaking plaster. But after a long silence, he merely asked what he should do. So I told him.

Around eleven that night my bell chimed. Fancy Phil. Not that he woke me; I'd gotten absorbed finishing an article by a Korean War veteran turned historian on the Second Infantry Division's role in the fighting at Heartbreak Ridge. (And, big surprise, thinking about Nelson.)

The night was cool, in the low sixties, and Phil was wearing a sweatshirt. Brown University. The "vers" stretched across his gut looked larger than all the other letters. I assumed he'd borrowed it from his son, although the gold Egyptian amulet on a thick herringbone chain was clearly his. "I talked to Gregory," Fancy Phil announced in a voice loud enough to broadcast that he knew I lived alone. I didn't want to think about how he knew. I invited him in. "You got time now?" he asked, but by then he was in the living room, on the couch, gazing at a bowl of potpourri on the coffee table, ruefully concluding it wasn't a snack.

"You asked Greg about Steffi Deissenburger?" I inquired.

"Yeah. You know, you hate like hell to ask your kid the one thing he doesn't want to talk about. But like I told him, 'Listen, Gregory, I know you got more'n you can handle. But you gotta stop shittin' me—pardon me for saying that—because I swear to God I'm keeping out of this. Except my friends—high-class friends—hear things, you know. And what I'm hearing is the cops think something was going on with you and that German girl that was watching the kids. And that's how come they think you . . . you know, did it to Courtney.' "

With sad but hopeful eyes, he glanced away from me and down at the potpourri again, so I excused myself, went into the kitchen, and brought back a plate with a bunch of red grapes and a couple of plums. "What did Greg have to say?" I asked.

"It took a while." He started on the grapes. "Men don't like to talk about . . . things they don't want to talk about. Know what I mean?"

"Emotional stuff," I suggested.

"Right. So I said to him, I said, 'Gregory, I'm your old man. There's nothing you ever done that I didn't do maybe a hundred times.' So finally he tells me. A few days after Courtney's missing, he's sitting with the German girl and she's showing him a list. So she can go shopping. Probably still buying those pukey-tasting health cereals Courtney made the kids eat. But anyways, all of a sudden, in the middle of reading over the shopping list, Gregory breaks down. Crying. Sobbing his head off because it's like all of a sudden he's beginning to get it, that Courtney might never get found. So the German girl pats his hand"—Fancy Phil motioned for my hand and offered a couple of demonstration pats I doubted would leave bruises—"like that. And so Gregory starts to cry even harder." Fancy Phil shook his head. "Can you picture what it was like for him to have to tell me this, even though I'm his own flesh and blood? I mean, about the crying and stuff. But I told him, 'Hey, kid, listen, I've sobbed my head off, too, and I didn't have no wife disappear on me.' I didn't say 'unfortunately' because my first ex is his mother. So anyways, Gregory puts his head on the girl's shoulder to cry. Like they say, 'A shoulder to cry on,' you know?" Fancy Phil leaned back, resting his head atop the couch cushion. He pulled a few grapes off the branchlets with his teeth. "All of a sudden," he went on, "the girl pulls back! Like Gregory's grabbed her. Whatever. So Gregory pulls back, too, and they finish the list like nothing happened. And then the girl went shopping."

"And?" I asked.

"And he swears that was it. *Nothing,* not one thing else, happened. He didn't lay a finger on her. It was that he just broke down for a minute and laid his head on her shoulder."

"Phil."

"What?"

"Do you believe him?"

"It's funny." He spoke more cautiously than usual, but that might have been because he had a mouthful of grapes. "If anybody else told me that story I'd be thinking: Big bull. But I'm his old man. I know my kid. I even know how my kid lies. All kids do. He doesn't now. But when Gregory was a kid, he'd get three words of a lie out and his ears would turn bright red. I'd give him a smack and say, 'Don't lie to me, you little pisspot!' My ex used to say, 'Philly, stop with the pisspot, for crissakes!' "

"And you think Greg's telling the truth now?"

"I think someone should get hold of this German girl—" I shook my head. "I didn't mean hurt her," Fancy Phil explained. "I meant to help her try—"

"No," I said softly.

"You don't have to whisper with me, you know. I'm not some nut who's gonna blow your head off that you gotta get to calm down."

"I wasn't whispering," I replied. "I was talking softly. You know Theodore Roosevelt? He said, 'Speak softly and carry a big stick; you will go far.' "

"You trying to teach me history?" Fancy Phil shook his head, the way people do when dealing with a hopeless case.

"It couldn't hurt."

"Fine. History." He put his hands on his knees and, with a weary grunt, pushed himself up from the couch. "It so happens I know history. Theodore Roosevelt was before Franklin Roosevelt."

"That's right."

"So listen, call me right away if you hear something." I said I would, and yes, of course he could take the rest of the grapes and the plums with him.

It was nearly eleven-thirty. Too late to call anyone and I didn't have the energy to start the new book I'd taken out of the library. I'd already seen the AMC movie *The Sundowners* at least three times, so TV was out. It was hit the Ben & Jerry's or give myself a pedicure. As I was twirling a tissue to separate my toes, I realized: Hey, it's not even eight-thirty on the West Coast—in Courtney Bryce Logan's hometown. Not too late.

So I riffled through my clippings, found the one I'd printed out from the *Olympian* Web site, and within a minute was on the phone with one Lacey Braun, the high-school classmate of Courtney's who'd been quoted as saying Courtney was "shrewd." A curious adjective. Okay, maybe not all that curious, but I had no other ideas.

Lacey hemmed and hawed for a minute or two but finally admitted it was because of an incident that had occurred in her senior year of high school, something that had happened between her best friend Ingrid and Courtney. No, she didn't want to talk about it. Hem, haw again, and then a third time, but at last she gave me a name, Ingrid Farrell, as well as a phone number.

" 'Shrewd,' " Ingrid repeated. "Well, Lacey's right. That's what Courtney was." I heard two puffs and a slurp. "Ow, hot! Sorry, I just made myself a camomile-clove tea a second before the phone rang."

"Could I ask you a couple of questions about Courtney, Ingrid?"

"I never saw her again after high school."

"But you may know something that could be helpful," I urged.

Ingrid emitted a dubious "uuuuuuuh." Finally, four actual words emerged: "What is this for?" she finally asked.

"I've been hired to check out Courtney's background. Just to make sure the wrong person isn't . . ." My voice trailed off more because dealing with Lacey and then Ingrid felt like too much expenditure for too little return. "The wrong person could be accused of her murder and . . ." I was suddenly too sleepy to offer her an image of an innocent being gassed or fried or whatever they did in the state of Washington.

"You're not a reporter?"

"No."

"It's not nice to say anything bad about the dead," Ingrid informed me. I thought I heard a regretful note.

"I guess not—except if it can help the living."

"I mean, it was a high-school thing."

"What was?"

"See, Courtney Bryce was always doing stuff. You know?" She took a long, noisy sip of tea. "President of every club. Helping out teachers. Courtney Bryce was the smartest, best, nicest girl in the whole school."

"Right." I stifled a yawn.

"Everyone always said, 'Oh, Courtney, she's wonderful.' " I waited. "Well, it's like this: She was running the Crunch-Munch sale. Fund-raising. Candy bars. It was chocolate then. I think now it's energy bars made from rainforest nuts and stuff. That's what seniors do every year to raise money for a sit-down dinner on Prom Night."

"Uh-huh," I said. My back and shoulders began to ache for bed. I massaged the back of my neck.

"Courtney stole eight hundred dollars in cash from the Crunch-Munch sale. And got away with it."

"What?"

"We had all this cash. I was treasurer. So I had to put it in a sealed envelope and give it to Mr. Cooper, the principal. And I did. Courtney was with me when we went to Mr. C's office. And he opened the safe. It was late Thursday afternoon, like almost four o'clock, so he said he'd deposit it first thing Friday."

"A wall safe?"

"No. This big heavy thing on the floor. And so his phone rang and he picked it up and Courtney and me were just standing there and I went to check out pictures of old graduating classes to see if I could find my dad. Courtney was looking at all of Mr. Cooper's books. My back was turned to her. So was his. Anyhow, then he got off the phone and shut the safe. The next morning it wasn't there. The cash."

"Is it possible the principal took it?"

"Of course not! I mean, he did this every year, holding the money for the seniors because a lot of kids get it in late. He called Courtney and me down separately. Guess who got blamed?"

"That's an awful story!" I said.

For a long moment, Ingrid was silent. Then she said: "Do you know what the worst of it was? He called Courtney down first. By the time I got there, he was totally, totally convinced she never would have done it. That I did it. No, the worst of it was, ninety-nine percent of the kids thought it was me, too, except Lacey and one other girl. Everyone else believed Courtney. The school made my parents pay it back and even my parents . . . Water under the bridge, right? But my name was totally mud. And that kind of thing stays with you forever. I mean, I've never been invited to one class reunion. And I was volunteering at the county animal shelter. Well, one day I walked in—this was two or three years ago—and nobody said a word, but I knew somehow someone had heard the story. And then told it to everybody, and everybody *believed* it, people who'd always thought I was a good person. A story, a lie, from way back in high school!"

"Did Courtney avoid you the rest of your senior year?" I asked.

"Well, we never hung out. But whenever there were other kids around, she went out of her way to be sweet to me, like she was full of pity for my being such a bad person. Everyone thought, wasn't it great of Courtney to be so fantastically nice to Ingrid after the terrible thing Ingrid tried to do—and almost got away with."

Chapter Ten

A giant brown eye stared back at me from a magnifying mirror as I plucked my eyebrow. Cautiously. A few months after Bob died, I'd decided it was time to start looking like a human being again. I dug out my old tweezer. Alas. When I finished, one brow was so much higher than the other that for several weeks I looked inappropriately ironic. Soon after, I'd bought the mirror.

So there I was, bright-eyed at six A.M., hell-bent on an hour's worth of self-improvement. What had wakened me? Rambunctious bird business outside my window, or maybe CourtneyLoganangst. In any case, I showered and exfoliated enough to go down a dress size. Then, so intently was I concentrating on my eyebrow's image in the magnifying glass, that when I lifted the portable phone from the edge of the sink, I didn't catch the opening words of Steffi Deissenburger's early morning conniption fit. However, it wasn't necessary. Each time I tried to butt in she squawked: "How, *how,* how could you visit the Leedses' house on my day off? *How?*" again and again, turning up the volume with every "how."

I recalled Nelson telling me, a couple of decades earlier, of something he'd heard at a cop seminar: a technique for dealing with people who'd gone over the edge—something like Calming a Psychotic Who Has an Assault Rifle in One Hand and a Fistful of Plastique in the Other. The idea was not to be confrontational and say something like: What's your problem, dipshit? It was to ignore the madness and pursue pleasant discourse. As in: Gee, you like the Uzi nine millimeter, too!

So I enthused: "Steffi! I'm glad you called. Too bad I missed you yesterday afternoon." Only then did it occur to me that Steffi wasn't behaving irrationally, that she had a right to be steaming. Plus that Nelson had muttered something about the congeniality tactic probably having only a thirty percent chance of working, and if it didn't, you were dead (albeit good-natured) meat.

Just as I was about to beg her pardon and offer extravagant apologies, Steffi replied: "It would have been better if you telephoned." Stress still vibrated her voice. Her German accent was heavier—"would have been" became "vut hof bean"—as if her last year in America had not happened. Nevertheless, she was no longer squawking.

"You're right," I said quickly, "Forgive me for not calling ahead. It's just that I happened to be in Connecticut and thought I'd pop in and say hi." In the mirror, my humongous eyelid flickered at this lie. "You know, I was wondering about something you said about Courtney."

"Perhaps I did not explain when I spoke." Steffi was now sounding only mildly snippy. "Courtney was my employer. I did not know her well."

"You lived in the same house."

"Yes, that is true. But when she was at home she was in her office nearly all the time. For hours. I was with the children. She was at the computer or on the phone. Her door was closed."

"Just out of curiosity . . ." I said (turning from the mirror so I didn't have to see my crow's-feet in the early-morning sun, which, magnified, looked deep as pterodactyl tracks). "How did you know Courtney was on the computer so much?"

"The light of the phone line."

"She couldn't have been talking to someone?"

"She could have been." Her reply was still somewhat testy. Still, Steffi did not seem to have the heart to hold a grudge. An explanation quickly followed of how her boyfriend Stefan was studying economics in Dusseldorf and how they emailed each other several times a day and how difficult it was for her to get his letters with Courtney being on-line so long—How could she only be talking for hours and hours? Yet she insisted Steffi keep the other line free for incoming calls. Stefan looked a little like Dave Grohl. The drummer from Foo Fighters.

"He sounds wonderful." I put my hand over the mouthpiece so she wouldn't hear my yawn. And Steffi kept going. I was finally able to cut her off while she was still at the beginning of confiding Stefan's carefully laid career plans. Nevertheless, her obvious loneliness, living in a foreign country on eight or so acres with a husband, wife, and two three-year-olds, saddened me. On the other hand, perhaps when she was on Long Island, her solitude had inspired fantasies about Greg Logan. Enough to make her want to murder Courtney Logan? That would be a nifty solution. Fancy Phil would be happy. The only problem was I didn't think I could buy it. "Steffi and Stefan sounds like a great team," I added cheerfully.

"Thank you."

Now that we were pals again, I inquired: "By the way, Steffi, did Courtney work all day, every day? Didn't she ever go out with friends or have friends over?"

"Yes. Now and again. Women friends."

"Do you happen to know any of their names?"

"There was Kellye Ryan. She was a visitor many times. Have you seen her? Tall, thin, like a supermodel. Very beautiful. Fine, fine clothes. And nice. Very kind."

"Anybody else?"

"Yes, three or four. I can't remember their names. I saw them. They always said hello—they were nice women, although not so friendly to me like Kellye—but often Courtney would ask me to take the children someplace out of the house so with her friend, she could have a quiet talk."

"I see. Oh, by the way, remember we spoke about Gregory Logan?" Steffi's answer was silence. "That Courtney had said if he called while she was out to say she was shopping. Because she didn't want him worrying about her: He had too much on his plate."

"Yes." Wary. She was stretching out the monosyllable as long as she could.

Phone to my ear, I stepped from the cold tile of the bathroom onto the comforting softness of the bedroom carpet. "Did you find Greg like that, under pressure?"

I waited. Well, I told myself, she sure doesn't talk off the top of her head. I sat cross-legged on the bed, reaching behind me to prop up a couple of pillows against the headboard. I felt around my night table for a pen, came up with a long-lost lip-liner, and jotted a few notes about what Steffi was saying on a milk-mustache ad in *Entertainment Weekly*. At last Steffi spoke: "No. Mr. Logan seemed—I do not know exactly how to say it—like anyone else. Of course, I do not know American men very well, you understand. After Courtney disappeared, he was what you would call a man under pressure. Very, very unhappy. The police were visiting. Often he would call his father. You know about his father?"

"I think so," I mealymouthed. "He's supposed to be a gangster, right? Fancy Somebody."

"Yes. Fancy Phil Lowenstein. A man with many jewels. Very friendly. Informal, I should say. He said to me, 'Call me Phil.' He himself often called me 'honey,' but I believe that was because he could not remember my name."

"Did Greg Logan speak with anyone besides his father after Courtney disappeared?"

"His mother, I think. His sister. A friend from college. His lawyer of course."

"Did he pay attention to the children during that time?"

"Oh yes. He was very nice with them. Always. Before and after."

The early, pre-car-pool silence beyond my open bedroom window was broken by the screech of a jay, a stupid-sounding *Waaa?*, as if the bird couldn't figure out what was obvious to every other creature. "You know, Steffi, from what I hear around Shorehaven, the police believe Greg had—well, a romantic interest in you." She didn't chuckle at the foolishness of such a notion, so I plunged ahead. "I suppose it's one of the reasons why they suspect him." Still no response. "You know, I have two kids not much older than you are. I can hardly imagine . . . It must have been a terrible situation for you."

"Yes."

"I give you credit, staying there as long as you did."

"They were good children," Steffi explained. "With their mother missing . . . It was very sad."

"You were so devoted to them. It must have been tense in the house, I mean after Greg Logan . . ."

"Yes. He was . . . He watched me all the time. When I read to the children, or watched television with them—he allowed them to watch television. Courtney would not be approving of that."

"But you knew his eyes were always on you."

"Yes."

"Awful. Did he ever actually touch you?" When she didn't reply, I said: "I'm sorry, Steffi. It's just that I feel protective. As if you were one of my kids."

"He was crying one afternoon, about Courtney. I touched his hand, with pity, you understand, a light touch. He put his arms around me. He pulled me to him."

"My God! What did you do?"

"I tried to pull away, but he would not allow me to. He kept saying,

'I need . . . I need' . . . but he was breathing too hard. I could feel his tears or maybe—*Schweiss* in English—yes, his sweat. I could feel wet on my neck. I told him, 'You must stop this!' but he did not. I said it louder, so loud I was afraid the children would hear, but I had to get away."

"Of course! You did the right thing. And then did he let you go?"

"Yes."

"But he kept looking at you."

"He never stopped."

I led her back to talking about Stefan. Within a minute she was cheery again, telling me of the hobby they shared, collecting Monty Python memorabilia. Beguiling though her tale was of Stefan's pursuit of a *Life of Brian* T-shirt, I managed to get myself off the phone.

Downstairs in the kitchen, quartering an orange, I felt almost certain Steffi did not have it in her to shoot Courtney Logan twice in the head, then deep-six the body in the swimming pool. And as far as the he said/she said versions of Crying Greg, I didn't see much in Fancy Phil and Steffi's accounts that was inconsistent. Maybe Greg had put his arms around her, maybe not. Perhaps he was looking for solace, perhaps nooky (though my vote was for solace). In any case, the awkward moment had lasted less than sixty seconds. Were his eyes always on her after that? If so, it was impossible for me to know if the cause was lust or mortification.

When I noticed myself arranging orange pits in a row, I perceived my mind had meandered. I'd been going over the Zee Friedman timetable on Courtney. From what Zee had said, business hadn't seemed up or down in July, yet she claimed Courtney had been "bummed." But by early fall, she'd noted, Courtney was detached; her mind, according to Zee, was someplace other than StarBaby. She'd gone from trying to breathe for Zee to letting her wing it. I sauntered over to the refrigerator and retrieved a still-unopened container of no-fat pineapple cottage cheese I'd successfully avoided. I checked: seventy-two hours past its freshness date. Lacking courage to break the seal and confront what could be going on inside, I chucked it into the garbage.

Now that I thought about it, Zee's assessment of Courtney's September and October detachment had been backed up by Kellye Ryan: By September, Courtney's mind was no longer on StarBaby. So what had it been on? Monkey business? Money business? Was she phasing out Greg, in love or lust with somebody else? Or had she simply moved on to some new, more sophisticated investment bankerish interest than StarBaby?

Since becoming a widow, I'd tried hard not to indulge in the lonely person's Happy Hour: talking to oneself. About a year earlier, in the drugstore, I found myself befuddled, dithering between a condom rack and a display of batteries and was startled when I heard my own loud voice demanding: "Why am I here?" But now I gave in and had a chat with me.

That was because my kind of thinking never turned out to be pure reason. Instead, my thought processes were a mishmash of random ideas, intuition, and untoward meddling by my subconscious. What I wanted was logic, so I inquired aloud: "Is there any way to determine whether it was sex, money . . . or absolutely nothing preoccupying Courtney?" One of the orange quarters smiled up at me. I ate it, then answered myself: "What have I learned about Courtney? That she was different things to different people. She was nice, very nice, really nice, having an affair, was asexual, was a poison-gas person. Oh, right, and a perfect human being. In death, she's a Rorschach test. Was she that much of a cipher in life?"

I finished the orange and chomped on a petrified oat-bran pretzel while waiting for the coffee to drip. As I could not talk and chew at the same time I reverted to thinking. How had people reacted emotionally to Courtney? Steffi, who'd worked for her and lived in her house, appeared not just to like her but to revere her. Greg had either loved her (or liked her enough to stay in the marriage) or downright hated her enough to kill her. Not only was it easier for me to believe the love stuff, what with Fancy Phil having hired me to clear his son, it also was more comforting to picture the single parent of two young, traumatized children as another innocent victim of Courtney's murder rather than as the monster who could execute such a crime.

My client, Fancy Phil himself, hadn't liked his daughter-in-law. Yet he hadn't seemed to hate her. He'd compared her personality to *lukshen*—the Yiddish word for noodles, i.e., something limp, bland, and tasteless—a description that could in no way be construed as a compliment. On the other hand, blahness did not seem enough of an affront to get a person on a mobster's hit list.

Or on anybody's hit list. So had Courtney Logan been truly blah, truly nice, truly the supermom and diligent young entrepreneur? Or had she hidden some aspect of her life from those who supposedly knew her best? Had her detachment meant a preoccupation with love or money, something that had led to another person wanting or needing to wipe her off the face of the earth? Or had she been heading for a quickie with her inamorato on Halloween night? Had he (or she, positing a jealous wife of said inamorato, or an inamorata of Courtney's) murdered her? And if so, how come her body wound up in her own swimming pool? Had some meandering maniac decided trick instead of treat? "Beats the hell out of me," I announced, and poured myself a mug of coffee.

But wouldn't the killer have been taking a sickening risk? To transport a dead body back from wherever to the Logan house on Bluebay

Lane, across a lawn, through the gate of a high, wrought-iron fence onto the deck around the pool? Or had the deed been done at or right near the Logan house? Wouldn't two shots to the head in the garage or backyard, even with a silencer, have made some noise? And unfastening the tied-down-tight pool cover to shove the body into the water couldn't have been easy. Okay, maybe it made sense to stow her there. Algae-killing chemicals in the water might prevent a god-awful smell, whereas burying a body in the wooded area beyond the backyard was the quickest way to make a Nassau County Police Department beagle look good. But think of the danger! Greg might have come home early. A trick-or-treater could have cut through the backyard. Steffi or Morgan or little Travis might have peeked out a window.

Okay, let's say the killer had been lurking outside the house waiting for Courtney to return. She put the car in the garage and . . . *whammo!* Except if she'd just come home from Grand Union, where were the apples she'd gone out for? Though it was certainly possible, I had trouble picturing a gunman shoving a gun back into one pocket, then four organic Winesaps into another.

Another thought. Another mug of coffee. One percent milk. Half an Equal. I sat back down at the kitchen table. Had Courtney's body been put in the pool in order to implicate Greg in the killing? If so, why had the killer refastened the cover so tightly? I recalled when I'd first heard Mack Dooley, the Logans' pool man, on the radio in May. He'd said something about the cover looking fine: "tied down real tight" the way he'd left it in the middle of September when he closed it up.

Did the killer want people to believe Courtney was simply missing? If that was the case, why risk putting her body in the pool? No murderer would rely on incompetence from the Nassau County PD's Homicide unit—that they would *not* look under the pool cover. Because the department had a good reputation. Obviously there might be the predictable politically connected losers or lazy guys, like the guy in charge of the Logan case. Still, most of the detectives were thought of as well qualified. Or terrific, the way Nelson had been.

I put on a pair of gray slacks (which delighted me by buttoning without my having to inhale) and a white shirt, then tied a yellow cashmere cardigan around my shoulders in that trendy, capelike style that made adult females look as if they were playing some communal game of Wonder Woman. Slipping into a pair of Gucci loafers I'd bought in Rome in 1985, I was so *comme il faut* I looked like a chic distant relative of myself. So I dropped by both Susan Viniar and Kellye Ryan's houses. And all just after nine o'clock.

Susan's housekeeper led me upstairs into a home gym with floor-to-ceiling mirrors. I found her straddling a menacing-looking machine, pulling down a bar that resembled a deformed wishbone; the bar was attached by pulleys to—I squinted. Yikes!—ninety pounds of iron plates. The weight did not seem to faze her in the least.

At Kellye's, after I rang the bell and called out my name, she herself reluctantly opened her own door. No live-in housekeeper. Not quite in supermodel gear yet: Her black hair was wrapped around giant foam cylinders. Strips of parchmentlike paper were glued to her nose, forehead, and chin—a beauty treatment, not rampant weirdness. Whatever she was doing to the rest of her was doubtless even less inviting, because she kept gripping the neck of an ankle-length cotton robe to make sure not an inch of skin was showing. "A North Shore Child and Family Guidance luncheon," she explained. "I'd love to invite you in for a cup of coffee, but like, you know . . ." We chatted at the door for about ten minutes.

Afterward, I drove to Starbucks and sat in the parking lot with a container of iced decaf. Okay, what had I just learned? Not much. Neither woman had altered her view: Susan was still convinced Courtney was sexless; best friend Kellye sensed Courtney was preoccupied, the way a woman with a lover might be—and, Kellye added, clutching the sky-blue robe even tighter to make sure whatever glop she had on her neck was invisible, Courtney had "that glow, if you know what I mean."

Well, at least between the two of them I came up with a list of ten other women who might know Courtney well. So I spent most of the day and early evening visiting and phoning upwardly mobile thirty-somethings.

After dinner, around seven-thirty, I phoned my daughter the lawyer. What could Courtney have been doing? Was it possible she'd made a mint doing on-line trading—hundreds of thousands? millions?—and someone learned of it and wanted to get their hands on the money?

Like Dreadful Dan Steiner, Kate thought it was unlikely although conceivable. "Mom, even in a bull market, I don't think it's easy to be a genius for more than a month or two. I don't know. Maybe she had a special knack for it and picked the right Internet stocks. I mean, you hear amazing stories about fortunes being made, but my guess is most of them are probably myths."

My response, I regret to say, was one of those vocal maternal sighs designed to make offspring feel they owe you something. Anyway, Kate offered me another minute despite the predictable lunacy (senior partners pounding on conference tables, clients screeching) of whatever merger or acquisition that she was working on. "Listen, Mom, if this Courtney was on-line for hours on end, she could have been reading tech reports on particular securities or on certain industries. Or watching a tape of stock prices. Maybe she wasn't investing. Just interested or trying to learn. Or she could have been investing small time. From what I hear, even that can get addictive. Or maybe it was something having zero to do with trading. Like hanging out in chat rooms, talking to friends she'd made. Or looking at porn sites, having cybersex, or bidding on baseball cards. There are a million things she could have been doing." Kate paused for a breath. "Hey, how about trading on insider information from one of her old colleagues?"

How about it? One thing I knew: That whole day, no one said anything to make me leap up and shout *Aha!* On the other hand, though I was wide awake, my mind was tired. Like soap bubbles, shimmery ideas of who-done-it or how-done-it rose and gleamed for an instant, then popped into thin air. So around eight-thirty, just as the sun was setting, I tooled over to Nancy's. For a while we just sat silently in her office gazing out at the pink-and-orange June sky—luscious pastels, what you'd see at an Estée Lauder counter.

"Pretty," she observed. The colors of the sky glowed on her cheeks and forehead, giving her the complexion of a flamingo.

For someone who found looking in mirrors a pleasant experience, who paid a fortune for clothes, who planned what earrings she'd wear a week in advance, Nancy's office was remarkably unpretty. In fact, it was a mess of a space, with an old rocking chair with a splintery rush seat, a sagging daybed, piles of books serving as endtables, and two dusty afghans left over from the few months in the early seventies when Nancy had gone through an Earth Mother phase and bought a used loom. Nevertheless, the office was the only room in the house that had survived her husband Larry's latest renovation. No pointed arches, not one gargoyle.

Nancy's only decoration was on one wall, where she'd taped up some of her early freelance writing efforts: "Bubble, Bubble, Soil and Trouble: What You Need to Know About Phosphate Detergents" and "One Hundred Ways to Say 'No' to a Man" (a notion, alas, that had never occurred to Nancy). Now the articles were yellowed and dry, held up by Scotch tape so old it had turned bronze. Flakes of desiccated paper crumbled from the curling edges of the pages and adhered to the baseboard and rug.

"So?" she inquired, sipping a little water or a lot of vodka.

"I spent the day talking to young mothers," I reported.

"Did you get anything? Besides bored?"

"Were you boring when you stayed home with your kids? Was I?"

"I wasn't. You were."

"Shush. I want to talk about Courtney."

She nodded. In an instant her expression transmuted from snide to solemn. In the grand tradition of best friends, Nancy resembled one of those exquisitely calibrated instruments that sense the first rumbling of a quake a thousand miles away. Unlike a mere good friend or a pal or a chum who might proclaim, Hey, let me know if you need anything/I'm always here for you/If you feel like company just call, Nancy, in a split second, would sense the slightest shift in my seismic activity and respond accordingly. "I'm all ears," she said.

"A couple of the people I interviewed thought there'd been a change in Courtney this fall. She seemed kind of depressed over the summer, maybe about the business, maybe about something else."

"Something male?" Nancy inquired.

"Possibly. In any case, she was still working to make a go of StarBaby. But come September, she acted detached from it. The last couple of weeks before Halloween, there were a few times she got all dolled up and was away for the entire day. Her husband doesn't get home till around eight. And she told the au pair to tell him she'd gone shopping. Most of the time, though, she stayed in the office for hours on end, maybe on-line, maybe talking. Zee, her videographer, says she was just going through the motions, businesswise, with StarBaby. Her best friend sensed something else was occupying her—a guy. Courtney supposedly had 'that glow.' On the other hand, a woman in her group who really wasn't close to Courtney told me she thought Courtney was utterly asexual."

"How did she have her children? By budding?"

"Now, the best friend is superfashionable. Very attractive, too, except for inordinately long canine teeth." I did my Bela Lugosi imitation for a few seconds, until Nancy closed her eyes. "She seems to have a good heart. But I think the other woman in the group is infinitely brighter. She picked up on something about Courtney that I'd picked up on after talking to a whole bunch of people: She was . . . incomplete. The woman, Susan, told me Courtney reminded her of the pod people in *Invasion of the Body Snatchers.*"

"Excellent," Nancy said. "Another evening of high culture. I can always count on you to elevate any discussion."

"I really understand what she meant by pod people. Courtney had all the qualities of a winner—fine education, good job after college, decent-to-terrific husband, money, lovely children."

"Except she wasn't a winner? Something was wrong with her?"

"Not wrong. It was that something wasn't quite right. Listen, some people liked her or thought she was a decent sort. The au pair looked up to her. But except for the best friend, no one had a single tear for her. No one seemed to have the wind knocked out of them by the awfulness of murder."

"Well, it's been a while since they found the body."

"It's three weeks today," I told her.

"But she's been gone since October thirty-first. After a few days, people must have assumed some kind of foul play. So finding her body wasn't a shock."

"Listen, imagine if the same thing happened to someone we were peripherally friendly with, say Mary Alice. She certainly is a peripheral friend. But wouldn't you still be stunned?"

"No. I'd be dancing in the streets," Nancy said.

"You would not."

"Doing the tango up Northern Boulevard."

"No. You'd be stunned."

"Fine. Whatever you say."

We were quiet for a minute, Nancy studying the quotes on a paperback she'd bought, me combing the fringe of a brown-and-gold afghan. "I keep thinking about something you said," I told her. She set aside the book. "About Courtney being third-rate and StarBaby not being a star. Was that something you heard at *Newsday*?"

She flung back her head in a southern-belle-taking-umbrage gesture and muttered a weary "Mah Gawd!" When my only response was to keep combing afghan fringe, she added: "No, you turkey. It's something I heard my inner voice say. Courtney Logan quits her job when she has her first kid. Have you heard one tiny little word about her having been dying to get back to Wall Street or wherever she'd been? Or missing it?"

"No."

"She was running one of those cute home-office businesses that seemed to be going noplace fast." Before I could challenge her, she added: "I swear I'm not being snotty. If the company had potential, she wasn't the one who could take it there. Ambition's fine, but you also need what we used to call in Georgia stick-to-it-iveness."

"Because no one down there ever heard the word 'tenacity.' "

"Do you want my opinion or not?" she demanded.

"Go ahead."

"Courtney strikes me as one of those people . . . They have all the right credentials but they end up going through life appalled that instead of being, say, CEO of J. Walter Thompson, they're running the second biggest ad agency in Florence, Alabama. I mean, look at her. Cute as a button. Must have won a Little Miss Dimples contest back home. Smart. Princeton, *magna cum laude*. With an Ivy League, MBA husband. Worked at that big investment banking firm."

"Patton Giddings," I said quietly. "Listen, Nance, I think it's time for me to go farther."

"Which means what?" she inquired, somewhere between huffy and belligerent. "Seeing your cop?"

"No! Literally going farther. If there was a guy in Courtney's life, the way her best friend says, no one in town has a clue as to who he is. Or at least no one I've come up with. If there was some big fight or a business deal here in Shorehaven that blew up and made someone want to kill her, I haven't heard a peep about anything that could lead to me finding out about it. And I haven't sensed anyone trying to hide anything either. Frankly, for someone so active locally, she doesn't seem to have made more than a superficial impression on people."

"Thus your pod-person thesis."

"Listen, Nancy, she just could have been a plain old nebbish. Or maybe she was hiding something dark and dirty. But I think sooner or later I have to go into the city because I'm coming close to the end of my rope here."

"What's at the end of your rope?" Nancy asked.

"Don't ask."

"I'm asking."

"Fancy Phil."

Chapter Eleven

"What's wrong?" Fancy Phil Lowenstein peered across the yellowed laminate of our table in a booth in Coffee Heaven. A half step up from greasy spoon, the place stood in grubby contrast to the recently renovated, excessively quaint white clapboard railroad station across the street, about eight miles up the track from the Shorehaven stop.

A few leisurely commuters, dressed down in chinos or suited up in seersucker, atilt from attaché cases and tote bags, let their eyes drift in our direction to check if . . . Yes! The Long Island Bad Guy himself was at his usual table. Uh-huh, today he was wearing—Je-*sus*—a giant sun medallion on a rope of gold and a belly-hugging sports shirt, gray, with wide, horizontal bands of red. The shirt was so tight it broadcast the news nobody really had to know, that his navel was an outie. Before he could catch them ogling, they turned to check the day's special: OJ 2 POCHED EGGS ON TOAST COFFEE $2.20.

Still, these suburbanites, basking in the shine of Fancy Phil's celebrity, suddenly seemed to be living more fully. Like drooping plants brought into the sun, they were revitalized by his light. Shoulders rose from their slumps. Eyes sparkled. "Two eggs over easy, *very* crisp bacon!" was ordered in a cocksure manner, as if being a mere few feet from the source of power had transformed men and women alike into wise guys. Mornings couldn't get much better than this unless a genuinely more transcendent celebrity, a Dick Cavett, say, or a Madeleine Albright, would pop into Coffee Heaven for a bagel and cream cheese.

"You don't like your breakfast, Doc?" my client inquired. My half-eaten egg white omelette lay on the plate like an exhausted invertebrate.

I myself was feeling fairly jaunty. "No, the omelette was fine," I replied.

"Because if you want, I can get Monte to make you a waffle. Or a real omelette, with the yellow in it." Phil himself had finished off a breakfast of scrambled eggs and all the accoutrements. Not a shred of hashbrown potatoes was left, nor a crust from the tower of toast he'd been served. Miniature foil containers of grape jelly and strawberry preserves, now empty, as well as a minor mess of small paper rectangles Phil had ripped off pats of butter, were strewn across the table. "Maybe some pancakes?" He grabbed a few napkins from the dispenser and dabbed the already clean corners of his mouth. "They got hot oatmeal. The kind that still's got a little crunch in it, not the mushy kind."

"No thanks, Phil. Look, I want to talk about money." His poker face was impressive, though the almost imperceptible slosh of black coffee in his cup showed me something had registered. "No, no," I came back quickly. "Not money for me. I'm in this as a volunteer, just as I said I'd be. I mean Courtney's money. I need to ask you some questions about her, and please understand I don't mean to be disrespectful—"

"What are you talking? Respect? You think I'm some godfather where you gotta kiss my ring?"

"No, because I have no intentions of kissing anything of yours. So, let's move along. If your daughter-in-law had a strong guiding force in her life, what would you say it was? Love—including sex—or money?"

Fancy Phil didn't even bother with a token "Hmm." "Money."

"How come you're so sure?"

He gave himself time to mull this over by calling out to the man behind the counter. "Hey, Monte, what's a guy gotta do around here to get more toast?" Monte smiled, undoubtedly knowing his role in this game, and gave a snappy, yes-sir! salute. Fancy Phil, knowing his role also, graciously inclined his head. Then he turned back to me. "It's like this." He massaged the first of his chins. "Picture a business thing, okay? You meet some guy. He looks right, says all the right words. Except you pick up little things. Let's say you're talking about a deal. But all of a sudden a girl walks by and he's checking her out. Then he turns back to you; he says,

'What were you just saying?' Now, the guy only lost his concentration for maybe half a second, but you know, hey, he don't have the . . . the focus for you to want to do a deal with him. A girl's a girl, but a deal's a deal. Like with Courtney. Focus. You talk about business stuff, and even though she was a good wife and mother, always googly-eyeing Gregory and calling the kids 'Sweetie,' in my heart of hearts—" Fancy Phil whacked the northwest corner of his paunch to show me where his heart was—"she'd drop the sugarplum shit—pardon me—if somebody three blocks away whispered 'spreadsheet.' "

"What did she like more about business?" I pumped him. "The wheeling and dealing? Or the money?"

"Well, she knew how to spend all right. Clothes. That house, the cars, the vacations. Bali the last time. Making Gregory go halfway around the world to go to the beach? Antiques, too. Let me tell you, for two kids playing it straight—"

"By straight you mean legal?" I cut in.

"Yeah. Legal. Legit. For two kids keeping their nose clean, Courtney and Gregory were doing nice. Living nice. Too nice, because Courtney was always spending. Getting plans drawn up for a greenhouse one time. Pressuring him to buy the house next door when it went up for sale. So's they could knock it down and have more land. Land. They already got two acres. Who the hell was she, Miss Scarlett O'Hara?"

I finished cleaning off the tops of the salt and pepper shakers with my napkin and willed myself not even to glance at the ketchup-encrusted seam between the table's top and sides. Instead I inquired: "So it was more money—what money could buy—than wheeling and dealing that interested Courtney?"

"Nah, that's not right either. Because you couldn't shut her up about business when she started StarBaby. Blab, blab, blab. And when she finally said everything twice, she'd talk about other people's businesses, too. Like telling you *Wall Street Journal* stories. Boring corporate crap: 'Schmuck-ola, Incorporated's quarterly profits exceeded all forecasts.' Like I really give a you-know-what about Schmuckola. But after a while, when StarBaby wasn't raking it in, she didn't have nothing to say about anybody's business. So put it this way: Courtney liked wheeling and dealing only if she was in the plus column."

"That money she took from her and Greg's brokerage and bank accounts," I said. "We've gone over how she put some of it back. But in the end, she wound up keeping for herself twenty-five thousand dollars of what used to be joint money."

"Yeah," Fancy Phil said. "That's right. She needed it for StarBaby."

"Can you remember when all that taking out and putting back on her part happened?"

"Lemme think. Gregory told me about it . . . I guess the second week of November, two weeks after she was missing, when the cops began asking him about that forty thou he took out from their joint account and put in his own name."

"That was the money that was supposed to make his bankers feel comfortable, right?"

"Right. You're running a legit business, you need an open line of credit, you don't want no uncomfortable bankers." He paused, then bunched up his lips and spat out—fortunately not in my direction—as if he'd just tasted something revolting. "Except those dummy putzes, those Homicide cops! They took Gregory's putting forty thou aside to make Soup Salad Sandwiches secure to mean *he* was the reason Courtney was missing, if you get me."

"You mean, the cops' theory is that Greg wanted to get his hands on the family money, and maybe he and Courtney fought. So he killed her."

"You ever hear such crap? Anyways, Gregory told me something like he had a talk with Courtney on Mother's Day, whenever that is."

"Mid-May."

"So a talk in mid-May, about her pulling money out of their joint accounts for that stupid StarBaby. Then later they had words again; I guess in the summer. That's when she dipped in and helped herself the second time. Can you believe such chutzpah? But he told me she calmed down moneywise around the time Morgan started kindergarten. So that's around Labor Day or a little after. Courtney said she was sorry and Gregory said *he* was sorry but he had to keep a certain cash balance to make his bankers happy. He told me everything was lovey-dovey after that."

I took a deep breath and asked: "How sure are you that your son is telling the truth?"

Fancy Phil answered "As sure as I can get" so quickly and so calmly I decided to believe him.

"From what I've heard . . ." I was interrupted as Monte came from behind the counter with what looked like an entire loaf of bread, toasted, as well as a bowlful of jelly containers and butter pats. When at last he stopped smiling and moved back behind the counter, I continued: "Courtney's usual pattern seemed to change in September. She lost interest in StarBaby. According to both her best friend and the young woman who worked for her part-time, her mind was elsewhere. It all jibes with what you're saying."

"Want a piece?" He held out a triangle of toast.

"No thanks. Listen, Phil, you're a smart businessman. What does it tell you if someone who is really interested in money and business starts neglecting the very business she'd thought would be the key to her making it big?"

"It could tell me a couple of things," he said carefully.

"Like?"

"Like with a woman? She could've had a boyfriend. But I don't think so. Not Courtney. She could've been, you know, having depression or something—a nervous breakdown. Or maybe she was getting born again, the Jesus stuff they do. But I don't think that either. If I had to guess, I'd say she found some other business that was more, you know, interesting than the one she had."

"Could she have gotten involved with something messy? Wound up paying blackmail? Or did she have it in her to possibly be blackmailing someone else?"

Fancy Phil shook his head as if I'd suggested something beyond idiocy. "When someone's in trouble, there's like . . . an invisible black cloud over them. They can go ha-ha a million times a day, but someone like me—you know, someone who knows what trouble really means—can sniff it out. And Courtney didn't have no black cloud like she was scared or in a jam or trying to pull a racket that wasn't going right."

"What about the opposite? Could she have found some other business interest more lucrative than StarBaby?"

" 'Lucrative.' " He chuckled without any discernible humor. "I know what 'lucrative' means."

"I'm sure you do. That's why I used it. I don't talk down to you, Phil. We're both too smart for that."

"Yeah, I know, Doctor. Anyhow, if you're right, and I say *if*, then yeah, some other lucrative business thing makes more sense to me than a boyfriend or blackmail. But that's The Big If. You could be going on a wild-goose chase. Mark my words."

"But there's a time you've got to trust your instincts, isn't there?"

"There's a time," he agreed.

"So regarding the love versus money approach," I went on. "If I believed it was love that drove her, I'd keep looking in Shorehaven. But as far as money goes, I need to follow Courtney's finance contacts. So what I'd like you to do is see if you can get something from Greg—"

Fancy Phil was squeezing the contents of a container of strawberry jam onto the corner of his thickly buttered toast. The jam looked like a clot of blood. "Done," he declared.

"But you don't know what I want yet."

"Whatever you want," he said, carefully seeing that the jelly covered every crevice of his toast, "I can do."

What I wanted was names of Courtney's colleagues. True to his word, Fancy Phil delivered, calling me just before noon with a list of names and telephone numbers. My Caller ID indicated he was phoning from a Shorehaven number. I figured it was safe to assume that he'd gone to the Logan house while his son was at work and made himself comfortable—perhaps in Courtney's home office—by Greg's invitation. Or more likely not. Fancy Phil probably considered his own need invitation enough.

I almost couldn't believe it was me acting so fast, but by four that afternoon there I was, marching up a downtown Manhattan street two blocks from Wall even though the blood supply to my little toe was being choked off by a patent-leather shoe. I felt sort of choked off, too. Even though this was the heart of High Finance City, it was a creepy neighborhood. The sidewalk lay in the perpetual dimness of shadows cast by office buildings that seemed to be leaning toward each other, tall, dank, and dreary, on either side of the narrow thoroughfare. Number twenty-two's gray masonry gave off a moldy odor as if it had been decaying since—I eyed the cornerstone—the second decade of the twentieth century. Once past the almost immovable revolving brass-and-glass door, I found myself confronted by a long-lashed security guard who reminded me of one of the teenage rapists in *A Clockwork Orange*. He gave me a slit-eyed gaze, even after Cecile Rabiea, vice-president of Patton Giddings, whom he phoned, told him it was fine to send Ms. Singer up to the thirty-fourth floor.

Patton Giddings was one of those institutions venerable enough to gain even more respect from looking seedy. The rug in the reception area was worn down to the mesh in spots, and what was left looked as if it hadn't been shampooed since FDR beat Hoover in '32. A secretary came and led me down darkly lighted halls. I wasn't quite sure what to expect in an investment bank. Certainly there were no shirt-sleeved hysterics screaming "Buy!" or "Sell!" Most doors were closed. The hallway was carpeted and I couldn't even hear my own footsteps.

Besides my tight shoes, I was wearing my several-years-old almost-Armani black pant suit, an austere, cream-color silk T-shirt, and the gold watch Bob had bought me for my fiftieth. If I wasn't exactly dressed for success, I felt fairly confident no one in the financial community would break out in scornful laughter upon seeing me. However, when I was ushered into the brave new world of Cecile Rabiea's ultramodern office, I immediately knew that the shoulder pads of my suit jacket (which could have replaced first and second bases at Shea) were clearly not of the twenty-first century.

Cecile, of course, was. First of all, she was probably six feet. I sensed she'd never been one of those tall and gawky twentieth-century girls who had wished themselves diminutive and adorable. No, as she stood to shake my hand, her bearing asserted: I'm glad I was born to be tall! She appeared to be in her mid-thirties, around Courtney's age, although she had lineless, pulled-tight-over-her-features skin and a chin-length helmet of dark brown shiny hair that, sooner or later, would have people referring to her as "ageless." On her right cheek was a mole precisely where a Madame de Pompadour might have pasted on a beauty spot.

"Thanks for seeing me, Ms. Rabiea."

In charcoal slacks with a matching, high-collared, zippered tunic, she was strictly contemporary. She looked appropriately got up to lead a hostile takeover of Briny Deep Fish Sticks or to captain a NASA voyage to Uranus. The only jewelry she wore was a plain, thin platinum wedding ring so understated that suddenly I had an overwhelming urge to take off my watch.

"Please call me Cecile," she requested, gesturing for me to take a seat in a chair that resembled a squared-off, leather toilet, although it was probably some incredibly brilliant design by one of those gaunt Milanese designers with black-framed glasses you always see in the *Times*'s Style section.

"Judith," I responded. "As I mentioned on the phone, I'm working on behalf of the family. So far, the police haven't made much progress."

"Are you a detective?" Cecile asked. Frankly, I could have done without the way her eyebrows started rising, ready to signal disbelief if I said yes.

"No. By training, I'm a historian. What the family wants me to do is a research project." Her eyebrows looked as if they were about to go up again, so I added: "Historical research often means trying to extract meaning from the past, so in that sense it's a form of detection." No gales of derisive laughter, no snort of incredulity, so I kept going. "I want to see if there's anything in Courtney Bryce Logan's past that might have played a part in her disappearance and murder."

Instead of more eyebrow theater, Cecile gave me an encouraging nod. "That makes sense," she said. "I vaguely remember a saying about 'Study the past . . .' "

" 'Study the past, if you would divine the future,' " I quoted. "Confucius said it."

"When was Confucius again?"

"Somewhere around the fifth century B.C."

Either I sounded authoritative or I was right, because whatever the test was, I passed. Cecile asked: "What do you want to know about Courtney?"

"How well did you know her?"

"We weren't friends, if that's what you mean," Cecile said, leaning back in her high-backed starship *Enterprise* black suede chair. "Look, investment banking can be a cutthroat field. Who'd want to have a close friend who knows your innermost thoughts, your vulnerabilities, when you might get into a competitive situation with her? On the other hand, neither of us felt any hostility toward the other—at least I'm sure I didn't. We were business-friendly, but not friends."

"How would you assess her capabilities?" I asked.

"Hard to say," she said cautiously. "We graduated college and came to Patton around the same time. If you come in without an MBA, the way we did, you're put in a two-year analyst program. It's really a kind of boot camp. You spend a hellish amount of time crunching numbers, doing computer models of businesses, and so forth. But you work alone, or with associates and partners, twelve, fourteen, sixteen hours a day, all-nighters—whatever it takes." Cecile was clearly not the sort who would try to be engaging, yet her manner was so forthright and low-key that the word "agreeable" came to mind and stood alongside "formidable." "So I never got to know her all that well," she went on. "I'd have known her even less if she hadn't been a woman. Thirteen years ago, when we started here at Patton, women were already more than a novelty. But we weren't an established fact yet. Every once in a while a small group of us would meet for dinner or drinks for mutual morale raising."

"What was Courtney like?"

"Like all of us. Focused on career. Ambitious. At the beginning, though, we were all pretty useless. I believe Courtney was a psych major and I majored in math, but—I can only speak for myself—I came here knowing next to nothing about investment banking."

"Did Courtney seem to know more than you did? Less?"

"I have no idea. The game in this business is to act as if you know what's going on as you try to grab onto the next rung of the ladder. Or at least not to look as panicked as you feel. Naturally, you have to scramble up the ladder pretty fast, or someone will throw it over."

"If you'd been in different fields, if say, she'd been a lawyer, could you have been close to Courtney Logan?"

Cecile Rabiea had obviously been conceived without nervous mannerisms. She simply sat motionless in her grand suede chair. Finally she said: "I don't think so. She was a bit too rah-rah for my taste. Happy, happy, Patton, Patton, go team go. I mean, she was perfectly fine. It's simply a matter of personal style."

"I understand." I peered around her spare but expensive office. "You seem to have done pretty well." She wasn't a person given to modest

shrugs or self-effacing You've-got-to-be-kiddings. "Was Courtney as successful as you before she retired to become a full-time mother?"

"No." I counted one-banana, two-banana to give her whatever time
she wanted. Cecile would say only what she wished to say. I sensed my
pressing her or prattling to cover the silence would be counterproductive.
Anyhow, by the time I got to the fourth banana, she went on: "The first
two years she did as well as I did. Most of the others got a thank-you for
having been with us, Godspeed, and have a nice life, but the two of us
were asked to stay on. But then . . ."

She swiveled back and forth, which I sensed was a prelude to standing and saying Nice meeting you. So I leaned forward and said: "Listen,
you have my word that anything you tell me won't have your name attached. You're one of five names and I'm only going to report what was
said, not who said it."

When her nod finally came, it said, Okay, I believe you. "What a lot
of people don't understand is that everyone on Wall Street is really smart,"
she began. "I didn't get where I did by having the highest IQ, because I
don't. I'm only as smart as the next guy. You get ahead in this business by
being persistent. I think that's the point Courtney couldn't comprehend.
There's no magic. You do first-rate work. Courtney did, from what I
heard. But after that, you've got to be tenacious. When they finally let
you get near a client or potential client, you offer him your information
and your insights. *Then* you call to wish him happy birthday. You ask him
all about his fly-fishing trip. You help him get more office space. You give
him hot news on one of his competitor's earnings-per-dollar sales. You
take him out to dinner with his wife and your husband. Pretty soon,
you're an established fact in his life. When he needs an investment banker,
who does he turn to? To you. Except Courtney apparently felt her work
alone could speak for itself."

"Didn't anyone tell her it wasn't enough?"

"I'm sure something was said. But if you don't have a good sense of
people, if you can't read the subtext beneath their words, then you're not
going to get it. And you definitely won't be able to fulfill a client's needs,
needs maybe even he hasn't identified yet."

"So she had something of a tin ear for"—I paused—"the human
stuff?"

"I wouldn't put it that strongly. She just lacked a little something, it
always seemed to me. Maybe depth. Maybe sensitivity. Not that she
wasn't nice."

"But she didn't have the right stuff?" I asked.

"If you're a professional cheerleader, or a wife and mother, nice and
pretty and bright is more than enough. But not if you're an investment

banker. Clients expect commitment. Solidity. Now subtract from that the fact that once the research and the spreadsheets were done, the reports written and the meetings held, Courtney believed she'd done enough. To win the client. To earn the big money." Cecile got up from her big chair. I rose from mine. "She never comprehended that at that point her work was only half finished." She walked me to the door. "Courtney wasn't capable of going the full mile. She could only make it halfway. I'm sure at some level she understood she didn't have it. I remember feeling sad for her, but I knew her leaving was inevitable. And sure enough, once she had the baby, she didn't even try to get back into this world."

So I checked off the first name on Fancy Phil's list. Then I spent the next day and the one after that traveling into Manhattan, speaking with Courtney's former colleagues—an investment banker here, a real-estate mini-mogul there, as well as the chief operating officer of some mammoth conglomerate that apparently couldn't stop itself from buying anything that had the word "broadband" attached to it. Actually, I was surprised all these hotshots were willing to see me without due diligence, or at least a few probing questions. My guess was they all considered themselves, to one degree or other, traffickers in information—gossip as well as the financial stuff—and they wanted to be inside the Courtney Logan learning curve.

So I wound up sitting in some nifty leather chairs and drinking Diet Cokes in crystal tumblers proffered by private secretaries, all of whom had soothing mommy voices. But in the end all these custom-tailored VIPs could offer were similar recollections, that Courtney had been bright, ambitious, and friendly, although not quite top drawer professionally. That is, until I visited Joshua Kincaid.

"Hey, call me Josh!" he'd insisted before I could get to the second syllable of "mister." A smiley man, he wore a dark blue loose-weave shirt that looked like a screen door at dusk, tucked into black silk slacks. He was the least investment bankerish of the people on Fancy Phil's list. No wonder: He'd gotten an invitation to go elsewhere after one year at Patton Giddings and had wound up in his family's business. Now he was president of Kincaid, Kincaid & Kincaid, Mortgages.

We sat on a couch in his midtown office and worked on a plate of zucchini and celery sticks his secretary brought in. "Keeps my mouth busy when you're talking," he explained, "otherwise I'd never shut up. Bad habit, talking. This works, except by late afternoon . . . Do I have to tell you?" Apparently he thought he did. "Gas. Detroit could use me as an alternative energy source."

"Right," I managed to get in.

"That's why I walk home every night." Josh was sandy-haired and fair, with pipe-cleaner arms and legs that looked even longer and thinner because he was so lanky. The more he chattered the more it seemed as if he'd had a successful personality transplant from some short, Falstaffian donor. "So—let me think a second—I guess the last time I heard from Courtney was like about a year ago. May, June, I forget."

"What did she—"

"She wanted financing. For her company. Whatever it was called." I didn't even try to slide the word "StarBaby" in edgewise. "So I said to her, 'Courtney, if you want a jumbo mortgage, I'm the man. But we're not in the banking business.' Naturally, that took around fifteen, twenty minutes for all the back-and-forth I-think-the-world-of-you-but-I'm-giving-you-the-bottom-line. To tell the truth, if the baby-video thingie had sounded good, I might have put some of my own dinero into it, but it sounded like she was no way near getting it off the ground, much less fly, much less stay up. Because we aren't talking seed money. Uh-uh. Courtney wanted heavy bucks and she was nowhere near ready for such a big step and anyone with an IQ higher than cheesecake would have known it. You know what was really pathetic?"

"Wh—" I think I managed to say.

"That the Courtney I knew at Patton Giddings would have turned her own proposition down in two seconds flat. Maybe one. And I think she knew that. It's soooo weird. Everyone always said what a bubbly personality she had, and she did. But this time when we talked, her bubbles had bubbles. She went so over-the-top on the baby idea that I knew at some level—Christ, I *hate* myself when I say 'at some level'—Courtney had to know she wasn't going to make it. But she was desperately trying anyhow, and I give her credit for that. Except she really wasn't all that skillful at hiding her desperation, and someone who's really good, someone I'd want to back, would be. Good at hiding desperation, I mean. And you know what's even weirder?"

"What?" I asked, realizing that by the time his next sentence was finished I would have missed my chance of catching the 4:43 to Shorehaven.

"Right after Courtney was missing, guess what? *Another* woman—a banker in New Jersey. She disappeared without a trace, too!"

Talk about weird: my reaction. Not one shiver of Dear God! passed through me. Not one gasp. I can only guess it was because I have neither the temperament nor the cheekbones for high drama. I was tempted to say, Yeah, Josh, right, weird. Or maybe I was suppressing my excitement because I didn't want false hopes. In any case, if the notion of some connection did zip through either my conscious or subconscious mind, even for a second, I didn't seriously consider the possibility of danger. Like, Egad, a serial killer targeting smart women in greater New York. Or, some heinous plot by evil masterminds is afoot that I must steer clear of. If I had been the least bit fearful, unlike all those plucky protagonists in movies, I would have walked away from the Courtney Logan case, hopped the 5:03 back to Long Island, and taken guitar lessons. Or Chinese cooking lessons. Or had a face-lift and spent the rest of my years looking like Cindy Crawford's Semitic aunt.

But at that moment all I was aware of was that I'd spent two days of interviewing people in custom-made haberdashery and all I'd gotten was that Courtney was cheerful, smart, but not quite top-drawer professionally. Thus, when Josh's secretary followed up the zucchini and celery sticks with iced tea with an actual sprig of mint along with a plate of Oreos, I decided this might be a lead worth pursuing.

"Wow," was how I responded. "*Another* missing woman. Did you know her?"

"I met her once. We did the home mortgage for some major client of Red Oak—the Red Oak National Bank, little dippy three-branch operation—and Emily was there for Red Oak to make sure his feathers didn't get ruffled, not that we were out to do that."

"What was her name?"

"Emily something. Hispanic. Or Latino. I'm not sure: Is there a difference? I'm always afraid I'll use the wrong one and insult them. Or it could have been Italian. Anyhow, she was okay. Not a major deal at the bank, I don't think. But she seemed to have done a lot of work for this client and he seemed very comfortable with her."

"Do you remember who the client was?"

"A guy with English teeth. You know, two hundred teeth in one small mouth, like they have. Except he wasn't English. Probably New England. Or super preppy. I remember he kept saying 'cahn't' instead of 'can't.' Except they never say 'cahn' for 'can,' do they? So you know they're full of it."

"Do you remember his name?"

Josh sucked on an ice cube while he ruminated. Then he crunched it and offered: "Richard Gray? Gray Richards? He inherited like fifty-one percent of the shares of a company that manufactures containers for the pharmaceutical industry. His sister has the other forty-nine. Heavy, heavy money. Dumb, dumb guy."

"And this Emily was his personal banker, his contact at this Red Oak place?" Josh nodded, but before he could start talking again I asked: "Why didn't the bank give him his mortgage if he was such an important client?"

"The government won't let you lend more than fifteen percent of capital to any one borrowing entity, so with a small operation like Red

Oak . . . probably has two hundred million in assets, well"—he chuck-led—"you can do the math." If I had a day and a half and a calculator.

"Tell me what happened with her disappearance," I went on.

"I don't know. Like one day she was there and she went on vacation and she never came back and no one knew where she was."

"How old a woman was she?"

"Early thirties. At least that's the impression I got. I could be wrong, ha-ha. Come to think of it, I vaguely remember her introducing herself as an assistant branch manager and she was hand-holding an important client like Pharmaceutical Container Man and I thought, like, '*Assistant* branch manager?' and guess what I thought next? 'Glass ceiling.' Just so you know I'm a sensitive guy."

"Did they check to see if she had embezzled any—"

"Of course," he said, managing not to snicker at my too obvious question, although barely. "She didn't. So what else can I tell you? This Emily was zero-point-zero-zero percent like Courtney. I think whoever called to tell me about her said she was single and ultraserious and from what I can remember not good-looking and didn't have a personality be-cause I *can't* remember. You know what I mean? Like a total blank. Not *totally* total. I get"—he closed his eyes and swayed his head like a fortune-teller—"an aura of dorkiness. If I'm thinking of the right person. Actually, no. Not dorky. A loser."

"Could her path have crossed Courtney's?"

"Anything's possible," Josh replied, pulling an Oreo apart and scrap-ing off the filling with his top front teeth. "Is it likely? Statistically, I'd say like two shots out of a hundred. Red Oak is way down in South Jersey, and whoever was telling me about her disappearing mentioned—I think, but I wouldn't swear on a stack of Bibles—that she also lived somewhere around Cherry Hill. And Courtney had been out of it for years, for how-ever old her oldest kid is. Also, I doubt if a diddly little bank like Red Oak had much business with Patton Giddings, although anything's possi-ble, and, like Patton Giddings told me, basically, I don't know shit about investment banking. So for all I know maybe Emily and Courtney were best friends."

"Did they ever find any trace of her? Or her body?" I asked.

"I'm hardly on the A-list of calls to make when the cops or whoever trip over Emily something's body," Josh replied. "But I never heard any-thing else."

It was only when the train from Manhattan came up out of the tun-nel that I allowed myself to tingle with anticipation. How many young women in New York and New Jersey who are somehow involved in fi-nance could vanish into thin air or, in Courtney's case, into the family swimming pool? Sure, it was possible that the answer was forty-seven. But I had a gut feeling that somehow there was a connection between Courtney Logan and—I went straight from the Shorehaven station to my computer—Emily Chavarria.

Bingo? Maybe. According to the *Courier-Post,* Emily Chavarria, age thirty-one, a graduate of the Wharton School of the University of Pennsylvania, an assistant branch manager at an office of the Red Oak National Bank in Cherry Hill, New Jersey, left for a three-week trip to New Zealand and Australia on Friday, October 22. A week and two days before Courtney's disappearance. She was never seen again. On Monday, November 15, the president of the bank, concerned that Emily had not only missed the eleven A.M. trust department meeting but hadn't called in—two occurrences utterly at odds with her perfect-attendance, perfect-person record—had his secretary drive the fifteen minutes to Emily's place not far from Cherry Hill. When there was no answer at the door, the secretary called the police and, getting a key from the apartment complex's property manager, she and two cops entered the premises. No sign of disturbance. No sign of luggage. No sign of Emily Chavarria. Not then. Not since.

Chapter Twelve

Bless the World Wide Web. The articles from the local New Jersey newspapers I came up with mentioned Emily Chavarria belonging to two groups: an organization of New Jersey bankers and the South Jersey chapter of a national group called FIFE—Females in Financial Enterprises—which I guessed was preferable to WIFE.

I called Fancy Phil and gave him the assignment of finding out if Courtney had been a member of FIFE. Again he muttered about a wild-goose chase, I muttered back that if it was a wild-goose chase, I was doing it on my dime, not his. He grumbled, I'll get back to you. I was relieved it did sound as though he meant I'll get back *to* you rather than *at* you, a concern I would likely not have had if my first client had been a podiatrist. Anyhow, I went back to the articles. Emily came from a small town, Leesford, Oklahoma. I checked out Leesford on the Yahoo white pages: Only one Chavarria was listed. I called Chavarria, Pete, and got his wife on the phone. "Mzzz. Chavarria," I began, to avoid the Ms./Mrs. quandary which, for all I knew, might not have been completely resolved in Oklahoma, "my name is Judith Singer. I'm an investigator on Long Is-

land. I've been looking into a case that has some similarities to your
daughter's disappearance."

"Uh-huh," she replied.

"I hate to bother you during what must be an upsetting time for
you—"

"We don't . . . know where . . . she is," she cut in, pausing between
every two words. She didn't sound obviously broken up, but more like
someone not inclined toward conversation, though whether that was out
of taciturnity or grief I couldn't tell.

"I understand that. I'd just like to ask you a few questions, maybe
come up with some parallels between the woman who is missing on Long
Island and Emily." She didn't say anything, so I went on: "I know she was
scheduled to make a trip to Australia and New Zealand. Did you hear
from her, or get any postcards or anything?"

"No."

"I see."

"The police in New Jersey. They said . . . it didn't look like Emily
went."

I decided not to ask how they knew, because her answer might exhaust her willingness to talk. So I made a guess that the Jersey cops had
found she didn't board her plane—or something like that—and instead
asked: "Does Emily have any close friends on the East Coast?"

"I guess. I wouldn't know their names." Ms. or Mrs. Chavarria had
what I guessed was an Oklahoma twang, the sort of accent that makes
most people sound open and uncomplicated. Not her. Yet even though I
assumed she must be going through hell, there was something about
her—or maybe about me—that did not automatically evoke sympathy,
which made me feel both guilty and wary. I sensed my reaction might
mean something, because even though Greg Logan had been a cold fish
the night I'd gone to speak to him, I still had felt terrible about his loss. "I
told the police that," she added.

"Right. Do you know if Emily had a boyfriend?"

"I don't know. She came home for Christmas, but she only stayed
two days."

"So maybe she didn't get a chance to keep you up to date."

"Maybe," Ms. or Mrs. Chavarria replied.

"Was she going someplace else?"

"No. Christmas and New Year's is busy at the bank."

"Do you know if Emily ever went up to New York City, or to Long
Island?"

"No."

"Did she ever mention a friend named Courtney? Courtney Logan."

"No."

"Her maiden name"—I almost slipped and said "was," but caught myself in time to keep it in the present tense—"is Courtney Bryce."

"No."

"Can I ask: When was the last time you heard from Emily?"

"A couple of days before she went on her trip. Except the police say she didn't go. She called to say good-bye." There was no break in her voice at the word "good-bye." Not a flicker of emotion.

"Did she sound as if she were upset about anything?"

"No."

"Was she excited about her trip?"

"I guess."

"Did she say she was looking forward to it?"

"No."

Finding myself winding the telephone cord around my finger, I made myself stop when I noticed the upper joint turning cerise from strangulation. "Did the police from New Jersey ask you anything I haven't?" I finally asked.

It took a very, very long minute, but finally Ms. or Mrs. Chavarria answered: "They wanted to know where she kept her money."

"And did you know?"

"No."

"Did they say why they were asking?"

"Because she took her money out of the bank."

"All her money?"

"That's what they said. And out of her stocks and bonds."

After I gave her my number and asked her to call collect if anything else occurred to her, I hung up and stared at the phone as if I could see through the wires and circuitry. If only I could call Nelson was my first thought and Stop it! was my second. And my third was that years earlier he'd told me how most investigative work was supposed to be boring, following A to B to C and so on, in mind-numbing, skip-nothing sequence. However, he'd found the thoroughness of it comforting. Even if you were ninety-nine percent sure of knowing what G was, you still had to go through D, E, and F. For some mysterious reason, that time-consuming process sometimes led to bright, new ideas and almost always made for a stronger case.

Easy to be meticulous, I thought, if you're a cop and you have access to A, B, C, D, and so on. Go through missing people's houses, get to their bank or brokerage accounts, flash a badge, and ask your questions. I had no subpoena, no license, not even a business card.

However, I did have Fancy Phil, and he was turning out to be a not-

bad gumshoe. Courtney had been a member of the Wall Street chapter of
FIFE, he reported back, though in the past few years, what with living on
Long Island, having two young children, and running StarBaby, Greg
doubted she'd gotten to any meetings. I closed my eyes, trying to envision
a joint tea/meeting/cocktail hour between the downtown Manhattan
FIFEers and the South New Jerseyites, but I couldn't get a picture. I
probably exhaled a careworn sigh, because Fancy Phil demanded: Whatsa
matter? Nothing, I replied. But do you think you can go back and ask
Greg if Courtney was ever active in the association, or if she'd gone to
any event where she might have met members from other chapters?
There's a FIFE member from New Jersey who's been missing since November. What would stop me from asking him? he asked, sounding
cranky. Well, I replied, for starters he might think it curious, your asking
such a specific type of question. Curious? Fancy Phil declared. I'm his old
man. If Gregory can't trust me, he can't trust no one. If you think he
don't know that then you're not thinking.

I decided I needed to stop worrying the Courtney–Emily connection
to death. Unfortunately, I couldn't call Nancy, who would instruct me
not to be an utter ass. She and her husband had gone to a dinner party at
some *Newsday* executive's house where she was convinced Larry would
jabber on about Gothic architecture, mock her political observations, spill
red wine, laugh his raucous donkey laugh, and cost her her job. So I meandered into the sunroom, channel surfed, and came across *Stagecoach*
with John Wayne and Claire Trevor as the whore with the heart of
gold—one of my favorite westerns. I settled in for a night on the couch, a
squishy throw pillow perfectly supporting the back of my neck and my
head. Except I couldn't concentrate because I couldn't stop brooding over
what connection there could be between Courtney and Emily.

My first reaction was to consider more carefully Fancy Phil's suggestion that I was on a wild-goose chase. The two women had been in separate chapters of FIFE, which was probably a good-sized organization.
What were the odds against them knowing each other? As I'd always been
queen of the SAT verbals and among the deeply pathetic in math, I
couldn't begin to calculate what the chances were against two highly intelligent, reasonably successful and responsible women around the same
age winding up murdered or missing. Thus, unencumbered by fact, I
kissed off the wild-goose-chase hypothesis.

My next guess was that some third person—a nutcase, an icy, me-
thodical killer—had done them both in. Whoever it was might have been
cruel beyond belief—besides being homicidal—because he/she had
stashed Courtney in her family's swimming pool. Or maybe he/she had
just been pressed for time: trick or treaters out and about, people inside

the Logan house. Or he/she had to get rid of the body fast because he/she needed a day, a week, or, as it turned out, months, to get out of town? But when had he/she done the deed? Steffi and the children had seen Courtney driving away. Was it when she arrived back home with the mysterious missing apples? Could she have been murdered in the Grand Union parking lot and driven home in her own car? If so, how come there were no traces of blood from the head wounds? Or was she kidnapped, held, and killed a day or a week later? After all that time in the pool, how precise could the medical examiner be?

I turned off the TV, strolled into the kitchen, took out a bag of those pygmy peeled carrots, and started to chew. There was a big difference between the two dead/missing women, if indeed there was a Courtney–Emily link. Courtney's sapphire earrings that Greg had given her for her thirtieth birthday were where they were always kept, in the safety-deposit box. Other than the twenty-five thousand she'd helped herself to from around Mother's Day to Labor Day, her money was where it belonged, in joint bank and brokerage accounts and in her StarBaby business account. And possibly most important, there were no signs of planning; Courtney had actually said: "I forgot something. I just have to run to Grand Union for a minute."

Emily Chavarria, on the other hand, she of never missing a day's work, had been discovered missing only after the three weeks' vacation she was supposedly taking, when she didn't return to the Red Oak Bank. The New Jersey police had asked her parents about her money—specifically, where was it. How much had it been? Five hundred, five thousand, fifty thousand dollars? Five hundred thousand? Who knew? After all, Emily had been graduated from one of the best business schools in the country. She could have been a canny investor. On the other hand, maybe she'd lost a bundle guessing on the wrong dot-com stock.

I took another carrot, despite my chronic worry that I'd chew too fast, choke, not be able to do the Heimlich maneuver on myself, and would die not only needlessly but still sixteen pounds above the "large-boned" group on the height/weight tables. Anyhow, the difference between the two women was that there seemed to have been planning behind Emily's disappearance and, perhaps, murder. If she'd vanished or been killed after her last day of work, no one would look for her for three weeks. She'd left for her trip on a Friday, more than a week before Courtney disappeared. Just like someone with a perfect attendance record to finish up the complete week, I mused. Just like someone that meticulous to have a plan.

I was telling myself to stop imagining and start digging, that the guilty party, the person with the nefarious plan, had most likely been a third

person. Or, I mulled, going back to the Fancy Phil–wild-goose-chase theory, maybe there'd been no plan at all: Emily Chavarria's disappearance
and Courtney Logan's murder had nothing to do with each other. The
phone rang. I risked my life swallowing a not-quite-chewed bite of carrot
so instead of saying hello, I coughed.

"You okay?" Fancy Phil asked.

I coughed again and said, "Fine."

"Gregory thinks she could have gone to some meeting of that FIFE a
while ago. Probably before she got pregnant with Morgan. Or maybe
when she was pregnant but before she decided to stay home and be a
mother. But it could have been some other group. He's not sure."

"Morgan's five years old, right?"

"Yeah," he replied. "He thinks she went to Baltimore, but it could
have been Washington, D.C. What's this all about? That girl from New
Jersey who's missing? You really don't think—"

"Phil, it could be a wild-goose chase. I don't know." It occurred to
me I might be sounding crabby, but—I looked at the clock—it was almost
eleven and I was too tired to care. "But don't you want me to check on
this Emily Chavarria so I can rule out the possibility?"

"Do whatever the hell you want," Fancy Phil answered. A microsecond later he hung up the phone.

As I was getting into bed, I gave myself a figurative pat on the back:
You've got guts, I told myself, not being fazed by Fancy Phil's pique or
anger or fury, whatever the slamming down the phone had meant. Naturally, about twenty minutes later, just as I was floating in that brainless
state between wakefulness and sleep, I sat up wildly alert, panting with
fear. From outside the house, I'd heard the change of hum a car engine
makes as it slows down. It was just past the house. Whoever was in the car
could have been admiring the contrast between my purple pansies and
the violet ones planted around my mailbox. Except it was too dark for
that. Or perhaps the driver had merely shifted gears, although not being
one of those manual-transmission kind of dames, I couldn't be sure. On
the other hand, I didn't know Fancy Phil's precise address, but twenty
minutes would be a reasonable estimate as to how long it would take from
his town to mine. By the time I got up, locked the bedroom door, then
pulled back an edge of curtain to peek out the window, all I could see was
a pair of red taillights disintegrating in the blackness of the night.

Two days later, though, Phil and I were pals again, although not
chummy enough that I could expect an honest answer to the question:
Did you drive past my house after eleven Thursday night? So I didn't
bother asking it. Instead, I nodded respectfully as he related: "So I told
Gregory," Fancy Phil was explaining, " 'Hey, Gregory, it'd be nice to take

Morgan and Travis and that ugly nanny to a matinee of that *Sesame Street* show.' You wouldn't believe what that rat-bastard scalper charged me, but it's worth it. We won't get bothered." A weighty gold link bracelet on his right wrist and what looked like a cabochon emerald set in a braid of gold on his pinkie made no sound against the leather-covered steering wheel, but they sparkled in the sunlight.

At that moment his yacht of a car pulled into the Logans' driveway, right up to the front. Fancy Phil opened the old-money-green door with a key, punched four numbers into the alarm pad, and stood back, the compleat gentleman, to let me precede him inside. Well, with a compleat gentleman, one doesn't fret about being shot in the back or whomped on the head with brass knuckles. On the other hand, he seemed content just to follow me around.

"Who did the cooking?" I asked as we headed toward the kitchen. "The au pair, or Courtney?"

"Courtney. I gotta give her credit. She made an excellent meat loaf." As he tsked for a moment—probably more over loss of meat loaf than loss of daughter-in-law—I glanced around. Expensive. A floor of terra-cotta tiles of a hundred subtly different shades, that virtually announced: Not machine-made! Dark granite counters that gave off a blue sheen. Wood cabinets with glass doors that displayed blue-and-white dishes, some from a set of one of those classic Royal Copenhagen patterns, some that were likely antique pieces. There was every sort of drinking glass, from juice tumblers to brandy snifters. An elaborate stove. A double refrigerator with glass doors to display the Logan mustard collection and the family's preferences in yogurt. A floor-to-ceiling collection of cookbooks, from *Apples, Apples and More Apples!* to *The Elegant Vegetarian*.

I whipped out a pair of the translucent plastic gloves they sell in boxes (which I used to change the litter box whenever I baby-sat for Kate's loathsome, allergen-laden Persian cat Flakey). I wasn't quite sure why I felt compelled to bother with the glove business, but it had a hard-boiled detective-ish quality that appealed to me, and seeing Fancy Phil nodding appreciatively as if he approved of my cunning, I realized at the least it was a good marketing move.

Drawer by drawer, cabinet by cabinet, appliance by appliance, I went through the kitchen, but all I found was a small mound of black, hardened glop on the bottom of the oven, which I decided was more likely blueberry drippings than a clue, and an impressive accumulation of twist ties for plastic bags kept in its very own plastic bag. Finally, Fancy Phil and I leafed through every cookbook, then shook each one hard, a task he seemed to enjoy. Nothing fell out: no old grocery store receipts, no pre-mortem shopping lists, no "call so-and-so" notes.

By that time I was beginning to get that sluggish feeling of overload that comes with seeing an overambitious museum retrospective, so I passed on the rest of the downstairs. With Fancy Phil following me, I went upstairs and into Courtney's office. Pretty, done up in raspberry and pale green, feminine but not frivolous. Costly, no doubt. The trimming on the valance over the curtains had its own dainty fringe. I turned on her computer, an extravagant-looking IBM with one of those giant, flat monitors I'd never actually seen in person. The Windows clouds looked spectacular. Even better, no password was required. Five seconds later, of course, when I got to her financial program, QuickBooks, there was a blank box. I typed in "Courtney," "Court," "Gregory," "Greg," "Logan," "Bryce," "Lowenstein," "Olympia," "Princeton," and so forth, the way they do in movies, but gave up after her birth date and the kids' names failed.

"Was there any pet name Courtney or Greg called each other?" I asked.

From where he was sitting, on a window seat that overlooked the backyard and pool, Fancy Phil said wearily: "Beats the hell out of me. You done yet?"

"No. Listen, do you want to go downstairs and read"—from his curdled expression I gathered he did not find this suggestion appealing—"or watch TV?"

"Nah. I'll watch you." Oddly, the remark sounded more flirtatious than threatening, so I ignored it and double-clicked on Courtney's calendar database. No password! I studied her calendar pages from May through December, past the thirty-first of October when she disappeared. Play dates, Mommy and Me classes, weekly nail and monthly hair appointments, Saturday-night dates with people who had local numbers. Ditto with the dates that said "Filming" and "Meeting #1" and "Meeting #2." The contacts were all suburbanites with phone numbers from Shorehaven and the surrounding towns of Port Washington, Manhasset, Great Neck, and Roslyn. Zee Friedman's name was there for the weekends she worked. However, I found no sign of the name of the other assistant, the Wesleyan guy, who supposedly was holding Courtney's video equipment.

Steffi Deissenburger had told me that in the weeks before Courtney disappeared, she had gone out, dressed in suit and heels, very pretty, very business looking. She'd stayed away all day, returning shortly before Greg was due home. She'd warned Steffi that if Greg called to tell him she was shopping, an activity which he'd have no trouble in believing his wife capable. Nowhere were there any indications of these appointments, assignations, shopping expeditions, or whatever they were.

"Done yet?" Fancy Phil inquired, reasonably patient.

"No," I said, or possibly grouched. My hands were clammy under the plastic gloves.

I went back to two years before Morgan was born, when Courtney was still at Patton Giddings. This was easier because there were more blank days; whatever calendar she'd kept for business appointments did not seem to be on this computer. What was there, however, in 1994, on April 8, 9, and 10, the weekend after Easter, was FIFE EAST—BALTI-MORE.

"Hot shit!" Fancy Phil exclaimed. I turned on the printer and copied that month as well as all of 1999, when Courtney disappeared in October, until May 2000, when she was found. "Good work."

"Thanks, but it's not good work until I find out if Emily Chavarria was at that meeting also."

"How do you find that out?" he asked.

"Beats me. I'll figure something out."

"Wanna go out for a drink, Doc?" he asked.

"No thanks. I want to check out their bedroom. Her chest of draw-ers or whatever and her closet. You can go down and make yourself a drink. Trust me: I'm not going to heist her panty hose."

"Nah. I'll keep you company," Fancy Phil said.

To make an hour-and-a-half-long story short, I went through every drawer built into her walk-in closet, every handbag in the handbag cub-byholes—many Kate Spades and something that had cost a navy-blue alli-gator its life. I searched every pocket of every garment and I felt inside each size-six shoe on her rows of slanted shoe shelves, five pair of which were Manolo Blahnik, a label whose price I once inquired about upon seeing a pair of brown-and-black spectators with a flawless little bow and was told a dollar amount that actually caused me to gasp.

Deciding against using Fancy Phil as my stenographer, I wrote down from which article of clothing and which handbag I found the stuff I laughingly decided to call evidence: a fold-up hairbrush, two Clinique lipsticks in Copper Rose, a Clinique compact, a wad of purple bubble gum I assumed was Morgan's and not Courtney's wrapped in a sales re-ceipt, a Montblanc pen, and a sales slip from Barneys in Manhasset for an eighty-five-dollar candle and a fourteen-dollar lip balm. There was also a twenty-dollar bill in a pair of gray wool slacks. In other words, unlike the half ton of junk that could be salvaged from my closet and dresser, Court-ney Logan had left little behind; she'd been neater and more organized than I, though not quite obsessively orderly.

"Wanna go for cocktails?" Fancy Phil inquired, pausing an instant be-fore "cocktails" as if seeking a word refined enough for a lady.

I couldn't understand his sudden desire for my company, but I figured I ought to do better than my earlier No thanks. "I wish I could, Phil, but I have a date and I have to do all the girl things to get ready."

Refinement no longer required, he wiped his nose with the back of his hand. "Who's your boyfriend?"

"An English professor at the college where I teach."

"A *professor*?" he said, obviously controlling an overwhelming urge to shudder at the horror of such a union or perhaps at the notion of a man teaching English. I couldn't really tell. "You gonna marry him?"

When, slightly aghast, I said, "God, I hope not," he gave a genuine if monosyllabic chuckle. Then he said, "You're a good kid, Doc."

Actually, I had no Saturday-night plans. Postmodernist Geoff had found someone else willing to share expenses and was safely in England. With any luck, I was rid of him at least for the summer, if not forever. I'd spotted him during exam week walking across the quad (and brushing arms in a significant manner) with Promiscuous Patti of the music department and suspected she might be his companion in the Lake District. Anybody I actually wanted to see was being otherwise amused and I didn't have the patience to listen to any of my après-Bob single-women acquaintances recounting all-men-are-louses/all-men-are-little-boys/all-men-only-want-one-thing sagas.

On the other hand, I was too steamed up about Courtney–Emily possibilities to watch a movie or read a mystery. Instead, since Nancy wasn't around to stop me, I called Nelson Sharpe and spoke to his voice mail. He called back less than a half hour later.

By seven P.M. we were sitting across from each other at a table out on the gray wood deck of Fisherman's Folly, breathing in the salt air of Long Island Sound and whiffs of gasoline from the boats at the marina next door. "This isn't a social meeting," I said to Nelson after a waiter with a shaved head and a tiny, curly pigtail so unkempt I wouldn't have been surprised if he oinked set down Nelson's gin and tonic and my Campari and soda.

"You said that on the phone," he snapped. "You don't have to repeat yourself." He set his wedge of lime on the side of his cocktail napkin.

When we'd been lovers, we'd met during the day, when my kids were in school, so I'd only seen him in a jacket and tie or on the way to getting naked. Now, in a red plaid short-sleeved shirt and khaki slacks, he looked as if he'd embarked on an entirely different line of work—construction foreman or phys-ed teacher. His forearms were more thickly muscled than they had been. I tried not to imagine the second wife running her hands over his arms while they made love. I decided not to think that he was pumping iron to impress her, but as his accommodation to some new department fitness regulation. "I appreciate your seeing me on such short notice," I said congenially.

"Cut the crap, Judith." We smiled at each other and sipped our drinks. I didn't inquire: What did you say to your wife to get out on a Saturday night? He glanced at my ringless ring finger, then looked into my eyes and asked, "What do you want to know?"

"Have you heard anything more about the Courtney Logan case? I mean, there hasn't been anything in the papers or on TV for a while now. Are the Homicide guys just going through the motions because they think it's the husband?" Before he had a chance to talk, I added: "I'm not asking you to betray your oath or tell me classified police secrets."

"You're really smooth at this," he remarked.

"Thank you."

His eyes were still on mine. Over the years since we'd parted, I'd recalled so many details about Nelson, but this I'd forgotten, his ability to win any staring contest in the world. Never actually a contest: Nelson didn't appear to be holding your eyes to confront, the way an animal does to establish dominance. At least it had never seemed that way then. His velvet-brown eyes seemed always gentle and a little sad. I remembered long ago thinking he gazed the way he did because he was searching for something he desperately needed. Sitting there, listening to the soft lap of surf against the wood pilings of the deck, I told myself such romantic notions ought to have been tossed out right after my early adolescence, along with the stuffed animals and the pressed corsages. I pulled my eyes from his and turned my attention to my own lime wedge, squeezing it into the red bubbles of my Campari and soda. Naturally, I'd forgotten what I'd asked him.

Fortunately, he remembered. "I hear about the case every now and then."

"Have you heard anything about a missing woman in the south part of New Jersey in relation to it?"

Nelson shook his head. "Who is she?"

"She's a banker. She was scheduled to go on a three-week vacation to Australia and New Zealand. She left a little over a week before Halloween, when Courtney Logan went off to buy apples and never came back."

"It might mean nothing."

"I know. But it might mean something."

He took out a business card from his ID case and said: "What's her name?"

A little too late it dawned on me that if I gave Emily's name, the Nassau County cops would either be on the Turnpike in two seconds flat to

interview Emily's neighbors and colleagues or request the Jersey cops to
do it. I'd never get a shot. So I looked Nelson right in the eyes and lied:
"I don't know."

"You're lying."

"That's not very nice." Possibly I dilated my nostrils to illustrate how
offensive his accusation was.

"You're a lousy liar, Judith."

"I am not. You just know me too well." We finished our drinks and
ordered dinner while I filled him in on what I'd learned about FIFE and
Emily, without giving her name. However, I did offer up the name of the
Red Oak Bank in the spirit of fellowship.

If I wasn't ebullient, sitting out on that deck in the pink-and-blue
light of an early evening in June, at least I was as happy as I'd been in
years. I didn't want to count how many years. Looking at the menu, I
told myself it was because I was actually getting a chance to talk about
what truly enthralled me, and with a pro, no less. But by the time I decided on a small Caesar salad, without anchovies, and grilled halibut, I realized that most of my pleasure was being with Nelson. l still loved looking at him, hearing his voice again, being in his company. My sex drive,
which I long assumed I'd misplaced somewhere in my late forties, was
definitely in working order.

"How did you find out about this woman's existence?" Nelson asked.

"I was speaking with a former colleague of Courtney's who'd stayed
vaguely in touch with her. He didn't strike me as a genius. He'd gone
from investment banking to joining his family's company, giving mortgages or something. Anyhow, he'd met this New Jersey woman once doing some mortgage deal. Later someone told him about her disappearance. All he was saying was something like 'Weird, two women just
vanishing like that.' "

"What was his name?"

"What do I get in return?" I asked.

"My regards. Tell me his name."

"What do you think, this guy killed both of them?" Nelson said
nothing. "Trust me, he's not a murderer. A little blabby for my taste. Immature."

"Thank you for the psychological profile," he remarked.

"For the record, even though Courtney had been in finance and this
woman was, too, he wasn't able to come up with any connection between them." Still, I gave him Joshua Kincaid's name because I couldn't
come up with any reason not to. I felt pretty confident that since Nelson
wasn't in Homicide any longer, the name wouldn't get to them at least
until Monday morning. Which gave me Sunday. "What does it mean,

when someone vanishes into thin air? Do you assume they've been murdered and go looking for a killer?"

"If they're like your two women, leading a seemingly normal life?
Even if it's not some psycho raping and killing, it's still pretty often homicide. Most of the time the perpetrator turns out to be the boyfriend or
husband. If this Courtney or the other one was leading a wild life, with a
mountain of debt or some clear sign of irresponsibility, then we'd think in
terms of them skipping and trying a new life under a new identity. Those
types usually screw up just because they are so careless. It's not easy to disappear." Nelson fell silent for a moment. Too many intelligent men make
a big deal about thinking. They purse their mouths, close their eyes, and
say hmmmm, or they massage chins, or rotate their pens between their
fingers—while you breathlessly await the jewels of cerebration that will
fall from their lips. He, on the other hand, had a natural fluency of
thought to speech. When he needed to stop and think, he merely
stopped. No big deal, no hmmmms. "Even all those rich guys," he continued, "the master-criminals-egomaniacs who steal millions: Whenever
they move on, they usually leave a lot of pissed-off people behind. Ultimately, those people talk and the guys get caught."

"So you're thinking the other woman is dead, too?"

"Just sitting here like this, talking? Yes. But if I was a Jersey cop without too big a caseload, I'd keep looking."

"For a Courtney connection?"

"Sure. But mostly I'd want to look at her whole life."

"So you don't think it's a wild-goose chase?"

"I'd say it's something we should look into."

" 'We' meaning . . ."

"Not you and me, Judith."

My salad and his clam chowder arrived, which was fortunate because
I couldn't think of a withering rejoinder. I speared a small leaf of romaine
and suggested that in all the information he'd heard about the Courtney
Logan investigation, there might be a byte or two he could pass along that
wasn't Eyes Only or whatever big cop secrets are called. "Like your
Homicide guys are apparently all excited because Greg Logan withdrew
forty thousand dollars from their joint account and put it in his own
name. That was only in response to Courtney having taken twenty-five
thousand out of their joint accounts to throw away on StarBaby or cashmere bathrobes or whatever."

"Don't you think his lawyer mentioned that?" Nelson asked.

"So?"

"So, maybe someone did follow up." Except for an occasional flare of
temper, he'd always been a low-key, don't-show-your-cards kind of guy.

To another person, the "someone" following up would be interpreted as a reference to a detective in the Homicide unit of the Nassau County Police Department. But despite his low key, I knew the way Nelson played the game enough to realize he was the "someone" he was referring to.

"What did you find out?"

He gave me a small smile of acknowledgment and said: "The twenty-five thou she took: A buddy of mine in Homicide looked into it. There was no trace of it in any business or personal account. They couldn't find any photography equipment that would come to anything near that. Twenty-five thousand bucks just disappeared."

I left my fork in the salad, put my arms on the table, and leaned toward him. "Nelson, doesn't that tell you something?"

"What?"

"I don't know," I admitted.

"Listen—" I think he was on the verge of calling me "my sweetheart," which he'd often called me during our affair. But instead he said, "Judith, sometimes what looks like a clue is just a plain, old fact." I was about to argue that twenty-five thousand bucks would be a big, fat fact, but he held up his hand. "And sometimes cases don't get solved. Sometimes killers go free."

"I know, but I don't think Greg—"

"Why not?"

"He's too smart to have done it so stupidly."

"Let me tell you something." He clunked down his spoon alongside his soup bowl. "A lot of killers are stupid. Those cases almost always get solved in less than seventy-two hours. And sometimes a pretty smart person kills and thinks he's covered it up in a genius way, like the bad guy in Sherlock Holmes—"

"Professor Moriarty."

"—except they get arrested within seventy-two hours, too. Now take your friend Greg Logan."

"I'm not even going to bother saying he's not my friend."

"Good. He seems to have gotten everything he might have wanted: No wife, no nagging. Control over all his property, custody of his kids, bank and stock brokerage accounts. Okay, that's minus twenty-five thou, but either it's his cost of doing business or he found it and stashed it someplace. In any case, we would have solved this case in seventy-two hours, too, if the idiot who was in charge had done his job."

"Looked in the pool, you mean?"

"That? Sure. You know what almost seven months in a three-quarters-filled swimming pool does to a body?"

I pushed my salad plate away and asked: "Are you going to give me a

graphic description that will make me realize this sort of thing is too ugly
for me and I should stick to history?"

"I'm going to try."

"Don't they put chlorine in the water?"

"Fifteen gallons of liquid chlorine and algacide."

"You read the reports!"

"Reports, autopsy findings, a fast look at the video and crime-scene
pictures. I did it for you, my sweetheart." He said it in a mocking way,
but couldn't carry it off. Two red stripes of embarrassment appeared on
the tops of his cheeks. "So, do you know what all that time does to a
body, even with the chemicals?" he challenged. "See, it decomposes from
inside out, so the gases made it float to the top. It's *really* disgusting after
months in cold water. What's left of the outside of the body gets a waxy
look. You wouldn't have wanted to see Courtney Logan after they pulled
her out." He paused, waiting for me to tell him to stop. When I didn't, he
took a couple of ostentatious spoonfuls of clam chowder. "Of course her
face wasn't identifiable, and part of her head had been blown away by the
two bullets. But we had her dental records. Hey, do you know how the
skin on your hands and feet get when you're in the water a long time?" I
nodded. "Well, imagine how it would look after seven months."

I pulled back my salad plate, stabbed a crouton, and ate it. Nelson
looked annoyed that I didn't seem at least mildly nauseated. "How can
you tell whether a homicide victim has been murdered someplace else
and then moved if it's been in water for months? I mean, if she were shot
right by the pool, would it be different than if she were shot someplace
else and brought back?"

"There could be trace evidence at the scene. You know, signs the
body had been dragged from a short distance. Or an out-of-place bit of
material that indicates some distant location. Like a really unusual soil
sample that could tell us she wasn't killed on Long Island. But after seven
months, it's unlikely, and in Courtney's case, it didn't happen."

"Was there enough left of her to take fingerprints?" I asked.

"They got two or three, I think. Matched prints on her stuff in the
house."

I picked up a bread stick. "You read everything?"

"I read a lot of it," he answered cautiously.

"Did anything in all the evidence you read about strike you as odd,
or worth exploring further?" Slowly, he rocked his head from side to side:
maybe yes, maybe no. "What?"

"I'm not going to tell you."

"But you're good at this and the guy in charge of the case isn't!" He shrugged. "Wouldn't you want to see it solved? An innocent man may be—"

"I knew you would say that," he remarked.

"So what's your response?"

"If I see anything that can point to someone as the killer or exonerate your boyfriend's son, I'll be sure to mention it to one of the nonassholes on the case. Okay?"

"Nelson."

"What?"

"Are you ticked off with yourself for calling me your sweetheart or with me for staying on the case even though you warned me off?"

"You know what women always say?" he finally said.

I smiled. "What do we always say?"

"I feel like I'm being used."

"That? You know I'm not using you."

"Yes you are."

"Nelson, I'm talking to you as a . . . coworker."

"No. You're jerking me around to get information you shouldn't have."

The pigtailed waiter approached, tray in hand, and eyed us in the way a disapproving parent might look at children who didn't clean their plates. "Do you want me to hold your entrées?" he inquired, so overly polite as to be rude. Nelson was still giving me the evil eye, so I indicated to the waiter that he could take my plate. While he was at it, he grabbed Nelson's bowl, then promptly replaced it with his dinner, fried scallops and french fries. Finally, huffing as if he were used to serving a more sophisticated clientele, the waiter set down my fish and left us to our own devices.

"How about this?" I said. "I'll tell you some of my thoughts and you do with them what you want."

"Like . . . ?"

"Like first seeing if the New Jersey woman and Courtney had any connection. Didn't you say in the week or so before Halloween, Courtney put seven hundred plus miles on her car? She could have gone to Cherry Hill and back a few times."

"Maybe she drove to Colonial Williamsburg."

"Maybe Miss New Jersey had financial dealings with Courtney. All her money had been cleaned out of the bank. And Courtney was down twenty-five thousand."

"Even if they had some dealings, then we'd likely be looking for a third person."

"But the woman might have killed Courtney," I objected.

"Or Greg Logan could have done the job on both of them, stashed the bucks someplace, and is biding his time."

"If Phil Lowenstein had even an inkling his son might have killed Courtney, do you think he would want me looking into this?"

"Aren't you hungry?" Nelson inquired.

"I love lukewarm fish. Listen to me. Courtney Logan embezzled from her high-school candy-bar sales."

He started to laugh. "That's fifteen to life."

"Shush. Something was wrong with her. She told the young woman who did the videotaping for her that she had another person working for her. But there's absolutely no evidence of him. Courtney was lying."

"Maybe she was trying to puff herself up."

"And when she went out and the au pair didn't know where, she was supposed to tell Greg that Courtney was out shopping."

"What did you tell your husband three afternoons a week when we—"

"Not shopping, but how tactful of you to ask." When he didn't apologize I said: "Courtney told the au pair that Greg had too much on his plate. Except no one else, including the au pair, ever saw him as pressured or stressed. And as far as an affair goes, only one person thinks she could have been having one: her best friend."

"Well," Nelson said, "you're the historian. How often in the history of the world does a woman *not* tell her best friend?"

"That's my point. Courtney didn't. The best friend is very pretty and sweet but probably not the sharpest knife in the drawer. She said Courtney never told her anything about a guy. She just suspected it because Courtney seemed so distracted. Except I don't see them as best friends. Like everything Courtney did, there was this quality of superficiality to it.

"Nelson, over and over, people keep saying something was missing in her. At work she was this bundle of ambition but never gave it a hundred percent. StarBaby wasn't thriving and she lost interest. She tried to get Greg to open Soup Salad Sandwiches on the West Coast, but that was too big for him and my guess is she thought of him as small potatoes. She did all the suburban lady things, but dropped out of organizations she'd been really active in. I'll bet anything if she hadn't been killed, 1999 would have been the year of her last pumpkin cake. Baking, interior decorating, shoe buying, Mommy and Me classes. She wanted bigger things than just that. And I'll bet quiet, nebbishy, smart Miss New Jersey offered her a chance to satisfy some ambition that needed satisfying."

"You're telling me a story. 'Once upon a time there was a little girl named Courtney who looked at her candy-bar-sale balance sheet—' "

"I'm telling you a theory. I'm telling you what I know deep down is true, and don't say anything like 'Oh, the DA will really be impressed.' "

"What's New Jersey's name?" Nelson asked.

I found myself in the middle of another staring contest. I lost. "Emily Chavarria." And I spelled it for him.

When I got home, I set my alarm for six A.M. I wanted to get to New Jersey early, before all the Sunday-morning beach traffic.

Chapter Thirteen

All the way down the Turnpike, I kept pushing thoughts of Nelson out of my head. I was nervous that in the midst of some erotic reverie, I'd swerve into another lane and hit one of those interminable silver tank trucks, the ones with huge "Flammable" warnings. Instead, I sang along to a Dinah Washington CD and pondered how come New Jersey, an otherwise normal state, would elect to honor its notables by naming after them the service areas at which travelers urinate and eat suspect frankfurters.

I exited onto Route 73 and finally, despite my Internet driving directions, found The Meadows, Emily Chavarria's town-house complex, just outside Cherry Hill. I hadn't foreseen a gated community. How the hell was I going to get past the guard? Lowering the Jeep's window, I felt a droplet of sweat trickling from behind my ear down my neck. My mouth went so dry I was surprised I could part my lips. In a white shirt with a gold shield that proclaimed EVERALERT, the private security guard scowled at me with bulging eyes, then looked away. His Adam's apple bounced. "Yah?" Apparently he'd decided I was not an imminent threat to The Meadows.

"Hi!" I smiled. He didn't. I cleared my throat. "Uh, did Sergeant Wilson get here yet? To the place where Emily Chavarria lived?"

"Again?" The guard sighed with the weariness of an old hand who's seen it all far too often. "I thought they got done with that months ago."

"I guess not."

"No," he said at last, "nobody's got here yet."

"Oh," I said, trying to appear deflated, a performance that was lost as he was eyeing some sort of screen in his booth. "I'm supposed to give him . . ." I patted a brown paper bag on the seat beside me that contained an apple core and an empty water bottle. It made a crisp, official sound. "From the lab."

"Name?" he mumbled, picking up a clipboard.

"Dr. Singer." One of the boons of being a woman of a certain age is that we are often viewed as terminally lackluster and, thus, incapable of any interesting vice, including guile.

"You from the lab?"

"Yes."

I was already looking ahead. The complex was a series of wood and fieldstone structures that looked more than substantial enough for an up-wardly mobile assistant bank manager. He wrote down my name, directed "First left, first right," raised the barrier, and even managed a one-finger salute.

Emily herself, or the new owner of 807 Squirrel Court, had set a huge stone squirrel beside the front door of the town-house to greet visitors. Despite its toothy smile, I moved on and rang the bell of the attached house next door. A woman about thirty, with purplish-red hair—the result of that rinse that makes everyone who uses it look as if their ancestors hailed from a part of the British Isles with extremely peculiar climatic conditions—answered the door.

"Good morning!" I said, in a jaunty, dropping-in-at-nine-thirty-on-a-Sunday voice. The woman tightened the belt on her pink, waffle-weave bathrobe. "I'm Judith Singer. I've been hired by the family to look into Emily Chavarria's disappearance." I didn't say whose family, a sign of my growing skill at subterfuge. I suppose it was to my credit that I felt a pang or two of guilt.

Maybe the woman picked up my discomfort because she opened her door wide and stepped back so I could come in. "Hey," she greeted me. "Beth Cope." A man about the same age strolled into the hall. "Judith Singer," she introduced us, "my husband, Roberto Anello. Hon, Judith is a detective. She's looking into Emily's disappearance."

Roberto, in a corresponding bathrobe in blue, flared his nostrils, but he was only suppressing a yawn. Lacking the hair for a purplish-red rinse (or for anything else for that matter), he scratched his scalp. Then, having come to some sort of decision, he asked with considerable courtesy: "Do you have any ID?"

Oy, I thought. "Sure," I said. I opened the latch on my handbag, took out my car keys, cell phone, and Palm Pilot and poked around in the utterly ID-free abyss.

I was saved by Beth's "Hey, no problem" and Roberto's silently seconding the motion, because, within seconds, I was in their kitchen. I sat across from them at a table between a red leatherette booth, the sort found in diners. As the walls were festooned with an Eskimo Pie clock and archaic signs like PEPSI COLA'S THE DRINK FOR YOU! and OBERMAIER'S YUMMY PIES, I concluded they were 1950s aficionados. Ergo, I fit right in.

"You were living here last October, when Emily supposedly left for her trip?" They nodded simultaneously. "Did she talk to you about it at all?"

"Not much," Roberto said. "It's like we—Beth and I—met that night after work like we always do and went grocery shopping. Friday shopping." Beth beamed as her husband spoke. "We came in around sevenish." She nodded vigorously in agreement. They seemed such a pleasant couple, and obviously pleasant to each other. I found myself wishing that Kate would have a relationship like that instead of with MTV Adam and his zoot suits.

"I guess we remember because we told the police all about this sometime in . . . I guess back in November," Beth added. "It was incredibly spooky. I mean, Cherry Hill is not the kind of place people vanish from."

"So Emily's putting a suitcase into the trunk of her car—" Roberto went on.

"Which was . . . ?" I asked.

"A Toyota something," he replied. "I think an Avalon." I noticed, he wasn't actually bald. A layer of pale fluff covered his scalp, the sort of near hair you often see on a newborn. "And I said, 'Hey, Emily, need any help?' because the suitcase was half the size of her and she looked like she was struggling. She said no thanks. Then we asked her where she was going. She said Australia and New Zealand. For three weeks. I thought, Hey, what a great trip!"

"And you know what I thought?" Beth chimed in. "Three weeks on one suitcase? She's a better woman than I am. She only had that one suitcase in the trunk and then she closed it."

"She was driving herself to the airport?"

"I guess," Roberto said. "Personally, I'm not a great believer in long-term parking."

"Did she seem excited about the trip?" I asked.

"Not that I could see," he responded. "She had a flattish personality.

Besides being quiet. I mean, she wasn't quiet and weird or quiet and nervous. Just . . . quiet. She wasn't, what do you call it? A big talker."

"It's like this," Beth added. "We were just 'Hey, how's it going?' neighbors."

"Okay," I said. "Even if she didn't say anything, do you have any sense how it did seem to be going for her around the time she left and didn't come back?"

"I couldn't tell," Roberto answered, "but Beth has a theory."

I looked to her. "Well," she exhaled meaningfully. "I feel bad saying this but she was as close to being totally dull as a person can get." I nodded. "And she looked dull. No makeup except this kind of awful frosted coral lipstick that must have been a freebie, one of those cosmetic company mistakes that become gift-with-purchase. You know what I mean. Anyway, Emily wasn't homely or anything, but she didn't have lots to work with. Small eyes. Hair about here"—she indicated the middle of her neck—"which is neither here nor there. Except in the last couple of months she started to look better. Much better. Not noticeable makeup, but whatever it was worked because she suddenly looked like she had some life in her face. And she let her hair grow and it was definitely, definitely highlighted. I mean, September, October, and it kept getting blonder and blonder instead of darker."

"She still wasn't what anyone would call a babe," Roberto interjected.

"But I told Roberto: 'I bet she's someone's babe!' "

Beth and Roberto turned out to be the best The Meadows had to offer. One woman screeched from behind her closed door: "What? What? Who? What?" I shrieked "Emily Chavarria" until my throat hurt and I began to worry that someone six town houses away would call the cops. Across Squirrel Court, another couple knew her, but not as a neighbor—only as a photo in a newspaper captioned MISSING. Everyone else was out praying or golfing.

Unable to figure out what to do next, I longed for guidance, *Detection for Dummies*. I drove around Cherry Hill aimlessly. Eventually, I wound up in the parking lot of a giant mall, the kind of place that has too many stores selling the sort of candles whose scent is so belligerent no packaging can contain it. I opened the car window, turned off the engine, leaned back in the seat, and closing my eyes, thought about what it takes to go to Australia besides a fondness for marsupials.

Arrangements. Had Emily bought a ticket and then simply not shown up? Were Australia and New Zealand a cover for other plans, like establishing a new identity in some far-off place? Maybe she'd bought a ticket to Lima, Peru, or Lima, Ohio, and was, at this very minute, snickering over her *rebanada* or Froot Loops as she contemplated her successful murder of Courtney Logan. Or was I being too hasty? Was Emily also a victim? Was there some evil genius preying on FIFE members or on smart women or some other category I couldn't figure out? Were any other members of FIFE mysteriously missing or murdered? Was some rogue FIFEer running amok? Was there some connection between Greg Logan and Emily Chavarria I'd missed?

Before I finished each question, another would pop up. I opened my eyes for an instant just to make sure there were no Hannibal Lecters sautéing fava beans outside the open window of my Jeep. Safe. I tried to imagine Emily's life. Coming to an Ivy League school from a small town in Oklahoma. Whether shy or nerdy, quiet. Living a quiet life, seemingly brightened only by coral lipstick.

Yet according to Beth and Roberto, she'd begun coming out of her shell. As the days grew shorter, her hair grew blonder. Her face brightened. To me, this Emily didn't sound like someone singing the blues. In fact, Beth had suggested the possibility of a man. I could relate. Was it a coincidence that with the mere notion of Nelson back in the general vicinity of my life, I'd gone to the hairdresser the previous week to become a bit more intensely brunette? If I'd had blond tendencies, the way Emily apparently did, no doubt I, too, would have spent fall getting sun-streaked.

So who was the new guy? Definitely no one I could come up with on a late Sunday morning. In fact, the only man I could think of mentioned in connection with Emily was the bank client Joshua Kincaid had called Pharmaceutical Container Man. What the hell was his name? In noir whodunits, the detective calls his secretary and says, "Listen, dollface, what was so-and-so's name?" And with two cat-claw nails, doll-face takes the chewing gum out of her mouth and says . . .

Right! Richard Gray or Gray Richards. And he owned fifty-one percent of his family's company. Could Emily have been yearning for one of those plain-girl-takes-off-her-glasses-and-rich-guy-who'd-overlooked-her-goes-hubba-hubba moments? She sounded too serious a careerist to mix business and romance, but Josh Kincaid had mentioned something about her hitting the glass ceiling, so I wasn't going to rule it out—especially since I had nothing else.

I checked my voice mail. Four messages! To many, no big deal. To me, a wildly eventful morning: Fancy Phil reported that Greg had never heard of anyone named Emily Chavarria. My son Joey announced he'd been hired by the *New York Times*'s Arts and Leisure section to do an article on the Coen brothers. Nancy, her Georgia tones sugary as pecan pie, demanded, "Where the fuck are you?" And then Nelson, in his bland cop voice: "I'll see you at noon today, Sunday—" I glanced at my watch. Nearly eleven. Even flying, there was no way I could make it back to

Long Island. "—at Carlo's Big Cheese Pizza, Forty-seven Donovan Street, Cherry Hill." Cherry Hill?

If stomachs can have seizures, mine did, contracting over and over before finally solidifying into a pain-producing object north of my navel. How the hell had he known? I tried some relaxation breathing I recalled from a yoga video I'd watched two or three times: in through the nose, hold, hold, hold, out slowly through pursed lips. All right, he'd called at ten forty-two, so clearly he was in or near Cherry Hill. Either there had been a magic moment when he'd spotted me tooling around in a red Jeep with New York plates and a St. Elizabeth's College faculty parking sticker or he, too, had gone to check out Emily's house and discovered from Everalert or Beth and Roberto that a lady from the lab/investigator for the family had left just a short time before. From the tone of his voice, it didn't sound as if he were planning on a fun lunch.

Being one of those drivers who needs very specific directions—"Immediately after an off-white stucco house with a cutesy mailbox decorated with little girls holding a daisy chain, bear right onto North Peanut Street . . ."—I spent a good part of the next hour locating Carlo's Big Cheese, then trying to outwit a traffic circle in order to reach it. So when I walked into the place in a state well beyond frazzled, I felt grateful that Nelson had always been one of those people for whom noon meant precisely that. I'd have time to select a table not in direct sunlight, check to see if the ladies' room was go-able in, and lighter of bladder and spirit, sit down and breathe some more.

Except there he was. No casual short-sleeved, extensor-muscle-baring shirt like the night before. Gray suit, white shirt, blue tie. While it didn't shout "Cop," it said something loud enough for Carlo, or whoever the guy in the tinted glasses behind the counter was, to have seated him at a discreet corner table.

"Sit down, Judith."

Although it occurred to me to inquire "Is that a command or an invitation?" I merely sat. What I finally did say was: "You didn't mention last night that you were going to Cherry Hill." When that did not produce a response, I got up, left my purse on the chair, and went to the ladies' room. When my return received no reaction, I stood beside my chair and said: "Listen, I've lived through a not-great marriage and both my children's adolescences. So if you're planning on continuing the silent treatment, know that I'll find it incredibly boring and I'll be forced to lunch elsewhere."

"I wasn't giving you the silent treatment," he finally replied.

I sat down. "What was it, then?"

"I was at a loss for words." I wasn't ready to smile yet, which was fortunate, because he was in ice-cold mode. "I was amazed at how stupid you were," he continued, "going to the guard and saying you're from the police lab."

"It got me in," I retorted.

"It got you in, but if you're going to pull that kind of crap, you shouldn't leave your real name."

"Next time I'll have an alias ready." Nelson stood. I thought he was walking out, but he only strode across the restaurant and said something to the man behind the counter. When he came back I said, "Can I assume you didn't tell him to call the Cherry Hill cops and have them come and arrest me for false something?"

"I told him a plain pizza." I nodded. "Are you still drinking Diet Coke?"

"Still. So, did you just hear about me from the security guard or did you get a chance to meet Beth and Roberto?"

"I met them."

"Good. Nice couple. So you know that Emily left with a suitcase."

"I know," he said, hooking his finger over his tie, loosening the knot, then opening the top button of his shirt. "Now tell me what you make of all this."

"Then will you tell me?"

"Come on, Judith. I gave up a day off to look into this business. I don't have time to fool around." God knows what kind of a smirk crossed my face, because he added: "Cut it out."

"Fine."

"Talk."

"I wish I had a lot to tell you," I began, "but all I've done so far is speak to the neighbors. So you probably heard what I heard: Emily was acting as if things were looking up. I don't know what was going on with her at the Red Oak Bank. Come to think of it, I don't know what was going on with her *not* at the Red Oak Bank. But at the very least it seems to me when a woman changes her appearance for the better, she has a different sense of herself, or some new expectations. Maybe she'd gone for therapy and had new feelings of self-worth, which for her meant lightening her hair and contouring her cheekbones."

"What?"

"Never mind. Some makeup thing. Or it could be she found a man."

The pizza guy came from behind the counter, set a Diet Coke before me and a beer in front of Nelson, both in giant red, green, and white paper cups with the slogan EATA PIZZA spiraling from bottom to top. "Did you happen to find out if there was a man?" Nelson asked.

"No. Does that make us even or are you ahead of me?"

"Even."

"Let's talk about Emily's travel plans," I proposed.

"Go ahead," Nelson said.

"Well, I was sort of hoping that after last night when we'd discussed how Emily seemed to have made plans and how Courtney seemed to have made none—beyond buying apples for her kids—you might have come up with some information on where Emily did go. From credit cards or something."

"You're really an ace at this detective stuff, Judith." For the first time since I'd walked in, he smiled, openly, generously, as if he'd forgotten he was angry. " '. . . credit cards or *something*'?"

"Go ahead," I said. "Talk about whatever you want to talk about."

For a little longer than was comfortable, he looked into the foam on his beer. "You know, I have a problem about talking to you." I started to be amused, but then he added: "I'm serious."

He was. "What's the problem?"

"I have to think about anything I say to you, Judith. I could be more, whatever, open with you. Except there's a direct line between you and your friend Phil Lowenstein."

Maybe I shouldn't have been stung by this remark, or stunned either, but I was. "Do you think I would betray you, Nelson?"

"No; no, I don't. But like I tried and tried to tell you, Phil isn't a nice man. He's a dangerous and sometimes violent man. Look, under normal circumstances, even though all these years have gone by with us not seeing each other, I know . . ." For a second he put his hand over his heart. "I know you would never do anything to hurt me. Even under abnormal circumstances. But what if this guy put a gun to your head? It wouldn't be out of character, you know. What if you reported certain information to him and he wanted to know where it came from? So you'd say, 'Sorry, Phil, it's a privileged communication.' Do you think Phil is just going to say, 'Okay, I respect your right to protect your sources'? Or do you think he'll grab you by the throat and start squeezing until you manage to cough up my name?" He took a paper napkin from the napkin holder and folded it in half, then in half again. "Listen, my job is on the line. Other than my kids, it's pretty much my life. If it somehow got out that information I gave you found its way to Fancy Phil Lowenstein, I lose my living, my reputation. Forget being shamed. I'd be risking jail."

"I want to live to see grandchildren," I said quietly. "So if there were a gun to my head, well, I don't know what I would do. So I guess it's best if you don't tell me anything."

We sat in the sort of silence that is only possible between two old friends or two lovers so assured of the other's admiration that there is no need to charm or even to speak. I don't know how long we didn't talk, but finally the guy in the tinted glasses appeared beside our table and set down the pizza. I was getting busy fighting the mozzarella when Nelson said: "Just on the basis of a preliminary check, Emily didn't use the Amex or Visa that were in her name after Thursday, October twenty-first, the day before her final day of work at the bank."

"You don't have to tell me this."

"And forget her not getting on a plane. There's no record of her even buying a ticket to Australia or anyplace else since before Christmas 1998, when she went from Philadelphia to Oklahoma City to visit her family. So if things were looking up for Emily, or she had big expectations, I'd like to know what they were."

We sat in Carlo's until the leftover slices of pizza congealed. We left the Courtney Logan case and chatted about safer subjects. The public's Gore–Bush blahs versus the electricity we'd known as kids watching JFK run against Nixon. Police-department politics compared to the politics of academia. Who was worse, Kate's boyfriend or his son's fiancée (whom Nelson referred to as the Syosset Slut), who wore microscopic leather miniskirts and too-tight tube tops. Neither of us got near the topic of Nelson's having a wife.

When we got outside it was not only hotter, but more humid. I didn't want to leave, but I didn't want to stand there and feel my hair growing into a deranged frizz. At that instant he touched my arm and said: "I'll drive."

The words "I think I'd better be getting home" seemed to be on their way from brain to mouth. Nevertheless, I found myself opening my handbag and dropping in my car keys. I don't remember much about the short ride except staring at the blank screen of one of those global positioning systems and thinking, What if he can't? What if I don't? What if it's awful? What if the motel room or wherever he was taking me smells of insecticide? What if one of us (no doubt him) really doesn't want to see the other again afterward? Would there have to be one more tryst for courtesy's sake? What if he'd been imagining me as I was twenty years ago? What's going to happen when we leave and I have to go home alone and he goes back to the guidance counselor? In matters of the heart, I've always had a tendency to look on the bright side.

He pulled into a Holiday Inn. Since in our earlier days we'd met in one of his friends' apartments, I immediately started agonizing over motel protocol. Check in together? I linger while he goes to the front desk? He pays? Dual, egalitarian credit cards? Untraceable cash? "I have the key," Nelson remarked as we pulled into a parking space.

"I guess that makes you an optimist."

"About you, yes." As we walked through the halls and took the elevator upstairs, he held my hand. His skin felt so hot I knew, besides his excitement, that my fingers were freezing. "Judith," he said as he slipped the magnetic key card into the slot, "this isn't going to be painful. You're not going to need anesthesia. Relax."

I stood beside the low, king-size bed that overwhelmed the small room. A sliver of sunlight slipped inside where the curtains didn't quite meet and made a diagonal across the bedspread. I was saying, "God, don't you wish we could get past the next couple of minutes and—" when he kissed me, a gentle, leisurely kiss to show me No, I don't want to get past anything.

Amazing, I suddenly realized, how completely I remembered his lips, the prickles of his beard, the same aftershave that smelled like lemons and witch hazel. He was only a couple of inches taller, so it was the easiest thing in the world to kiss him. I thought, I want to do this for hours, but I found myself pulling off his jacket, his tie, unbuttoning his shirt. After he eased off my cotton sweater, I was the one who threw back the spread, hauled off his undershirt, drew him onto the bed before I'd even bothered to slip off my shoes. "Please," I whispered.

"Listen," Nelson told me, "I don't know about you, but I don't have to be anyplace until tomorrow." He slid his hand behind my back and, in a move I hadn't forgotten, unhooked my bra and tossed it aside in a single fluid motion.

All through the afternoon we kept murmuring the helpful hints lovers offer each other: "Easy," "Slower," "Faster," "Harder," "More."

At the end of the day, he said, "You know how women are always needing reassurance and how men aren't supposed to be good at giving it?"

"I've heard words to that effect."

He propped himself up on his elbow. "So, here goes. I loved you way back when. I love you now. And I loved you all those years in between."

"Same here, big boy," I told him.

"No. You have to actually say it." So I did.

I left him an hour later. I can't say the possibility of intimacy hadn't occurred to me, because even before having dinner with Nelson the previous evening, I'd shaved my legs so closely I'd taken off the first two layers of the epidermis. However, I didn't want to stay the night with him. Toothbrushes, deodorant, and makeup were all buyable in New Jersey, but I didn't want to have to bear the chilly loneliness of daybreak after a night of his warmth. He drove me back to the parking lot of Carlo's Big Cheese and we parted with soft-spoken I-love-yous.

I got back to Shorehaven with time to spare until sunset and drove over to Nancy's without even calling first. Maybe subconsciously I wanted her to wag her finger at me and howl "Adulteress!" but instead, after agreeing to stay for Larry's barbecued swordfish kabobs, an admittedly high price to pay, I dragged her upstairs to her computer and asked her to access a couple of *Newsday*'s databases, like Lexis and Nexis.

"Have you taken leave of your senses? No, don't even bother answering. Do you have any idea how much the charges are? How can I justify—"

"You don't have to justify anything. Just say you used it for some personal research and pay them back."

"Why can't you go to the library?"

"Because it's seven-fifteen on a Sunday night, that's why."

"Wait till tomorrow."

"Now."

"Oh Lord! I can't—"

"Nancy, I don't have time for your Butterfly McQueen act. You know how a person should be willing to lay her life on the line for her best friend? Just access Nexis and we'll call it even."

Muttering "shit-ass-rat-fuck," she got on-line and typed in all the permutations of Gray or Grey and Richard or Richards, the Pharmaceutical Container Man. It took only seconds and some scrolling backward to discover that in April 1998, Richard Grey and his sister Marlena Grey Eugenides offered shares of their family's company, Saf-T-Close, in a public offering.

"Let me think," I said. "That's one of those IPOs. Initial public—"

"I know what it means, turkey. But what does it *mean?*" Nancy asked.

"I think . . . I'm not one hundred percent positive, or even seventy-five percent positive, but I think it means that Emily Chavarria knew that the bank's big client, Saf-T-Close, was going to sell stock to the public. Maybe she got in on the ground floor and made a bundle."

"What's wrong with that?"

The truth was, I had no idea. "Keep looking," I ordered her, a little imperiously, but I was standing beside her aching to get on-line and she refused to relinquish control of either her chair or the mouse. "Boring, boring, boring," I muttered as she clicked on various thrilling items, such as Saf-T-Close hiring Charles W. Swarski Jr. as its new director of marketing and its earnings per share increased by eight percent in the quarter ended December 31, 1998. Then I said, "Look!" On October 11, 1999, Chapman-Bohrer, a major drug manufacturer, announced its acquisition of Saf-T-Close at fifty dollars per share. " 'At close of business the previous Friday,' " I read off the screen, " 'Saf-T-Close's final price on the NASDAQ was thirty dollars per share.' "

"All right!" Nancy cheered. Almost immediately, she deflated. "What does this have to do with Courtney Logan?"

"Insider trading!"

"What about insider trading?" she persisted.

When I tried to explain and the words didn't come, we agreed to reconnoiter and meet again in five minutes. Nancy made a beeline to her

bedroom phone to call her broker at home and I stayed by the computer
and called Kate on another line. Fortunately she answered, making it un-
necessary to expend enormous stores of energy being civil to Adam.

It used to be, Kate explained, that insider trading applied to sales or
purchases of stock by a company's employees, people who have confiden-
tial information about the company's plans. These days, she said, it also
applied to people who are tipped off by an insider even if they don't work
for the company or owe it any legal duty. A banker like Emily could be
one of these people. If Richard Grey tipped her off about the sale, she
couldn't buy Saf-T-Close at a lower price and then flip it the next day or
week and nearly double her money.

I said good-bye to my daughter and sat down at the computer and
went back to the April 1998 announcement. The price of the IPO was
eleven dollars per share. If Emily had a piece of the IPO, which was probably legal, she could have made a nice profit on Saf-T-Close. But what if
she wanted more? What if, besides her profit on the IPO, she wanted to
put even more money on a sure thing, the acquisition? How would she
work it?

Nancy returned and took off her imaginary hat to me. "The broker
says the deal with insider trading is that you get someone else to buy the
stock and not set off the SEC's computer alarm or whatever."

"So Emily could have gotten Courtney to buy the stock," I mused.
"But how much good would that do? Courtney only had twenty-five
thousand."

"For someone smart you're so fucking muddle-headed," she said with
her usual delicacy.

"What are you saying?"

"I'm saying, peabrain, that if indeed any of this is true and not a fig-
ment of your overheated imagination, then Emily might have given
Courtney some bucks, big bucks, with which to buy said shares of Saf-T-
Close and maybe agreed to give her a nice percent of the profit for her
trouble. And maybe, you nit, Courtney wanted to keep the money all for
herself. I mean, what less can one expect from a person who has the
panache to embezzle from a Crunch-Munch sale? And maybe Emily got
pissed, made some careful plans"—she took a deep breath and kept going—"came to Shorehaven for a tête-à-tête with Courtney, and two shots
later—"

"Courtney is dead and Emily is free to start a new life where there
aren't any glass ceilings!"

Chapter Fourteen

The woman from FIFE sounded unduly nasal, as if she were holding her nose in a juvenile attempt to disguise her voice. "You're the second call about this today," she said. For a second I was flummoxed, not a reassuring state of mind on a Monday morning. Who? What? Why? Who else could possibly . . . ?

"Oh," I replied, "you mean Captain Sharpe of the Nassau County Police Department." I did my best imitation of a warm chuckle. "I guess he's one step ahead of me this morning."

"I'm sure if he wants to share the details, you can get them from him," Ms. Lovely said, clearly not finding my warm chuckle either credible or endearing.

"Probably not. It would take me a week to convince him to give me the correct spelling of Emily Chavarria's name." The day before, Nelson had been willing to share information with me (to say nothing about what else he'd shared). But not only didn't I want to rely on his generosity again, I didn't like the idea of being a damsel in distress who needs saving by a hero. "Look," I went on, "I'm doing this on behalf of the family. Obviously they're frantic. All I need to know is if Ms. Chavarria and Ms.

Logan were at the same meeting at any time, if they could have met. Please. For the family."

"All right, all right. I told the captain . . . They were at the same meeting in '94, in Baltimore. It was in April. FIFE East. But as I explained to the captain, there were over forty delegates. I, personally, have no way of knowing if they ever said two words to each other. I wasn't even here in 1994." Both times she said "the captain," she got a little breathy. I figured Nelson had been troweling on the gruff charm.

"Is Ms. Chavarria still active in the organization?"

"The captain asked that, too."

"I suppose there's a certain investigatory mind-set." I figured "mind-set" was one of those corporate words coined to evade the need for actual thinking and would warm the cockles of Ms. Lovely's heart. "Was she still active?"

"Yes, in the South Jersey chapter and in FIFE East. Not in National."

"And what about Courtney Logan?"

A hurricane of a sigh came over the phone. "Paid her dues. Was she active in the Wall Street chapter? I'm afraid you'd have to call them."

"Okay, whom should I call?"

"I can't give out such information."

In movies, private investigators are always slipping people twenties to get information. I couldn't imagine saying, Hey, Ms. Lovely, if you cooperate, I'll stick a couple of sawbucks in the next mail. So I merely said: "Look, I know you must be horrendously busy—"

"I am and I really have to—"

"—and I wouldn't be bothering you if not for the family. If you could tell me the name of the head of the Wall Street chapter—" Before she could slip a word in edgewise I added: "And also, if you could email or fax me the list of people who were at the Baltimore meeting, I know they'd be grateful." With another whooshed exhalation, she gave me the name and agreed to fax the list. I was on the verge of asking what, if any, other questions Captain Sharpe had asked. But at that moment she got another call and got rid of me fast.

The president of FIFE Wall Street was a hotshot at Merrill Lynch, so I wasn't expecting anything. But she took my call and told me no, Courtney Logan hadn't been to any meetings or events that she could remember. She herself had of course heard the name and about the murder, though couldn't recall ever meeting her. However, she really should write a note of condolence to the husband, poor guy. I was nearly in shock over her acute niceness, but nevertheless was able to give her Greg Logan's name and address.

Shortly after that, a faxed list of the Baltimore attendees arrived. Now that I had it, I didn't know what to do with it short of entering every name on a search engine and seeing if any articles on serial killers or missing women came up. But I decided I had other fish to fry first, so I shoved it into the desk drawer I used for papers and clippings I really wanted nothing to do with yet couldn't bear to throw out.

Then I paced around the room for the seven whole seconds such a circumnavigation took. When I'd returned to graduate school after Bob and I decided not to have another baby, I'd taken over the fourth bedroom as an office. It was so small that whenever I felt guilty about only having two kids, about not adding another Jew to the world to help replace the lost ones, I'd think that the third child would have untold resentments at having gotten stuck with what, essentially, was a cell with sheer white curtains.

I sat back down and returned to the *Courier-Post* Web site, where I downloaded the piece about Emily's mysterious disappearance. Then I spent a half hour muttering "Shit!" until I finally figured how to extract the photograph from the body of the article. Ten minutes later, after reaching Steffi Deissenburger, I emailed the photo to her. I thought it was a pretty nifty idea until the increasingly familiar dread returned—that I actually was on Fancy Phil's wild-goose chase, and in the end, Emily would have been a side trip to nowhere. The killer would turn out to be Steffi, or Steffi + Greg. Having thus screwed up, I would incur Fancy Phil's fury and Nelson Sharpe's contempt. Or vice versa.

On that happy note, the phone rang. "This is Steffi Deissenburger." I probably thanked her twice. "It is not a bother," she said. "I cannot tell one hundred percent if this woman was a visitor. But"—I held my breath—"I think she could be, or might be, someone who was visiting Courtney. I did not see her for long. Only for a minute."

A tingle of excitement, followed by the warm flush of hope that feels too good to be a hot flash. My heart began to pound. But wanting to sound composed, I said, with over-the-top sincerity, à la Judd Hirsch as the shrink in *Ordinary People*: "Tell me about it."

"Sometimes when Courtney had a friend visit," Steffi said, "she would ask me to take the children from the house. So she and the friend could enjoy a quiet conversation. Did I tell you that already? This is what I did on that day. I took Morgan and Travis to the library, then to lunch, then I think to the big playground in Christopher Morley Park."

"When was this?"

"I believe it was in . . . I cannot say exactly. It could have been the end of summer."

"Please," I urged her, "go ahead."

"I brought the children back earlier than Courtney had asked. Travis was—he was crying. From being cranky, you see. He had not had a nap and he was a child who needed one. Sometimes he even took a nap in the morning."

"What time was it when you got back to the Logans'?"

"Before four. Courtney asked me to keep the children out until four o'clock so she and her friend—"

"Did she mention the friend's name?"

"I don't think so. Or I don't remember. I am not sure."

"Sorry to have interrupted you. Please go on."

"I drove home, and as I am parking the car, a woman comes out from the front door. Courtney is there and they kiss good-bye."

"A hugging kiss?" I asked.

"No. A fast kiss like Americans do who do not know each other so well." Steffi made the staccato smack of a social kiss. "The woman sees the children, so Courtney waves to me to come over. She says, 'This is Morgan and this is Travis.' "

"She doesn't introduce you?"

"No. I believe she is a little angry that I came home before four o'clock, although she may just be tired. And the woman says something like 'They're so cute,' even though Travis is crying. He was very, very cranky and it was a long day for him. Then the woman gets in her car and drives away."

"Did Courtney say anything to you about your coming back early?"

"No. I started to apologize, but she said to forget about it, that it was all right and she had a nice visit with her friend." I got a clear mental picture of Steffi at that instant: her contrite expression, her heavily made-up face, her placid posture, her nervous hands.

"Courtney didn't call the woman Jane or Mary or anything? Just 'my friend'?"

"I think just that. I don't remember."

"Okay, you said the woman got into a car. Do you remember what kind it was, or the color?"

"No. I don't think it was a German or a Swedish car. I have been to both countries and their cars are familiar to me. And the color . . . ? I don't remember. It may have been dark."

"Did you notice the license plate?" I ventured. "Was it from New York or some other state?"

"I don't think I saw. Travis was crying and I felt, you know, bad about coming home early. Courtney had asked me to please to keep them out and if they got to be a problem to go to Baskin-Robbins and buy them ice cream."

"That doesn't sound like her," I remarked. "Ice cream?"

"Well, you see, she understood how young children were. She wanted to make it easier for me to handle them. She was very thoughtful in this way."

"Right. Now, would you say the woman was younger or older or the same age as Courtney?"

"I would say a little younger, but not too much. Thirty or thirty-one."

"And what did she look like?"

"Like the woman in the photograph you emailed to me. Very plain. Dark blond or light brown hair. She wore it back, like a chignon, but not so elaborate, if you understand. Not very tall, but she wore shoes with those high but very heavy heels. I don't know what you call them. And a plain gray business suit with a white blouse under it. Not well cut, the way Courtney's suits were. Like a little gray mouse the woman looks, was what I was thinking. She—what is the word?—oh, carried. She carried herself as though she did not wish to be seen."

"Would you say shy?"

"Maybe shy, someone who is not easy at being friendly—except with a few who know her well."

"Was she easy with Courtney?"

"I did not see her enough to know." She paused, and I held myself back from throwing another question at her. "It is like this," Steffi continued. "I watched her when she was looking at the children and I thought, She is fond of them not because she likes children but because she thinks so well of Courtney and they are Courtney's. So she has admiration for Courtney. Maybe I was wrong and she is still shy, even with children. But she did not seem to know how it was with them, or even to like them. She kept looking at Travis as though he would see her and understand he had to stop crying."

"What was your general feeling about her?"

"Perhaps lonely," Steffi said cautiously. "She did not act like a woman with a husband or nice boyfriend. You know? As if there is someone in the world who wants you. Still, I did not see her longer than one minute. I cannot even tell you more than maybe, *possibly*, this woman was the woman in your email."

After speaking with Steffi I found myself at loose ends, only in part because I couldn't figure out what to do next. Her offhand remark about the confidence of a woman with a husband or boyfriend who knows there is "someone in the world who wants you" kept replaying in my head.

At ten-twenty (according to the perpetually erroneous clock on the lower right of my computer screen), I was at the height of aggravation at myself. I hadn't been able to dismiss the why-doesn't-he-call anxiety about Nelson as well as the so-why-don't-you-call-him-and-stop-the-playing-hard-to-get-game response (to which I added a schmuckette-that's-what-you-get-for-sleeping-with-a-married-man kick in the ass). I was starting to get unusually inventive, constructing a scenario in which Nelson drove home from the motel the previous afternoon, slept with his wife out of guilt or desire, had a heart attack, and at that very moment was being laid out with a boutonniere in his lapel in some Methodist funeral home. The phone rang as I was subtracting the carnation and adding an American flag because he'd been in the air force and was a cop.

It was Nelson. Alive. His greeting was the one he'd always used two decades earlier, saying I love you, to which I responded with my customary "Who is this, please?" He told me he'd like to come over, I said good. Thirty-five minutes later he came through the door. He kissed me thoroughly before saying "I'm here on business."

"I could tell," I answered, trying to ignore the hideous houndstooth jacket he was wearing again. I led him through the living room into the sunporch, a small room common in Tudor-style houses built in the 1920s and '30s, the old-time equivalent of a den. It was there I watched my old movies, listened to music, stretched out on the couch to read mysteries and the occasional literary novel, biographies, magazines—anything not having to do with being a historian. I gestured to a seat on the couch for Nelson.

I sat cater-cornered to him in Bob's old leather recliner, a chair that had begun making embarrassing squealing sounds not long after he died, no matter how much silicone and oil I offered it. In my weirder moods, I thought of the chair as haunted, though not malevolently so.

Anyway, I told Nelson what Steffi had said about the emailed photo, that she had seen someone resembling Emily saying good-bye to Courtney and driving off. Then I offered him what I'd found out about the Red Oak Bank's client Richard Grey and about Saf-T-Close's going public in '98 and its acquisition by Chapman-Bohrer on October 11, 1999.

"That's fantastic!" he said. "How did you find that out?"

"Luck. And the Web."

"I'm impressed, Judith."

"Wow. Now I am, too," I told him. "Nelson, can you look to see if Emily or, more likely, Courtney bought any of this stock? If Emily did it, it would be a clear case of insider trading. So she couldn't do it legally. But if Courtney knew about Saf-T-Close's being acquired early enough, through Emily, she might have made a killing."

"On that twenty-five thousand she pulled out of those joint accounts?" Nelson asked.

"Well, I don't know about that. I mean, if the stock went from thirty to fifty, I figured that's about a sixty-six percent profit. But what I'm

thinking is that—assuming there is an Emily–Courtney connection—that
Emily gave Courtney her money to invest."

"And then?"

"And then maybe Courtney held on to it. And Emily, who had
planned to disappear from the bank, made a side trip to Shorehaven. I
don't know if she got back her money, but maybe she got back at Courtney." Nelson did not make a big production out of thinking. Still, I knew.
"What are you thinking?" I demanded.

"I'm thinking that if this story you're telling me turns out to be true,
which I'm not saying it will, then it will be a stinkeroo to figure out.
These two weren't teachers, or cops. They were financial sophisticates."

"And we're not."

"Unless you sneaked in an MBA along with your Ph.D."

"Nope."

"Okay now, my turn. I may be onto something also." Late morning
light streamed through the louvered windows and lit up his hair. With his
snub nose and large, choir-boy eyes, he looked vaguely angelic. He
reached into the inside breast pocket of his jacket and extracted a folded
sheet of paper. "Listen to this."

"Can I see it so I know what you're talking about?"

"No. Listen, Judith . . . The last thing I want to do is hurt your feelings, but I'm going to say it straight out. You're not my partner in this."

"So how come you're here?"

He flashed one of his annoyed looks. "To talk."

"To talk about stuff you really shouldn't be talking about?"

"Probably." He seemed remarkably casual about such a lapse, although I supposed that anyone doing the sort of work he'd done for all
the years he'd been doing it could not be easily flustered. "Do you want
to listen?"

"Of course."

"This is just between us."

"You don't have to tell me that, Nelson."

Instead of countering with anything smug or scathing, as almost anyone else would do, he simply opened the paper and ran his finger down
what appeared to be a column. Naturally, such a showing of cool impressed me exponentially. "I was checking out incoming calls to Emily's
house and office. Okay, five of them came from the same number in the
917 area code. You know what that is?"

"The code for a lot of pagers and cell phones."

"Right. It's used around the tristate area. So, a couple of things. The
cell phone was bought on September seventeenth, 1999, a Friday, at an

AT&T place on West Thirty-ninth in Manhattan. That was over a month before Emily Chavarria and Courtney Logan disappeared."

I leaned forward. "Was it in either of their names?"

"No. It was bought and paid for by someone named Vanessa Russell."

"Cash or credit card?"

"A Discover card," he replied. "First of all, whoever Vanessa is or isn't, she—or someone who used her cell phone—made those five calls to an 856 area code, which is—"

"Cherry Hill," I said. "Home of the lovely Holiday Inn overlooking— Okay, who did Vanessa call in Cherry Hill?"

"Only Emily Chavarria's voice mail at the bank. Now let's see how good at this you are," Nelson said. "The calls varied in length from a little over a minute to almost four minutes. What does that tell you?"

I did some hmmming. "Does your watch have a second hand?" I inquired. He nodded. "Okay, time me: 'Hi, Nelson. This is Judith Singer of Sixty-three Oaktree in Shorehaven. I'm calling you about the whole business with Emily Chavarria and Courtney Logan. I'd appreciate getting whatever information you have. You can call me at 516-537-1409.' "

"Twenty-one seconds."

"Which means either she was leaving a hell of a long message—"

"You got it. Checking Emily's messages."

"Which would most likely have to be done by Emily, because she'd have to know the password or code or whatever to retrieve them."

"Most likely," he agreed, "but not definitely."

"Were any of those calls made after Emily disappeared?"

"Three of them."

"If the phone is in the name of Vanessa Russell . . . How did you find it so fast?"

"Doesn't take long if your contact from the phone company feels like being a nice guy. Everything's computerized. Almost all of the other calls to access Emily's voice mail were made from Emily's house. One was made from a pay phone at a restaurant in Manhattan. The rest were from that cell phone."

"So Emily was around even after she didn't go to Australia but disappeared."

"I'd give it a seventy-five percent shot," Nelson said.

"I'd give it a ninety," I retorted.

"In a homicide investigation you shouldn't give anything those odds. If you were a guy, I'd say you haven't been doing this long enough to know a pile of shit from a hot rock."

"But I'm not a guy."

"Right. So maybe you're being a little overoptimistic about your deductive talents. But I still haven't gotten to the good part."

"What's that?"

"That someone using Vanessa Russell's cell phone called Courtney Logan's house on Sunday, October twenty-fourth, and then again on Thursday, October twenty-eighth, three days before Courtney disappeared."

"Oh my God! That definitely ties Emily to Courtney."

"No, that ties a user or users of a certain cell phone to both Emily and Courtney. Maybe it was Emily herself calling. Maybe not."

I bounded out of the chair, muttered "Excuse me," and hurried to the kitchen. Returning with a bag of organic celery hearts, I plopped down on the couch beside Nelson and offered him one. Looking at me as if I'd proffered a bag of rocks, he shook his head. I pulled off a stalk and began to munch. "Eating calms my nerves," I explained.

"You think I don't know that?"

"Oh, shut up! Now, Vanessa Russell of cell phone and Discover-card fame: Is there really such a person?"

"I don't know yet. There was no answer at the home number that she gave on the application for cell phone service, a 718 Brooklyn number. I called her where she supposedly works, with a 212 area code, but there's no such number. I'm having someone check out her home address and number and also with Discover to look at her credit history, if any. But I can't take too much time on this. Courtney is a homicide and Emily is a missing person in New Jersey. Not my jobs."

I set down my celery and put my hand into his; I'd always loved the way his hand made mine look dainty. "You wish it were your job, don't you?" He nodded. "Can you try to make it yours? Like on the theory it involves an organized crime figure you're already investigating for . . . whatever. I mean, Fancy Phil was Courtney's father-in-law."

"I already tried that the day after they fished her out of that pool. The powers that be knew exactly what I wanted to do, which was to horn in on a homicide case. They said leave it alone."

"Was it an actual order?"

"No, it was one of those friendly suggestions that if you don't take to heart, your ass is grass and you wind up getting an unfriendly suggestion that it's time to start filling out the pension papers." He gave a what-the-hell shrug that was utterly unconvincing.

"So what are you going to do?" I asked.

"What I'm doing. A little looking here and there. A little listening. Mainly to you. And to a couple of my old friends still in Homicide—though not on this case."

"They're part of the old regime and don't get the juicy cases? That's department politics?"

"Smells like it."

"Nelson, do you honestly think Phil Lowenstein had anything to do with Courtney's murder or Emily's disappearance?"

"Damned if I know."

"You know," I told him.

He rose from the couch and I did, too. "Twenty percent chance," he said.

"Two percent, and I'm not going to split the difference. Even if he wanted to find out what I was doing ringing Greg's front doorbell and offering my services—"

"You did that? Are you nuts, Judith?"

"Marginally. But if Fancy Phil was interested in hearing what I had to say, he could have done exactly what he did do, hang out in a corner of my garage until I pulled my car in and closed the door. 'Hi! Wanna see my new pinkie ring?' "

"He surprised you in your garage?"

"He's such a playful fellow. Look, if he'd wanted to get me wiped out, I'd have already been run over by a cement truck. No, he *hired* me. I'm working on his behalf, even though I refused to take any money from him."

I suddenly realized I was following him to the front door, without a detour to the upstairs. He gave me a fast kiss on the forehead. "Gotta go. Can I see you tonight?"

"I can't." He looked on the verge of asking me to change my plans, so I added: "It's a long-standing date with friends from high school. There's no way I can weasel out of it."

I said nothing about not wanting to weasel out. After he left I went back onto the sunporch and sat where Nelson had been sitting. The cushion was still warm from him. Did I really *not* want to see him? Of course not. Doing anything with Nelson was better than listening to my friend Marcy's unfailing lament over what managed care was doing to her practice of medicine and hearing Helena's ode to the golfing life in Boca Raton. (I suspected my descriptions of St. Elizabeth's History Department Frolics were equally electrifying for them.) But I was afraid of an overnight with Nelson, not only that all the nights after that would be unbearably lonely, but that somehow I would wind up being the lever to pry him out of his supposedly lousy marriage. If anything was going to happen between me and Nelson, it would have to be on a separate agenda from whatever was going on between Nelson and the guidance counselor.

Naturally I had an almost irresistible impulse to bring the entire matter before Nancy, except I wanted to avoid her inevitable harangue even more than I wanted to hear her advice. Instead, I made notes on the case for the rest of the day, went into the garden to cut some roses, and left for dinner in Manhattan with my pals. As expected, nothing was new with them, beyond a new grandchild for Marcy and new moisturizing regimen for Helena. I heard about both at great length.

Driving home from Manhattan, I was so exhausted I blasted a rap station and turned the air conditioner to its iciest to keep from nodding off. I'd never been one of those frisky types about whom it is said: If you want to get a job done, give it to the busiest person. A full day for me was teaching a class, making egg salad, and watching a Bette Davis movie. While I did crave the sense of being alive that I got from murder, all the exhilaration and agitation of the past month had worn me out more than I wanted to admit.

I was heading down Oaktree Street. Even before I got to the driveway, I saw my way to the garage blocked by a colossus of an automobile. I got alert fast. And turning in, I spotted a heavy, hairy braceleted right arm as the front passenger door of the giant car swung open. Fancy Phil. It was like a massive intravenous shot of caffeine.

"What's up, Doc?" He at least had the decency not to guffaw at this allegedly humorous reference.

Glancing at his Cro-Magnon driver, I turned to Fancy Phil: "How come I have the pleasure of your company at this time of night?"

"Let's go inside and we'll talk."

His multichinned face, illuminated by the outdoor lights, was one large, friendly smile. Around his neck he wore a star of David so unavoidably huge on his black knit shirt, so goldly garish that I could only assume it was not only meant to be noticed, but also to reassure: My people = thy people. "Not inside," I said, smiling back. "It's such a beautiful night." I gestured upward to what was either Venus or a satellite and took a deep breath of rambling roses and car exhaust. "Let's stay out here." I walked up the path to the three steps that led to the front door, sat, and patted the flagstone beside me.

Fancy Phil followed me slowly and somewhat stiffly, as if he were Frankenstein walking after just a few moments of life. He did not sit. "What's the matter? You scared of me again? I thought you got over that."

It's always hard to choose when your gut says one thing and your brain says another. "Phil, do you have your driver's number?" In case he thought I was referring to the man's ID from Ossining State Penitentiary, I added: "His phone number."

"Yeah. Why?"

"Then please tell him to take a ride for a half hour or so. You'll call when you need him."

He glanced down and saw my house keys in my hand. If he was even half as brainy as I believed he was, he'd realize the electronic gizmo on my key chain was a panic button for the house's alarm system. He flashed me a look that said, Hey, if you want be ungracious, fine by me. Then he wiggled his index finger and his driver/goon opened the window. "About half an hour," Fancy Phil said. "I'll call you." Quietly and elegantly, the great, dark car backed out and drove off. Fancy Phil turned back to me. "So, you gonna invite me in now?"

"I'd rather take the night air." For some reason, I was not afraid. Uneasy, sure. Maybe even apprehensive. But no chill of fear, no shiver of panic.

"What kinda crap is this, Doc? If I was up to something, I wouldn't be hanging out in my car in your driveway, so all your neighbors could memorize the license plate. You think you can't trust me?"

"I think you've got something on your mind and I'd prefer to hear it under the stars."

The residue of his smile vanished, but he lowered himself down and, with a barely perceptible grunt, sat beside me on the step. His white linen slacks were stretched so tight around his thighs they looked about to explode from fabric fatigue. "So?" he inquired.

"So what do you want?" I asked.

"I want to know everything you got."

"I'm not planning on keeping it a secret, Phil. I'll tell you as soon as I feel I can present a coherent narrative." I saw the look he flashed me, but I also realized he understood exactly what I'd meant.

"Listen, Doc. I like you a lot."

"Good. I like you, too."

"If I didn't have a wife and, you know, a good friend already, I'd actually ask you out on a date. So liking you so much, admiring your smartness, I don't want to make you upset. Or angry with me. Or even, God forbid, afraid of me."

"Where do you come from, Phil?"

"What? Way back? Brooklyn."

"Me, too. And we had an old saying there: You're pickin' on the wrong chicken."

"I never heard that."

"But you understand what it means," I said.

"Yeah."

"For several reasons, none of which I want to elaborate on, it would be best for you if we could resume our old, friendly relationship and cut the business of 'God forbid, afraid of me,' which translates into 'You should be scared shitless.' Now, do you want a report on what I've been doing?"

"Yeah." He pretended to scan the sky for glorious celestial objects. "Can I come inside now? I swear I'm not gonna hurt you or make a pass. I'm just upset, is all."

It is rarely wise to ignore your head and your gut and proceed on faith, but I sensed this was one of those times. "Let's go." I took him into the living room, turned on all the lamps, and left the curtains open. The place smelled of the roses I'd cut before I left for the city, and any trepidation I may have had disappeared when I saw him gazing from vase to vase to vase, from red to apricot to yellow. "Beauty-ful," he commented.

"Thanks."

Fancy Phil lowered himself onto a club chair and pointed to a hassock. "Can I put my feet up there if I take off my shoes?"

"Sure, even if you don't take them off." I was about to sit a few feet away in a matching chair, but I asked, "Do you want something to eat? Drink?"

"No." He patted his belly, not without fondness. "I gotta take off a few. You got any sour balls or anything?" I peered into the depths of my handbag and picked out the two mints wrapped in cellophane I'd taken from the restaurant where I'd just had dinner as well as an almost full pack of sugarless gum. "Thanks, Doc." When he finished ripping the cellophane with his teeth and gulping the mints whole instead of chewing them, he said: "Look, I didn't want to scare you. I just wanted to catch you when you got home. It's that the clock is ticking. They called Gregory and wanted him to go back to their headquarters and go over his information."

"Again?"

"Yeah."

"The cops from Homicide?"

"Yeah. His lawyer told them, you should pardon me, to go take a flying fuck. But you know and I know, they don't got anyone else waiting in line to take the hit for this thing. Their not making any arrest is an embarrassment for them. I'm . . . I'm scared any minute they'll trump up some phony crap just to make the public think they solved the case. What Morgan and Travis have already gone through . . . How could they take their father getting dragged off?"

"It would be a nightmare," I agreed. I didn't want to think about Greg behind bars for Courtney's murder, his children seeing him in an orange jumpsuit on their increasingly rare visits.

"Okay," I said. "We've got to give them something that will divert their attention from Greg. So let me give you a rough sketch of what I've found out."

Chapter Fifteen

The moon was almost full. Outside the window, across the street, the mist over my neighbor's front lawn glowed in the light; it looked as if a Spanish colonial had risen from a swamp on some extraterrestrial landscape. "I don't see the end to this yet," I told Fancy Phil.

He slipped off his white suede loafers and put his bare feet up on the hassock. "See?" he said, wriggling his toes for emphasis. "Feet don't come cleaner than this."

My duties as hostess apparently included smiling my approval of his personal hygiene, so I did. Then I went on: "It's not only details of what happened with Courtney that we're missing. It's the big picture, too. There are so many blanks to fill in. I want to be able to give you a chronology or some kind of logical progression."

An enormous pink jewel set in a ropy gold ring on Fancy Phil's right hand gleamed in a cone of light cast by the lamp. "Do I look like a guy who's gotta have a progression?" he inquired.

"Maybe not, but that's the way I work."

He placed his right arm in front of his sizable waist and, with surprising grace, considering he was sitting, offered me a magnanimous bow. "You're the doctor, Doc. Go ahead."

"Okay. Let's start with the assumption that Courtney had an aspect of her life she didn't want Greg to know about. That's not to say there was some deep, dark secret, like an affair or a complicated financial deception. It could have been that she was going to a friend's house and smoking marijuana and watching dirty movies. Or going to Bloomingdale's and trying on clothes all day."

"I got news for you, cookie," Phil said, twisting around his ring to better admire it. "Nobody's got a life that's an open book." He saw me eyeing his ring and held up his meaty hand for me, fingers splayed, so it could catch every photon of light and better show off the gem. "Is this a ring or what?" he demanded.

"I've never seen anything like it."

"Quinzite opal," he declared. His nails looked far better manicured than mine, topped with a clear polish with a hint of pink to echo the color of the opal. "Those stories about opals being bad luck? Craziness. But I guess it keeps down the price. Not that I care. I pay top dollar for quality."

I gave him a look I hoped would say: Sadly, we must leave the subject of your jewelry. "About Courtney's life," I said. "She told Steffi, the au pair, that if Greg ever called and she wasn't around, to tell him she was out shopping. No big deal. Not the kind of lie that if Greg found out would shake the marriage to its foundation. Still, something was going on. In the week or two before Halloween, Courtney was away three or four times for a whole day, from after breakfast until seven or seven-thirty at night."

"That don't sound like marijuana," Fancy Phil reflected. "And not Bloomingdale's either. Because you know what happens, you try on clothes for ten hours? Seriously, you could end up in traction." He unwrapped a few pieces of the gum I'd given him earlier and popped them into his mouth.

"You're probably right," I said. "Anyhow, according to Steffi, on those days, Courtney dressed up, nicely, elegantly. Not in anything sexy, not the kind of thing she might wear if she were having a sizzling affair." (Twenty years earlier I'd worn jeans or corduroys to mine, though I concede I did go flambé in the underwear department.) "It sounds as though she was dressed for business."

"Maybe she had some guy who wanted class, not tits and ass." Delighted by his rhyme, Fancy Phil smiled, albeit a reserved gangster smile that displayed only the hint of teeth.

"Do you really think so?" I inquired politely. He shook his head hard: no way. "Then I'll go on. According to one of StarBaby's clients, when Courtney came to talk about the company, she wore a simple pair of slacks and a silk blouse. Not a suit with a skirt and high-heeled shoes, not with her hair up. The au pair confirmed that."

Fancy Phil smoothed down the chest hair in the V made by his open-neck shirt. His gold chain and star clanked. "Courtney was platinum card all the way. I told you, Doc, for someone who liked simple, that girl spent a fortune—like on clothes. Gregory and me was talking about it last weekend. He came over for supper with Morgan and Travis. My wife made her own pizza. Can you believe that? Plain for Morgan, with all kinds of fancy mushrooms for us. Not canned mushrooms. Fresh. Macaroni for Travis. Anyway, Gregory was never cheap, like about Courtney's clothes. A guy wants his wife to look like a million bucks."

"But not necessarily cost it."

"You got it, sweetheart. Listen, if you're in the money, sure, why not? Buy your wife a fur down to the floor, a diamond bracelet that says 'diamond bracelet' loud and clear—not one of those crappy tennis things. But Gregory don't have those kind of bucks yet. Maybe he won't ever, what with everything having to be legit. Not bucks for the big-time stuff Courtney was dying for. Not to rent a house in Italy for a month with not just a maid, but a cook. A *cook*? Tell me, what does it take to make spaghetti? And the money Miss Simple pissed away—she should rest in peace. Eight hundred dollars for a pair of pants. That's what Gregory told me, and that was just for starters."

"She'd been an investment banker," I remarked. "I'd have thought she would have a more realistic understanding of what their finances were."

Fancy Phil shook his head sadly. "It was like this. It wasn't about Gregory. Courtney was positive I had all the money in the world. So whenever she had to have something, she'd hint in front of me. And to tell you the truth, sometimes Poppy Phil would reach into his pocket. Like one time she hinted about a new car to drive the kids around with, with more safety things. Could I say no? Of course not. I got her that Rover. And okay, the TV screen that comes out of the ceiling and gets projected on. For that dumb StarBaby. When she saw I wasn't going to go for it, she said she really meant it for the kids to watch *Sesame Street* on. Okay—so call me a schnook—I got it for her. But if she wants a sable? She has a mink already. But she was hinting big time: One of her girl-friends' husbands bought her"—his voice rose to a falsetto squeal—" 'the most beautiful sable coat for her thirty-fifth.' That was how Courtney hinted. Never said *I* want. I'm thinking to myself, a squirt like her puts on sable, she'll look like a sable holding a pocketbook. And I'm also thinking: *No way*. Not a sable, not a fox, not even—pardon me—a fucking bunny rabbit. I don't wanna cut off my son's balls and buy my daughter-in-law a fur. Also I got a wife. Third wife, and she's the kind of girl who thinks number three means she gets to have three furs." Having gotten that off his chest, Fancy Phil said: "What am I talking? Go ahead. Any more on Courtney's secret life?"

"On October fourteenth, she had her Land Rover serviced. The thirty-first was the last day she could have possibly driven it, right?"

"Yeah? So?"

"Between those two dates, she put seven hundred sixty-two miles on her car."

After two seconds of calculation, Fancy Phil asked: "Where the hell did she go?"

"Remember when I was talking to some of Courtney's former colleagues in the financial community, how one of them happened to mention what he called a weird coincidence: that a banker in New Jersey, someone he dealt with once, had also been reported missing. Emily Chavarria."

"Yeah. The one you asked me to ask Gregory about. He never heard of her."

"Right. Thirty-one years old, had gone to a good school. She was supposed to be smart, though not extroverted like Courtney. Quiet. Or maybe just shy. From what the guy who'd worked with Courtney at Patton Giddings told me, Emily must have been more than competent because she was hand-holding one of the bank's biggest clients. Yet she seems to have hit a glass ceiling that was set pretty low." Fancy Phil's head cocked to the side with an unspoken "Wha'?" So I explained: "A glass ceiling is about discrimination. It's an obstacle nobody inside a corporation will admit to that keeps women and minorities from rising to positions of power. But even though she was young, Emily didn't find another job and take a hike. So maybe she was resentful. Maybe she felt entitled to more than she was getting or going to get from the bank."

Fancy Phil put his feet down in the space between hassock and chair and leaned forward. "You're just guessing at that."

"Absolutely."

"Keep going. I'll stop you when you start sounding stupid."

"So far so good?" I asked.

"So far."

"From Shorehaven, it's about a two-hundred-twenty-five mile round-trip to where Emily lives and works. Or worked. Now, one of her bank's biggest clients was a man who'd inherited the majority interest in a family company. And there came a time when he took his company public, sold shares—"

"You don't gotta explain the market to me, Doc. The SEC once tried to get me for stock manipulation, those dumb-fucks."

"Anyway, later on, the company was acquired by a large corporation. Of course, if you're a banker for a company and you know this sort of thing is going to happen—"

"Insider trading," Fancy Phil cut in. "Yeah, yeah. The goddamn SEC makes such a big stink about it."

"I think they call it a felony," I replied.

"They're so stupid. Anyhow, what's the name of the guy's company?" he asked.

"I'm not prepared to tell it to you right now, Phil."

"C'mon."

"I'd rather not."

"Why not, goddamn it?" he suddenly bellowed. No suburban niceties for Fancy Phil; no "Quiet so the neighbors won't hear."

I never had anyone angry at me who had a criminal record, one element of which was smashing somebody in the face with a brick. At the sight of the fire in Fancy Phil's beady eyes, my guts began to turn liquid. His face was a dangerous red, getting redder. I had to steel myself not to turn away from his glare. "Why won't I tell you?" I demanded, surprised at finding my own voice rising. "An insurance policy."

"Cut it out!"

"No, Phil. Not after I get home late from the city and Surprise! There's Phil Lowenstein and some muscle-bound moron waiting for me."

"He's not that dumb."

"Look, it would make me incredibly happy to help Greg, so you and I can be friendly after all this is over."

"I'm friendly now!" he bellowed. Placing his left hand over the star of David, he raised his right high: I swear to God! "Hey, aren't I sitting here with you? Listening polite."

"You're very polite. And very intelligent. Greg's lucky to have you in his corner. And I like you, Phil. I don't want to get you angry or hurt your feelings. But when I saw your car and got a look at your driver . . . So this is just a way to make myself feel more comfortable."

"I'm not gonna argue with you, even though you're wrong." He sniffled once, noisily, to show the hurt I'd inflicted. "Keep talking."

"It looks like this Emily had a tie to Courtney, besides that FIFE meeting—that's the organization they both belonged to. After Emily disappeared, someone called her voice mail at work from a cell phone a few times. Now unless she'd given her password to somebody else, she was alive and curious enough to check her messages."

"Whose name was the cell phone in?"

"A name that appears to be a phony, although it's being checked."

"I hate it when the flavor of gum goes south so goddamn fast," Fancy Phil muttered as he added another piece to the wad already in his mouth. "Who's checking the name of whoever bought the cell phone?"

"Someone with easier access to that sort of information than I have."

"Which means that's another thing you're not telling me." No rage this time. He merely grumbled.

"Right. But listen. Here's the Courtney–Emily link. Whoever had that cell phone also called your son's house two times, and the last time was a few days before Courtney disappeared."

"No shit!" he exhaled.

"No shit. Maybe they were just trading rice pudding recipes. But it's my gut feeling that there was some business deal between Emily and Courtney. There's the matter of the company being acquired by a larger one, and also the matter of Courtney making twenty-five thousand dollars disappear. Who knows what else? If I had to guess, it's that Courtney fronted for Emily in buying that stock of the company before it was acquired. They knew, because of insider information, that the price would go way up. I'm not saying that's exactly what happened. For all I know it could be some other shady or unshady deal. The question is, how do I find out? Could there possibly have been a brokerage account Courtney had that Greg hasn't mentioned to you?"

Fancy Phil gave me a who-knows shrug, but was silent. I waited while he buffed the stone of his ring on his white slacks. Then he said: "If those two girls was in cahoots and this Emily was smart enough to buy a cell phone in some alias—"

"The credit card she used is probably a phony."

"Sure," he said offhandedly, as if such methods were kindergarten tactics to him. "So if she's got the brains to buy a cell phone in a phony name, she and Courtney sure in hell aren't going to trade in their own names."

"Right. Do you have any idea how they might have done it? Trading the stocks?" I figured Fancy Phil wouldn't get insulted if I assumed he had knowledge of the illegal.

He didn't. "Maybe do that Internet trading, someplace where they don't ask too many questions. Except that's usually Amateur Hour."

"Not with these two," I suggested.

"Yeah, you could be right. If it was me? Offshore corporation."

"I've read about it, but I don't think I really understand."

"You could trade in your name: Dr. Judith Singer. But if you do that, what's the point? The point is hiding yourself. The way I *heard* it's done"—I couldn't swear, but I think he winked—"is that you set up a corporation in the Bahamas or Cayman Islands or British Virgins. Okay? You with me? Their laws basically say they can't give out the name of the person or the people behind the corporation. Trust me, it's done all the time. That way, it means the pig people at the IRS can't trace you and those bastards at the SEC can't go for your throat. See, it's the corporation that buys and sells stocks or whatever. No names."

"But Courtney was murdered. Wouldn't the police or FBI be able to get those islands' governments to give up information on who's behind the corporation?"

"Do I look like a lawyer, sweetheart? But the answer is, even if they get the name or names, what good is it gonna do them if this Emily was smart enough to start the corporation in an alias?"

"Don't you need to show ID to start up a corporation?"

"Yeah, you do. But, Doc, if a lady banker from a good school has got the smarts to figure out how to get a fake credit card, and then has the balls to use it, don't you think she's already got a phony ID? You come up with a halfway decent-looking birth certificate, you got your new identity, and a passport is a piece of cake. It costs, sure, but it can be done."

"So if we don't know the alias Emily chose to set up the corporation, we'd have a hard time tracing her."

Fancy Phil's mouth turned down at the edges. He looked as glum as I felt. "Hard time? Impossible time."

"You mean even the bank or lawyer or wherever she has the phony corporation won't know who she truly is?" I asked. "There really would be no way of tracking her down then."

"Right," he conceded.

"If Emily set up this corporation to buy the stock, and if she gave Courtney the money to do it for her—beyond whatever money of her own Courtney may also have invested—would both of them have had access to that corporation?"

"Could be," Fancy Phil said.

"Why wouldn't Emily just use the corporation and bypass Courtney entirely?" I asked. "I mean, if she created a corporation using a false name and fake ID."

"Maybe she wasn't convinced that she couldn't be traced. If she was a shy girl, maybe she was scared to go someplace like the Caymans, deal with a local lawyer. Maybe Courtney had more brains about this stuff than this Emily: She'd been at a big place that did international deals. The other girl was stuck in some dipshit town in New Jersey. Or maybe Emily talked over her plan with Courtney and then Courtney put on pressure not to be left out of the deal."

"Blackmail-type pressure?"

"Could be. She wouldn't have had to say it out loud. No 'Include me out and I'll rat to the feds.' This Emily would be smart enough to understand without words. Know what I mean? Or maybe they were happy partners in this thing, but each of them set up their own corporation."

"Why?"

"Because after this deal, Emily planned to disappear. Why else all that business with Australia? Or because even happy partners can learn to hate each other. Or because this Emily was smart enough not to trust Courtney."

"But then why would she kill Courtney?"

"Because Courtney *knew.*"

"Knew what?"

Fancy Phil took a gum wrapper from his pocket and spit out the wad of gum. "Courtney knew the money from insider trading existed, right? Courtney knew Emily existed. And Courtney might not have been satisfied with what she got. You told me she lost her interest in that dumb StarBaby after the summer, that she seemed to have her mind on something else. She could have tried to get the hook into Emily for more: 'Fork it all over or else.' " He wrapped the gum carefully and stuck it in his pants pocket. "Of course, that's if your story's right: 'Once upon a time there was a bad girl named Emily who led a good girl named Courtney down the garden path.' You make it sound real possible, even though it's hopeless to find this bitch."

"Maybe hopeless is too strong a word," I suggested.

"I said 'hopeless' and I mean 'hopeless,' " Fancy Phil retorted. "Shit, I can't believe that little blond pipsqueak Courtney could get messed up with something like this."

"At least we have a link between these two women, Phil. You can have Greg's lawyer bring it to the cops. For my part, I'm still going to try to dig up more."

"How?"

"Should I tell you I have secret methods? Or should I tell you I have no idea, but maybe I'll think of something?"

Putting his hands above his knees, Fancy Phil managed to launch himself out of the chair. "I hope you can think of something. Because remember that wild-goose chase I was worrying about? For my Gregory's sake, let's pray you don't got us both on it."

After he left, I walked around in a haze, fluffing up the cushions on the club chairs, rearranging perfectly satisfactory arrangements of roses, turning off lamps. Hopeless, he'd said. I couldn't believe this was the end of the line. I trudged into the kitchen to set up the coffee machine so all that would be required of me in the morning would be the push of a button.

When a few lucid thoughts returned, they were random ones: Regret that I'd chosen to investigate murder rather than teach a quickie summer course on the social and intellectual history of the United States, a subject I was completely unqualified to teach (not that that would deter Smarmy Sam). Fear that Nelson would not be proud I'd gotten as far as I had, but rather, disappointed that I'd turned out to be irrevocably second rate at the one thing at which I had hoped to excel.

Then I made myself sick over how awful it was that Emily Chavarria had not only outfoxed me, but the police as well. Greg Logan could still wind up paying for her crime with the rest of his life. When I went to bed (as always on my half, as if lying on Bob's side would be an act of flagrant discourtesy), I fell almost immediately into the deepest sleep.

Arising with the sun, I had an intuitive awareness that something lousy could be happening in my life, much like the way I'd woken up mornings as a teenager when my period was overdue. I could almost hear Fancy Phil's "hopeless" echoing through the house. I dragged myself into the bathroom, and sparing myself a confrontation with my own image, I turned my back toward the mirror as I brushed my teeth. Who knows what happened next? Maybe the whirr of the electric toothbrush diddled a nerve fiber on some brain cell, or maybe I was just thinking "teeth." But teeth led to chew, and chew led to gum, and suddenly my mind's eye was watching Fancy as he spit the gum he'd chewed into a wrapper and then managed to poke it down into the pocket of his too-snug slacks.

Used gum led me to more used gum. I recalled the night I'd called on Greg Logan and how, in taking out my curriculum vitae from my handbag to show him, I'd also pulled out an ancient wad of Trident wrapped in a random piece of paper. The one minuscule globule of moisture left in the gum had glommed on to my CV and I'd almost handed it over to Greg.

What was it about gum? By this time the toothbrush had nearly abraded the enamel of a molar, so I turned off the brush and rinsed my mouth. Gum? I turned on the shower, waited till it went from ice-cold to scalding to its usual lukewarm, and stepped in. Oddly, the thick fog of my melancholy began to lift. No mopey standing under the water hoping to be washed clean of whatever was plaguing me, no sniffling "I Gotta Right to Sing the Blues" as I soaped up.

It wasn't until I was drying off my nether reaches that I stood up straight and said, "Oh my God!" Dropping my towel, I pulled my ratty bathrobe off the hook and raced downstairs and into the sunroom. There, in one of those idiotically oversized wicker baskets that look so deceptively felicitous in decorating magazines, was my "Check it out!" book bag from the library. I'd stored the evidence from Courtney's closet in it, the stuff I seized the day Fancy Phil took me to the Logans'.

There it was: grape bubble gum. A child-sized piece, not a great wad like Fancy Phil had been chomping on. Still, from what I knew of Court-ney, this was not a treat she would allow her daughter. In fact, had she picked up Morgan at her Nuclear Physics Readiness Playgroup and espied her chewing something purple and sweet smelling, she would have said: Spit it out.

Since at that hour the sunroom was not living up to its name, I hur-ried into the kitchen and examined my find under the brightest light. My memory hadn't failed. The gum was wrapped in the customer's copy of a charge receipt. American Express. Whatever had been bought cost $3,078.62. However, the nature of the purchase and the name of the buyer was stuck to the gum and therefore unreadable. No reason to give up, I thought. The gum could have been so dried out after months in Courtney's cordovan shoulder bag that it would no longer have a gummy nature. I tugged gently on the paper. Nothing.

After turning on the coffee machine, I walked across the room and studied an article I'd clipped years earlier, one of Nancy's first freelance ef-forts. I'd taped it onto the inside of the door of the broom closet. "Go, Go Goo," it was called, with advice for removing common stains, candle wax, and, yes, gum. Naturally, from Kate and Joey, I remembered the ice-cube-on-hair trick, but she'd also recommended putting a gum-rid-den object in a plastic bag in the freezer, then chipping the gum away. Or dry-cleaning it. Or using peanut butter as a solvent.

But should I, could I have a go at the evidence? I went to call my lawyer. Kate answered first, then an instant later Adam picked up an ex-tension. From the woolly sound of their voices, I realized they were only moments into the getting-up process. I posed my question anyway. First they both made a huge to-do that *they had nothing at all to do with criminal law* and *I should not rely on them for a legal opinion.* Then their best guess— *and it was only a guess*—was that as long as I was brought into the Logan house by a member of the family who possessed keys and the alarm code, and since I had not done this snooping on behalf of the authorities, it was okay to have the receipt in my possession. I saw no point in mentioning the grape gum. When Adam hung up to get ready for work, Kate said: "Mom." Her voice was gentle, maternal.

"What?"

"Consider not doing it."

"Doing what?"

"Let's put it this way," she remarked. "When I was in high school or college, say I called you about having something like this receipt in my possession. If I'd asked vague questions about its legality, and you knew that receipt was either remotely or closely connected with a murder investigation, what would you have said?"

All I could truthfully say to her was: "I would have said, 'Are you nuts, Kate? Leave it alone!' "

"I rest my case," my daughter said softly.

The minute I hung up, however, I went right back to the degumming dilemma. Peanut butter was a substance, along with bittersweet chocolate, that I dared not allow in the house. Not that I would employ something so blatantly gooey as peanut butter to separate paper from gum. However, I did stick the receipt into a plastic bag, pop it in the freezer, and got busy quartering an orange. I'd only halved it when I retrieved the bag.

What should I do with this evidence? Turn it over to Nelson so he could give it to a police laboratory—if he thought it a lead worth pursuing? That made sense, except the police lab might turn it over to Homicide, and they, in their proven idiocy, might conclude that the Jane Doe who'd bought a $3,078.62 sable boa or whatever had absolutely zero to do with Courtney Logan's murder. Thus the cops would continue on their merry way, looking for a smoking gun to help them nab Greg.

A laboratory, I was thinking as I returned to the orange. A laboratory I could trust. I considered calling Fancy Phil and asking if he knew any drug kingpins and whether they might have a rogue chemist on their payrolls. But what if the kingpin had an unstated beef with my client? Or what if there was a DEA bust and the receipt was seized along with forty-three tons of cocaine? Besides, I concluded, a rogue chemist might not agree to chat with the cops if he/she discovered anything worth pursuing.

It wasn't until a few hours later, when I was in the middle of the householder's chore I most detested, bill paying, that it dawned on me that although I didn't know a lab, I did know a chemist. Jenny McFarland and I had been on a committee to try to improve the lot of adjunct professors. I'd always felt that she and I could have been great friends if not for vast differences in age, politics, religion, marital status, and cultural interests. We disagreed on everything except that we were awfully fond of each other. So I called her at her house in Forest Hills Gardens, in Queens. While I baby-sat for her five children (who were so well behaved I wondered if Jenny had been sprinkling some tranquilizing chemical over their Cocoa Puffs), she drove over to St. Elizabeth's to try to separate American Express receipt from grape gum. She didn't even ask why. I'd told her it was important and a personal favor and that was enough for her.

Three hours, six diapers, and untold readings of *Where's My Teddy?* later, Jenny returned with a huge grin and a piece of purple gum in a small, transparent container—as well as a slightly holey, somewhat oily receipt from Louis Vuitton on East Fifty-seventh Street in Manhattan for three-thousand-bucks-plus worth of luggage. For all I knew, that could wind up being one small duffel bag. The lucky owner was not Courtney Logan, not Emily Chavarria, and not Vanessa Russell. Standing beside Jenny, gazing at the receipt, I experienced what the heretofore meaningless cliché—jumping out of one's skin—meant.

"Another name! Samantha R. Corby!" I crowed into my cell phone as I sat in my Jeep in front of Jenny's house. When I explained who Samantha R. was and how I'd learned about her by going into the Logan house, and finding and ungumming the receipt, Nelson threw a fit that included using every curse word he'd learned since fifth grade. I promised him I would go straight home and call no one, especially Fancy Phil, until he came over after work. He ordered me to put the receipt on top of a piece of plain paper, not paper towel, not newspapers, and *leave it alone.*

Well, I needed to get back to what that ass Warren G. Harding called a "return to normalcy." When I got home, I returned to my month's stack of bills and praised myself for being, unlike Samantha R., so restrained a consumer. I spent the rest of the day pruning whatever tree or bush happened to get in my way. Then I sat on the patio listening to Louis Armstrong and Ella Fitzgerald sing together. When they got to "I Won't Dance," I thought how easy it was to say that in song, how hard in life. I was dancing. Having started again with this man I felt I'd been born to dance with, what was going to happen to me? An endless adulterous whirl? A gentlemanly thank-you to me as the song ended, then a return to the lady he'd brought to the ball? It wasn't that I was trying to avoid thinking about the receipt. The truth was after so many years of lifelessness, I was so overstimulated I couldn't think straight.

The last thing on my mind was sex—except around five-thirty I admit I did take a second shower, then spritzed a little Femme in strategic areas. But having exhausted myself thinking about my future or the lack of it, I somehow found the energy to obsess about the case again, trying to figure out a way to discover if "Vanessa Russell" or "Samantha R. Corby" had left any trace at all. I couldn't imagine calling some banker in the Bahamas and saying: Listen, I know you're not supposed to give out information on your depositors, but could you make an exception in this case because I'm a nice person? I don't need much, just the address where you send the statements.

A little after six, I opened the door for Nelson. His slow step over the threshold and his pulling me toward him in the most leisurely way was a clue I didn't have to be a detective to decipher. I was about to suggest Work first, play later, but the warm path his hand made as it snaked under my blouse and made its way up my back changed my mind.

The only awkward half-moment was when we reached the top of the stairs. I realized I couldn't bring him into my bedroom. God knows why. Rationally, I knew Bob's ghost would not suddenly materialize in his customary stance—arms crossed over chest, lips compressed in vexation. Still, I stood unmoving, until Nelson suggested quietly: "How about one of your kids' rooms, or a guest room or something?" I led him into my office, where I took *Mr. Truman's War: The Final Victories of World War II and the Birth of the Postwar World* off the couch. We made such splendid love that when it was finally over, I virtually floated down the stairs, back to the American Express receipt on a piece of white printer paper on the kitchen counter.

I didn't mention I'd already made two copies of it and put one of them in the mailbox to Fancy Phil. As *Cosmopolitan* used to instruct us girls in the sixties, there's no need to tell your man everything. The two of us gazed down at the receipt. I said: "Now don't tell me getting out the grape gum is a felony with a minimum ten-year sentence at a maximum-security institution because I won't believe it."

But Nelson wasn't listening. He was mechanically buttoning his shirt and staring at the receipt. "This is the place for the expensive pocket-books, right?" he asked.

"Right."

"And you found this in one of Courtney Logan's pocketbooks."

"Yes. In a shoulder bag. Not a Vuitton. Nice leather, though, if I remember correctly."

"Let's get back to this." Nelson pointed to the receipt. "Either the card she used was a fake or stolen or a legitimate card she got using a false name. Unless it turns out it was Emily's card, and Courtney just happened to pick up that receipt. Or maybe there really is a Samantha R. Corby around, and when the kid or whoever spit out the gum, Courtney just picked up that piece of paper."

"They're all possibilities," I agreed. "But listen, Nelson. Under normal circumstances, you get a receipt, you put it in your bag. It's yours. If you're insanely organized you keep it. Or you throw it out when you get home. But most of the time a receipt just lives there for a while, until spring-cleaning or whatever. Now, if you're preoccupied with more important things—the way Courtney was after the summer—and you catch your kid chewing gum, you reflexively wrap it up in whatever you've got—a tissue or in any piece of paper you've thrown into your handbag."

"So you're saying that in your opinion, most likely Samantha R. and Courtney are one and the same."

"Well, this isn't a normal situation, what with suburban women being missing or getting murdered and fake credit cards and questionable stock trades and all that, but still, yes, in my opinion they're one and the same."

"So how come"—he broke down and borrowed my reading glasses—"how come it says 'Luggage' here?"

"Because they sell luggage, too," I explained.

"Courtney was murdered on the thirty-first?"

"That's right."

"Doesn't it strike you as funny," Nelson said, "that six days before she was killed, at a time of year hardly anyone takes a vacation, and a little too early for Christmas shopping, she was buying luggage? Where was she planning to go?"

Chapter Sixteen

I beamed at Nelson. "You can find out where Courtney was planning to go!" Standing motionless about two feet apart in front of the cabinet where I stored my mixing bowls and baking gear, we were gazing down again at the American Express receipt. I'm not sure why we couldn't seem to move from it—whether we were still awed at finding that rectangle of paper that could prove a memento of Courtney Logan's secret life or if each believed the other would make a grab for the receipt and run like hell: him to police headquarters, me to Fancy Phil.

"What do you mean, I can find out?"

"I mean, don't you have a number to call and get a printout of whatever charges were on that card?"

His eyebrows strained toward each other. He couldn't figure out how come I was asking a question that had such an obvious answer. "Of course I do." If he'd been his children's age, he would have said Duh.

"I don't get you," I told him. "I know it's not your unit, and maybe if this case gets solved you won't get enough credit, or any credit. But don't you have an overwhelming need to know? *Now?*"

"My sweetheart," Nelson said sweetly. He'd always been a lot of good things—thoughtful, friendly, intuitive, tender, fair. Loving, too. But sweet he wasn't.

"What's the bad news?"

He put his arm on my shoulder and pulled me close so my head bent to his shoulder, the kind of playful embrace football players give each other. "Judith," he said so warmheartedly that I immediately understood why a criminal would confess to him. "I've already done much more than I ought to. Going to New Jersey, checking Emily's phone records, the cell phone purchase. And then talking to you about them. You may not think so, but I've gone out on a limb."

I pulled away not so much in anger, though I was less than delighted, but because I couldn't converse with my neck stretched out and my head resting on a shoulder that felt surprisingly bony for a guy with actual muscles. "I know you have. I appreciate it. I'm grateful for the faith you have in me."

Thankfully, he dropped the sweetie-pie and good-buddy acts. "I haven't told my guys in Homicide how come I'm so interested in the Logan case. They think it's because of the Phil Lowenstein connection, or because I miss the unit so much. I definitely haven't told Carl Gevinski. He's the asshole in charge of the investigation. It's been just you and you alone."

I leaned against the cabinet, but far enough from the receipt that he'd be assured I couldn't execute a deft spin and snatch, though I suspect he knew that for me, deft was not an applicable adjective. "I don't know what to say, Nelson. The last thing I want is for you to get into trouble on my account. And I understand that it probably wouldn't look good for you to be consorting with a person who has ties to Fancy Phil, a guy involved in a case you're investigating—although obviously that could be explained."

"Explained is one thing. Believed is another."

"I don't want you to compromise your integrity or your livelihood."

"I know that."

"The only solution I can think of is to let you call the shots if you can promise me an honest and thorough reinvestigation of Courtney's murder. If you can't, I have a responsibility to Phil and his son—" He didn't like the last remark. He slammed his hands down into his pockets and began one of his staring contests. "If you can't share any of this information with me, then I'll write up whatever I already have and let Phil turn everything over to Greg's lawyer." Naturally, he was still looking directly into my eyes. Supposedly with men the staring business is about who gets to be the alpha male, but since I was willing to yield to Nelson the right to the biggest chunk of woolly mammoth, I didn't have to feel like a bug-eyed fool. So I signaled my beta status by glancing back at the receipt. Nevertheless, I wasn't about to forgo my argument. "Greg and his attorney have an absolute right to know what I've found," I informed him. "Look, she won't like it; no criminal lawyer is going to be thrilled that Fancy Phil has had a secret, parallel investigation going on, except her detective hasn't produced any miracles. But chances are, the guy being a pro, he has a contact at American Express who's either sympathetic or bribable. He can find out what Samantha R. was buying before Halloween."

While Nelson stayed in the kitchen to make some calls, I went upstairs to slip into something more comfortable, which in my case was a pair of baggy navy shorts (my legs being fairly sensational until three inches above my knees), a big white shirt, sleeves rolled up, and thongs. Still, I didn't know if Nelson was staying or going until I came back down and saw him standing before the open refrigerator with a bunch of tired parsley in his hand. "Believe it or not," he told me, "you have a better refrigerator than most single women."

"That's because I eat more than most single women. Are you cooking?"

"Sure." Right after high school, Nelson had gone into the air force and been assigned to a stove instead of a jet fighter. He bragged his most brilliant dish was barbecued chicken for three hundred, though he'd always claimed he could pull together a decent meal for a smaller group, like two.

"What are you making?" I asked.

"Pasta with a sauce made out of whatever you got." He pulled out an onion, a stray clove of garlic, and a red pepper so old it had imploded upon itself, then opened the freezer and discovered half a French bread I had no memory of buying, eating, or serving.

"How do you know so much about single women's refrigerators?" I asked.

"From when I was between marriages. And you know, on the job."

With that cheerful thought, I got busy setting the table. "Do you know what I'm thinking?" I asked.

"You're going to tell me, aren't you? Where do you hide your canned tomatoes?"

I pointed to the pantry and said: "About Emily. That Josh Kincaid I told you about, the one who'd worked with Courtney at Patton Giddings, who met Emily at a real estate closing? The way he described her—"

" 'Her' meaning Emily?"

"Yes. He made her sound so bland and quiet that she must have been close to invisible. I guess she had a good relationship with the bank's big client, that Saf-T guy. But I don't know about other relationships. When I spoke to her mother, she didn't know anything about Emily's friends. Maybe there weren't many, or any. By the way, the mother was not from the big conversationalists, to put it mildly. And Emily's neighbors, that nice young couple you spoke to also—Beth and Roberto—their description was of someone really quiet or extremely shy."

As Nelson was opening the cans of peeled tomatoes, I got to thinking that this sort of intimacy was probably more threatening to my peace of mind than the sex part of the relationship. Such welcome coziness, and from the very man I'd yearned to be cozy with for much of my adult life. I recalled that in the first years after we parted, I'd often excuse myself when the family was watching TV together in the evening and go upstairs to a bathroom, lock the door, and sob. "So what about her being quiet or shy or unassertive or whatever?" he asked. "How many hundreds of times have you seen neighbors of a guy who's just gunned down ten people being interviewed? They all say, 'But he was such a nice, quiet person.' Quiet people kill. Shy people kill."

"I know. But it's so weird to me to have to think of someone that retiring as a criminal mastermind. Look, she accepted the glass ceiling at work. Her whole career she'd been at only one job, and it didn't sound like a particularly thrilling one."

"Not everybody is ambitious."

"I know that. She could have done better, but she stayed and stayed in a boring, safe job. Sure, maybe that was how she was, someone who didn't like challenges. But that's what's so amazing, that she plotted this whole criminal scam, using insider information. She had Courtney, or Courtney and some offshore corporation, buying the stock low and selling it high."

I had to give him credit; he could listen and chop the onion with the boldness of a television chef at the same time. "First of all, my sweetheart, this is just your theory. It could be that Emily Chavarria and Courtney Logan met each other at that women's thing in Baltimore and became friendly. The reason Emily called Courtney a few days before Halloween was that she was going to a party and couldn't decide whether to go as Snow White or the Seventh Dwarf."

"I know it's just a theory," I conceded. "Anyone could have killed Courtney. Greg, the au pair, the high-school classmate who wound up taking the blame for the candy-bar-money theft, Mr. or Mrs. Fancy Phil, the guy who built and serviced the Logans' pool. Just give me another theory that fits as many facts as mine does. I'll be glad to consider it." He turned away to think and chop.

All I wanted to do was stand there and watch him, so I made myself go upstairs to my office. I got on-line and did one of those People Searches. A few Vanessa Russells, though I sensed none of them was Emily since killers probably prefer unlisted numbers. Still, I printed out the page.

I pushed back from the desk to avoid one of my flake-out attacks: I'd begin at a music site ordering a Sinatra CD, wind up reading personal accounts by Japanese-Americans of life in internment sites during World War II, then shut down the computer having no memory of why I'd turned it on in the first place. Focus, I ordered myself: Even a big baby like Josh Kincaid had landed himself a job at Patton Giddings. True, after a year he'd been asked to leave, but if he hadn't had the family mortgage company to fall back on, he probably could have chosen from a couple of non-dead-end, semi-interesting jobs in finance. I had no idea how much discrimination against women there was in the field, but even assuming a great deal, Emily might have gotten out of the Red Oak Bank and gone elsewhere. Well, I thought, maybe she had a mad crush on an unattainable man there and couldn't bear to leave. Or maybe, despite having the Mr. Saf-T seal of approval and thus kept on by Red Oak, she was a noticeably dim bulb or a bad egg nobody else would hire.

The aroma of sautéing onions wafted into the room and I felt myself getting teary—not from the onions but from the perfection of having Nelson in my house and the knowledge that sooner or later he'd be leaving for his own. For his wife. From wife, it was just my usual happy hop to contemplating the possibility that she'd decide on a late-in-life baby—Surprise, honey!—thus guaranteeing their marriage for the next twenty or so years.

I pulled my chair back to the computer and typed in "Samantha R. Corby." Eight S. Corbys, with addresses and phone numbers. I printed out that page, too, then switched to a general search engine and gave "Samantha R. Corby" a shot. Nothing, which didn't cause me to reel with shock. However, knowing the mindless literalness of computers, I typed in "Samantha Corby." One item came up.

I double-clicked and there I was, at the Web site of the Wiggins, Idaho, *Star,* a newspaper that made the *Shorehaven Beacon* read like the *Christian Science Monitor.* Right there, in the November 19, 1999, issue, in a small box titled "Welcome New Neighbor!" between "Arlene and Arnold Chester" and "Dr. and Mrs. Alwyn Rossi" was "Samantha Corby." I had no idea of what to do next, but since no mellifluous calls of "Dinner!" were rising up the stairs, I pulled up a map of Idaho and made Wiggins the center of that universe. Just a few millimeters above it, a direction some might call north, past towns called Bellevue, Hailey, and

Ketchum was Sun Valley. Resort, I thought. Famous resort. Hadn't some Olympics been held there?

I got on the phone. The woman at the *Star*, who sounded as if she might be the paper's entire staff—or the only one there so late in the day—said the names for "Welcome New Neighbor!" came from local real estate brokers. She gave me a few numbers. I kept making calls until Nelson bellowed: "Ready when you are!"

I came down bubbling about my Samantha Corby discovery. "Could be," Nelson said, actually pulling out a kitchen chair for me.

Whatever parsley he hadn't used he'd stuck in a glass and set it on the table as the centerpiece. "When Steffi talked about the woman she saw leaving the Logans', the woman who might be Emily," I said a few minutes later as I pierced a couple of pieces of fusilli, "she described her as a little gray mouse." Busy admiring either my shirt or my cleavage, Nelson nodded in a polite, uninterested way that was almost husbandly. I thought I deserved a little more heed, having already lauded his tomato sauce at length, with absolute sincerity. He was a natural cook, at home in any kitchen. He'd even discovered my vegetable patch and picked some lettuce and radishes for the salad. "Nelson."

"What?"

"I want you to pay a lot of attention to me right now." He smiled, nodded okay, took a bite of the garlic bread he'd made, then refilled our glasses from the bottle of red wine I always kept on hand for Nancy so she wouldn't get d.t.'s or bitchy or whatever. "Okay," I said, "remember 'little gray mouse,' but put it on the shelf for a minute."

"It's on the shelf. I'm listening, Judith. I'm fascinated by everything you say."

"Good." I made a big deal of clearing my throat, probably because I wasn't completely clear about what I was going to say and I guess I wanted Nelson to approve of every syllable. You think you get to a point in life when other people's opinions don't matter. You are who you are; you won't be destroyed if someone doesn't like you or mocks your ideas. I knew Nelson liked me—loved me—and he wasn't going to laugh his head off if he thought I was wrong. He'd say straight out that he disagreed with me. At best he'd be kind. At worst, polite. Sure, if I'd say something blatantly idiotic he'd respond with "Give me a break," but I knew he was well aware I wasn't a blatant idiot.

"Come on," he said encouragingly.

"To me, it seems that when you're searching for the whodunit in a murder case, you have to have the pertinent facts. But if the facts aren't enough to help you to solve it, you also have to search out the emotional or psychological truth. I keep thinking about the sort of person Courtney was and I keep coming up with the feeling there was something fundamentally wrong with her."

"Homicide victims are dead because someone perpetrated a crime against them," Nelson retorted. "They're no better or worse than anybody else. Saints get murdered. So do monsters. If you're right about Courtney, she was involved in a serious mess. She was greedy, arrogant, and a lousy judge of character."

"Right, but let me go on from this. At first I thought of her as a perfectionist, but I think it's equally about control. She wanted to be in charge. She was the one who set the rules. No sugar for the kids. Only an hour of TV. The au pair had to wait until after the kids were asleep before she could watch television in her own room. The young woman who did the videography for StarBaby told me that until Courtney lost interest, Courtney practically breathed for her. She didn't hire an interior decorator the way a lot of women in her economic class do. She did it herself. Perfectionism or control, but nothing was left undone. The chandelier in the front hall: it had teeny lampshades over each bulb, and each shade had a scalloped trim. She lined the bathroom wastebasket with a doily."

"I can't believe someone thought she deserved to die for that," Nelson said.

"No. That's not why Mack Dooley got a big surprise when he took off the pool cover. But before I get to that, let's talk about how other people saw Courtney. Greg? He's not going to say he hated her. There's no way of knowing what he felt. The same with the au pair. She seems to have genuinely idolized Courtney, but if she had a mad pash for Greg, requited or unrequited, she's not going to tell me that Courtney was a domineering pain in the ass."

"Do you have a mad pash for me?" he asked.

"No, I'm just toying with you until I can find something better."

"That's what I figured you'd say."

"Courtney was pretty, or at least cute, kind of a Princeton amalgam of Sandra Dee and June Allyson." Nelson laughed, but then he'd always reacted that way to my movie analogies, so I flicked my hand to brush him off. "But so many people seemed to think there was something not right about her.

"First and foremost, that woman she went to high school with, Ingrid Farrell. Ingrid took the hit when Courtney stole that candy-bar money. It's really not a juvenile prank, because everyone believed Ingrid was guilty. Even Ingrid's parents believed she'd done it, and so they made restitution. The cloud of that incident has been hanging over her ever since. It was a terrible thing for Courtney to do. Okay, next: Jill Badinowski, one of StarBaby's clients: She described Courtney as being an ice-cold businesswoman, that she could be selling videos of babies or poison gas, it made no difference. Fancy Phil told me that if you looked for personality in Courtney, it wasn't there. He described her as *lukshen,* Yiddish for noodles."

"Noodles are a no-no?"

"No, they're a yes-yes, but plain, without seasoning or sauce, they're really blah. So Fancy Phil saw Courtney as bland. On the other hand, he recognized how manipulative she was, trying to get him to buy whatever she and her husband couldn't afford: a Land Rover, a super-duper TV. She even tried getting Fancy to buy her a sable coat."

"So what are you saying?" Nelson wasn't challenging me, just trying to find out where I was going.

"I'm not one hundred percent sure yet. What does it sound like to you?"

"I don't know. So far, what strikes me is that candy-bar thing. I know I kidded you about it, but it's not cute or pretty. It stinks. The sable coat is pushy, but it's not the end of the world."

"One of the women in her group of about seven or eight mothers of little kids didn't really know Courtney very well. But she was very smart, very insightful, plus she used a movie analogy in describing Courtney."

"Always a sign of high intelligence," Nelson observed.

"Of genius. She compared Courtney to a pod person in *The Invasion of the Body Snatchers,* just a shell of a person, drained of all humanity." I waited for a laugh or a good-natured shake of his head, but he merely sipped his wine and waited. "Zee Friedman, the videographer, said that when little Travis came into the room while they were talking, Courtney got this blissed-out look on her face, like a Madonna. And when Greg came home from playing golf, Courtney acted as if he were the hottest guy in the world."

"What's wrong with that?"

"I love my kids with all my heart and soul," I said, "but when they were little and came running into the room and interrupted what I was doing, believe me, it wasn't Mary and Jesus time. And after you're married for six or seven years or whatever, and you're with a business associate, you don't get all steamed up when your husband comes home. The au pair picked up on it, too; she said when Greg was around, Courtney acted like a bride on her wedding day. And her best friend Kellye Ryan noticed the 'Ooh, isn't he hot?' bit. She didn't buy it for a minute. In fact, she thought Courtney was having an affair—although she's a minority of one. Most everyone else didn't see her as sexual at all." I rested my head against the back of the chair. "Is she coming through clearly to you yet?"

"No."

"Cecile Rabiea, who came to Patton Giddings the same time Courtney did, said her work was good, but she wasn't able to go the full route, to court the client, help the client. It wasn't that she was lazy, it's that somehow she couldn't get the human element right."

"Fine, but she's still not clear."

"Courtney didn't comprehend other people's needs, not really. She could have been immature or insensitive. On the other hand, she could have been seriously deficient or defective. And another thing: She wasn't showing people her true colors. Maybe she didn't have any colors. Too many people described her in terms of being slightly off. You know, like a pretty good actress playing roles like wife, mother, neighbor, investment banker. When you're talking about a person's essence, a pretty good imitation isn't good enough. That's why people were struck that there was something off about her."

"Where you taking this, Judith?"

"Where do you think I'm taking this?"

With his fork he made tracks through the tomato sauce on his plate, around, rather than through, the pasta. "That Courtney was some kind of . . . Whatever they're calling it these days. Psychopath? Sociopath?"

"I think so. I know I shouldn't take that one incident with the Crunch-Munch sale in high school as emblematic, but it showed a coldness that's scary."

"But that's not fair to Courtney. She isn't around anymore to defend herself."

"I know. But if she were a sociopath, she'd probably be articulate and have a smooth defense—the way she convinced her high-school principal that Ingrid Farrell stole the Crunch-Munch money. Courtney didn't have a conscience."

"How do you know?" he insisted. "If she did steal the money, maybe it was bothering her all these years. What could she have done? Gone back to wherever she came from—Washington—and confessed? That's not realistic. She had a husband, kids, a position in the community."

"I know. Stable family life. And she wasn't violent or argumentative the way a lot of wackos are."

"Right," Nelson said.

"But if she's turned out to be such a good person, full of remorse but unable to apologize without jeopardizing everything, then how come she got involved with Emily?"

Nelson reached out and put his hand over mine. "But that's just a theory, Judith. All you have on that is that when Emily was supposedly on vacation, the cell phone that was used to call her office was also used to call Courtney's house. And also that about six years ago the two of them went to the same conference in Baltimore."

I set down my fork so I could cover his hand. "A hand sandwich," I noted. He smiled. "I know you're being kind, Nelson. Thank you."

We took our hands back. "It's okay." His tone was gentle. "Listen, don't be hard on yourself. Nobody, including me, would want to give Phil Lowenstein bad news."

"I want to give you another theory."

"Sure."

"It's about little women," I began. "Not the book—"

"The movie?"

"Be quiet. You know, I saw pictures of Courtney in the papers and on TV. She wasn't a beauty, but she was really good to look at." Nelson nodded cautiously. "Then I went to try and convince Greg to hire me, and don't shake your head and mumble 'I can't believe you did that.' I did it. Period. End of discussion."

"Not quite. You were a jerk to do that, Judith, knocking on the door of someone who's pretty obviously a murder suspect. Now it's end of discussion."

"Fine. Anyway, I was sitting in his living room and on the table next to me was a framed photograph of Greg and Courtney in tennis clothes. They looked adorable together. Both were clean-cut, athletic looking, but there were nice contrasts, too. He's dark, she's fair. He's tall, she's short. I remember, her head was resting against his chest. Actually, he's not all that tall. She was just short. My guess is about five-feet-one or so."

Nelson swirled the wine in his glass. "Uh-huh."

"So I was thinking again about that picture. And also, when I went through her closet, which I don't want to dwell on because just the thought of it probably makes your cop hackles rise, whatever hackles are. Anyhow, her shoes were a size six."

"Well, that solves the case, doesn't it?"

"You know who else was short? Emily. When Beth and Roberto were talking about her, they said she only had one suitcase for her trip. He offered to put it in her trunk because she was, you know, a little woman, but she said she could manage. And remember the 'little gray mouse' Steffi talked about?"

"Where are you going?" he demanded. "Do you think she was carrying body parts or gold bars in the suitcase and didn't want anyone to feel how much it weighed? Or she had little bitty Courtney inside? Maybe Courtney went to buy apples but then drove down to New Jersey and Emily, who hadn't gone to Australia, killed her, then brought her back to Long Island and slipped the body into the pool." His manner wasn't sarcastic, but tough-minded, the devil's advocate.

"No, I'm not saying that."

"Good."

"I'll get there, Nelson. Just hear me out. Emily had brown hair. But after the summer, she started letting it grow. And voilà! It started getting blonder. Beth told me she suddenly looked like she had some life in her face."

"A boyfriend?"

"Could be. Or maybe she was all charged up about the new life she was going to have, financed by whatever scheme she and Courtney had cooked up, and yes, Nelson, I know it's just a theory. Here's another theory: Maybe Courtney was giving her a makeover."

"Okay."

"Little Courtney was making over Little Emily to look like Little Courtney."

He was gazing right at me, but this time it was no staring contest. He was looking for an answer. I think he was close to realizing what I was trying to say, except he was slowed down by simultaneously reasoning it out and thinking of reasons why I couldn't be right. "What are you trying to say? What do you think was going on?"

"I think Courtney was creating a substitute Courtney. I think the body in the pool—"

"Impossible!"

"—is Emily Chavarria."

Chapter Seventeen

"Don't just say 'impossible.' Think about it," I pleaded with Nelson. "Emily coming to Shorehaven and shooting Courtney doesn't make sense."

"It makes a hell of a lot more sense than—"

"I'm talking about character. Personality. Whatever you want to call it. When I found out there was an Emily and decided there could be a link, I thought, Hot damn! She did the dastardly deed. But the more I learned about her, the less likely she seemed to be capable of carrying off this kind of a murder and cover-up."

"What about the money side of this, if there was one?" Nelson asked. "Was Emily capable of that?"

"Intellectually, without a doubt. But I bet even there, Courtney took over and was calling the shots. But what Emily did or didn't have is find-outable. Even if all her money disappeared from her bank and brokerage accounts, you can find out how much was in them and when she took it out."

"You think her timing for withdrawing everything would have to be before that bigger company took over Saf-T-Close?" He seemed not so much attentive as tolerant, letting me express myself.

So I did. "Sure, she wanted to get all she could to buy that stock she knew was going to go way up. But forget her for a second. Look at Courtney. She was assertive, she was ambitious. She was athletic, for God's sake. Do you think Emily the mouse would have been strong enough to kill a Courtney wherever and then get the body into the pool?" He was shaking his head: pure speculation. "Give me a break, Nelson, come on."

"I'm giving you a break, believe me. But what do you want me to do? Throw out any rational thought that comes into my head because it doesn't fit your theory?"

"No. Not at all. Just give me a little more time." It struck me that the request for more time might sound obsequious or pathetic, as in "Don't go home to your wife yet." To make up for that, I heard myself breaking into my I-am-Woman-hear-me-roar voice that was so thunderous I unnerved myself. "Listen to me! Emily was obviously struggling with that suitcase." I quieted down a bit. "That's why Roberto offered to help her. She wasn't that strong. But I bet if you check out Courtney some more, you'll find out she could lift . . . whatever Emily weighed."

Nelson pushed his chair away from the kitchen table, sat back, and crossed his legs in that triangle shape men make, so their privates remain on display in case anyone has doubts. He gave his mouth a curl to the side that I knew meant: I hate to say this, but . . . "Fingerprints, Judith. Remember fingerprints? The ones in Courtney's house and car they got after she was missing match the prints they were able to get from the body." I started clearing the table, not to run away from the conversation but to organize my thoughts. "And another thing," he said.

"What?" He drew back his lips and tapped on his teeth. They appeared to be in good shape. "Teeth?" I said. "Oh, you mean the dental records."

"They seem to go with the teeth from the body in Courtney's pool."

I made a big deal of putting the leftover pasta in a plastic container so he'd know I'd cherish it for days to come. I was beginning to see why prudence suggests not mixing romance and business; it's hard to think straight when desire and pique mix. "Don't worry," I said, too brightly for my taste, "I can fit all of this into my grand synthesis of unprovable hypotheses."

He lifted his glass in a toast. "I'm a good listener."

"Think about the little gray mouse again. She was in Courtney's house." Seeing he was about to interrupt, I added: "Okay, she *may* have been in Courtney's house. I bet if you gave Steffi some more pictures of Emily she could identify her even more positively."

"So Courtney did what?" Nelson inquired tactfully. "Wiped every surface in the house so only Emily's prints would be there?"

"Probably, although I'll bet if Nassau County's finest had really been conscientious, they would have found other little prints from some other little adult. Don't forget, when they picked up those prints, they were looking for a missing person, not a murder victim. And they probably did it days or even weeks after Courtney disappeared."

"We'll never know, will we?"

"Maybe not."

"What about the car?" Less tactful now, and on the road to bluntness.

"The car . . ." I said slowly.

"Because you yourself told me the au pair said that gray mouse who might be Emily . . . Her car was in the driveway."

"That doesn't mean she didn't drive Courtney's car some other time. Look, I'm Courtney, okay? I don't want my own prints on my car. So I wipe the steering wheel, the window buttons, the gearshift, the seat belts, the car seat for the kid really, really well. What else? Oh, the door handles, inside and out, the back gate on an SUV. Now every time I use it, I either wear gloves or something over all my fingertips. Pieces of Band-Aid or something." He mumbled either "genius" or "ingenious" in a sardonic tone which I naturally ignored. "I also have my husband drive it," I continued. "But at some point I ask Emily to drive. Maybe instead of going for apples I met her in a central location and said, 'Hey, I've been driving car pools all day. Give me a break,' or some such thing. So to the Missing Persons cops, the Land Rover will look like a normal family car because the parents' prints will be up front and the kids' and their friends' prints will be all over the back. No prints from a kidnapper or carjacker or killer or whoever supposedly snatched Courtney."

"I like that," he said. "Very creative."

"Oh, go stuff it!"

"You're making Courtney out to be a master criminal."

"No, not a master criminal, but a damn good one. Why not, Nelson? If I can imagine all this, she certainly should be capable. She's a *magna cum laude* graduate of Princeton. That means she was more than smart in college. She was organized. Meticulous. You could see it in her house. Everything was *done*. Every lampshade was the platonic ideal of that particular kind of lampshade. She had botanical prints matted and framed and hung on a ribbon. There wasn't one empty table; every single knickknack was planned, not too many, not too few, size and color-coordinated. It was a flawless, soulless house."

He rose from the table and kissed me just as I was coming up from fighting with a bowl that didn't want to go in the bottom dishwasher rack. "Is that it," he asked, "or is there more?"

The night before, when I'd momentarily wakened for a bathroom intermission, I'd promised myself that whatever happened in this relationship, I was going to behave like a grown woman—not a middle-aged girl. No innuendos. No cutesy hints. I would not refer obliquely to his marriage in the hopes he'd respond with a declaration that included the words "getting a divorce" and "redecorate your big bedroom upstairs." If I wanted to discuss his status, I'd promised myself, then I had to say it straight.

Thus, I stifled the emerging Are-you-sure-you-have-time-and-don't-have-to-get-home? and told him: "I've got a lot more." We sat back at the table, clear now except for the glass of parsley. "The gift Courtney had for analysis, for looking at all the angles of a problem, was sharpened at Patton Giddings. Numbers crunching, evaluating businesses. Remember, her work was good. It was her people skills that didn't make the grade."

"Okay, but what about the dental records?" He caught the look in my eyes. "Oh no. Don't tell me you're going to say she switched them, Judith Eve Bernstein Singer."

"She did switch them, Nelson Lawrence Sharpe. The X rays that they slip into those cards? Emily's has got to be in Courtney's and vice versa. I bet if you locate Courtney's dentist, you'll find a new female patient . . . probably in September or early October. A new patient who was about Courtney's height, with blond streaks, a little younger than Courtney. Is that creative, too?"

He had that annoying tender look people give to klutzy, big-footed puppies. "Yes."

"Good," I responded. "Well, we can solve this difference of opinion very easily."

"Excellent. How?"

"Get Courtney's dental records from Olympia, Washington. I bet they won't match the teeth on the body. Or Emily's records from Leesford, Oklahoma. They will match."

"Jesus H. Christ," he said softly, and shifted in his seat. Now he was looking away from me, viewing the wall with my arrangement of framed California fruit-crate labels, although I don't think he saw them. After what seemed a long time but was probably only a minute, he turned back to me. "I don't know what to say. This is a theory. A long shot."

"What's the downside? You annoy a couple of dentists?"

"I'd need a subpoena to get those records. And this is an interstate matter."

"Can't you wangle a subpoena? Or just make a call and be charming?"

"I'm not charming."

"You are, too."

"I've got to think about it," he stated with finality. Then he stood. "By the way, Nelson, there may be another way to solve our difference of opinion."

Maybe he thought I was being too overbearing, or attempting to keep him from leaving. Still, he behaved kindly, even indulgently. "I'm still listening." He even smiled.

"All that fingerprint evidence and the teeth business are considered conclusive, right?" I asked.

"In a lot of cases."

"So did anyone on the Logan case bother to compare DNA from the body with DNA from Morgan or Travis?"

Nelson sat back down. "Oh shit!" he replied.

By the time he left, he was still wavering. Though taken with what I had to say, he was not completely convinced that he hadn't fallen for a story, my diverting fusion of random facts. Nevertheless, he was intrigued by the Courtney–Emily link: the Baltimore meeting; the cell phone that had made calls to Emily's office and Courtney's house; the possible identification of Emily by Steffi Deissenburger. He was aching to bust open the case. But I'd studied the FDR years long enough to have a pretty good feel for politics. I understood that the last thing Nelson would do was go out on a limb and risk making a fool of himself in front of the department's top brass and the new chief of Homicide.

The next couple of days were rough. I was never much good at waiting around for things to happen, but I didn't dare try anything rash. So I kept a lid on it. Just to show Fancy Phil I was still on the case, I had another breakfast with him. Raisin Bran for me. For him, two stacks of pancakes, a plate of French toast. His morning jewelry was a ring with a giant seal that looked as if it had been snitched from the Vatican, and a double length of huge gold chain links that might have been a combo of jewelry/equipment for a sex game I did not want to envision. I kept my Emily-in-pool theory to myself, but reported to Fancy that I was pursuing leads on the two women in both Shorehaven and Cherry Hill.

Nelson called mid-afternoon. I could hear him trying to keep the excitement out of his voice. He'd been able to get a copy of Samantha Corby's charges from an ex-cop he knew who was now working in the compliance department of American Express. Heavy-duty purchases in the best of the best stores in Manhattan during October, a car rental there, and meals at some pretty tony restaurants. For a few minutes I puzzled over why she hadn't shopped locally, then realized, given her spending habits, she couldn't pass herself off as Samantha Corby on the north shore of Long Island, being well known already as Lady Bountiful, aka Courtney Logan. Among the other charges were some first-class tickets to Miami and a hefty Miami hotel bill. I couldn't believe she had the gall or carelessness not to worry about running into someone from her New York life there. Then to—*Bingo!*—Nevis in the British Virgin Islands for two days. Offshore whatever! I gloated. Visiting her money! Nelson countered with: How about scuba diving? After that interlude, Samantha Corby had gone back to the Miami area, to Key Biscayne, for two weeks, then on to Boise, Idaho—about one hundred fifty miles away from Sun Valley—where she spent over four thousand dollars on ski gear.

"The charges stop the end of December," Nelson said.

"What?" Since he wouldn't fax me the list of charges, I'd been cradling the phone between ear and shoulder and scribbling notes as fast as I could. "What do you think happened?"

"I don't know."

"But you have a theory."

"Come on, Judith," he said. "I can't stay on with you. I've got a lot to do."

"What's your theory, and don't give me your I'm-being-tolerant sigh. Why no charges after December?"

"If there's actually a Samantha R. Corby—and so far there isn't any—I'd say she overdid it on her Christmas spending and needed time to recoup."

"But if it's Courtney?"

"Then she could be as smart as you think. All the American Express bills were paid in full."

"Why is that smart?" I asked, musing if I was a sociopath and had no qualms about murder, I could probably live with stiffing Neiman Marcus.

"Because if you're going to get lost, you pay your bills. The last thing you want are bill collectors or skip tracers hunting you down. They stay at it longer than cops can and they have more money to search with."

"Then what happened after December?" I asked.

"You know as much as I do."

"No, Nelson, you know more. You're a detective."

"I thought that's what you are."

"Don't banter with me now. I'm not in a bantering mood. Just tell me what you think."

"If it's Courtney? She's either dead or, more likely, using another name. And if she dropped Samantha, which would be super-cautious but also super-smart, she probably dropped Sun Valley, too."

All that kept me from going into a complete funk was the belief that even if Courtney had gotten away, there remained the possibility of clearing Greg Logan of the murder charge that had been hounding him since his wife's disappearance. A DNA test would do it. Actually, the other thing that kept me out of funkdom was Nelson's calling at seven-thirty that evening asking if he could come over for a while.

This time we made love in Joey's ex-bedroom, under a *Metropolis* poster. He waited until he was dressed again to give me the news that Courtney Logan had been cremated. Before I could howl in despair, he added that the medical examiner's office always kept tissue samples for later testing. In this case, with the body so decomposed after all those months in the pool, they'd kept teeth and bone instead of tissue. The pulp cavity of a tooth and the marrow of a bone would retain blood elements that could be tested. Not conventional postcoital sweet nothings, I admit, but I was exhilarated—until he said he was going to wait to get dental records from Washington or Oklahoma before he put his ass on the line and pushed for the DNA test. Also, he was swamped with his own cases, so please, no pressure.

The next morning I tried Fancy Phil. No luck with him. Maybe he really had turned over that new leaf and was at that moment studying Talmud. Or if he was still the same old Fancy, he could have been occupied with some new white-collar crime or with his old, reliable: assault with intent to kill. He finally responded to his beeper after noon. Just to keep him from getting too inquisitive, I asked him to get the names of Courtney's gynecologist, dentist, and accountant, figuring that with Fancy Phil, teeth (and their implications) would be overlooked when bracketed by vagina and money.

Having not much to occupy me after Fancy, I called the Red Oak Bank, said I was working for Dewey and Bricker, and asked for the person who had done secretarial work for Emily Chavarria.

"Helloooo," I heard at last. Gina Berke trilled so high her voice probably fell more into the hearing range of rodents than humans. "How may I help you?" I gave her a story about Emily being missing for so long now, and how the family had scrimped and saved and had come to Dewey and Bricker Investigations in Oklahoma City. Would she know offhand who Emily used as a doctor and dentist in New Jersey? Before she put me on hold, I considered saying Thanks, ma'am to sound more western, but decided not to push my luck. When Gina picked up the phone again, she gave me Dr. Alan Jerrold, D.D.S.—"Can you believe he's still on my computer?"—and Jack Goldberg, M.D. While I had her at her screen, I asked if she'd ever made any hairdresser appointments for Emily.

"God, it's funny you're asking that. Not till the last couple of months. You should have seen her before. Very plain Jane. You wouldn't have ever thought of her as a blonde, but she started looking *so* good."

"A new boyfriend or something?"

"I don't know. Emily didn't talk all that much. Very, very, very shy socially."

"Could she talk for banking business?"

"Oh yeah. Sure. She was . . . I forget the word, but really, really good at what she does. Did. Sorry."

"I heard she was close with Richard Grey," I said.

"I don't know if she was close. He's engaged."

"I meant in a business sense."

"Oh, sure, Mr. Grey would have trusted her with his life. When she didn't come back . . . He was beyond the valley of upset, if you know what I mean."

"Right. And her hairdresser?"

"Mane—M-A-N-E—Magic." And she gave me the number.

"By the way, just out of curiosity. Was Emily sickly or kind of weak? Or strong?"

"She never, ever missed a day of work."

"So I've heard."

"But she looked like if you'd blow her over, like, she'd get blown over."

When Fancy Phil called back with the names of Courtney's accountant, gynecologist, and dentist, he wanted to know why I needed them. Greg was curious, too.

"Does Greg know about me yet?" I asked.

"Look, Doc honey, I'm asking him a lot of questions, you know? So he must know I got someone looking into something, but he don't know it's you. How come you're asking about her gyno and her dentist and CPA?"

"No reason. I guess I'm grasping at straws, Phil."

"You know, that's one of those stupid sayings, 'grasping at straws.' Not that I'm blaming you. But who the hell invented something that goddamn stupid?"

"Beats me." I took down the names and said I'd get back to him.

Courtney's dentist in Shorehaven was Winslow Gaines, D.D.S. I had a hazy recollection of hearing the name from Nancy. Assuming Gaines hadn't been Ginsberg a generation earlier and speculating that between the Millers' church and Larry's country and yacht clubs, she, of all my friends, would have the best chance of knowing a Winslow Gaines any-way, I called her at *Newsday*. After both of us vented our spleens about the disgusting attacks on women and girls by forty men in Central Park and made a date for dinner that night, we got to Winslow. Not only did Nancy know Win, a member of North Bay Yacht Club, she'd *known* him, chuckle-chuckle, about ten years earlier. Didn't she ever mention him? The knowing had lasted less than a month because of his fondness for dental humor. Without too much of a fuss she said, All right, I'll call him. I know he'd adore hearing from me again. As always with Nancy, I simply could not imagine an American girlhood that could have engendered that much ostensible self-esteem. If I'd had a hat I would have taken it off to her. Anyhow, she commanded me to meet her at his office around six o'clock. I asked if she didn't want to check with him first. She said, Oh, please!

For a man in his early sixties, Winslow Gaines was quite a hunk. Tall, broad-shouldered in his white dental tunic, with white at the temples of his light brown hair and a cleft in his chin. He had the ho-hum hand-someness of a soap-opera star. He certainly was friendly enough, though it was hard to get his attention, as it kept wandering to Nancy, who, I could tell, had changed from the usual slacks and shirt she wore to work into a sleeveless beige linen dress cut to bare a little shoulder and a lot of leg.

"The last time Courtney came in?" he said as he sat down at the re-ceptionist's computer. His staff was gone. The waiting room, with its pic-tures of sailboats and copies of *Yachting World* and *Classic Boat,* along with *What's New in Tooth Whitening?,* was empty. The dentist was not a natural cyberguy, hitting the keys slowly with his index fingers. Nancy, standing behind him, hands familiarly on his shoulders, rolled her eyes at his bum-bling. When he turned back to glance at her, she flashed him a provoca-tive smile. "Let's see," he muttered. After poking a few more keys, he swung his office chair around to me. "How did the dentist break his mir-ror?" he demanded.

"I don't know," I told him.

"Acci-DENTAL-ly!"

I chortled along with him while Nancy said, "Come on now, Win. You're looking for Courtney Logan."

Finally, he pointed to the screen. "Here she is! Last came in on Octo-ber twenty-sixth, in 'ninety-nine. Complained of tooth pain, but it was periodontal. I remember telling her that her home care was pretty far from exemplary, and she was on her way to serious gum disease if she didn't mend her ways." He shook his head sadly. "You know, after she disappeared, and then all that stuff later, finding her . . . You remember things like that. Nice, nice woman."

"How were her teeth?" I asked.

"Not bad at all. But like most people with good teeth, you think everything will be fine forever. Oral hygiene is way, way down on your list of priorities. You can't live like that."

"Around that time," I told him, "someone else might have come in, probably a new patient. A woman. Also on the small side, like Courtney. Streaky, blondish hair, on the quiet side."

"Do you know her name?" he asked. I suggested Emily Chavarria, Vanessa Russell—the name of the cell phone's owner—and Samantha R. Corby. He typed in the names, but none came up on the screen.

"Do it by date," Nancy directed him. When he turned around looking befuddled, she shooed him off the chair, sat herself down, and began to type.

"Why did the guru refuse Novocain at the dentist's?" he asked me. He was lounging against the wall, arms crossed over his chest, looking incongruously bon vivant.

"I give up."

"Quiet!" Nancy demanded. "What does NP mean? New patient?" Win nodded. "Seven new patients in October. Look at these names," she commanded him.

He whispered "He wanted to transcend dental medication" to me, gave me a wink, then leaned over toward Nancy until the side of his face was touching hers. He pointed to a box that said AGE and immediately eliminated four from the group as being children. Of the others, two were women, one of whom was fifty-seven years old.

The other was twenty-eight. "Polly Hastings," Nancy announced. "An alias if I ever heard one. Win, do you remember Polly?"

"I don't think so."

"Twenty-eight, angel. You must have some memory."

"Doesn't ring a bell," he answered.

"Look! She came in on October the twenty-sixth!" Nancy said.

"What time?" I asked.

"Two o'clock."

"And Courtney?"

"Two-fifteen."

"Oh my God!" I said. "She could have snatched Emily's file for a minute. All she had to do was go into the room Emily was in to say hi."

"Or while the X rays were drying," Nancy chimed in.

"What's going on?" Win asked. "Who's Emily?"

"Or she found a way to get into the records room," Nancy said.

"Patients don't walk into the file room," Win said. He looked as much confused as disturbed, although in either case, handsomely so. "This new woman was just in for a checkup. Oh, Wendy gave her a cleaning and took X rays." I took out the photograph of Emily Chavarria I'd gotten off the Web and emailed to Steffi. He studied it and shook his handsome head. "I mean, she's not really, uh, that memorable, is she? Well, maybe it's not a great picture."

"Imagine her all dolled up," I suggested. "Longer, blonder hair. Makeup. Does she look at all familiar?" I asked.

"I'm sorry, I have no recollection."

"Well, give us a copy of her X rays, then," Nancy directed him. I think he was about to explain about doctor-patient confidentiality when she took his hand and led him farther back into the office. I assumed she was taking him to the file room, or (if the good Dr. Gaines was still having compunctions) for a few magical moments on a chair in one of his examining rooms. To while away the time, I sat down at the computer and managed to retrieve Courtney's record. Good health, it appeared. No allergies. In the four years she had been a patient, she'd only had X rays, cleanings every six months like clockwork, and what I guessed was some sort of custom-fitted gizmo made for teeth brightening.

"I hate to ask what took you so long," I said to Nancy later.

"Then don't ask."

"Fine." We were sitting at the town dock watching the day wind down before going out to dinner, although the gulls were busy with theirs. They flew, then rode the wind, then zoomed down to the water for their entrée.

"Besides having to work my wiles to get the X rays, do you know what else I got from Win?" she asked.

"I hope nothing that will require medication."

"Dubious. I got 'What ride in amusement parks do dentists like most?' Don't bother to guess. 'A molar coaster.' The man cannot control himself. And his wife: I see her at the club and she always looks vague. She probably punctured her eardrums. Well, in any case . . ." She waved a manila envelope. "We have Polly Hastings's X rays. What are you going to do with them?"

"If he swears to give them back or have a copy made for me, I'll give them to Nelson. To see if they match Courtney's childhood and teenage records from Olympia, Washington. I bet they do, because Courtney went and switched the X rays, hers for Emily's. If Nelson can't get the information, I'll give it to Fancy Phil, and maybe Greg or Greg's lawyer can work out some deal with the Washington dentist."

"Let me be clear. These really aren't Polly's teeth," Nancy drawled.

"Well, Emily's teeth. These are what you were talking about, from the old switcheroo, so they're actually Courtney Logan's. Right?"

"Right. If they aren't, I'm making a major fool of myself." Her silence spoke loudly. "I'm not making a fool of myself with him, Nan."

"Still the same old fire?"

"Still the same. It's not just fire. I love him." Way out on the bay, we watched as a sunfish bounced happily through the wake of a grand sailboat.

"This is the strangest relationship."

"Nancy, loving a man is not strange. Some might say sleeping with so many men that you stopped counting because you couldn't remember if it was seventy-one or seventy-two is a bit peculiar."

"It's not peculiar," she said somewhat huffily. "It's promiscuous. What did our man in blue say about his wife?"

"I didn't want to talk about her."

"Why not? Afraid he'll say he's staying?"

Clearly, although I didn't say so.

The next morning, to get away from Nelson and Captain Sharpe, both of whom seemed to be exerting an undue influence over my life, I got on a flight leaving La Guardia Airport for Salt Lake City. By mid-afternoon Idaho time, I found myself on an exceedingly small plane being piloted by an excessively young woman over the Sawtooth Mountains. It landed in Hailey. That's about ten miles from Sun Valley. And six miles from Wiggins, where I found Samantha R. Corby's rented condo.

Chapter Eighteen

At the fourth real-estate office, I got the news: Yes, they had rented to Samantha Corby. But she was long gone. "God, she left . . . Why do I think before Christmas? If I'm thinking of the right person. You understand this is not the field if you're looking for long-term relationships. The rental market, I mean." Doreen Brinkerhoff, the agent in charge of renting the furnished condos in Knob Ridge Villas in Wiggins, stood beside a file cabinet. She stuck a ruby-nailed finger through her tangle of shoulder-length black corkscrew curls and scratched her scalp. "Even if they buy. Usually it's an investment property, so they're hardly here." Probably in her early forties, Doreen was firm to a fare-thee-well. Her skin was so tanned that it had the color and texture of the tobacco leaf outside a cigar. "Let me look one place more." She shoved the drawer shut and, despite a minimal denim skirt and platform sandals, squatted down for a look in the bottom drawer. She struck me as the sort of woman to whom life has offered many reasons to be cynical, yet her hard-featured face was benevolent.

I took out the photos of Courtney I'd gotten from the Web and from Fancy Phil and bent down to let her see them, not daring a squat on general principles, and additionally not after all those cramped hours on air-planes. I gave Doreen a choice: tennis Courtney, bridal Courtney, mommy Courtney holding baby Morgan, baker Courtney holding lattice-top pie. "Does this look anything like the woman you think could be Samantha?" I asked.

Her turquoise eyes—the color, I suspected, not of her irises but of her contact lenses—swept over the pictures. "I . . . think . . . it . . . could . . . be. I only met her one time." She went back to the file drawer, though it was so choked with folders I didn't know what she could possibly find.

"What makes you hesitate?" I asked.

"Honestly? I don't remember. Maybe . . . Shorter hair? Younger?"

"Samantha Corby looked younger than this woman?"

"I think so. God, if you got to rely on me, I hate to say it . . . You're in deep you-know-what. Oh! Look! Do me a favor. You see where it says '2BR 99'? That's the two-bedroom units in 1999. Pull it out for me. I just did my nails this morning." After a fair amount of tugging I was finally able to jerk out a thick file. "Depending on how the season is going," Doreen said, "we sometimes have to rent by the week. That makes for a real fat file." Swiftly, she was standing and flying through the pages. "Here! Hallelujah! Look, Judy. Samantha rented through December thirty-first, but she left on the twenty-first." I had long since given up correcting Judy to Judith when dealing with people who were not likely to be soul mates.

"Does it happen to say why she was leaving early?" I asked. Doreen shook her head. "Okay, big question: Did she leave a forwarding address?"

"Uh . . . No. It says . . ." She took a page from the file folder and handed it over. In schoolmarm penmanship someone had written "Will call re security deposit." Since Doreen didn't stop me, I turned over the page. The paper trembled. That was because my hand was shaking. On the back was a photocopy of a check from Samantha R. Corby to Wiggins Way Realty drawn on the Key Biscayne Bank & Trust—as well as a Florida driver's license with her photograph.

In the mountains, it was a cool, windows-open day, but I started to sweat. After I wiped my face with the tissue Doreen handed me, I took out my glasses and stared at the full face picture. I couldn't tell if it was Courtney. A resemblance, sure, but the formerly blond hair now appeared dirty blond or light brown in the black-and-white photocopy. It was shorter, too, curling under mid-neck. The once clear brow was covered with a fringe of uneven bangs. It could have been Courtney. Or Courtney's younger, less attractive sister, had she had one. Or someone completely unrelated. I copied down Samantha's home address on Key Biscayne, her height, five-two, and her date of birth, 08-04-71. On the bottom of the card it indicated that Samantha, a caring soul, was an organ donor.

"Do you want to fax it somewhere?" Doreen inquired. "You can use my fax."

I faxed copies of both sides to myself and also to Nancy at home, in case I needed it sent anywhere before I got back. "This is really awfully nice of you," I told her.

"Please. It's been real slow and it's exciting having a detective—"

"Researcher."

"Oh, come on, Judy!"

I accepted her knowing smile. "Well, if it is so slow, Doreen, would you mind seeing if the condo she was in is rented now?"

"Sure. But look, after she left, maybe there were five, ten, fifteen other people between then and now." She seemed to think I had some private-eye purpose in mind, like lifting fingerprints or searching for money under floorboards, and as I could see she was relishing the notion, I didn't set her straight. Strolling over to her computer, she typed in an address. "Sorry. Summer people in it now. How about this? How about I show you where it is. It's a short walk. And if you don't say I sent you, maybe you could knock on a few doors."

I should have known from Doreen's calf muscles that a nice walk for her would be at least two miles. After fifteen minutes bouncing along at an altitude over five thousand feet, I was convinced I was going to faint, or at least swoon. It wasn't only being higher than zero feet above sea level. I felt so detached from everything and everyone I cared about. I could have been renting somebody else's life, somebody whose job was to chase down a woman who might have called herself Samantha R. Corby.

But the country was glorious. The cloudless sky was a shade of brilliant blue new to me. And there really were purple mountains majesty rising behind downtown Wiggins. Notwithstanding, I held back from humming a few bars because from the little I'd seen I sensed this might not only be the whitest town in America, but also one content with the distinction.

When we got to the other side of Wiggins, Doreen said: "Listen, Judy, off-the-record? Girl Scout's honor? With someone clean-cut like Samantha Corby whose bank says okay, the check won't bounce, we sometimes don't bother with references—not if we're under the gun like we are in November when she rented."

"Now that you mention it," I said, "you're right. I didn't see any references on the sheet you showed me."

"That's because whoever first showed her the place probably didn't ask for any. I mean, it's not like this is New York, nothing personal." Before we said good-bye, I wrote down my number for Doreen, although we both agreed that if Samantha hadn't called for her deposit since December, she was unlikely to now.

The Knob Ridge Villas were a series of flat, off-white two-story buildings with gray roofs, unremarkable in any way except, I supposed, in their ability to disappear against a backdrop of snow. In June, they simply looked wan. I could not picture the Vuitton Queen, the Land Rover Lady, the Armani Madonna living in a Knob Ridge Villa. On the other hand, if months earlier Courtney Logan had wanted to disappear without having to hide out in a trailer park in Rapid City, South Dakota, if she wanted to ski or have a first-rate martini or be just a few miles from *al dente* pasta and urbane men, well, this could be the place.

It was getting late in the afternoon, and chilly. Already I was yawning. But since I hadn't rented a car and wanted to walk back to the Wiggins Inn having made some progress, I started lifting the brass doorknockers on the villas of Knob Ridge. Most of the condos had the comatose air of a resort off-season, after the end of snowtime and just before the summer rush. Only four people answered their doors, although I surmised a few more were at home. Two of the four had only been renting since the end of April, when the ski season ended.

H. Jurgen opened her door about three inches, keeping her hiking booted foot planted right behind it, in case I tried to smash my way inside. No, she had no idea where Samantha had gone. They'd shared a chairlift a couple of times. She hardly knew the woman. She looked at two of the Courtney photos, then back to me, shook her head, and without another word, closed the door. I heard the fall of a deadbolt.

H.'s neighbor, Victor Plummer, was a scrawny man in his seventies with a few tufts of white hair. He lived two condos up from where Courtney had been. While not a gent of the old school, he appeared to be marginally more courteous. He didn't know where Samantha had gone either, but she'd been a nice girl. He'd heard Vivaldi coming from her place once, and not *The Four Seasons.* He looked at all my photos. "Could this woman be Samantha Corby?" I asked.

"Can't tell," he said. His gaunt face was shadowed by its old handsomeness, like the photographs of FDR at Yalta, although you'd have to picture FDR with a very deep tan and a Denver Nuggets T-shirt. "Who's she?" he asked, pointing an arthritic finger at the photographs.

I was on the verge of finding him endearing, albeit brusque. "She's a woman named Courtney Logan. She's been missing since—"

"What is this?" he demanded angrily. "I don't have time for this kind of crap."

"Look, Mr. Plummer, the family is very concerned about her." I pulled out my notepad and hurriedly wrote my name and phone number on it. "Please, if you remember anything about Samantha, or if you hear anything, I'd be grateful—and so would the family—if you'd call me collect." He, too, closed the door in my face, but at least he grabbed the piece of paper first.

By the time I made it back to the Wiggins Inn, I was shivering. Exhausted, too. A long day and a useless one. The inn didn't believe in room service, so I had a bowl of pretty good mushroom soup and a roll, and called it a night.

The mattress in my room had been shaped into a V by previous guests. I know I slept because I opened my eyes and was startled to discover it was morning, but I felt I had witnessed every second of the night. I kept thinking how stupid I'd been to spend my own money coming across country to discover that Courtney Logan was no longer in Wiggins, something I'd known before I left my house for La Guardia. Could she have moved to some other part of the Sun Valley area and was living under another name? If she'd left, where would she go from here? Back to Washington? To some other country? How much money did she have to invest in her own disappearance? And naturally, what if this whole thing came down to nothing and I'd been on Fancy Phil's wild-goose chase?

On the first half of the plane trip home, I finished the book on Truman I'd been reading, then slept from someplace above Sioux City, Iowa, back to New York. When I got back to the house, there were three messages. One was from Nancy: "I'm assuming you are either schussing down mountains with a dude named Chet or you are back and holed up getting your brains banged out by that cop who will inevitably break your heart, you besotted, romantic fool. In either case, I would appreciate a call just to know how things went." That meant she was worried, especially after receiving the fax with Samantha's name and picture on a driver's license. I called and told her that while I might be besotted, I was not a fool, romantic or otherwise.

"Oh please!" She heaved a vast southern sigh. "You might as well walk around in a jester's costume. In any case, I have had a thought."

" 'So rare as a day in June.' Can you remember what it was?"

"I was thinking about how Courtney or that little mouse person died. Just because they found her in the pool, you get the image of a watery death."

"But in fact it was a gun," I remarked.

"Yes, two bullets. The more I thought about it, I remembered an offhand remark either you or I made at the time, that the second shot was for insurance. And I thought—I being a woman of constant cogitation—damn, isn't that just like everything you've told me about Courtney Logan."

"Which is?"

"Thorough. All the lampshade gewgaws, the bric-a-brac, everything just so. One shot in the head would do it. All right, if you were Fancy Phil or one of his associates, you might think something like: Remember in 1977, how Vinnie the Vulture got shot in the head but was still able to identify his assailant by dribbling his name in spittle. But if I were going to kill someone by shooting them in the head . . . Judith, once is enough, especially if you're going to stick them facedown in water and tie back the pool cover nice and tight."

"It does go with her personality," I agreed.

"So following up on that thought, on *Newsday*'s time and money, I called Summit High School in Olympia and thoroughly beguiled the assistant principal. He toddled over to the yearbook office for me and found *The Apex*—isn't that clever?—for the year Courtney graduated."

"And?" I demanded.

"Many, many, many activities and honors for our girl, as you can well imagine. Including a rating of Distinguished Expert in the NRA—as in National Rifle Association—Marksmanship Qualification Program. Not that it takes a Distinguished Expert to shoot someone in the head point blank."

"Not at all."

"But it does show a certain degree of comfort when it comes to pulling a trigger."

"Wow. Thank you. I'm really grateful that you—"

"Judith, don't go effusive on me. There's more. I could get no satisfaction from the old battle-ax at Emily's school in Oklahoma. But I called the mother—who was not America's sweetheart. She did manage to string enough words together to tell me that Emily—and I quote—'never messed with guns.' "

I recalled Zee Friedman remarking how she'd overheard a one-sided conversation Courtney had a week before she disappeared, in which she'd said, "You promised." Zee had thought she sounded desperate. Had the caller been Emily and had Emily pushed Courtney too far?

Nancy's message was followed by two from Nelson. "Just calling to say hi. By the way, I found out something interesting about your hometown girl. Call me at work. If I'm not there, leave a message." In his second call, his voice gave away his concern by trying to come across as cool: "Hey, hope you're having a good day. I'm working late, so you can beep me whenever you get in."

After I beeped him, I took the portable phone, placed it on the edge of the tub, then soaked in a hot bath, usually a fine place for bright ideas to bubble up. But nothing much bubbled. Oh, I'd check the Key Biscayne address to see if it was authentic and if anyone named Samantha R. Corby had lived there and left a forwarding address. And of course I'd give Nelson a copy of the fax so he could, if he wanted to, call or subpoena the Key Biscayne Bank & Trust and see if they had information on Samantha—any other checks she'd written, her balance, and so forth.

I knew that if Courtney had executed the perfect crime, I would never have thought that the body in the pool was anyone but hers. Still, it was a damned good crime, as crimes go. Good enough, because of her thoroughness, to ensure her freedom. Deciding to delete the possibility of a wild-goose chase from my consciousness, I pumiced my feet and wondered how long she'd been planning her escape from marriage. Why couldn't she have just said "enough" to Greg? Or simply taken a powder?

My guess was maybe that was what she was originally planning. Being the quintessential suburban wife, the perfect mother, after all, had not worked out. Maybe after her final throw pillow there was simply nothing left to buy. Perhaps Greg, with his refusal to try to open Soup Salad Sandwiches on the West Coast, had proven unworthy of her awesome efforts. Possibly she found child-rearing not only draining, but incredibly boring—a conclusion that would inevitably be drawn by someone who could not love.

But Courtney being Courtney, she couldn't endure failure. Greater New York hadn't been so great for her. First the knowledge that she'd failed at Patton Giddings, then the realization that being a housewife would bring no applause, no money. The only reward was satisfaction. How could she break free? She could resign from Patton Giddings, or wait to be asked to leave; in either case, she'd be done with them forever.

But even if you quit as a wife, you're still stuck with an ex-husband, a nuisance almost by definition. And the children! Be rid of them, give over custody to Greg, and you'd still be obliged to return to the scene of your failure to visit them, or worse, have them intrude upon your new life. Not only that: You would have a legal obligation to contribute to their support.

And people would gasp, How *could* she? If she went to Sun Valley or Milwaukee or Beijing as Courtney Bryce Logan, someone from her old life, hearing about her, spotting her, might say to someone in her new life: Do you *know* what that woman did? So she had no choice but to disappear, to be missing. Emily Chavarria could have been part of Courtney's original scheme or an afterthought, but at some time it became clear that Emily, knowing about the insider trading and who knows what else, could not be allowed to live.

I climbed out of the bath, enveloped in a cloud of freesia, and grabbed a towel. How well could Courtney hide? A magazine article I'd read recently said it was impossible to become a new person through plastic surgery; to some degree you would always be recognizable. Still, I'd passed by several longtime acquaintances around town within the last year or two not recognizing them after what one of them referred to as "a little work." They'd had to tap me on the shoulder and say, "Judith, it's *me*." Karen or Linda or Jean. So who knew?

Nelson's call caught me in my closet as I was making the cataclysmic decision between white or beige underwear. "Where were you, for Christ's sake?"

Since I couldn't come up with a clever response to show him I was very much an independent woman, I told him: "In Sun Valley."

I chose beige and held the phone about a foot away from my ear as he yelled "What the hell is wrong with you?" while he banged on something several times, hopefully his desk. While Bob almost never shouted, he could hold a grudge longer than the Hatfields and McCoys. If Nelson still had the temper he had years before, it would soon blow over. "What if Courtney had been there?"

"See? You already know she wasn't," I pointed out. "Not just because I'm alive. Because we both knew there was at least a ninety-nine percent chance she wouldn't be. Otherwise, trust me, I wouldn't have gone." I told him about the photocopy of Samantha Corby's check and license I'd gotten from Doreen in Wiggins and about the cold shoulder I'd gotten from both H. and Victor, Samantha's former neighbors. "Now you," I said. "You said you found out something interesting."

"I'll come over in a while. To pick up that photocopy." I went back into the drawer, came out with black underwear. Obvious, perhaps, but also effective. "Is that okay?" he asked as I ditched the beige.

"Sure."

"I'll tell you what I came up with when I see you."

It was getting near the summer solstice, so it was still light out when Nelson arrived. I'd already set a couple of citronella torches on the grass around the patio and made sangria with the wine we'd left over a few nights before—once I'd sniffed and determined it wasn't vinegar. I had just dried my hands after slicing up a peach when he came around the back. "Hi," he said, and from behind his back brought out a great bouquet of daisies, although I'd seen several of them peeking around his sides. They were beautiful, and we went into the kitchen and spent a few minutes kissing and finding the right vase. By the time we got outside, the daylight had turned softer and more gold, the lovely silkiness that comes to the light before dusk. We wound up sharing a chaise and a glass of sangria. "I've been thinking about how to handle this Courtney business," he said.

"You mean politically, for you."

"And for you. If anything comes of it, you should get credit from your boyfriend."

"Fancy, you mean?"

"Fancy. So first let me tell you what I've done while you weren't answering your phone and I didn't know what . . . You should have told me you were going, Judith."

"I don't know about that," I said carefully. "But that's a subject we can talk about some other time." I squelched: If you want there to be another time and you're not here to say good-bye.

"I told you I wasn't ready to go to the brass on the DNA. But unless I had something concrete, I couldn't go to them at all."

"What if I told you I got X rays from Courtney's dentist here in town?"

"You didn't."

"I did."

"How?"

"My friend Nancy got them. The dentist is a former lover of hers, but then, who isn't?"

"Not me." We spent a minute or so sipping sangria and making out, then went back to the case.

"So what are you going to do?" I asked.

"You mean, what *did* I do. I thought about calling Courtney's parents out in Washington, making some excuse about needing her dental records for the investigation and not wanting to waste time having to get a subpoena for them."

"How long does a subpoena take?"

"An investigative subpoena from the DA's office? A few minutes. But then I thought, no, they already must have a relationship with somebody from Homicide. They might call to check on me. And who knows what kind of a kid Courtney was? Maybe her parents knew bad stuff about her that other people didn't know. They'd have the presence of mind and the experience to call a lawyer before doing anything."

"So, what *did* you do?"

"I called Emily Chavarria's house. Got the father—"

"I hope he's better than the mother."

"Sounded like a decent guy who's been through hell. Anyway, I commiserated with him and told him the last thing I wanted to do was scare him, but if he could get Emily's Oklahoma dentist to overnight me her records and X rays, it would help rule her out."

"And?"

"And they got here this morning."

"*And?*"

"I brought them over to this great guy at the medical examiner's office, somebody I've known for years, and asked him for an unofficial opinion." I waited. "Judith, they match the teeth from the body in the Logans' pool."

It was only a combination of relief, too many sangria-soaked peach and apple slices, and jet lag, but I gave the glass over to Nelson and closed my eyes, too wiped out to say anything more than "Congratulations." I heard the clink of the glass as he set it on the patio and rested against him while he stroked my hair, something he'd figured out years earlier to bring me back when I was ready to go over the top. "Now what?" I finally asked.

"Now I'm going to go to the brass, tell them what I've found out. I'll also let them know that I've heard whispers about Greg Logan's lawyer having some questions about the ID of the body. And in case it hasn't dawned on them, I'm going to tell them very delicately that someone had his head up his ass on this case because no DNA test was ever done."

"That will make them do it!" I enthused.

"No. Not right away. What that will do is make them wait a day or two—till they figure out how to cover themselves. Or it may make them hem and haw and want to get rid of me. So I'd appreciate it if you'd . . . Shit, I hate to do this. But let Fancy Phil know you have some doubts that the body was Courtney's, that it could be someone else's who had zero to do with Greg Logan. Trust me, by seven A.M. Monday morning, all over Nassau County, you'll hear the sound of Greg's lawyer screaming for a DNA test."

A little later, after I realized that if I made and/or ate dinner I might die of fatigue, I told Nelson to go, that I had to go upstairs. Though I was sure I'd go straight to sleep, this time he walked me upstairs, came into the master bedroom with me, and stayed for an hour. No shade of Bob came to haunt our lovemaking, no shadow of Nelson's marriage held us back.

"When do you want to talk about us?" he asked before he said goodbye.

"Tomorrow," I mumbled. "Whenever we both want to."

"Want to what?" he inquired, in a sensual murmur which usually means: I want to do it again.

Once again I told him good night, sent him home, and slept until the phone rang the next morning. "Is this Judith Singer?" a woman's voice asked.

I cleared my throat to get the languid sleep hoarseness from my voice. "Yes it is."

"Hi, my name is Ellen Berman. I live in Garden City. One of my friends in town went to Princeton with Courtney Logan. She heard something about your looking into the case. Anyway, she gave me your number. I really feel funny about doing this. But I worked at Patton Giddings until the end of last year. I knew Courtney. I don't want to get involved, but I feel—I don't know, an obligation . . ."

I sat up and quickly told her, "Oh please. There's no reason to worry about getting involved."

"Well, this may be a big nothing. I hate to waste your time. But I was talking to my friend about some of the conversations I had with Courtney and a couple of bells rang. Maybe I could meet you for a cup of coffee sometime?"

"Sure. How about later today?"

"Today? Well, I'll actually be near Shorehaven. I have to go to that big picture-framing place. Just tell me where to meet you."

"Would you like to come over here?" I asked. "I can guarantee you a semi-decent cup of coffee."

"Are you sure it wouldn't be—"

"No trouble at all!" I gave her directions to my house from Main Street.

"Around eleven or so? Is that okay?" Ellen asked. "God, I hope I'm not wasting your time and your coffee. But there are a couple of things about Courtney"—she hesitated for a minute—"that somebody ought to know."

Chapter Nineteen

Ellen Berman rang my doorbell at ten-thirty, a half hour early. Since I would have wasted the next thirty minutes alternately fantasizing she'd give me a major lead like, Oh, Courtney's dream was to live at 43 degrees latitude and 98.6 degrees longitude, or dreading she'd have an insipid tale like, Courtney shoplifted a teaspoon in her Old Master pattern, I was glad to see her.

"Am I too early?" She was pretty, a little like Audrey Hepburn in *War and Peace*—the thick browed Audrey. She had those great, dark doe eyes.

"No, this is fine," I assured her, opening the door wide. "Glad you're here. I didn't put on any eyeliner, but if you can survive that horror, I'll put up a fresh pot of coffee."

"Thanks!" No sweet tremulousness like Hepburn: Ellen had the easy manner of the naturally outgoing. Her clothes were outgoing, too, in that astutely mismatched designer way. Cropped orange pants, a shocking-pink cotton sweater, snazzy cork-bottomed clogs in pink, red, and orange. Her jewelry was a simple gold watch and thin hoop earrings. Instead of heading for the living room and into the sunroom, I led her toward the just-straightened-up kitchen. Just then she asked: "Would it be okay to use your bathroom?"

"Sure. It's straight through—" When I turned back to point her in the right direction, I saw she had another accessory. A gun.

No matter how many scenes you've seen in movies where the camera looks straight into the barrel of the gun, it doesn't prepare you for the ugliness of looking into that long metal nose with its single nostril. It's a creature out of Hell. My body told my mind that I didn't have long to live; whatever force holds cells together began to weaken. I'd heard that people lose control of their bladders or defecate in this kind of horrific moment. Others simply black out. My body considered all three options, but instead crashed against the wall right where we were, just outside the kitchen. Even though the answer was obvious, I asked with disbelief: "Courtney?"

No answer. Her eyes darted back and forth over that five-foot-long passageway between center hall and kitchen. I glanced around and saw what she was looking for. Yes, this was the perfect spot. No windows, not even a small, ornamental pane of leaded glass. No windows, no witnesses.

"Is that—" I began.

"No questions," she snapped, though still in that chipper, extrovert voice. No more peppy little blonde: She had the deep gold tan of a wealthy brunette. She'd lost weight, too, and now was model-thin if not model-tall.

"Is that the gun you used on the . . . other person?"

"Of course not," she said dismissively.

Her thumb moved, or maybe it was only my head shaking in denial of what was happening. But though I had no knowledge of guns beyond seeing Nelson's in its holster and watching *Shane,* I had the sense she was flicking the gizmo that would take off the safety lock. "Not the other person. Emily!" My words exploded, and the force made her head jerk back. "Is that the gun you used on Emily?" No answer. In that second of silence that followed, I thought how terribly sad it was that I would never know how it would have turned out with Nelson. But since that was a future I wouldn't have, and I had almost no more present, I sent up a silent blessing for Kate and Joey. Then I got out the first four words of the *Shema,* the prayer Jews are supposed to say twice a day and right before their deaths. But I stopped myself because I was still alive, and where there is life I was obliged to fight for it. Thinking "I'm dead" would doom me.

"What do you know about Emily?" she inquired, as if asking about a mutual acquaintance.

Slowly, not so much because I did not want to startle her but because I didn't have much strength, I pushed myself from the wall into an upright position, regretting the year I'd picked Learn to Crochet over Tae Kwon Do. "Do you mean the Emily Chavarria who was found on May fifteenth in your family's swimming pool?" I asked her. Just then, a thought flashed into my head: How the hell did she find me? I didn't go around thumbtacking index cards on bulletin boards or sending out "Wanted" posters with RSVP JUDITH SINGER in the lower left corner. "Oh," I said. "Did you find out about me from that man in Wiggins I gave my name to? Your neighbor Victor?"

"You got it!" she replied brightly. I was still having trouble thinking of her as Courtney Logan. I didn't dare look directly at her any more than I'd make eye contact with a slobbering Doberman. But after a couple of glances, I saw her hair had been dyed, very skillfully, the darkest brown, with a touch of auburn. My color. Her eyes, too, were like mine, somewhere between dark brown and black. Of course, I looked like one of those late-nineteenth-century photographs you see at Ellis Island, Pensive Semite in Babushka, and she like Audrey Hepburn. What I couldn't figure out was what kind of loyalty a man like Victor would feel toward Samantha/Courtney. "When I moved in," she explained, as if she'd heard me ask, "I told a couple of my neighbors I was on the run, that my husband had been abusive." Maybe she wanted me to tell her how clever a strategy that was. I didn't, so she explained: "I said he was very rich. He'd been stalking me. He'd hired detectives. I told them about beatings. I told them he'd threatened to kill me. I begged them to let me know if anyone came looking for me."

"How were they able to reach you? You moved, didn't you?"

"Question time is over." The horror of her was her niceness. She had a gun and was about to kill me. Her Audrey Hepburn eyes were still shining. Her voice was cheery: Life is really neat! What made me even more terrified was my knowing the buoyant gunslinger standing less than two feet away had once earned an NRA Distinguished Marksman qualification.

But the next second brought a respite: Though question time was over, answer time was still going on. "I gave them a number in St. Louis where they could call me or leave a message," Courtney was saying. "Of course, I'm not in St. Louis. But I call that number twice a day, religiously." Well, I had called her thorough. "And I'm going to keep on doing it until the second anniversary of my escape, just to be extra sure."

"Escape out of where?"

"Out of *here*! Trust me, the only thing that could drag me back to Shorehaven was to deal with you."

Because my credo is that it's always better to know the truth, I decided to give Courtney a dose of it—not for her own good, but for mine.

"Your problem is bigger than me, Courtney. Your father-in-law knows all about you. The Nassau County cops just got onto you. *Newsday* could break the story any minute."

She gave a heh-heh chuckle I supposed qualified as the "mirthless laugh" villains are forever emitting in noir mysteries set in Los Angeles. "You're trying to buy time," she observed. "Sorry, I'm not selling any."

I lost my fight to keep my eyes away from the gun. She could see my fear was exhausting me. It was hard to get enough air to push out my words. "They know about how you switched dental X rays at Dr. Gaines's office, how you—"

"Listen to me," Courtney commanded. "Don't even attempt to match wits with me. I know all about you, how you got involved in that dentist case here in town, whenever, a hundred years ago. Well good for you. You get an A for this one, too—for all you found out all by your-self." I wish I could say that in looking at her I could see the wickedness or the madness. Truth was, she looked pretty and well put together, though more *Elle* than Long Island. Only her eyes looked somewhat life-less despite their luster, a hint that something about her was not a hundred percent. However, I guessed it was less an emanation of evil or sign of pathology than the brown contact lenses.

I prayed Fancy Phil was right in his where-to-hide-money theory and that she hadn't gone to the Caribbean to scuba dive. "How would I be able to find out about the offshore corporation in Nevis? The federal authorities traced that." I can't say Courtney looked scared, but for the first time she looked disquieted. With the index finger of her free hand, she stretched out the collar of her pink sweater—even though it was loose fitting enough that it couldn't be annoying her. "And what about your dental X rays? The Nassau County cops are checking the ones from Emily and the ones supposedly yours from Dr. Gaines against yours from Olympia, Washington."

"What else do they know?" I couldn't believe she still had that read-any-good-books-lately? breeziness.

"Why should I tell you?"

"Because I have a gun," Courtney said reasonably. She did one of those perky, apologetic shrugs—Sor-ry. Her gold hoops sparkled in the light from an overhead fixture in the passageway. "And you don't." Just as I had begun to feel safer, seeing an extra minute or two of life, she sud-denly seemed to be growing taller in her cork-bottomed clogs, more res-olute. "What else do the cops know?"

"Listen, Courtney, New York's got the death penalty again. Do you want to add another murder so if you're caught it's guaranteed?"

"Stop it," she said with an indulgent smile. "I'll live a long and happy life. Unfortunately—"

"I don't want to hear about your life!" I told her. "I don't want to hear any big bullshit about how clever you were, because you weren't."

"Listen to me!" she ordered. "I—"

"No. You listen to me, Courtney. I don't want to hear what a brilliant plan you conceived. And I don't want to hear that the whole thing really wasn't your fault. I've seen too many movies where the killer explains why it's never his fault. Her fault. It *was* your fault. But unfortunately this is life, not a movie. You have the gun. I don't have the agility to knee you in the balls even if you had balls. I don't have the strength to twist your arm so you wind up killing yourself. But know this: You're not that smart. You're a screwup, plain and simple. If you weren't, we wouldn't have found out about it. Meanwhile your husband has been living under a cloud—"

"It so happens," she hissed at me, "that even before the whole thing with Emily, I was planning on leaving after I took Morgan trick or treating. I didn't want to disappoint her by not going. And I also did it on the thirty-first because I knew, I *knew* Greg would be at a dinner meeting in the city with Jim Cooley from Upper Crust. I *wanted* him to have an alibi."

Maybe she was waiting for me to tell her how thoughtful she was, but I decided to disappoint her. My only chance at getting out was to be able to make some clever move, although with her standing a couple of feet away and the gun pointing somewhere in the general direction of my heart and lungs, clever wasn't coming. The only way I could buy time was to keep her talking, since I doubted she'd be the type to appreciate the Bergmanesque qualities of a meaningful silence. "Not that I'm being critical," I went on, "but didn't it occur to you that the trick-or-treat experience for Morgan might be tainted by the trauma of having a mother disappear and never return?"

"See? This is why it's useless to talk to you." I tried to swallow so I could speak, but I found myself choking on my own gulp. "It so happens I gave it my all. You and everyone else will never know how hard I tried to be the best mother there is. Maybe I wasn't the best wife in the world, but I tried there, too. Part of it was I didn't have the best material to work with." There was no need to ask Courtney what she meant, because she was on a roll.

"He was the biggest disappointment. Good-looking in that exotic way, very intelligent, a real natural athlete. You look at those blobby parents of his and you wonder how in the world did they produce someone with such amazing hand-eye coordination. And his speed! He's all the way back and suddenly he's at the net. And money. He had money and an MBA, which can be an unbeatable combination. Except what did he do about it? Next to nothing. He had no daring. He took a really good idea and worked and slaved and turned it into a mediocre business." I decided it best not to bring up StarBaby. "And do you know the most pathetic thing about it? Greg was perfectly content to be second rate." Courtney rubbed her lips together the way you do before you blot lipstick. "He knew damn well he was settling for safety and security over the chance to be a player. And he knew that sooner or later someone was going to come in and copy his formula and make it the next Starbucks. Do you know what he said?"

"What?" Her right arm, the one with the gun, must have been getting weary because she was propping up her forearm with her left hand. All I could think of was what in the world I could do to disarm her. For once, I was overjoyed to be sixteen pounds over the legal limit, except I couldn't come up with a way to throw my weight around that would result in both my getting the gun and staying alive.

"He said he could live with that. I told him in a kidding-around way that I didn't know if I could. And he said, 'Well, Courtney, you're just going to have to *learn* to live with it.' And then his whole fixation on being legitimate. Believe me, when I told him I was proud that he wasn't interested in the family business or the family values, if you know what I mean, I meant it. But it permeated every aspect of his life. He was panicked about anyone thinking he was coarse. Panicked. Half the time we'd go out with other couples, really terrific, successful couples, and he'd hardly say anything because he was so panicked. Except his excuse was that he was reserved. Reserved? And taxwise there were probably hundreds of deductions he could have made legitimately, but he wouldn't let the accountant take them. You can be understanding for a while, but for how long? And the really sick thing? He was on the phone with his father at least once a day, even on weekends. Talking about baseball and the market, like his father was a normal person. Greg never heard of the term 'arm's length.' "

I was tempted to ask her about her children but was afraid of setting her off. Sooner or later, unless she decided to fire in the meantime, I'd have to do something. But my legs were performing a pathetic shimmy and it was all I could do just to keep standing. The unsettling thing about Courtney, as if I needed more unsettlement, was that for an egocentric crazy sociopath, or whatever the diagnostic term is, she was as intuitive as she was.

Just as I was thinking, Huh? What about your kids?, she said: "As far as the children go, they're better off without me. I know that may sound like a rationalization, but it's the truth. They always loved Steffi, our au pair, better than they loved me. I felt badly I couldn't leave Steffi a letter with some instructions or guidelines, though that was obviously out of the question."

"What about Emily?" I inquired. Courtney did her lip-rubbing business again, then kept them pressed together, as in "mum's the word." "I know you two met at a regional FIFE meeting in Baltimore. But I couldn't piece together how the relationship developed."

Her lips parted. "I wouldn't call it a *relationship.*" Each time she began talking again I'd get an instantaneous flush of hope, followed by a growing desperation and paralysis. The reverse psychology which had worked earlier, telling her I didn't think she was smart and that I didn't want to hear her version of events, might not work again. "There was much too much of a hero-worshiping aspect to it," she was saying. "I mean, the woman was a *tabula rasa* looking for someone to write on her. Self-confidence in negative numbers. Which was sad, because she had a mind. But if I hopped on one foot, she'd hop. I bought a Lana Marks bag and guess who else did? One time I told her, 'Emily, you can wear a really great pants suit and the bank won't fire you, I guarantee it.' So of course she had to buy a couple of pants suits, but I got sixty thousand emails asking where she should buy it and what designer and all that."

"Her name wasn't on your database," I said.

She laughed, throwing back her head, although not so far that she still couldn't keep her eye on me. And the gun didn't move a millimeter. "That's because the month before I left I got a new hard drive. My nightmare was that Greg would spare no expense trying to find me and hire one of those computer people who can read stuff you think you erased." She shook her head in weary recollection. "You wouldn't believe how long it took to import a lot of that stuff and reenter the rest. Not just database stuff. My other files, too, minus what I didn't want to show up. Days and days and days I was my own secretary."

"You weren't involved with on-line trading?"

"You mean day-trading? No. That's so dilettantish. For total losers and a couple of geniuses. I admit I'm not that kind of a genius." For a moment she looked pensive. "Emily traded on-line, but she didn't sit around all day staring at a computer screen like a day-trader. I wouldn't call her a genius, but she was terrific at it. She made herself some good money."

"What was her nest egg? From the first public offering of Saf-T whatever?"

"Very impressive," Courtney remarked. "How did you track that down?"

"Someone else did."

"Who? All right, play games. I don't care. You'll see where it will get you. Well"—she grinned—"technically you won't see." With her first real smile of the morning, I noticed the old Courtney dimples. "What were we talking about? Oh, Emily. Emily got in on the ground floor with the IPO, invested her life savings, thirty-five thousand. She doubled her money the first week. Then she sold all her Saf-T-Close stock and began making serious money. I mean, from something like her initial seventy thousand investment, she ran it up to almost *seven hundred thousand* in on-line trading by the next summer. She'd get home from the bank and that's all she'd do, not that she had a lot of other opportunities. Anyhow, every time she made a killing she had to call me up and boast. Well, finally this boring person in New Jersey was worth almost three-quarters of a mil! That's when I said, 'Let's have lunch. We haven't seen each other in ages.'"

"When was this?"

"I don't know," she said irritably. "So we kept having lunch. And then she told me about the Chapman-Bohrer buyout. Anybody would think, Oh, Courtney's the evil genius behind all this, but Emily was the one who suggested it."

"Suggested what?"

"You know. That I should buy stock for her in my name and she'd give me fifteen percent of whatever she netted. The naïveté, the gullibility. That she could trust anyone, even me. Then she said if I wanted to buy for myself, whatever money I wanted to put into it— *She* said, 'Why don't you have your parents buy your shares for you? They have another name.' Like a couple who makes fifty grand or so a year would be buying twenty-five thousand dollars' worth of Saf-T-Close. For someone smart she was not smart."

"That was the money you took out from your joint accounts?"

"Right again. Very, very good. But buying under another name gave me the idea of the offshore corporation. So I set that up and gave Emily the papers to sign as coprincipal, except three guesses what I did with those papers."

"Why did you have to kill her?"

"I take full responsibility for that," Courtney said. "I just didn't think something through that I should have."

"What was that?"

"That once she comprehended—and that took forever—that we weren't best friends and that I hadn't bought tickets to Australia for us and that there was no chance in hell she was going to get her hands on the money, she wasn't going to take it lying down. She threatened to blackmail me."

"How?"

She did not directly answer. "Well, I didn't want her to go back to her bank and say, 'I didn't go to Australia and New Zealand because my friend Courtney fucked me over.' I wanted her to make a clean break so they'd think she was missing. So I got her a hotel room in the city and told her there was some problem with the offshore corporation because our lawyer had left the island. I said, 'Just sit tight. We'll take our vacation as soon as I clear this up. I'm working night and day on it.' I got her a cell phone so she wouldn't make calls to my house from the hotel. I said, 'We can't afford to have any phone records if the SEC ever decides to take a look.'

"But then she finally figured out something was wrong. And then the blackmail threats began: She was going to tell Greg. Then she'd go to the SEC, which I personally doubt she would have done. But of course that would have totally fucked up my plans about getting away. And then she came out to Shorehaven. Unfortunately, she'd been to the house a few times, so she knew where it was. She could practically get there on automatic pilot."

"And?"

"And, I said, 'We can't stay here, Emmy. You're making too much noise, carrying on like this. Let's go for a walk.' And of course she said okay. She even waited while I ran back upstairs to get out the gun. I told her I had to change my shoes and she believed me. I even got her to drive my car one last time."

"Where did you shoot her?"

"Where? In the head." She spoke with exaggerated patience, the way an unkind person might do with someone who is slow.

"I mean, where were you?"

Courtney exhaled, as though exhausted by the memory. "In Piney Woods Park, behind the old Fiske mansion, on one of the trails."

"You shot her twice."

"One for good measure. Just to be sure. That's how I am. This was just a couple of days before Halloween, the day I was planning my escape. But I had to put everything else aside. Anyhow, I shot her and I put a pile of leaves and branches over her and said a little prayer that I wouldn't screw this up. Then I had to go home, pick up Emily's car, and drive it to one of those dumpy car cemeteries with all the old wrecks. Isn't it amazing, how the mind works? I must have passed the place a year or two before, going somewhere. All of a sudden, on my way home from the park right after I'd shot her, it came back to me. Then I had to get rid of the plates. I threw them into a Dumpster at a construction project."

"And her body?"

"I was so nervous. You should have seen me! But I knew I couldn't let it stay where it was. But then on Saturday after it got dark, Greg was still at the office and I told Steffi, the au pair, to take the kids to Roosevelt Field and go to F.A.O. Schwarz and the food court for dinner. She was so good about working on weekends if I needed her. So I wrapped her—Emily—in one of those green plastic things you put on the floor when you paint. What do you call it? A drop cloth. I put my watch and rings on her. I got her into clothes similar to what I was planning on wearing on Halloween, wrapped her in the drop cloth, and put her in the back of my car—"

"But her fingerprints were on your car. And in your house. You obviously wiped your prints off in order to make the police think that Emily's fingerprints were your fingerprints—the same fingerprints that would match the body. She visited you at least a couple of times, right? When you had Steffi take the children away for the day, and again when you went to the dentist."

She shook her head, smiling at a recollection. "If you're dying, no pun intended, to know how I did it, I had her drive me to the dentist's office. I'd made an appointment for her under a made-up name, and when we got there I said, 'Ooh, your teeth need to be cleaned.' Cute? She didn't even know she had an appointment. I just said, 'Go in, Emmy. They'll take you. Oh, listen: I made the appointment under another name. I don't want anyone being able to connect the two of us.' Steffi was with the children."

"I guess there were other times she came to your house, too."

"So?"

"So what I'm thinking is that maybe you planned out this . . . Emily's death a little more than you're describing."

"Did you ever hear of 'FO and D'?" Courtney asked too sweetly. I shook my head. "No? We used to say it in school." For the first time she looked angry. "Fuck off and die!"

I spoke right away, trying to keep my voice soothing. "Did you ever consider that the pool wasn't a good place? That they might have found her before she"—I wasn't able to come up with a euphemism, so I said—"decomposed?"

"Of course I thought about it. But this wasn't how I'd planned to do it. She came to the house and I had to improvise. All you can do in any situation is your best. I had to shoot her in the goddamn middle of nowhere. What if there'd been a hiker around? Then the next night I had to go back and get her, which was incredibly spooky. I bet you're dying to know how I got her into the pool." I nodded. "I drove my car. It's a Land Rover. Greg said a Range Rover would send the wrong message, which just about sums him up. I drove across my neighbor's property after dark with the car's lights off. I got to ten feet away from the pool, then I carried her. In the dark. Talk about deadweight. But she was out of the car, into the drink, pool cover tied back down in five minutes."

"You weren't worried that once you were gone the police would look in the pool?"

"Of course. I agonized. But my escape plan was in place. Worse comes to worse, they'd pull back the cover and say, 'Gee, that's not Courtney. It's someone who's her size and who has blond hair, or almost blond, but—gee, where could Courtney be?' It was a calculated risk. But I'd be in another city. I'd be in another life! Let them look for Courtney. They wouldn't find her."

The blond business. Was Emily simply mimicking the woman she venerated? Or had Courtney talked Emily into going blond? If so, she'd formulated the pool burial not at the spur of the moment, but in early September, when Emily started changing her hair color. "How had you originally planned it, before you had to use the pool option?"

"FO and D." She was getting bored with me.

"Where did you get the gun?"

"Oh, that was about two, three years ago when we were skiing in Utah." Her manner turned reflective, as if reminiscing about a pleasant vacation. "I was a nervous wreck, sending it home in my luggage, but it was the only thing I could think to do. Like the airline really noticed. But I just thought that with someone like Phil Lowenstein in the family, we should be armed."

"Did he or anyone else ever threaten you?"

"No. But why not be protected?"

"Greg didn't know you had the gun?"

"Of course not. He probably would have thought it was coarse or something. And he was definitely too much of a wuss to have a gun in the house." She combed her hair off her face with her left hand. "I know you've been playing for time, trying to think of some way out. Not that I blame you. You're smart, but as I said, not as smart as I am. I hate to say it, but—"

With my left arm I slammed her gun hand against the wall. With my right, I jerked her gold hoop earring down. She screamed as it tore through her earlobe—I think as much with horror as with pain—and covered her ear with both hands. Now the gun was pointing toward the ceiling. Blood began oozing out between her fingers and down her neck. Reaction time was a factor, I knew. With mine being sluggish and hers fast, it would only be a second or two until she'd get back enough control to wrest her right hand from her ear, aim, and shoot.

I grabbed for the gun, but she tightened her grip. I couldn't get it loose and found myself swaying as she writhed and screamed, "My ear! My ear! You ripped my ear!" With one hand I grabbed onto her wrist and tried to keep the gun pointed up, although her wrist was slick with blood. Then I remembered something I'd heard at a self-defense forum at a Take Back the Night rally on campus: If you're trying to release someone's grip, don't go for his thumb. So I grabbed Courtney's pinkie and bent it back, and farther back, until her next scream told me I'd broken it.

Although I already knew that because now I had the gun.

Except we were at a standoff. I had the gun, but I needed the phone, which was in the kitchen. Courtney alternated between holding her ear and howling "I'm going to bleed to death!" and "My finger!" and making swipes toward me to try to get the gun back. The shoulder and sleeve of her bright pink sweater were blood-soaked, and for an instant it brought to mind Jacqueline Kennedy's suit after JFK was shot. My teeth started to chatter and I clamped my jaw shut.

But then I had to open it. "Courtney," I shouted over her caterwauling, "you better hear me. This isn't a democracy. I rule. Either you come into the kitchen or I'm going to shoot you, and with any luck, I'll kill you."

I pulled out a chair into the middle of the kitchen. I must have had a reason for that, though I don't recall. She sat. After throwing her a dishtowel for her ear, I grabbed the phone. God knows what I shrieked to the 911 operator. Then began the endless wait for the cops to arrive.

The vibrations from my chattering teeth spread downward until I was shivering all over. I have no doubt she saw it, because I wasn't more than five feet from her. Nevertheless, she did not try to take advantage. Instead, hunched over in the chair, both hands pressing the towel over her ear, she seemed to have withdrawn for a consultation with herself. No more bawling, no more attempts to get back the gun.

When the two cops came, one gingerly took the bloody gun from me. It was evidence and I suppose I wasn't radiating an Annie Oakley aura of expertise in the firearms department.

With that, Courtney began to weep. Loud sobs, buckets of actual tears. "Thank God you're here!" she cried to them. "Thank God!"

"Listen," I warned them, "she's the one who killed that woman they found in the pool last month!"

"Don't listen to her," Courtney exhorted them. "My name is Amy Carpenter and . . ." She stopped to weep some more but only for a moment. "She thinks I'm having an affair with her husband and I swear to God I'm not. Look what she did to me! Please, let me get to a doctor. Oh please." She looked up at them. Her doe eyes, only slightly red, brimming with tears, were so moving they almost tugged on my heartstrings. The two men glanced at each other, then back to Courtney. She showed them her ripped earlobe and then held up her broken, swollen pinkie.

It occurred to me that what I might be seeing in their eyes was sympathy. "She's not Amy Carpenter," I told them. "She's used lots of aliases. She's Courtney Logan, for God's sake!" A mistake.

Tall cop spat out: "Courtney Logan is dead."

"No, no," I told him. "She's not! The woman who's dead is—"

"Oh God! Please don't make me sit here like this. Please, get me to a doctor," Courtney wept. "I'm so scared I'll bleed to death." Shorter cop, gazing at her, looked as if his pity was turning to love, mixed with a dash of horror that someone would drop dead on his watch and he'd have to fill out the reports. Sensing this, she looked up at him, a lovely crystal tear resting on her lower lashes, on which, somehow, she'd had the luck or foresight to apply waterproof mascara.

Two more cops arrived. Second tall cop was grimacing at the blood-soaked towel and therefore didn't bond with Courtney. His partner, Female Cop, looked over at the first two and inquired, "Hey, guys. You call an ambulance?" A perfectly reasonable question, I thought.

"This lady," Tall Cop said, pointing to me, "is saying the other one—" His somewhat icy tone thawed as his finger moved toward Courtney. "She's saying this one is Courtney Logan. The one that got shot in the head and put in her own swimming pool."

"If you'll just listen for a minute," I began.

"Shut up, lady," the short cop barked.

"Hey, guys. Yes or no? You call an ambulance?"

"I'm going to throw up," Courtney announced with a note of genuine nausea in her voice. "Please, could someone get me to the bathroom fast?" All four cops took a step toward her.

"Not before one of you calls Captain Sharpe at headquarters!" I shouted. Four heads turned to me. I saw four faces with foreheads creased, as if they'd only taken one semester of the language I was speaking. As I was repeating myself, Courtney made a run for it.

Cleverly. Instead of standing, turning, and rushing for the kitchen door, like a person escaping, she rose from the chair in a crouched position. It barely seemed as if she had moved. Then she raced toward the door. The cops took a long instant to comprehend she was not making a run for the bathroom. Too long. Courtney was out the door and crossing the patio. "I have to get to a doctor," she cried. "I have to!" God, she was fast!

She had almost reached the grass when two of them got to her. But instead of kicking or biting, fighting to get free, as I'd expected, Courtney collapsed, falling to the flagstone, arms limp, torn earlobe lying on the stone. Tall and Short knelt beside her and called out "Ma'am?" over and over. After a minute, when she didn't stir, each took a side and tried to help her up. However, despite her being not much heavier than a paperweight, they could only haul her up so that she was on her knees.

I was calling out to Female Cop, "Could you please call Captain Sharpe and tell him you're at Judith Singer's house with Judith and Courtney Logan?" when Courtney made her mistake. Grabbing onto Short as if attempting to draw herself up, she tried to open his holster to take his gun. I had to give him credit. Before I could see it coming, he either swatted or smashed her so she was down on the patio again. Then he flipped her over onto her stomach and handcuffed her.

At that point Female stepped back into the house and said something about calling for an ambulance and backup and what was that captain's name at headquarters? I can't recall what else she said, because when I next opened my eyes I was on my living-room couch and the emergency medical technician who was taking my blood pressure was saying, "Everything's fine, dear."

Chapter Twenty

"I hate to say it, but you're going to have to regrout your tile." Nancy stared down at the black and white tiles in the passageway. "All that blood." She glanced over to me. "Are you sure you're all right?"

"Just a little shaky."

"Seriously, how about a double Absolut? It won't turn you into me."

"I already had a double Xanax," I told her.

We strolled back outside and sat on an old beach towel I'd spread on the grass on the side of the house. A cool day for a picnic, but the sky was radiant and the vision of the gun looking down its nose on me seemed fainter in the brightness. Cops were still in the kitchen and out on the patio, although all the crime-scene work seemed over. They chattered the way coworkers do on mornings after the Oscars or a World Series game: Can you *believe* what happened?

"Did Courtney look anything like the shot of her we originally ran?" Nancy asked. "Or did she look like that nauseating, nostrils-on-parade picture that was in the *Beacon*?"

"Neither. She dyed her hair dark brown, got really dark brown contact lenses, and lost weight." Nancy's eyebrows lifted. "She didn't mention which diet. You know those corky clogs that add a couple of inches? She had them on, so I got the impression of someone five-three or five-four."

"What was she wearing?"

"You always go right to the heart of the matter," I said. "A pink and orange getup. It could have been Ralph Lauren, but you'll probably tell me it wasn't."

"Describe it." I did. Wearily, she shook her head. "No, no, no, you poor, benighted fool. It sounds like Escada. By the way, where is your Little Boy Blue? Or Big Boy Blue? Does he know what happened yet?"

"Of course. He was here for a while."

"Holding your hand, no doubt."

"No doubt. But he went back to headquarters to have some jurisdictional dispute over the case. He worked on it, he wants it—for its own sake and as a way back into Homicide—but the *schmendrick* from Homicide who screwed up the case wants to keep it. He said he'll be back."

Though Nancy didn't change her expression, I somehow found it necessary to add, "He *will*. And not just for that." When she did not reply, I changed the subject. "I can't believe I actually fainted."

"So Victorian of you."

"I know. And one of my least favorite eras."

"You forget Dickens, but you're in shock. God, you were so incredibly brave. To say nothing of effective. Can you talk about it some more or are you just going to stare up at that tree?"

"The noble oak," I murmured.

"Noble sycamore, you ass. If you want to sit here in comfortable silence, that's all right with me, even though I came here so you could ventilate."

In the capacity of official best friend, Nancy had arrived in time to hear me giving most of my statement to a young, gum-cracking detective. I'd spoken about the Ellen Berman pretense, the gun in Courtney's hand and all she'd told me, my tearing off the earring, breaking her finger, and then the gun in my hand. For good measure I'd thrown in Courtney's break for freedom, the scuffle, the handcuffs. "No," I said. "I'd like to talk about it."

"Do you think Emily just surprised Courtney by coming over before Halloween and that's why she got killed?" Nancy asked. "Or was the whole thing planned?"

"Planned is my guess," I said, "although I'm still not sure how detailed the plan was, especially about Emily. Certainly the killing wasn't a whim. Listen, whatever Courtney says is suspect. Maybe Emily did surprise her. Maybe she invited Emily over to get a few more fingerprints on things, have a nice drive with more fingerprints, then murder her in the woods. But it seems to me she'd used her charm to get Emily to go blonder and blonder for a reason, to be a better Courtney substitute. So she must have been thinking of the pool, hoping she'd be left there till the cover came off and the body would be in lousy shape. Or maybe she'd planned on burying Emily in Piney Woods Park, but digging a deep enough grave was too much of an effort. She did seem to spend the fall making plans—getting credit cards and fake ID, probably driving back and forth to Cherry Hill and maybe scouting out places to ditch Emily's car, getting Emily a cell phone in Vanessa Russell's name. And one of the days she sent the au pair Steffi out of the house with the kids: She told Steffi to take them to Baskin-Robbins if they started to kvetch. That was totally out of character. But she wanted to be sure no one could possibly connect her with Emily."

"Do you want my two cents?" Nancy asked.

"Sure."

"I think that the minute she had the opportunity to make some serious bucks with Emily's on-line skills and the insider trading, Courtney started planning her own takeover—of the money—and Emily's murder. She strung Emily along, but once she got her mitts on all that money, there was no way she was going to share. Dead Emily was a given the minute Courtney got the money in a nice, warm offshore account."

"It was only a matter of timing, then?" I asked.

"Timing and opportunity. Courtney probably wanted out for ages." Delicately, Nancy picked a few blades of grass off her brown-and-white spectator flats. "Anybody else would think she had the perfect life, or at least a decent one."

"I know. But to her, it was a failure. She hadn't made a mark in investment banking. She got turned down for a loan for StarBaby. And StarBaby itself: It wasn't going to tank, but it does sound as though it was going no place fast. Her best friend, Kellye Ryan—"

"Our Lady of Prada?"

"Yes. Kellye and the young woman who was videotaping for her, Zee Friedman, the one I'd love to fix up with Joey: They seemed to think that by the summer Courtney was depressed. And then by the fall, her mind was somewhere else. A new lease on life—that didn't include StarBaby."

"Don't forget the husband," Nancy interjected. "I bet she didn't see him as a man who started a new business and was making a go of it."

"Of course not. She saw him as a loser, a guy who didn't have the guts to be big."

"Big was an issue for Courtney," Nancy observed. A uniformed cop

walking by nodded politely. Suddenly, dazed by the power of Nancy's innate man-attractant, he tried to smile suavely. By that time, of course,
Nancy had lost track of his very existence.

"That's part of why I think Courtney was planning something before
StarBaby's lack of success got her down," I went on. "Look, she took
twenty-five thousand dollars out of their joint bank and brokerage accounts last spring and summer. I'm sure the police will subpoena her bank
records, but she didn't put that money into her StarBaby account."

"Maybe she spent it on something worthwhile, like clothes," Nancy
suggested. "Or—listen to this—she took the on-line plunge and lost the
whole damn bundle trading stocks on the Internet!"

"That was one of my guesses." The tranquilizers were starting to take
effect. I stretched out on the towel and watched leaves swishing in the
breeze. "Or she could have used some of it to buy fake ID and open bank
accounts. I bet that would be hard to find out, though. She used so damn
many different names. Nelson said it looked to him as if Courtney had a
great source of phony ID. From that ID, she was able to get credit cards
and driver's licenses in different names. Usually, good ID like that costs a
bundle. So either she was willing to spend a healthy amount of money on
it or she got some sort of quantity discount."

"Where would you buy ID like that?" Nancy asked.

"Why? Whom do you want to be?"

"I don't know. Someone thirty-five. Remember when I was thirty-
five? I was thinking, Holy shit, I'm old. Next stop, Death. Now? I would
start over somewhere, pass myself off as a thirty-five-year-old— Okay, a
thirty-five-year-old who's lived hard. Not in Snore Valley. I suppose it's
a cliché, but I'd pick Paris. What I can't comprehend is where did a
mommy from Shorehaven come up with first-rate fake ID? She wasn't a
criminal."

"Of course she was! And smarter than most. As far as the ID, there's
supposed to be some on the Internet," I reported. "Except Courtney
strikes me as being too smart to order something like that, a birth certificate or a driver's license—and then go present it to get a passport. She'd
be risking arrest. She'd be risking a police or FBI sting. And she'd be risking blackmail by the scumbucket who sold it to her."

"So where else?"

"She probably could finagle a birth certificate with a raised seal from
some county in a sparsely populated state . . . I don't know. Like Montana
maybe. Some functionary in New York or Florida wouldn't be able to say
'Hey, that's not what a Montana birth certificate looks like.' Maybe she
just made it her business to find someone who sold high-quality stuff. It

shouldn't be different from drugs or any other contraband. Unless you really trust your source, it's terribly risky."

"So the source could have been some sewer sludge guy—or Courtney herself getting a phony birth certificate?" Nancy asked.

"Right. If it was Courtney, she'd need mail drops. I'm not sure if municipalities would mail a birth certificate to a box number. For all I know, it's the same with end-of-the-month statements from on-line brokers. But considering what else she was willing to do, I suppose a mail drop would be easy enough."

"She certainly had a sense of entitlement," Nancy observed. "Princeton."

"Please, you don't need three credits in sociopathy to graduate from Princeton. She was—she is—a bad person."

"Can you imagine, stealing from your joint account with your husband while you're still sleeping in the same room? Tacky. What's fascinating to me is that when her best wasn't good enough, what did she do? Turned around and became another person."

"Unmitigated chutzpah," I murmured.

Nancy twisted her hair into a topknot, then let it fall back onto her shoulders. "Too bad she became disagreeable."

"The murder business, you mean."

"Yes, that poor mouse woman. And you, almost!"

"But Courtney was always willing to do whatever it took for her own ends. Remember how she took the Crunch-Munch money and put the blame on Ingrid Farrell?"

"You've got to wonder," Nancy reflected, "what kind of a guy Greg Logan is. Not only putting up with her sticking her hand in the till. She must have shown her true colors at some point. Couldn't he know or intuit she was a bad seed?"

"Some people thought she was fine. Kellye Ryan seems to have been genuinely devoted to her."

"Possibly Kellye is not the person for whom the phrase 'Still waters run deep' was coined."

"That's true," I agreed. "Courtney's pool man thought well of her."

"Always the authoritative judge of virtue."

"So did her au pair. And Emily, of course. Although the pool guy didn't know her very well. And Emily, may she rest in peace, is dead. And the au pair is so good-hearted she'd probably think . . ."

"What?" Nancy asked. "You were going to say something about her thinking Hitler was a nice guy, but then you remembered she was Austrian. Am I right?"

"You're in the right neighborhood," I muttered. "Okay, yes. But getting back to how people viewed Courtney. A lot of them thought there was something not quite right, not the real McCoy about her. But it's still possible Greg was conned the way Emily was. Listen, it's significant she betrayed the two people who were emotionally dependent on her. One she killed, one she left with a shattered life. Not just that, even though she claimed she was being kind by giving him an alibi, she made him top suspect by putting the body in the pool. And I'm not even mentioning her two kids."

"Was it the emotional dependency itself that drove her bonkers?" Nancy inquired.

"Could be. She is really, really sick. Nelson said he's met more than his share of those. Psychos or sociopaths or whatever. Most people think of them as madmen like Charles Manson, or obsessed losers like Timothy McVeigh. But he says a fair number of them are smart, attractive, charming. Like con men, who don't just need the money; they need to pull the scam, to destroy lives. And I think with Courtney, her craziness—"

"Or overwhelming greed."

"Or need. Whatever it was, it gave her the power, the energy to be convincing." I got up from the towel and straightened out my shirt. "Guess what?" I said.

"You're going for a nap."

"How did you know? Seriously?"

"Give me a break. And after the nap? Him?"

"No. My client, Fancy Phil Lowenstein. And Gregory Logan."

It took me nearly two hours to tell Greg and Fancy Phil all that had happened from the beginning of the case. We sat in the Logan living room the way I had the last time. Not a speck of dust, the nap of the rug vacuumed to attention, but it didn't look as though it had been used since my last visit. The room was still a shrine to Courtney's grimly impeccable sense of design. But as I wound down my story, I noticed the tortoise-shell-framed photograph of husband and wife, Courtney and Greg aglow and agleam in their tennis whites, was no longer on the table beside the antique leather-bound books and the fat-bottomed onyx vase.

"I don't know what to say," Greg told me at last.

"Say you're sorry," Fancy Phil boomed from his side of the striped couch.

"Dad, you and I made a deal."

"So don't say you're sorry." Fancy Phil was dressed conservatively: only a flat, half-inch-wide gold chain and its matching bracelet. His shirt was Hawaiian style with a repeating pattern of Gauguin's *Tahitian Women on the Beach.*

Greg, in khaki slacks, white cotton cable-knit sweater, and sailing moccasins, sat in the wing chair where he'd been the last time I was there. He looked even more worn than the month before. His tan had faded to parchment, perhaps because he could no longer find golf partners, perhaps because he was now spending all his free time with his children. "I am sorry about how I treated you," he said.

"Listen, I was out of order, coming here the way I did," I told him. "It was just that I felt I had a chance of finding out at least something in this case. It didn't dawn on me that I'd be viewed as another in a long series of nuts intruding on your privacy. I should have been more sensitive."

"I'm not only sorry, I'm grateful. I owe . . . well, if not my life, then everything else to you."

"I'm the one who went over to her house and talked her into doing it," Fancy Phil announced.

"I'm glad you did, Phil," I told him. "You're a great father."

Greg nodded his agreement. "How do you think she was able to get away Halloween night?" he asked. "That's what I still can't understand. The car was in the garage."

"My guess?" I said. "She probably left the garage door open, backed out, and waved good-bye. She came back a little while later without her headlights on. It was dark by then. Sunset was before five that day."

"So what the hell did she do? Walk to Sun Valley?" Fancy Phil demanded.

"No," I said. "She'd rented a car in Manhattan a week or two before. On the Samantha R. Corby credit card. Maybe she had that car parked close by. A couple of blocks' stroll and she was off. Not to Sun Valley right away. She spent some time in Miami—"

"Bitch!" Fancy Phil said. Before his son could say a word, he said: "Sorry, Gregory. I'll leave it alone." He turned to me. "Before you got here we was talking. About a lot of things. About what he should say to the kids now." Then to Greg he said: "Whatever you tell them, kid, it'll be as good as anybody can say it."

"I'd have to check with Steffi Deissenburger," I went on. "But I wouldn't be surprised if the bye-bye Mommy game started in September."

"Why?" Greg asked.

"So she could have an adult witness to her driving off. Then she went to Florida. My guess is she already had at least a bank account set up there and some kind of address or mail drop. She might have even made a trip down there earlier, setting up whatever needed setting up. We know she charged tickets to Miami. She could do that in one day, fly there and back, and be home by seven-thirty."

"Do you think she had someone there?" Greg asked quietly. "A man?"

"I have no idea. I assume she went down there just to rest and establish a tan. Her story was she lived on Key Biscayne."

"What about . . . with Emily Chavarria? I mean, their relationship."

"Most likely a case of hero worship by a lonely young woman that Courtney exploited. But instead of being a good role model, she turned out to be a Svengali."

Greg nodded. Fancy Phil said: "A *what?*"

"How long do you think . . . How long a sentence will she get?" Greg asked.

"I haven't a clue," I told him. "Unfortunately, she can probably afford a good lawyer. Let's hope she can't charm a jury."

"Do you think there's a chance she could get off?" Greg went from looking pallid to looking ill.

"Gregory." Fancy Phil leaned forward toward his son. "Don't worry about a jury. Guilty, not guilty, she's never gonna get off."

On Long Island, roses are at their sumptuous best in the middle of June. At the end of the day I was out by the bushes clipping away when Nelson came by. I showed him a pale pink one with silvery outer petals. "I never remember the names of them," I said, "but this is an antique rose—brought over from France in the early nineteenth century. You know, around the time the pirate Jean Lafitte stopped plundering ships. He took time off to fight for the United States. He helped defend New Orleans during the War of 1812."

"Is that a history lesson or are you asking me to see the good side of Fancy Phil?"

"Both, I guess."

"If it's any comfort to you," Nelson said, "that week when we were tailing him . . . That particular time, we were actually after the guy he was supposed to meet."

"But Fancy never met him, did he?" I tried not to sound overly triumphant.

"I don't know. He was able to shake the tail. He's made tail-shaking into an art form."

I clipped another rose. Nelson took it from my hand and put it into the bucket of water with the others. "Are you ready to talk about us?"

"Today was a little on the stressful side, what with having to rip someone's flesh and grab a bloody gun and then a finger."

"I want to *un*stress you. Let's go sit down and talk."

I glanced toward the patio. "I want to stay outside, but I'm not in the mood for looking at Courtney Logan's blood droplets."

"Here's okay, then," Nelson said. "Look, I know you had more than your share today. I'll make it quick. I'm going to get a divorce."

"Listen, before you—"

"With you or without you, Judith, it was going to happen. It's not only that we're not happy. We're not—how the hell can I put it? We're not even good companions to each other. I married her because she was a decent person and pretty and I couldn't take dating anymore. At the time I thought that was love." He glanced away, then looked back. "I was kind of screwed up for a while."

"So was I. Probably from the day we said good-bye."

"Me, too," he said quietly.

"Maybe even before."

"Maybe me, too."

"But listen, Nelson. We've only known each other in one way."

"Which is . . . ?"

"As adulterers."

"God almighty! Do you think I'm a compulsive . . . fucker-arounder?"

"Not at all. Do you think I am?"

"No," he said. "Of course not."

"All that I'm saying is, if at some point you do get free—"

"It's a done deal."

"—and that's entirely between you and your wife, then you and I can see what it's like truly being together. Leading real lives together. Legit."

"Living together?" he asked.

"I don't know. Is that what you want?"

"Yes."

"Well, it's probably what I want. Or to be more truthful, I love you more than you'll ever know. I want you body and soul. But let's see how it works in the real world. I may hate your taste in music. You might hate my friends or your friends might hate me. We might love or detest each other's children."

"So we'll start out how?" He slipped his hands into his pockets, a casual pose, a way of looking cool at the start of a negotiation.

"We'll go on a date. We'll spend a weekend together. We'll be single. Free. Legit. We'll each go to work, we'll call each other. If I remember correctly, we'll talk more about the Mets than about politics because political discussions weren't our finest hour as a couple. What I'm saying is, we'll be—"

"Natural?"

"That's good. Natural."

"Judith, I want to marry you."

"I want to marry you, too. But before we buy the rings and send out the invitations, we should go for a walk, go to the movies."

"And then more," he said softly.

"Maybe."